ALL SOULS

INSPECTOR MATT MINOGUE MYSTERIES

ALL SOULS

AN INSPECTOR MATT MINOGUE MYSTERY

JOHN BRADY

STEERFORTH PRESS
SOUTH ROYALTON, VERMONT

For Nancy, Stanley, and David Colbert

Copyright © 2002 by John Brady

First published in Canada by HarperCollins Publishers Ltd., 1993
First published in the United States by St. Martin's Press, 1993

For information about permission to reproduce
selections from this book, write to:
Steerforth Press L.C., P.O. Box 70,
South Royalton, Vermont 05068

Library of Congress Cataloging-in-Publication Data

Brady, John, 1955–
All souls: an Inspector Matt Minogue mystery / John Brady.
p.   cm.
ISBN: 1-58642-043-7 (alk. paper)
1. Minogue, Matt (Fictitious character) — Fiction.
2. Police — Ireland — Clare — Fiction.
3. Clare (Ireland) — Fiction. I. Title
PR6052.R2626 A79 2002
823'.914—dc21   2001057754

FIRST STEERFORTH EDITION

A wrongdoer is often a man who has left something undone, not always one who has done something.

Marcus Aurelius

CHAPTER I

MINOGUE MADE ANOTHER quick study of the man's face. The eyes were lazy and red from the drink, the pocked skin still oily. Thomas Martin Nolan, known to his few mates and the man he had killed three hours earlier as Jelly Nolan, seemed sober. Nolan's eyes were fixed on a ventilation grate high up on the wall where gray lines of dust, years' worth, edged the metal. He drew on his cigarette. Nolan was twenty-two but he looked five years older. His red hair was cropped close, and the ends of his thin mustache curled into the corners of his mouth. His body was already thickening from too much drink and stodgy food. Nolan fingered the studs in his ear before he squashed his cigarette into the saucer with his left hand. Then he examined his hands carefully, pausing to stare at the nicotine-stained fingernails. Although Minogue had all he needed from the earlier session twenty minutes ago when Hoey and he had done the interview, the Inspector decided that he might as well get as much as he could from Nolan before Legal Aid showed up.

Nolan cleared his throat.

"Any more fags?"

Minogue shook his head. Hoey had left the room five minutes ago.

"Well, fuck you and the horse you robbed to get to Dublin on, you culchie bastard."

Minogue was suddenly seized by an urge to reach across the table and hammer Nolan in the face. He grasped the tabletop and searched Nolan's face again. Jelly Nolan had kicked a man to death outside a pub in Drimnagh. Nolan had known the victim, John McArdle, all his life. McArdle had worked as a deliveryman for a Dublin newspaper. He had loaned Nolan twenty quid a week ago and last night in the pub he had asked for it back. When Nolan wasn't forthcoming, McArdle had taunted him. Nolan had gone drinking elsewhere but had returned at closing time and followed McArdle down a lane. There he had felled McArdle from behind and kicked him in the head until the man lay dead in a puddle of cranial blood fed from his ears and nose. McArdle hadn't known that Nolan was in a corner already, running from a local shark to whom he was in hock fifteen hundred quid. Caught knocking off food, Nolan had also been sacked from his job stocking supermarket shelves. He had run out of friends, run out of a future. Minogue had heard of the shark, Carty, before. Cash Carty and his brother, Shocko, collected debts with legendary brutality.

Nolan glanced back under his eyebrows at the inspector.

"What's the big bleeding staring match about? Here I am doing your job for you. All I want is a few fags. You got everything you want there, haven't you? I signed your bleeding statement. I didn't give yous any runaround. So what's the big deal?"

He was sure he could take Nolan handily. He was also afraid he'd not stop with the first blow. Nolan frowned and leaned back in the chair. His white boilersuit reminded Minogue of a patient waiting for surgery. Detective Garda Shea Hoey opened the door of the interview room. He looked at Minogue, raised his eyebrows, and broke the inspector's stare fixed on Nolan. Minogue lurched out into the corridor. Hoey introduced a sleepy-eyed woman in jeans and a leather jacket as Kate Marrinan from Legal Aid. She spoke tonelessly to Minogue.

"Has he made a statement?"

"Yep," replied Minogue. "Got the caution in front of a witness, signed the waiver."

Not much older than Iseult, he guessed. Kate Marrinan had short fair hair with a touch of red. She looked at her watch, yawned, and swung a shoulder bag around front. Minogue's anger had ebbed. He wanted real coffee, a chance to chat to Kate Marrinan about her work. Both hopes were long shots and he knew it.

"He's all yours. Mr. Jelly Nolan. I think he's relieved to be in custody. Almost looking forward to being put away."

She wrote "Jelly Nolan" on a notepad.

"Aren't you getting ahead of yourself, Inspector?" She hadn't taken her eyes from the notepad.

"I've been accused of worse," he tried. "But I think people cod me with comments like that because of my easygoing disposition."

Kare Marrinan squinted at him. She remembered him now.

"Huh. I heard different. Who's codding who here?"

Minogue almost smiled. There were pleasant dangers to being known as a character in Dublin.

"We have seen to the rights of the accused in every respect," he began. "He was quite keen to tell us about what he did up that laneway and how he did it —"

"*If* he did it, you mean."

"Twelve o'clock today, his clothes and shoes will come out of the lab with evidence tags on them," Hoey weighed in. "Open and shut."

"Signed in at one o'clock," Minogue murmured. "He'll go to the Bridewell and get remanded over first thing in the morning."

What sounded like a sigh to Minogue escaped from Kate Marrinan. She hugged her shoulder bag and laid her hand on the door handle.

"Where's the fags?" Nolan called out. "And a bit of tea or something so as I can keep me bleeding eyes open."

The door opened.

"Who's she?" the detectives heard Nolan ask.

"I'm your legal counsel," Kate Marrinan said. "And I don't smoke."

• • • • •

Hoey and Minogue huddled in the doorway and watched the fine rain glow around the streetlights. Through the hush of rain, Minogue heard trains being shunted at Heuston Station at this western end of Dublin's quays. Hoey spoke through a yawn.

"I know what you're saying."

"Nearly let him have it, all right," Minogue murmured again. "I must be losing it or something."

"It wouldn't have done him any harm."

The rain was steady and gentle, as though it were being sprinkled methodically. Drains gurgled in the middle distance; a gutter drummed tinnily next to the door. Hoey took a packet of cigarettes from his pocket. He turned from Minogue and a folded airmail envelope fell to the pavement. Minogue picked it up and nudged Hoey's upper arm. The detective turned back in a cloud of smoke.

"Fell out of your pocket."

Hoey hesitated before taking it. He coughed once and plucked it from the inspector's hand. "The latest epistle. St. Aine to the pagans." Minogue registered the ironic tone but said nothing. "Says the people are very nice," Hoey went on. "The Zimbabweans. Did I say that right?"

Minogue wondered if Hoey kept all his girlfriend's letters in his pockets. "Sounds right. Here, I'll be in sometime in the morning proper. See if I can sleep this off. Maybe I'll wake up and find out it was just a bloody dream or something."

Hoey flicked a glowing butt out onto the street. It hissed and was carried as it landed. The two detectives watched as it was propelled along, spinning, by a lazy runnel of water. Trapped for several seconds on a drain grate, the butt bobbed before it snapped abruptly into the darkness below.

·   ·   ·   ·   ·

Minogue tried to stay clear of the bottle of Jamesons whiskey which he knew was kept beneath the kitchen sink. Kathleen Minogue had had new cabinetry installed that spring but the cupboard under the sink remained her detention area for whiskey. Her husband read its proximity to cleaning agents as her subconscious rebuke.

He was too restless to go to bed. He thought about tea — coffee would wake him up too much — and then he thought about a man being kicked to death in a laneway awash with rain. Kate Marrinan would doubtless try for manslaughter; that was her job: no hard feelings. *My client is also a victim, a victim of hopelessness, of alcohol, of inadequate education; he is prey to vicious social evils endemic to working-class areas — drug abuse, loansharking; he is a young man of inadequate personality . . .*

Minogue was an inspector in the Investigation Section of the Garda Technical Bureau. His office was on St. John's Road, hard by Garda H.Q. in Dublin's Phoenix Park. Although seniority would have allowed him to dodge an on-call shift after ten o'clock at night, Minogue insisted on his name being entered on the rota. He partnered Seamus Hoey, a Garda fifteen years his junior from Galway. In the six years he had worked with him, Minogue had been unable to figure him out. He liked Hoey a great deal and didn't mind his colleague's moods.

He heard stirring upstairs: his wife turning over in bed, he decided. Kathleen had become a heavy sleeper since they had had the house to themselves. Their daughter, Iseult, had moved to a flat in Cabra, to be with her fella, Pat the Brain, Minogue guessed. Kathleen knew this too and pretended not to know. Iseult worked mostly with embroidery out of a shared studio in Temple Bar. This last year she had been given a grant to travel the length and breadth of the country working up murals on school walls. Sometimes he liked to think of his daughter as beginning a mural in Donegal and painting it all the way down to Kerry, cutting a swath of color and life across the island.

Daithi, the Minogue's son, had gotten on with some outfit that had recently been bought by Microsoft. Minogue half-understood his son's restlessness, his continued search for other work in the States. Daithi had displayed an American girlfriend on a visit home eighteen months ago. He had spoken feelingly of the States being full of opportunity. Kathy had slept in the attic, talked glowingly of her Irish ancestors, and been unremittingly cheerful during her two-week stay. She had an enthusiasm for learning more about the Celts and learning Gaelic. Even Kathleen had been impressed.

The rain seemed to have let up. He moved away from the window and again considered the Jamesons. Maybe read for a half-hour to settle his thoughts down. He pulled down glossy folders from the top of the television set and studied the floor plans. Kathleen had the bug about selling their house and moving into these apartments or a townhouse. What about a garden, he had asked. What for, was her answer to that. Land, he had told her — something to walk on, somewhere to plant things that she thought still came mysteriously from the supermarket. No need to be sarcastic, she had replied, and then took the high road: why not something different from the run-of-the-mill? A terrace, a Japanese style of place with lumps of rock and shrubs and what have you, somewhere he could sit and read. He had retired from the fray at that stage and had spent his energies in avoiding the topic since.

He yawned and studied the floor plans. Fitted kitchens, security systems, prestigious addresses, easy access to the city. Huh, he thought. "Easy access to the city": Dublin? Must be a joke. He felt the resentment prowling behind his thoughts then. He dumped the folder on the chair and hotfooted it to the kitchen with the words sour and ugly in his mind: lifestyle, state-of-the-art, unrivaled. Kathleen worked as a secretary for an auctioneer and came home with these brochures almost daily now. Her employer could get them a deal, she argued. How could he tell her that the last thing he wanted was a deal? Kathleen had been the thrifty and sensible gatherer all these years but he had lately begun to see in himself a stronger urge to shed. He grasped the bottle of Jamesons and cast about for a tumbler. He paused then and, leaning against the counter kitchen, stared at the sink. Manslaughter'd have Jelly Nolan on the street inside five years. If Cartys, the loan sharks, didn't do for Nolan one way or another, inside or outside the nick, that is.

Minogue's thoughts fastened suddenly on Shea Hoey. Hoey was drinking. He, Minogue, second-in-command to Jimmy Kilmartin — the Killer, as he was known for his leadership of the Murder Squad — had not approached anyone about it. Hoey had had a smell of drink to him two days in a row last week, Minogue remembered. Looked washed out. What to say, what to do.

The Jamesons was sharp and it cut at the back of his throat. There was nothing new about Gardai drinking hard off-duty. Hoey's girlfriend, Aine, had signed up to teach for a stint in Zimbabwe and had flown out in September. Minogue had met Aine twice. She was cheerful, freckled, and opinionated. That was teachers for you, he supposed. Hard on the heels of his last gulp from the tumbler came an urge for more. Duty-free, Minogue's familiar gargoyle jeered nearby. Might as well at that price, go on, can't you? He took the bottle into the living room, slipped out of his shoes and lay on the couch.

·　　·　　·　　·　　·

The prevailing winds sweep in from the Atlantic and skim spume from the waves before they slam into the cliffs and inlets of west Clare. Carried up over the cliffs come the faint and massive slaps of the water's battery, the screeches of seabirds, the winds' roar. Behind the cliffs' edges, the grasses flatten and hiss as the gales buffet the headlands of this western edge of Clare and Ireland and Europe known as the Burren. The winds whistle through gorse and heather before they move across the patchwork of fields and drystone walls which creep up the Burren hillsides. Above the fields, boulders appear as a thickening crop that the soil cannot resist pushing to the surface. Higher yet, on the plateaus where the boulders give way to fissured limestone terraces, the gales race on. But in this wilderness that looks to be the work of nature alone, a careful eye can spot marks of ancient settlement. The Famine completed the work of centuries of erosion and left the Burren almost deserted. Behind them, the waves of settlers have left their ruined castles and churches, their deserted villages, their ancient ring-forts, and their graves.

Over Fanore and Kilcorney, through Lismara and Tuamashee, the winds course, battering and caressing, rippling the surfaces of turloughs, those seasonal lakes brimming with dark water. Like cattle laboring home full, the clouds move with the wind over the towns and villages and the long wet ribbons of roads that lead across the midland plains. With rain on the wind, the whole island can be wet within hours of those first clouds descending on the Burren. Although the hills on the west coast draw down heavy, dreary rains, they still leave enough for the midland pastures and even for Dublin city. In the Kilmacud suburb of that city, Minogue, long exiled from the precincts of the Burren, slept fitfully on the couch.

Kathleen Minogue, Dublinwoman, opened the bedroom curtains just in time to see the Dublin Mountains fade into the mist as the rain rolled down into the suburbs. She plugged the kettle in, tiptoed back to the doorway, and surveyed her husband. He stirred and laid an arm over his eyes. Asleep in his jacket even, she thought. She was caught between exasperation and pity. He was very long.

"I know what you're thinking," he murmured. She started. His eyes stayed closed as he raised his forearm from his eyes and stretched. The kettle wheezed and ticked stronger in the kitchen.

"Don't be so sure of yourself," she said.

Awake but fuzzy from the whiskey, Minogue tried to pull back a piece of his dream as it fell into obscurity. All that remained was a face indistinctly recalled and fading fast: a man, young, smiling at him, asking him or telling him something. Familiar, gone. At least it wasn't Jelly Nolan's face.

"Looking over the wreckage and wondering, I'll bet," he said. "Go on, tell me you aren't now. I'm a detective, You can't cod me."

"We have an early start on Halloween here with you on the couch. Frankenstein or something."

"Now I know where Iseult gets her wit."

She folded her arms and watched Minogue's eyelids flutter. A tight and pleasant ache cradled itself in her stomach and rose up in her chest. At my age, she thought. Last week he had reached for her in bed, stifling her giggles. She remembered him keen and gentle, whispering to her, saying her name as he coiled about her. Not heavy at all but arching easily, waiting. She flushed and tightened the belt on her dressing gown.

"Raining again," he said.

"Go up to bed, can't you."

"I will not," he declared. He sat up and rubbed his eyes. "And what's more, I have news for you. You can tell that boss of yours, that go-by-the-wall auctioneer, that aftershave gurrier, that you need a holiday. Are you listening to me?"

"A holiday," she echoed. "In this? Where were you, in dreamland? It's nearly winter, mister."

"Santorini. I saw a picture of it in a window the other day. Blue and white and nothing else."

Kathleen Minogue headed back to the kitchen. He followed her.

"I heard that all they do there is get twisted drunk and dance on the tables," she said.

"What's wrong with that?"

She made a face at him and scalded the teapot.

"God. Have a sup of tea with me and you'll wake up and talk sense."

"There are more tears shed over answered prayers," he muttered.

"Smart remarks department is closed today," she said. Minogue stared out the window.

"Have you forgotten we're going down to Clare tomorrow?" Minogue groaned inside. He had forgotten. Maura Minogue, a sister-in-law whose cheerfulness and vivacity seemed invincible to Minogue — the more a miracle, he considered, because she had been married to his brother Mick for over thirty years — had been on the phone to Kathleen. Maura hadn't asked for anything, but she had cried on the phone once. His nephew Eoin had recently been arrested and charged with possession of a gun, which the Guards had taken from a bag in the boot of his car. The bag belonged to his friend but Eoin, weaned on his father's Republican cant and full of a touchy and twisted sense of loyalty to the friend he had given a lift to, had delayed his own acquittal by making haughty speeches to the Guards. Eoin was to inherit the farm from Minogue's ailing brother, Mick, who was now too arthritic to do anything but token jobs on the farm. Farmers had fallen on hard times in the last few years. Now that she was marooned on the farm with Mick, finances a bit sticky maybe, Maura's morale was hitting bottom, Minogue surmised.

"Did you hear me?"

Kathleen had read her sister-in-law's conversation to mean that Maura wanted him to try and talk Mick and Eoin into selling part of the farm while there was still value in it. Minogue closed his eyes.

"I hear you."

· · · · ·

By the clumps of sodden grass that covered the rubble, a figure stood still. The rain dribbled off the rim of his cap and the breezes tousled his beard and hair. The rain had saturated his coat completely now and he felt cold drops roll down along his spine. The noises had stopped. He took his fists away from his ears and opened his eyes. Just the ruin and wet grasses and bushes under a low sky with the rain steady over everything. The cold had begun to fasten about his chest. He had been standing there for almost half an hour. The dog had tired of exploring and now lay at his feet. Occasionally it would get up, shake itself, and nudge at the man's knees with its snout. He would soothe the dog with words and strokes before returning to stare at the remains of the cottage.

The more he tried to imagine it, the harder it got. The frustration clawed at his heart again and he heard himself whispering aloud, trying to concentrate. The rain seemed to be getting heavier. In the few months since his release, he had come here many times. He had seen the odd car slowing as it passed the ruin, the driver eyeing him, but he never returned their cautious nods of greeting. Once he had thought of calling out to them: Yes, it's Jamesy Bourke, all right, back to set things right at last. You can tell the whole bloody world that too, damn you! He thought back to the fear that had seized him just two days ago when he had started throwing the pills into the fire. Each day now he committed the day's ration of seven pills to the fire. The first time he had done it, his hand had reached out reflexively to save the melting pills from the embers, as though that part of him knew better than what his mind had decided.

But now the images that came to him had become clearer than ever. In spite of the fears, the pictures that sometimes exploded in his mind had not been the ones he had had back in the cell, the ones he remembered with a vague but overwhelming dread. Wonder drugs, they called them, but he had known all along they were used to keep you stupid too. For a moment he saw in the steady rain the face of the social worker who visited weekly in his shiny Volkswagen, faking cheer and sympathy on that pink, unlined face behind the glasses. He had come to hate that face too. It belonged to another one he had to surrender to if he was to keep alive his chance of getting his life back. You run a very grave risk — he heard the words again against the slowly waving bushes that still

{ 9 }

rooted by the ruin which was also the ruin of his life — a very great risk of relapse if you don't maintain the treatment. Grave, relapse. Fuck him.

All that remained were the stones and the slab that had made up the floor of the cottage. Sort of like a grave but no one tended it. Jane was buried out in Canada. Murty Maher, the farmer who had rented the place to Jane, had bulldozed the walls after the fire. Bad luck on the house no doubt, and Maher had kept away from the place ever since. His hands seemed to remember that night better than his brain. The skin burned nearly black from trying to pull down the door as it was burning, but he hadn't felt it at the time. Drunk, of course, too drunk. Some things he remembered but they had never fitted together: the way the flames burst out the windows after exploding the glass, the roar of the fire, the thatched roof she had liked collapsing with a whoosh. The heat on his face, his own screams that ripped at his throat so that he thought he had swallowed part of the fire itself, a Guard's face inches from his own, shouting at him while he dragged him away by the neck. The hospital, the jail, his dejection at the trial were clearer memories. He hadn't been interested in living, he recalled.

The wind blustered and flung rain into his face and he turned away. He looked at the shrubs and bushes that had run wild as they leaned with the wind. Stray leaves flew around him. His coat was heavy on him, pulling down his shoulders. He hadn't slept last night and he still didn't feel bad. Maybe he'd try to take a snooze when he got home and changed. A slap, like a hammer-strike on wood, was carried faintly on the wind to him. Thunder? The dog stood slowly, her ears pricked and her head rolling from side to side to hear better. She whined and looked to him. He called to her and began to make his way down to the road, stepping up over the mound of rubble that had been pushed out from the house to block the laneway against tinkers drawing their caravans in and settling. He stopped then and turned for a last look at what had been Jane Clark's house. Here his own life had stopped too: like the floor dropping beneath him, he had tumbled into a nightmare that had lasted twelve years. And it still wasn't over. He'd never met any of the Minogues. He had known them to see but, like the rest of them now, he knew they would be wary of him, pitying at best. Yet again the thought wormed into him that even Crossan had promised he'd get in touch with Minogue, the big-shot Guard in Dublin, just to get rid of him. He'd got to Crossan's office in Ennis before the week was out, by God, and see what he had done. A. Crossan, Barrister-at-Law, he recalled on the plate by the door. Huh, Crossan had changed like the rest of them. He'd had twelve years to do it in, to get on with his life. The office and the secretary with her eyes like bloody saucers when he had walked in. Crossan no more than fucking Dan Howard didn't want to be reminded of things that they'd written off as dead and buried years ago. But Crossan was all he had for now.

The anger tingled in his arms before it burned his chest. The rainwater ran across the road in little rippling waves like the sea ebbing on the strand. The drugs would only keep him asleep. That was like letting part of himself stay dead. It was time to wake up. Better this way than hanging on, hanging around with half a life. He called out to the dog and his heart lightened when he saw the wagging tail, the willingness. There were prisons with bars, he thought as he set out for home, and there were other prisons too. His prison now was his own memory, but he had been locked out.

· · · · ·

Kilmartin was waiting for him. Minogue bowed to Eilis, the secretary of the Murder Squad, as he passed. She spared him a smile and a mock curtsy in return for his.

"Your Worship," she intoned in her native Irish.

"Aha," Kilmartin called out. "Hardy Canute himself. Howiya?"

"I'm a bit shagged."

"Well, that's life in the big city, pal."

Minogue glanced at the mass of his friend and colleague, Chief Inspector James Kilmartin. Eilis scratched a match alight next to him.

"A real beaut," said Kilmartin, thumbs behind his belt now.

"Kathleen doesn't think so," Minogue baited. "Says it's depressing."

"I didn't mean the fecking weather. I meant last night. The job done above in Drimnagh. Signed, sealed, and delivered."

"He had enough drink in him to get manslaughter, I'm thinking," said Minogue. "So does Legal Aid. The way I heard her anyway. She'll go wild when she hears he confessed. Expect a call, I'd say."

Kilmartin's expression turned thoughtful.

"God, you're crooked today," he murmured. "'Her'?"

"Kate Marrinan."

Kilmartin rolled his eyes. "Jesus. That one? A grenade disguised as a barrister. She gave me a few kicks in the balls when she was defending that fella what killed the fella with a hammer . . . Hogan. 'Victim of society' shite, right?"

"She didn't give me the treatment last night anyway."

"Wait till court, bucko. Jesus wept. She's an expert on everything. Did you hit the sack at all?"

"Enough of it. Is Shea in?"

Kilmartin's brow creased with the effort of holding back a comment. Minogue wondered if Kilmartin knew of Detective Garda Shea Hoey's habits lately.

"You know I'm off starting tomorrow. Get a break for a few days."

Kilmartin's brow shot up. He nodded toward his office. As Minogue followed him, he saw a yawning Hoey slope in past Eilis's desk.

"Just give me a hand in drafting a press release to warn all the gutties and head-cases that they're to wait until you come back from your holiday to —"

"You're a howl, Jimmy."

"Just a bit of levity, Matt. Don't get your rag out over it. Course there's no bother. Sure haven't you overtime built up like a bank?"

"Good, so."

"Yes. Morale is everything." The Chief Inspector nodded his head as he spoke now. "A bit of R and R to keep you sharp. It builds morale, let me tell you. You can throw your hat at the technical stuff if you haven't the morale built up. Amn't I right?"

The phrase echoed in Minogue's thoughts: Build the morale? Sounded like Kilmartin was trying out a phrase he had heard in his hobnobs with senior Gardai. The new Garda Commissioner, John Tynan, had made Kilmartin and other senior Gardai jittery. Kilmartin knew that Tynan was planning a major reorganization of the Gardai. The new Garda Commissioner's back was not for slapping and Kilmartin, the tribal chief with his repertoire of bombast and charm, still struggled to find a purchase on the metropolitan modern, Tynan. Minogue bumped into Tynan more than chance allowed. Wary of him, he still liked the Commissioner's dry wit, especially its effects on the likes of Jim Kilmartin.

"But Jases, look outside, it's bucketing. Are you going to hide at home and do a bit of wallpapering and painting or something?"

"A visit to Clare for a day or two. Then I was half thinking of somewhere like . . . Santorini."

Kilmartin frowned but Minogue let him dangle for a few moments.

"It's in Greece."

"Well that's very exciting, I'm sure."

"Wouldn't mind a week there if we could get a cheap seat. Morale, don't you know." He frowned back at Kilmartin. "Build morale, like."

Kilmartin didn't register receipt of the gibe.

"Have you court?" he asked instead.

"Ten days' time," Minogue answered. "State has no plan to call me up. Yet."

"All right so. But listen. There's something I heard last night that I didn't like one little bit. Not saying there's a fly in the ointment as regards you and Kathleen having a fling off in wherever."

"Santorini. You have to ride on the back of an ass to get up from the ferry, I hear."

Kilmartin's brow creased again.

"Arra Jases you can do that below in Belmullet, man," he scoffed, referring to his home town in Mayo. He narrowed his glance.

"I bumped into Tom Boyle at a shindig. You know Tom, don't you? Got a kick up the ladder the same time Tynan got the throne."

Minogue remembered a slim, dapper Chief Superintendent Boyle from a drinks party at Kilmartin's new house in Killiney. Boyle now occupied Tynan's former position of Assistant Garda Commissioner.

"I know him not to run him over in the street, I suppose."

"Uh-huh. Well. Tom says that Tynan's a week away from a final decision about 'reorganization.' Says Tynan is a holy terror in committee. Won't listen to reason. Do you know what I'm saying?"

"I do and I don't."

Kilmartin flashed a wily smile.

"Come on now, Matty. Don't lay the ace and you with the knave in your fist. You and Tynan are thick enough when you want to be."

Minogue's thoughts had flown to the prospect of a large white coffee in Bewley's. A read of the paper, plenty of noise and chat. Sociable, solitary, solace — noisy Dublin's best secret.

"Well? Has he dropped any hint to you about folding up the Squad here?"

Of course the travel posters would have been treated to highlight the blue of the Mediterranean, Minogue thought, throwing up the whitewashed walls to startle the eye. Turquoise . . . but the pictures couldn't be all hammed. Fishing nets and boats bobbing in the harbor. He heard Kilmartin's tones straying into the combat zone.

"He doesn't use me as a sounding board, Jim. It's just social and how-do with him."

"That a fact?" Kilmartin asked with his eyebrows arched. "Well, Tom Boyle isn't one for idle chat, let me tell you. No flies on Tom, by Jesus. No sirree Bob."

Minogue turned his gaze on Kilmartin but didn't see him. He knew as well as Kilmartin that there had been a stay of execution on the current structure of the Murder Squad for several years. The Squad had been slated to move to Garda Headquarters proper in Phoenix Park, adjacent to the Forensic Science Lab and the nabobs who could look over Kilmartin's shoulder day to day.

But by dint of Kilmartin's work, the Squad had not yet been folded back into its parent group, the Technical Bureau. Kilmartin had parleyed, parried, and placated his way into preserving his fiefdom. He had taken in more trainees from Garda Divisions all over the country. He had circulated Murder Squad detectives through other areas of the Technical Bureau to broaden their expertise. Kilmartin had made exemplary use of the new and emerging technologies. He had integrated computers and new communications protocols flawlessly. He had sat through complaint sessions with ranking Gardai from the country who were riled at having to run to Dublin for help in murder investigations.

"I really don't know any more than yourself, Jimmy."

Kilmartin changed tack.

"Maybe you don't give a fiddler's fart, Matt."

"Well, there are days . . ."

Kilmartin leaned in over his desk.

"Look, head-the-ball. You think I don't know what's going on? Me bollicks. I know you. Shy but willing, we say at home, like an ass chewing thistles. You know Tynan a damn sight better than I do. Find out what the hell he thinks we don't do well here. What we can do to keep him away. Budget? Public relations? More trainees? Christ, he can't complain about the stats! Didn't we clear 95 percent last year? Well . . . aside from the feuding, of course."

A feud between the IRA and the Irish National Liberation Army had blown a large statistical hole in the Squad's proud record. As though to taunt Kilmartin personally, both groups had taken up the habit of abducting a victim in the North and then killing him inside the border of the Republic — or vice versa. More often than not, this grisly ruse left the Royal Ulster Constabulary, whom Kilmartin despised, the kidnaping investigation and the Gardai the murder investigation.

Kilmartin's tone had grown moody.

"It's just that I know Tynan is looking right through me anytime I talk to him," he said.

Bewley's on Grafton Street would be just about right at this time of the day. The dinnertime mob gone. But the rain? Jam the car up on the path in Dawson Street and scamper over. With any luck it'd be robbed. How much would insurance pay out for an eight-year-old Fiat? . . .

"Well?" Kilmartin repeated.

"I'll give it my considered opinion. Will that do you?"

Kilmartin scowled and fixed Minogue with a one-eyed glare.

"When will you be talking to Monsignor Tynan, then?"

The irritation rushed back to Minogue.

"Jimmy —" Kilmartin waved away his response.

"I know, I know," he interrupted. " 'Tynan plays aboveboard.' 'He'd come straight to me to sort anything out.' 'He'd do right by us.' Hail Mary, Holy Mary, and the rest of it. All I'm saying is —"

"I'll phone and see."

"Ah, Jases! I'd sooner you said nothing than go around to him with a puss on you. He'll know I asked you."

Minogue rubbed his eyes.

"You're an iijit sometimes, Matt. All I'm trying to tell you is that the personal touch is what clinches things. I'm not asking you to butter him up. Look, I can tell you straight out that I know" — Kilmartin paused and pointed his finger at the desktop — "I know that Tynan thinks very highly of your —"

"He's never asked me once —"

"Shut up a minute and listen. I don't resent that one bit. Doesn't bother me one iota that you might have more of Tynan's ear than I do. Not one bit. And Tynan's not stupid."

"I'll pass that news on to him for you."

"Don't be a smart arse, you. Listen. Tynan has to make some response to the Divisional Supers, we all know that. They want their own glory. What'll decide Tynan in the end is not the computers and the stats. It'll be the human factor. It's our culture sure, man! Here, come on. You know what I'm getting at, don't you?" Kilmartin rapped his knuckles on his colleague's shoulder and gave Minogue a pantomime wink.

"Well . . ."

"Here, I'll tell you in plain English. What the hell does Tynan need from us so's he'll leave us alone? Am I getting through to you?"

Minogue nodded. Kilmartin beamed.

"Ah, you're a star! A real trouper. We'll say no more about it. Now, tell us a bit about this Saint place."

"Santorini. It's in Greece, I told you. Cradle of civilization, don't you know."

"Oho! Greece is right. You'd want to watch you don't end up on the flat of your back there with the runs, boyo." Kilmartin nodded solemnly. "They cook up bits of meat and what-have-you there. Right in the street, bejases. A pal of Maura's went there and spent half her holiday in the jacks —"

Minogue stared back at his superior.

"I'm sorry to hear that, Jim. Very sorry."

Kilmartin guffawed.

"I'm sure you are," said the chief inspector, hearty again. "Now shag off with yourself, ya bowsie. But phone me when you get your leg in the door with Tynan."

· · · · ·

Minogue reviewed the statements taken from one Tommy-John Casey several weeks ago. Casey had been in a dispute with a relation over the rent of pasture in the townland of Inisgeall, County Mayo. Casey and his victim, Patrick Tuohy, had repaired to a pub in Ballina in the hopes, Casey maintained, of coming to an amicable arrangement. The two men had continued drinking until midnight, whereupon Tommy-John Casey left the pub, got into his car and ran over Tuohy on a narrow road a mile outside town. Didn't know what had come over him, Casey had repeated over and over again. Kilmartin had read the statement with Minogue. What came over him, Kilmartin had scoffed, was the car. Casey had been contrite and candid with the Gardai. Minogue, unimpressed, had pointed to the fact that Casey had driven a further two hundred yards along the road beyond the point where he had catapulted Tuohy over the hedge, smashing his windscreen and leaving Tuohy dying, his skull shattered.

He glanced over at Hoey. His colleague's face looked a little puffy. Lack of sleep, bachelor diet. Drink, of course.

"Well, Shea," he said. "Can I leave you in the lurch with Jelly Nolan? It's well cooked already."

Hoey blinked and cleared his throat.

"No bother," he said.

The tight smile looked bleak to Minogue. Murtagh, another of the detectives permanently attached to the Murder Squad, walked through the office with file folders under his arm. He whistled softly around the pencil protruding from his mouth. Minogue found himself smiling at the sight, then he remembered Hoey. How could policemen be so different? Hoey, the dark horse, moody and reserved; Murtagh, surely beloved and spoiled as a child, a cocky athlete who gleefully chased nurses in nightclubs.

Minogue closed the folder on Tommy-John Casey and sat back. A countryman himself, Minogue understood rows about land. Dublin people wouldn't, he believed. The primal hunger for land bred during starving centuries wasn't imprinted on them. Land hunger, land disputes, wills' probate fought over, aging bachelor farmers, family farms. But Jelly Nolan and his likes still remained ciphers to the inspector. He wanted to know as little as possible about Nolan's life. Self-protective, he knew, and he felt himself recoiling from the thought of just how cramped and ugly Nolan's life must have been. There had to be a better line of work than sitting across a table from the Jelly Nolans of this world.

His thoughts wandered to Kilmartin's probes about the commissioner. Damn him for sending him like a spy to Tynan. What the hell use was it trying to explain to Kilmartin that he had no influence with Tynan? Tynan: a jigsaw with no guarantee you'd find all the bits, ever. Maybe Tynan was trying to get Kilmartin and Minogue & Co. ready for the end of an era. The soft glove of a blunt hand in elegy, a broad hint that Kilmartin and Minogue would do well to retire before the Squad was dispersed. His eyes focused again on the papers. He considered phoning a travel agent and trying to book some airline seats but realized he didn't know how many days they'd be staying in Clare. Damn again. He shoved the Casey file in the Current Trial cabinet and saw that the rain had stopped.

· · · · ·

Minogue in Bewley's was a happy man. The stained glass below the restaurant's skylights seemed to be moving. Clouds, he judged. He stood in line for coffee and noted that the racket from dishes and chairs and cutlery seemed muted today. Minogue had just deployed his coffee and bun when the clink of china on the marble tabletop drew his head up from his newspaper. John Tynan, Commissioner of the Gardai, edged into the booth next to Minogue.

"Damn," said Tynan and headed out again. "Sugar."

Minogue tried to gather his wits as he studied Tynan's well-tailored frame marauding around the cashier's desk. What was Tynan doing here? Coincidence?

"Slow day?" said Tynan. He sat on Minogue's side of the table.

"It's always murder," said Minogue. "I'm charging the batteries. I was late into the night on a case. Just a break to, em, build morale."

Tynan eyed Minogue while he stirred his coffee.

"Building morale? I phoned the Squad and was told that you were, quote, 'doing research.'"

"Eilis might have given me the benefit of the doubt."

"Anyway. I'm on a walkabout myself."

Minogue smiled.

"That's it. Look surprised. No minders, no gun in my pocket."

Tynan plucked a slim cellular phone from his jacket pocket and showed enough of it for Minogue to recognize the device.

"What do you think?"

The Inspector knew of Tynan's ways. The new Garda Commissioner had taken to walking about town in civvies, getting a feel for how Dublin was policed. It didn't seem to bother him that he was annoying several senior civil servants and Gardai with his perambulations.

"Great," said Minogue.

Tynan looked around the restaurant.

"And how are you all?" he said.

"Good," said Minogue. "Jimmy's as ever. You know the style."

"I meant Kathleen and the children."

Minogue squirmed a little on the seat. "Great. We're empty-nesters now. Discretionary income up. We're getting quite selfish, I suppose."

"Oho," said Tynan with no real enthusiasm. "And the children?"

Minogue knew that Tynan had no children. Tynan had studied for the Jesuits many years ago. Rachel Tynan was a Protestant, a former teacher. Her laughter and pottery studio intrigued Minogue. He had watched Tynan at functions, exchanging asides with his wife between speeches, she laughing, he with a straight face. Tynan the cold fish, many thought; Rachel Tynan, whose face reminded Minogue of a peach.

"Oh, we monitor them at a distance. The routine seems to be that I reassure Kathleen. Then I get the willies myself when I see what they're actually up to."

Tynan took some more coffee from his cup and sat back.

"I need to pay yous a visit soon."

Minogue nodded as though considering the news.

"Throw around a few ideas, you know," Tynan added.

"Great," said Minogue. Had Kilmartin been tipped off about this?

"Busy enough, are ye?" asked the Commissioner.

Was this a probe? "There's always work. But we still don't kill one another that much, don't forget."

"Compared to . . . ?"

"Well, compared to the really civilized countries, I mean."

The Commissioner continued his survey of the clientele in the restaurant.

"We need changes, that's clear," he murmured. "It's a matter of how and where at this stage."

"So they say in the press, John."

Tynan gave him a glazed look.

"The Delahunty Factor, you mean?" Tynan asked, his mouth set tight. Minogue nodded.

An Inspector Delahunty, well-known and well-liked by his officers, had told a journalist that the solution to finding people with guns on them was to pull out your own — as long as you were Special Branch — and shoot them down in the street like dogs.

"'Make-My-Day' Delahunty. I've have more letters about that —"

"Were I not so discreet, John, I might speculate."

"Let fly, so."

"This same party let loose those comments as a way to see how our new Garda Commissioner would handle them, our new Garda Commissioner being but months in the office, I mean. And our new Garda Commissioner being a bit of an enigma as yet. One wonders if our new Garda Commissioner is one of 'de boys' or if he is one for rocking the boat."

Tynan almost smiled before turning away. Nothing to tell Kilmartin here, Minogue thought.

"I've taken a long hard look this last six months," Tynan murmured.

His eyes returned to Minogue's "And what I seem to be seeing is something I last heard of twenty-five years ago when I studied medieval society. Warlords squabbling over their own territories. Some of it's beyond an outrage. It's nearly comical."

Indolent and intent, his eyes bored into Minogue's for several moments.

"It's stifling. It's bad for morale. It's inefficient. And it's going to stop."

Minogue took in the force of Tynan's determination. Should he report the warlord term to the Killer, James Kilmartin? The commissioner was again looking at the faces around him in the café.

Minogue told him about the holiday he was planning. Tynan nodded and told Minogue that the islands were indeed beautiful. Minogue didn't ask how he knew but he filed away this fact about Tynan to tell Kathleen later. Tynan turned in his seat and stared at Minogue. He seemed cautious now.

"I want you to drop by my office after your jaunt below in Clare," he said. "A chat."

"Jimmy too?"

Tynan flicked away the question with a quick movement of his hand.

"Don't be fretting. It's smarts that should be the basis of entitlement to comment, not rank alone. So don't be kicking in the stall now."

"I'll be sure and phone you," said Minogue. He felt pleased and bewildered. Tynan finished his coffee, rose, and replaced his chair under the table. He looked down at the inspector.

"Like the suit? There's stripe to it but you'd need glasses to see it."

Minogue issued a wink that he hoped might convey a sybarite's approval. Tynan's baleful gaze swept the room again.

"Well," the commissioner murmured. "I'm going to see if what some journalists write is true. That some Gardai are not, em, sensitive to Dubliners of lower socioeconomic status."

A swell of sympathy and liking swept over Minogue. He hoped that Tynan was not too isolated. "See you, John," he called after him.

CHAPTER 2

Minogue hummed along with the radio while he waited for Donny-brook to unjam itself. It was early in the afternoon for traffic jams, he thought. At least the sun had come out. An ambulance passed him, heading into town. A crash? Several teenagers in masks — one of Mick Jagger — trudged by carrying a shopping bag with the outlines of bottles straining at the plastic. Good day for pulling a bank job, thought the inspector. The traffic moved. Minogue waved to a Guard directing traffic around a Toyota sports car which had taken down a lamp post on its way through the railings in front of a house. A youth with a sullen, pale face and a gash on his forehead sat in the backseat of the squad car. Joyriders, Minogue guessed. Were others hurt? The Guard was talking to himself and frowning. He didn't wave back to Minogue.

The inspector stopped in Donnybrook and quickly settled on a bottle of wine to celebrate the beginning of his break from work. Couldn't be worse than the bottle of homemade plonk that Iseult's boyfriend, Pat, had opened for dinner last week, the red stuff with the homemade label "Banshee." Kathleen was on the phone when he turned the key in the hall door. "Maura," she mouthed at him. "Matt's just in the door," she said. "Yes, that's the job, come and go as you like. . . ."

She handed the receiver to her husband. He exchanged it for the bottle of wine and raised his eyebrows. Kathleen shook her head.

"Down in the dumps again," she whispered. "I told her we'd be down for sure tomorrow."

Minogue tried to hide his irritation. He picked up one of the bars of chocolate that Kathleen had lined up for the Halloween callers tonight.

"Hello, Maura, and how are you all below?"

"Hello, Matt. Arra you know how it is. We're nearly swimming. The Stone Fields and Durrus are underwater these three weeks. It's fish we should be farming."

A name for every field and ditch, Minogue remembered. He had his nail under the wrapper now.

"Was it ever any other way, Maura love?" he tried. The foil slid up under his thumb and chocolate showed. "And how's Mick?"

"Well enough now. The joints are bad with him in the morning, what with the weather and the time of year. And of course there's the age. Like they say, closer to the wood. There's no avoiding that, is there? God has His own plans."

"We'll be down by teatime tomorrow, Maura. Make sure you have a pack of cards in the house and a bit of meat." Kathleen laughed, at his pronunciation of meat as mate, he believed.

"God, Matt, you're a caution. But listen now, I phoned for a reason. It's to tell you or Kathleen that there's an envelope of stuff here for you. It's from Mr. Crossan, the man we talked to about Eoin's predicament there . . . and he gave us the best advice. Very nice man, but his own way about things. Maybe you know him, do you?"

"The barrister Crossan?" He recalled seeing or hearing the name somewhere. Yes, with one of Kilmartin's cronies, that was it. Grumbling about Crossan demolishing some case brought against an IRA man.

"The very one. It was his work that got the charges dropped against Eoin the next day."

Maura's voice dropped lower. Minogue imagined her shielding her words from someone passing in the hall, Mick most likely.

"Well, it came up in the course of a chat that you were a Guard, and, of course, in no time at all he knew your exact department. Very interested he was and all. Well, Matt, I don't know how I should put this to you, I'm not much good at this . . ."

Minogue sensed the awkwardness betokened some transaction in the rural commerce of obligations felt and favors returned. He could feel Maura's nervousness, the effort it had taken her to tell him, and his irritation disappeared.

"I'm not the sworn enemy of the legal profession, Maura. Officially, at any rate. What's Crossan about here now?"

Her voice was almost a whisper now.

"He mentioned the name Jamesy Bourke to me. Do you remember him?"

"Bourkes out by Kilrannagh? Wasn't there some trouble with them years ago?"

"That's them. Jamesy's the only one left. He was in prison these years. He only got out a few months ago and he's living up above in the mother's place since. It's only a shed really. Walks the roads like Methuselah with the beard and a big stick he carries. Talks to no one except himself or his dog. They say he went cracked in prison. The locals're afraid of him too."

"Do you recall what he ended up in prison for?"

Maura's reply came in a whisper. "He murdered a girl."

Minogue placed the chocolate on his tongue.

"And that's what Crossan wants to get in touch with me about?"

"Well, to make a long story short. Mr. Crossan had left an envelope about it with me a week ago so's I'd give it to you and you coming down. But he phoned today, asking would you be down soon —"

"Was he, em, in some class of a hurry with this, er? . . ."

She paused before replying. "Well, Matt, now he didn't say as much, but . . . I think so. But if it's any trouble to you, don't have anything to do with it. I told Mr. Crossan that you were very busy —"

Minogue thought of her laughter, her radiant smile, the hospitality she had showered on them over the years. She and Kathleen had grown to be like sisters.

"Ah, you're all right there, Maura, oul' stock," he said. "Don't be worrying. Keep that thing out of the floods you have and give it to me tomorrow evening."

"God bless, Matt!"

Kathleen watched her husband unwrap another chocolate.

"Leave a few for the children, can't you."

He rolled the foil into a ball, placed it on the telephone table and began flicking it about.

"Did you know anything about that?" he asked.

"The barrister fella? Yes I did. If you want my opinion, he put her in a corner. If I meet him, I'll tell him to his face, too. They're all the same, that mob."

"What are you saying?"

"'The best in the county, Mr. Crossan,' Maura tells me. Of course she went straight to his office in Ennis when Eoin was arrested. She would have sold the bloody farm if that was what it'd take to get Eoin out. As it turned out, this Crossan wouldn't take any money from her."

"So why are you dropping rocks on him?"

"I maintain that he knew all along that Maura was related to you and that he knew she'd feel under the obligation to him. That way she'd put him in touch with you. That's the way country people are."

"Tell me more about country people, Kathleen."

Kathleen didn't take the bait but examined her nails instead.

"Probably knew they were hard up for money as it was. Probably has some dirty work for a client that's willing to pay him buckets of money." She looked up from her nails. "Wants something under the table from you, no doubt," she declared.

An IRA lawyer, Minogue reflected again, or so described by a disgruntled senior Garda friend of Kilmartin's. Conniving afoot?

"Maybe I should give him a well-aimed kick so," said Minogue. He reached for another chocolate. "And tell him it's from you."

•   •   •   •   •

The shot cracked in the dusk like a branch snapping. He laughed and lowered the gun.

"There's a grand kick off this," he said. "Not too much, and not too little."

"Jesus Christ, Finbarr!" shouted the other man. "Don't be such a fucking iijit! What the hell do you want to be doing that for?"

"You've had your bit of fun for the day. Why can't I have mine?"

The other man, a little taller than the one with the pistol now dangling loosely at the ends of his fingers, bit back a retort. He swung the stock of the machine pistol back and stuck it in his armpit. Too short. Not meant to rest there? He stood up and slung the strap over his head before returning the stock to his armpit. He pulled the strap tight by shoving the gun forward. That's more like it, he thought. He looked down in the grass by his feet where he had laid the plastic wrap and the ammunition clips that he had been filling.

"Was it good?" asked Finbarr.

"Was what good?"

Merry, heavy-lidded eyes met his. "The ride. Was she good today?"

"Shut up. I told you before about that." He pulled the barrel down to

{ 24 }

feel the strap on his shoulder again. Good, steady. He spread his feet.

"Only asking."

"Don't ask. Mind your own business."

His companion looked down into the bottle. "Very touchy today, aren't we, Ciarán . . . darling?"

The other man ignored the gibe. Finbarr suddenly raised the Browning and loosed off another shot.

"You stupid fucking yob!" hissed Ciarán. He reached for the pistol but Finbarr turned and held it out of his reach. "Put it away and stop playing with it. Do you think it's a bloody toy or something? Give it to me!"

His friend chortled, thumbed the safety, and dropped it onto the plastic. He raised the bottle again.

"Well now, Ciarán. For a man who was supposed to have had a good time there, you seem awful jittery to me."

"If I am a bit jittery, it's because I've been watching you swallowing vodka and waving that gun around!"

He unhitched his gun and laid it carefully next to the pistol. As he stood stretching, he turned on his heels. Around him lay the Burren. Like the last place on earth, he thought. He had worked on the buildings in England for six years until the slump came. This is what he had wanted to come home to? Below him was the cottage they had been gutting and renovating for the new owners. They had been hired by Howard, whose company acted as a go-between for the Germans who had bought the place. Do it right, Howard's foreman had told them, and there'd be plenty more work like it.

"Might as well have a bit of crack," said the one with the bottle. "What's wrong with that?"

"It's not crack we're about at the present time," said the other. He squatted down beside the guns and began wrapping them and the clips in the plastic.

"Jesus, it's not like we're doing stuff that really needs doing by a certain time now, is it? I'm getting fed up waiting around. Breaking windows is all we're about so far as I can see."

The one wrapping the gun was a few years older than his companion. He concentrated on fingering the rubber bands over the ends of the package.

"Well?"

"Well what?"

"When do we get to, you know —"

"To what?"

"Ah come on now. You know. Use the fucking things right."

"Jesus, are you mad? You can't just decide to go around the place waving these without having thought it out carefully. We'll do the German's place tomorrow night like we planned, and that's it for the time being. So don't keep on asking me."

He picked up the package and stood. It'd be dark inside of a couple of hours.

"What's to stop us doing a bank job or something?"

Ciarán didn't answer.

"Well, why not? It's like playing with yourself instead of having a proper ride —"

The other man whirled around and hit him in the shoulder with his fist.

"Give over, for the love of Jases, Finbarr!" He waved the package. "Do you think we're doing this for entertainment value, is it? You're such a gobshite sometimes. Here I am, getting you in on this like I used to get you in in London, and look at you —"

"Hey! Don't fucking preach at me. We're in it together!"

"Well, don't you be slagging me about her! And don't be swilling that stuff on the job either!"

"What job?" He pointed the bottle toward the cottage. "Sure my work is done for today. I can take a drink if I want to. We're not up to anything tonight. What's the big deal, so?"

"Just don't be firing off that gun here."

"No one can hear us up here, only the birds —"

"It doesn't matter. It's just a bad habit to treat it so casual is what I'm saying."

"Bad habit! Hah! Look who's telling me about bad habits!"

Ciarán tightened his grip on the package and watched his friend laugh and turn away. Something gave way in him then and he felt the anger drop out of his chest. They had shared digs together, fallen into taxis pissed together, taken the mail boat home together. His friend had only started going on the drink lately, really. No girlfriend . . .

"Well, is she still the holy terror she was the last time?" he heard him ask. If anyone was entitled to take the mickey out of him, it was Finbarr.

"She's worse," he murmured, the anger completely gone now. "I'm worn out."

"Oh, you boy, you! Did she? Tell me, go on. What did she want this time?"

If only he'd act a bit more serious even.

"You're such a cowboy, do you know that?" he muttered. "One of these days . . ."

He glared at his smiling, tipsy friend who stood now with his feet spread wide, swaying slightly while he looked out over the hedges to the rocky heights. Christ, he thought, the opposite of scenic. What the hell did foreigners want to visit here for?

"Come on," he called out, anxious to shed the feeling that seemed ready to settle on him like the evening waiting close by. "Come on and we'll put the stuff back. Get a pint in town."

·   ·   ·   ·

With the suburban Dublin traffic behind them, Minogue drove the Fiat fast along the Galway Road. He had had little trouble persuading Kathleen to go the Galway Road. Dinner in Galway city, a walk around the streets and then down to the farm by teatime. Even with the new, widened stretches of roadway and the bypasses, he still considered Clare a long way off. The weeks of rain had deepened the color of the grasses and left the air clear. He thought of last night's Halloween callers. It was either the effect of the Spanish wine or the fluorescent brightness of the cloth, but he had ranked a mummy as the best costume and given it the extra propitiation of a fifty-pence piece. How many years since Daithi and Iseult had gone out on Halloween? Space blended with time as the countryside rolled by the Fiat. He thought of trips he had made all these years. When the kids were babies: that time Daithi had them up half the night with teething and he had forgotten to bring enough changes of clothes.

With his backside numb, Minogue piloted the Fiat through Athlone toward the River Shannon. He nudged Kathleen when they reached the middle of the bridge.

"Now we're in business," he said. "We're in God's country now, madam."

She looked up from her magazine at the Shannon. Black and wide, it idled toward Limerick and the sea.

"'To hell or to Connaught,'" she murmured.

"Typical Dublin gurrier remark," he said, and nudged her harder. "It's west of the Shannon where civilization actually starts, woman."

She flicked the magazine upright.

"Huh. You're beginning to sound like Jimmy Kilmartin more and more."

They had had a half-bottle of wine with a not-bad dinner of chicken in Galway city. He negotiated an hour in the hotel foyer with a pot of coffee and the paper and very nearly fell asleep, but Kathleen prodded him to go out in the streets. Minogue liked Galway very much. He sensed that this City of the Tribes, this mecca for the traveling people of the West of Ireland, was infused with a vigor and abandon due to the immensity of the Atlantic at the ends of its streets. Its visitors were in keen and anticipatory transit, passing a little time here in this portal city.

A poster of a starving child, black, naked, and bloated, caught his eye in a shop window. FAMINE STALKS AFRICA AGAIN was printed in fading black letters atop the poster. Large, glassy eyes returned the inspector's stare. On the bottom was the follow-up. "Famine knows no borders. Give to Concern this Sunday." Hoey, he thought then. Cheer him up with a phone call from his home county. And gather up any gossip without having to fence with Kilmartin. He found a phone in the post office. Eilis answered.

"No, he hasn't checked in. Might be the flu. Or something."

The irony in her halting utterance suggested to him that she too believed Hoey might have been on a batter and was too hungover. Or still pissed. Try him at home? No. Talk straight to him when he got back to Dublin, before Jimmy Kilmartin came to the boil about it and jumped on Hoey first.

A rising wind in from the sea brought more clouds. Minogue carried the cake and bottle of sparkling wine Kathleen had bought to the car, and they headed out of the city. They crossed into Clare a half hour later and Minogue turned inland off the Coast Road. The road narrowed and the Fiat began its gradual ascent through the Burren. As Minogue drove slowly through the limestone wilderness, the masses of stone began to exercise a subtle effect on him. He imagined that they were all there was to the world, that the earth had been petrified and worn down into this landscape. Not even glimpses of distant green lowlands between the hills broke the spell. He thought of the miles of caves beneath him, few of them mapped, which had been carved out by the underground waters. Hours and even days after rain, the further reaches of the caves flooded without warning, emerging as wells and ponds that appeared and drained over days or weeks or years.

The votive wells and springs near the farm still flowed. His sister, home from Toronto on a visit several years ago, had brought her youngest, Kevin — a gangling, skeptical, and embarrassed North American kid — to Tobar Dearg, the Red Well, for an asthma cure, he recalled. Next to the well was the *cillín,* a children's burial ground. For many years Minogue had thought of asking Kathleen if they could rebury Eamonn here amongst this tight cluster of stones. He had never actually talked to her about it. The idea of exhuming their infant son, gone a quarter of a century now, and bringing that small coffin west across Ireland would be too much for her, he believed.

"Not enough earth to bury a man," he murmured as they breasted a hill. "Not enough timber to hang him. Not enough water to drown him."

"Name of God." Kathleen elbowed him. She sat forward in the seat and looked hard at him.

"It's just a saying about the Burren —"

"Can't you come up with something a bit more, I don't know . . . cheerful, man? Look up in the sky — the sun is shining. Finally get a bit of weather! Cheer up!"

Minogue nodded at the stricken uplands continuing to unfold around the car.

"Cheerful? All right. 'Holy Mary of the Fertile Rock.'"

"Fertile Rock? What sense does that make?"

"That's the dedication the monks put on Corcomroe Abbey back in the twelfth century or so —"

He felt the car slowing a little. A soft bump alerted him.

"Here, why are you stopping here?"

"We have a puncture. The backseat on my side."

Kathleen followed him out onto the road and looked at the tire. Minogue rummaged in the boot.

"Do you want help?" she asked.

"No, thanks."

She stepped over to the remains of a drystone wall and looked through a gap between the ridges across Galway Bay at the Connemara mountains. Minogue bent to loosen the nuts before placing the jack. Aware of her watching him now, he stopped and looked over at her. A breeze caught her hair and swept it down over her forehead. She made to smile but a frown spread across her face instead. Her gaze wandered away to the heights inland. Worried, he thought. What was she thinking about?

One of the nuts was very tight and he paused several times to secure his grip. He felt himself being watched but when he turned to Kathleen, her back was to him. He looked over the rocks. Nobody. The nut gave way suddenly and the wrench clattered onto the road.

"Mind yourself," she called out, and turned back toward the uplands.

He stood up, stretched his back, and rolled the spare wheel over. He eyed her while he tightened the nuts again. She looks as if she sees something up there that she doesn't want to see, he thought. Suddenly aware of his eyes on her, she looked over and shivered.

"God, it's like a different continent or something." Her voice trailed off but her frown remained.

·　　·　　·　　·　　·

Guided by the light from the kitchen window, the inspector stepped into the cobbled farmyard. He had forgotten how dark a country night could be. He hoped that the cutting night air would banish the headache he felt coming on. It was only half nine. He shivered as he walked over the stones toward the car. He stopped by the gate and let the memories swirl around him. A breeze hissed through the hawthorn still rooted by the gate. A dog barked twice in the far distance and then fell silent. Minogue shivered again. Fretting breezes and gusts batted turf smoke from the kitchen range down into the farmyard around him. The sweet smell almost warmed him. The back door of the farmhouse opened and the light spilled across the yard. Eoin came out into the yard, wrestling his way into a coat.

"The da's just getting himself ready," Eoin said.

Minogue sat into the back seat of the Opel. Eoin left the door half-opened and the interior light stayed on. Minogue studied his nephew's profile for several moments. The same high cheekbones as his mother, the same thick, wavy hair even, but he had his father's thin lips. Even Mick's mannerisms, Minogue reflected dispiritedly.

"That was great ye came down now," Eoin said. "Mamo has been a bit odd this last while."

"She's had it tough this last while, all right," said Minogue.

Eoin turned in his seat. "How do you mean, like?"

Minogue considered backing away.

"You said she's had it tough. Is there something she's been keeping from us here —"

"No, I meant the farming, of course."

"True for you, Uncle Matt. True for you."

"And that gun in the boot of your car," Minogue added. He heard his nephew draw in a breath.

"I wondered if you'd bring that up. I had no idea that Liam was carrying a gun in his bag."

"If you had known, would you have kicked him out of the car?"

"Think what you like, Uncle Matt. I don't have anything to do with that kind of stuff."

Minogue thought of the fire glowing in the Aga in the kitchen, Maura laughing, a hand of cards maybe. Tell stories, a glass of whiskey. But Kathleen had dispatched him to the pub with a twenty-pound note to loosen tongues. And that bloody envelope was still lying on the hall table for him.

"Tell me something, Eoin," he began. "Have ye considered selling a bit off, maybe? A few acres. Who knows, you could probably get planning permission for houses or something."

"We're farmers here," Eoin declared. "We put the food on your tables up in Dublin."

"You and some poor divils growing onions in the arse end of Spain, you mean."

Anger flashed out of Eoin's eyes.

"With all due respect, Uncle Matt, what do you know and you up in Dublin this thirty years?" His voice rose. "Dublin's a different world entirely. Maybe you've forgotten who we are here."

"Forgotten what?"

Exasperation rippled across Eoin's face.

"The family farm and all that it means. 'Twas the country people brought us our freedom in '21. The people of Clare and plenty more that won our land back from the landlords in Parnell's day. We took pikes in our hands when we had no guns. We deserve every blade of grass that's under our feet."

Eoin's eyes strained as they looked into his uncle's. Whatever he saw there didn't seem to be the right answer. He blinked and returned to tapping the steering wheel. A speech worthy of his father, Minogue thought, as Mick Minogue stepped awkwardly out into the yard and began his labored, sideways walk to the car. He thought of the afternoon's drive through the Burren. Notions of property or boundaries seemed to falter and then fade entirely on the slopes of the desolate hills. Minogue suddenly felt his nephew's angry bewilderment as something familiar now, without menace.

"I farmed these fields, Eoin," he murmured. "It was hard then, too."

"All right," Eoin said. "So you know what it's like to see some bloody foreigner with pucks of money come in and snap up scraps of fields that'd mean the world to us. They put up bloody holiday homes . . . They're killing our way of life. I don't want to end up making their beds and cooking their dinners."

Mick Minogue let himself slowly down into the passenger seat. The Inspector again studied his nephew's face. Its frown of sincerity and anger, regret then as the brows lifted, moved Minogue. Dublin is a different world? The cold coming in under his arms and along his legs made Minogue shudder. Eoin talked while he drove the three miles into the coastal village of Portaree. It was a conversation that his passengers neither wanted to keep alive nor let die. So-and-so had sold out their twenty acres. Talk was that the buyer had planning permission for holiday homes. A folk village and museum was to be built nearby, too. At least the buyer was local, Eoin added.

"Who?" asked Minogue.

"Who else?" said Eoin. "Dalcais. Tidy Howard's outfit. Dan Howard runs it now."

"With the blessing of that bloody association, of course," Mick grunted.

"Which?"

"The PDDA," said Eoin. "The Portaree and District Development Association."

"There's one bloody farmer in that outfit," Mick said between his teeth. "Townies grubbing for money. It's a long way from Tidy Towns they've come."

Dan Howard, Senior, had put Portaree on the map years ago by promoting it in Ireland's Tidy Town contest, and the village had won the title several times since. Window boxes and fresh paint had been taken for granted in the town for two decades now. In tribute to Howard's astute business sense in connecting tidiness with tourism with development, the local people had wryly tagged him with his honorific, Tidy.

"I didn't know Tidy was gone," said Minogue.

"Oh no," said Mick. "Not gone to glory yet. He's in a nursing home after a stroke. They say he's lying up in the bed like a vegetable or something. They're not sure if he has his wits about him. Poor divil. For all you might have said ag'in him when he was in the whole of his health . . ."

The Opel shuddered on a pothole and Minogue glimpsed his brother's grimace. The first lights of Portaree flared on the windscreen.

A craft studio, a restaurant with candles and American Express signs in its windows, and a big grocery shop slipped by their car. A flux of memories took over Minogue's mind. Save for market days and Saturdays, his Portaree had been like a town asleep. He remembered cycling in for pints, cycling home again, drunk and dreamy, sometimes bitter, with escape carved on his heart. Mick seemed to read his brother's thoughts.

"Money in town now," he said. "We'd fork souls into the mouth of hell if the money were right."

The pub was half full. Faces turned to the Minogues and heads nodded greetings. They drew up to the bar. Minogue noted the brass foot-rail, the oil lamps hanging from the wall. The dismal shebeen of his own youth had been made over several times by the Howards. A barman unknown to Minogue raised his eyebrows at him. Before Minogue had asked Mick and Eoin what they would drink, a fat man turned on his stool by the bar. He cocked his cap back on his head, settled it, and greeted Mick.

"Gob now, Mick Minogue, is it yourself that I'm seeing in a pub? It must be the Christmas."

He chortled and swallowed from a pint glass of beer. The barman looked on, bemused and careful. The man's face put Minogue in mind of a pear, his nose pitted and large. The recessed eyes twinkled and the fat man spoke in a tone of mock earnestness.

"Please God, we'll see more of you so then, Mick?"

Minogue gave the barman a look sharp enough to cause him to elbow up from the counter.

"Jamesons," he said. "Two of 'em. Don't make a cod of them with ice or anything. Two bottles of stout for comfort on top of them. Pint of lager. Please."

"Are you here for the meeting, is it now, Mick?" asked the fat man.

"What meeting are you talking about?"

"Beyond in the dining room. Master Howard's in town tonight. The Development Association."

"The Dan Howard reelection committee, you mean," said Eoin.

The fat man's cheeks made slits of his eyes when he grinned.

"God, they haven't pulled the wool over your eyes, Eoin," he said. "Wide-awake you are, boy."

He turned his attention to Minogue and squinted out from the pouches around his eyes. The inspector folded his wife's twenty and handed it to the barman.

"I know you from somewhere . . . Ah, yes! You're the brother, the Guard up in Dublin. Wouldn't know you from Adam if I wasn't seeing you here next to the brother. Wouldn't know you at all."

Minogue took custody of the whiskeys and the bottles of stout.

"Maybe if you did, you wouldn't want to," he said.

The fat man regrouped with a smile and a nod. The barman changed the channel on the television. Minogue followed Eoin to a table and sat next to his brother.

"Don't mind that half-wit," said Mick. "He's Deegan from up the Saint's Quarter. 'As I roved out.' Does odd jobs for the Howards. Since Tidy's gone, I don't think there's much love lost between Dan Howard and your man here. Always trying to get a rise out of one or the other of us."

Dimly the inspector recalled a family of Deegans. He rolled a soup-spoon's worth of whiskey around under his tongue and then nodded it back to his tonsils. The heat detonated in his chest first. Minogue, one: early winter in the west of Ireland, nil. A man took an accordion from a case at a nearby table. Good, thought Minogue as the whiskey crept further through his intestines. Now he had an excuse for Kathleen: There was a session, my dear. How was he supposed to fob off advice on Mick or Eoin?

The musicians were soon loose and free with their instruments. A teenager with a ponytail and the faint and distracted smile Minogue associated with expert musicians started to fiddle. The accordion player began to slip in the extra notes and flourishes which are the insignia of Clare composition. The bar began to fill. Deegan had left the bar for a seat next to the fireplace where he drank with two younger men. Minogue spotted him looking toward their table once. During a break in the music, Mick wanted to talk about hurling. Minogue made a big effort to appear interested, but the music and the drink had set his mind rambling. Several times he glanced down at his empty whiskey glass, but Mick didn't get the hint. His own glass had remained half full for the past twenty minutes. Mick's hands had closed on one another as he talked and his hands worked slowly at stretching the fingers. Many would never straighten again, Minogue knew. God, another drink, he decided.

"Well, look," said Eoin, and leaned sideways to see around standing patrons. "The man himself."

Mick broke off his monologue, looked up, and wrinkled his nose. Minogue caught a glimpse of several men as they came through the door and made their way toward the bar. A hand rose and waved across the heads of the crowd at someone unseen to Minogue.

"Who?" he said to Eoin.

"Dan Howard and the crowd from the PDDA. Howard makes a point of dropping in here for a jar after the meetings. Oh, and here's the wife. Jacqueline Kennedy, I heard her called the other day."

"A state visit," grunted Mick. "His own damn pub and all."

Some memory came faintly to Minogue, but it disappeared before he could place it. She had straight white-blonde hair, lately trimmed, framing a ruddy, tanned face. The inspector was observing a woman who looked after herself, who had money and plenty of outdoor pursuits to make light of her years. Horsey maybe, he thought, with that fresh-faced, American sort of health. She wore a green loden over knee-length boots. A burrowing presence low under his ribs seemed to grow still. Confusion snared his thoughts tight; he realized that he was staring at her. From her gaze the inspector knew that she was well aware of eyes on her. He watched her shrug off her coat. His throat was suddenly dry. He took a breath and tried to swallow.

"Never passes up the chance of shaking a few hands toward the next election," said Mick. "He has the music organized for the same night as the PDDA meetings. Cute hoor, by God."

Dan Howard was six feet tall but looked even taller in his double-breasted suit. Black curly hair tinted with gray sat over his rosy, dimpled face. His eyes twinkled, his smile was steady and wide. Howard's hand strayed to his chest and searched out his tie, brushing it tighter inside his jacket. He shook hands with a young couple sitting at the bar and smiled at the musicians. One of them hoisted a glass in return. Minogue watched Dan Howard's impish, benevolent gaze sweep around the room. His winks and waves continued. He gave a thumbs-up and a gleeful wink to someone Minogue could not see.

"See the little fella under his arm," said Eoin. "He's a German. A bloody millionaire. He flies over every month for these meetings. I'm not joking you."

Minogue caught sight of a white-haired man with heavy, horn-rimmed glasses on a head that seemed larger than it needed to be. Howard's wife wore a loden, he remembered. A gift, maybe.

"Fell in love with the place. Yes, he's taken a special interest in our little corner of the world." Eoin's sarcasm brought Minogue's eyes to his nephew's.

"Spillner. He brings people here every now and then to buy places. Clare's ambassador in Germany."

Minogue looked over again at the group by the bar. Howard was still looking around the crowd. His eyes lingered on Minogue as though he were trying to recall a name to go with the inspector's face, and he smiled broadly. Minogue nodded back. Someone handed Howard a glass of whiskey. The German had made his way over to the musicians and was talking animatedly to them.

Howard moved away from the bar and worked his way around the tables. He paused by one to shake hands with an elderly man. He inclined over another to listen to a joke, his smile broader with anticipation. His eyes focused on Minogue while he listened. He showed perfect, even teeth when he laughed. The fiddle player drew his bow across the strings, set his jaw and launched into a reel. Spillner pushed at his glasses, laid his glass down and began clapping.

Mick eased himself more upright in his seat and grunted.

"Look at him, would you, for the love of God."

The music had restored Minogue, renewed his thirst. He stood and made his way through the crowd, Damn it all, he thought, he'd do his best to spend the twenty-quid fee his wife had given him for parleying with Mick and Eoin. Danger money. He watched the barman uncapping the bottles of stout.

"So how's Dublin?" called out the barman.

"Ah, it's all right. A bit like Mars by times. But I like it."

The barman shrugged and turned to the till. The fiddle wailed high over the guitar now and Minogue's blood began to race with the music. His foot began rehearsing in miniature the steps to a Clare Set. Howard was still on the move. Minogue could not locate Howard's wife, but as he stepped away from the bar he spotted her sitting next to the German.

While he clapped vigorously she was looking at the musicians with a faint smile. She glanced over suddenly and returned Minogue's gaze for several moments. The inspector felt the soft compression about his chest again. A nudge on his arm from another patron drew him around to face the bar. The barman was shouting at him over the music.

"Your change!"

Minogue returned to the table and fended off money held out by Eoin. He wanted an excuse to stand up so that he could see her again. What was it about her that looked so familiar? Maybe she had been inspecting him to see if she could peg him from a family likeness. He thought of how her shoulders had rolled when she had slipped off the loden. And him like the world's biggest iijit standing there, forgetting his change, staring at her. He took a gulp from his glass.

It was then that the inspector noticed the customers moving away from the door. The man who now stood in the doorway seemed immune to the ruckus around him. He wore a thick black workman's coat, a donkey jacket, with the collar turned up. Though he was tall and wiry, his shoulders were hunched under a mop of white hair. His beard was still almost completely black. The inspector shifted to get a better angle and saw the plastic shopping bags dangling from the man's hands. Others in the crowd had begun to look toward the new arrival now. The barman looked up from a glass he was filling and frowned. Several people edged closer to the bar. Minogue looked back at the bearded man. There was something more to him than that furtive alertness that Minogue associated with people who were cracked. In the animal shyness and caution was defiance.

The barman left the glass on the counter half-filled and lifted the hinged countertop. Men around the bar made way for him. The bearded man noted him coming toward him but returned to looking around the groups in the bar. The fiddle player left the guitar and the accordion to account for the melody and began to soar and fall around it. The German millionaire was smiling broadly, swaying from side to side on his stool. The barman's face was set in an expression of resolute regret as he talked to the bearded man. The bearded man kept looking at the faces in the pub. The barman's hands went to his hips and he nodded toward the door. The bearded man looked at him for a moment, seemed about to say something, but pivoted. Minogue saw that the bags seemed to be crammed with newspapers. So still had the collie been in the shadows behind that Minogue was surprised when it stirred. Minogue looked up from the animal to find the man's eyes staring at him. The intensity held his eyes for a moment before returning to the barman's. The barman nodded at the door again and shrugged. The bearded man left. The collie trotted out, its eyes locked on the man's boots. Minogue looked to their wake until the door swung back, then sipped from his whiskey. Ah, good heart, he tried to decoy himself. The drop of malt, the soft drift into comfort; there's always whiskey.

Mick leaned over and murmured into Minogue's ear.

"That poor divil. Your man there, the go-by-the-wall. You know him."

Mick shifted slowly in his chair and Minogue saw his brother's face seize with pain as he moved.

"That envelope back at the house," Mick added, sucking in air.

"Was that Jamesy Bourke?"

"None other."

Minogue watched as Mick rubbed under his chin with the back of his hand.

"There's a family that's scattered to the four winds. The mother only died a while ago. Three year. I tell a lie. Four. Four come the Christmas. She lived there alone and died of a broken heart. Jamesy was let out under guard for the funeral and he was gone again until a few months ago."

"Let out," Minogue repeated.

"Don't you remember that fire? The dead girl? A Canadian girl? I suppose it's ten or twelve years or more now. She was burned to death in a cottage she was renting. It was Jamesy set the place on fire and she inside. A love thing that went sour on him. He got a life sentence as I recall."

Minogue thought of the envelope he had dropped into the suitcase back at the farm. Crossan, the barrister, was working in some capacity for Jamesy Bourke. Something lurched into his thoughts then. Had Bourke known he'd be here tonight? Had he come to talk to him?

"I heard he lost his mind in prison," Mick murmured. "Took a knife to a warder and had time tacked on to his sentence for it . . ."

"But he's — ?"

"Ah, he has medication and that." Mick flicked his head. "So far, so good, I suppose. No run-ins with anyone. Yet. But there's plenty of people didn't want him coming back here at all. They cross the street or turn around rather than have to pass him. The poor divil. Lonely there by himself. There's only Jamesy and his dog left above in the cottage. Very fond of the dog. You'd hear him talking away to the dog and they walking the roads, the two of them. It was the mother, God rest her, scraped that little house out of the farm after she was rid of it."

Mick shrugged and began massaging his hands again.

"There was bad luck on that family, there's no doubt," he added.

Minogue stood and began to thread his way toward the toilet. Dan Howard was still on the move, shaking hands with a man just in the door of the pub. When he turned Howard was gone. The musicians' faces looked redder but more determined, but neither the German nor Mrs. Howard sat next to them now. Newcomers occupied the table, faces vaguely familiar to Minogue. He nodded at them and smiled, trying to place them, believing that he knew the family at least. He sat down next to his brother with faint dismay still hanging in his mind. Eoin raised his glass and tipped it against his uncle's.

"Your health, now, Uncle Matt, and all belonging to you."

·   ·   ·   ·   ·

The edges of the road glistened under the streetlamps and the night air was astir with the breeze in off the sea. Minogue felt its presence as it rolled and lapped up to the shore below the village. He paused on the threshold of the pub and watched a rain so fine as to be almost mist bloom under the rim of the streetlamps. The door of the pub hissed closed behind him, swallowing the talk within. He listened more keenly now, but he still couldn't be sure that it was the hush of the sea he was hearing. The smell of seaweed from the harbor, mingled with turf smoke, thickened the air around him. Eoin blundered out the door, nearly pitching him into the street.

"Sorry, Uncle Matt."

Eoin fiddled with the car keys and Mick paused to blow his nose. Minogue heard a dog bark up the street. A man laughed raucously somewhere. The dog howled as though struck and then began barking again. In between barks, Minogue heard laughs and a guffaw. He walked beyond the car and stopped by the forecourt of a garage recessed in from the street. From there he saw Deegan poke at the shopping bag. Bourke held the bag of newspapers tighter. The streetlamp reflected off his eyes as they darted from Deegan to the other two. The dog made another run at Deegan but moved to avoid a boot from one of Deegan's cronies.

"What's in the bag, professor?" Deegan called out over the dog's growling. "Dirty pictures, hah?"

Minogue remembered that same tone of bogus kindness in the sadistic teachers of his youth. Jamesy Bourke wrapped his arms around the bag and his eyes fastened on Minogue. Eoin and Mick now stood beside him. Deegan caught sight of the Minogues and turned to face them. The two men with him, young, with the slack smiles of men who had been drinking, turned also.

"A man can't stop and water his horse without some quare fella lying in wait and looking on," said Deegan. "Isn't that a divil?"

He glanced at the collie and then raised his arms and hissed. The dog recoiled, barking furiously. Deegan laughed. Still chuckling, he ambled by Mick. The two younger men followed.

"Tell me something," Minogue said as they passed. "Is it just the Halloween or are ye like this every night of the year?"

Deegan slowed his jaunty gait. Minogue noted how thick he was in silhouette. One of the men's shoes scuffed on the edge of the footpath and he took an extra step to steady himself.

"Ah, the polis down from the big city, bejases," Deegan drawled. "Enjoy your little holiday now, can't you, and then go home to Dublin without worrying about us humble folk down here. We can look after ourselves."

The inspector turned back to where Bourke had been standing. He was gone.

• • • • •

Minogue laid the envelope on the chest of drawers and began to finger his laces loose. Kathleen looked out from behind a paperback.

"I think I remember it now," she said.

"He was released just a few months ago."

Kathleen retreated behind the book. Her tipsy husband stared at the picture on the cover. A girl with long hair and her dress off her shoulder had her leg around a Robert Redford type inclined over her. Smoke-puffing cannon and soldiers busied themselves in the background. He stood and let the trousers drop, sat down on the bed and drew the trousers around his heels. Was it cold in Dublin too? Hoey. Where was Aine again? Zimbabwe. Hot there, no doubt.

"Not a word out of him," Minogue murmured. "Just walked off." The damp air brushed against his bare legs. The room had been his parents' and the wallpaper was a half-dozen layers thick.

"Who? Mick?"

"Jamesy Bourke. I thought he might come over and say something. But he just took off, himself and the dog."

Kathleen laid the book face down.

"God, can't you stop reminding me about that fella? You come home with a few jars on you and the first thing, you want to tell me all the gory details about it."

"Wait a minute there. You're one of the ones helped set me up for this little 'job' that bloody barrister Crossan wants me to do."

"Did you talk to Eoin or Mick about the future even? No, you didn't."

"There was music."

"There was music. Of course there was music. There's always something getting in the way."

"I can't just waltz in and start talking about selling the farm."

"Maybe not, but here you are, to top it all off, sitting there this last half-hour reading that stuff in the envelope. Some kind of lunatic. God, it gives me the creeps, man."

"What time did Crossan phone again?"

"Half an hour after you left for the pub. Maura asked me first. I told her to tell him you worked better around food. Twelve o'clock, the Old Ground in Ennis, tomorrow."

"I was obviously working under the delusion that we were on a holiday of sorts here," he murmured. "But you seem to have my schedule well in hand. The setup at the pub with Mick and Eoin —"

"Ah go on, would you. I gave you twenty quid to kill the pain there."

"— and now you're setting up appointments with Crossan —"

Kathleen pursed her lips and shook the book as though to wring more satisfaction from it.

"Why don't you go back to reading what he sent you in the envelope," she murmured. "Can't you always say no to him?"

·   ·   ·   ·   ·

"Shit," he whispered. He felt the pliers still in his back pocket as he hunkered down. Be a really stupid thing to be running and drop them and have the bloody Guards find them and trace the tool to them. He drew them out, put them in his jacket pocket and buttoned it.

"What?" said the other man.

"Nothing."

He had snipped the phone easily at the gable end of the house where it came down from the pole. Scurrying back toward the ditch, however, he had slipped in the wet grass. He was angry and embarrassed at looking clumsy. He searched his companion's face for any sign of a smile. As if he himself had been drinking and deserved a going-over this time — a taste of his own medicine. His companion waited, preoccupied, the gun under his jacket. He patted the pocket to feel the pliers secure now and looked back toward the car they had parked in a recess by the wall. He could just make out the dark strip of its roof.

"Jesus. Pitch-black tonight," said the one with the gun. His friend was pleased to hear the tension in his voice. No drink on the job tonight. Maybe he was coming around at last.

"That's because you were looking at the lights in the house. Your eyes'll get used to it in a while."

"They'd better . . ."

"We're gone inside of a minute now, right?" The other man nodded. "Hold it up near as you can to the sight, remember. There can't be slack in the strap. Okay?"

"Okay, chief."

"Otherwise it could fly all over the place or go high."

"Yes, boss."

"Shut up with the smart remarks. Have you set it?"

"Course I have."

"Check it —"

"I *did* fucking check it! Ten times! Give over, can't you, for Christ's sake."

"No closer than about twenty feet now," the other went on, his voice strained with the effort to remain patient. "I don't want you hitting anyone in there. That's not the idea."

"I heard you the first time," snapped the one with the gun. "Wouldn't want the little man to be getting hurt now, would we?"

He took the gun out from under his jacket, shouldered the strap and stood up.

"Just let me get on with it, for fuck's sakes! Go on back to the car, you."

The curtains were drawn in both lighted windows. The gunman looked back down at his companion.

"Go on, fuck you! Don't be worrying! Git!"

The other moved off reluctantly. He reached the wall and looked back toward the house. Then he cleared the wall and got into the car. It took enormous effort to control his urge to stay by the wall and make sure his companion wasn't screwing up. Both windows in the Escort were rolled down. He stuck his head out and looked up at the sky. A patch of stars had appeared. He looked across the passenger side then. No sound. Christ, he had screwed up. He looked at his watch and the jolt of fright beat hard in his chest. Four minutes already. Lonely as the place was, a car could come by. He mentally reviewed the way home and tested his night vision by staring at the outlines of the walls. He knew he'd have to drive up to a mile with the lights off, and smartly too.

Jesus, do it, or get to hell out of there! He swore and slapped the passenger seat. He was about to get out and head for the cottage when he heard the hammering stutter of the gun. His heart leaped. Not too loud, he thought with relief. Glass tinkles and what sounded like a ricochet followed. The silence after the shots seemed even deeper. He strained to hear running feet. The burst had been about two seconds. He hadn't given in to the temptation to be a cowboy about it. The gunman came over the wall wide-eyed, his teeth showing. The driver had the door pushed open. The gun clattered against the door and the chortling man fell into the seat, breathing hard. The driver had the engine started. He let in the clutch and moved smoothly away onto the dark road.

"Make sure the safety's on."

"I did it already before I headed back," the other whispered, breathlessly, and began giggling. He fought to get his breath back as it turned to laughter. "Just after you went, the light in the jacks went on. Here's my chance, I said to meself!"

He paused to laugh again.

"Keep it down!" said the driver, his eyes boring into the darkness ahead.

"I gave him a few seconds to get the trousers down — ha ha ha — and then I gave him the surprise of his life, so I did. Oh, Jases, such timing! Perfect!"

"You didn't shoot in the window of the jacks, did you?"

He wanted to clatter his companion but he couldn't take his eyes from the road.

"No, I didn't! Don't be getting yourself in a state. I went for the living room. But you can imagine the state your man is in now, ha ha ha! . . ."

He laughed again and couldn't seem to regain control. The driver smiled. His passenger drew up his knees and panted, helpless with laughter. Relief, he knew, must have been very tense, of course, he must have been. He'd done all right — they'd done all right.

"All right, all right," he said. Ahead he could make out the coast road. "Don't get carried away now. Let's drop it off." He nodded toward the submachine gun resting in the passenger's lap.

The gunman turned suddenly calm and his eyes grew wide again.

"That's some gun, that," he said with whispered fervor. "It's the best fucking thing since —"

"Yeah, yeah."

"What are you fretting about? We did great. Don't be fretting, for Jases' —"

"I'll fret if I fucking want to!"

The sudden return of his anger surprised the driver. He immediately tried to lighten it.

"Someone needs to fret about you, you bollocks," he murmured.

His passenger folded the stock and laughed. The driver turned the headlights on and sped up.

"Sounds to me like you need another bit of how's your father . . . Wouldn't you try a pint or something instead?"

The driver felt some relief taking the place of his anxiety. Why get annoyed now?

"Are you buying, is it, for a change?"

"And fuck you too," grinned the passenger, and he slapped the driver hard on the thigh.

CHAPTER 3

M INOGUE AWOKE EARLY to the sounds from the yard. It was seven. He must have fallen asleep immediately last night. He did not try to get back to sleep but lay still for ten minutes, the eiderdown up to his nose. Faint dawn light brought depth to the forms in the room, sharpening the corners and picture frames. He listened to the rhythmic humming suction of the milking machine before he tiptoed into the hall. Maura was setting the table. She smiled at him and went to crack eggs into a bowl. He wondered if she had slept at all.

"Howaryou, Matt?" she whispered. "Are you good?"

"Powerful," he said. He put on his coat. "The air here is mighty."

"There's spare wellies there," said Maura. "They'd be a fit."

He slid into them and stepped out into the yard. A bright dawn was soaking in between the hedges on Drumore Hill. The sky was clear and sharp, and Minogue rubbed his hands against the chill. His eye caught the silver edges in the yard, the ruts and holes where water had frozen. Mick was watching his son moving cattle through the milking parlor. He nodded to his brother.

"The happy lot of the farmer," Minogue tried. "At one with nature and her bounty."

"My eye," grunted Mick.

The brothers watched Eoin washing teats. Minogue helped Eoin move cattle out until he received a tail flicked across his face for his troubles.

"God, these are very boisterous creatures," said Minogue. "Are you sure they're not goats?"

Mick shook his head but did not reply. Eoin wore a frown of concentration as he moved about between the cows. Minogue blew into his hands and watched his breath vapor and trail off in the morning air. A sudden shaft of light struck at the side of his head, the sun cresting over the shed across from the milking parlor.

"Fresh," said Minogue. He turned to his brother. "Aren't you cold?"

"If and I am, I can't feel it," replied Mick. His hands came out of his pockets. "I might as well have bits of stick on the ends of these arms this morning."

Minogue held back from words of encouragement, knowing that his brother would hear them as pity. The sun blazed in the doorway now. The glare caught the nap on a cow's rump and outlined every hair. He looked around the parlor again and smelled the milk and the dung and the straw and the sweetness in the cows' breath. What the hell more can I do that I'm not already doing, he thought. He walked to the doorway to get some sun.

Two cars were entering the yard. One stopped within feet of the milking parlor, the other by the back door of the house. Minogue tried to shield his eyes but the low sun blinded him. He knew the cars for what they were when he saw the antennae still quivering after the engines were shut off. A young Guard with a crew cut and a long bony nose with a kink in it was out of the car quickly. Another in a soft leather jacket followed him from the passenger side. Minogue stepped out of the sunlight to see the farmhouse better. Two other men were gone in the door of the house.

"Lookit," Minogue began. "There's only the woman of the house and my —"

The Guard with the long nose brushed by him. The other stared at Minogue and stood to the other side of the doorway. The inspector made for the doorway but Leather Jacket stepped in front of him. He heard running footsteps in the yard. Another guard, a curly-headed older man with a pepper-and-salt mustache and a bomber jacket, entered.

"He's out here, all right," he said, with barely a glance at Minogue. "Who are these fellas?"

"Who are you?" Minogue asked.

The one with the mustache looked at Minogue and then beyond him.

"Down here," said Crew Cut. "Him and the da."

"What the hell are ye doing?" Mick Minogue began.

"Take the da and this fella out to the house," said Mustache. "Or sit one of them in the car."

Minogue started to follow Mustache down to where Eoin was standing. He had gotten two steps before his arm was pinned. He was down on his knees with his head twisted in a lock when the shouting began. He too tried to shout but the Guard's arm covered his mouth. Minogue inhaled the leathery scent from the arm over his face.

"This one's trouble," the Guard called out.

Minogue's mind flared with the sharp pain as his arm was pushed farther back.

"What the hell are ye about?" Mick was bellowing.

"Keep off now," said Mustache. He and the other detective closed on Eoin. Minogue heard more footsteps behind him.

"Lace him up," said the Guard holding him. "The oul' lad might be throwing shapes here in a minute."

With the headlock released, Minogue bent forward to ease the armhold. His other arm was grabbed and he heard the soft clicks as the plastic restrainers were cinched home.

"Bloody gangsters, the lot of ye!" Mick shouted. Eoin's eyes darted from one Guard to the other.

"Shut up," said Mustache. The Guard who had been holding Minogue stepped by him and faced Mick. Eoin had a pitchfork in his hand. The Guard in the leather jacket drew a pistol from under his jacket and held it at arm's length, pointing it at Eoin.

"Eoin!" Minogue shouted. The cattle began lowing and stamping their feet as they jerked at the chains. "Leave it down, Eoin!"

One of the cattle began kicking at the bars. The milking machine droned on: sum-sum, sum-sum. Eoin dropped the fork and the Guards were on him.

"Jases," Minogue heard the Guard with the gun mutter. He realized that he was still on his knees.

"Get up and let's have a look at you," said the Guard. He slid the pistol under his arm and pulled Minogue by the armpit. "You're not here to help your man here pike hay, are you?"

Minogue turned to face him. He was a stocky, tired-looking man in his late thirties. His hair had receded to a point directly over his ears. His breath smelled of cigarettes. He narrowed his eyes as he searched Minogue's face. Minogue watched the surprise roll down his face until his mouth opened.

"Divine Jases," said the Guard and he looked over Minogue's shoulder at his colleagues. "This is what's-his-name. Up in Dublin. I done a stint, a training thing with the fingerprint section in the Bureau up in Dublin." His eyes returned to Minogue's. "You're one of them, aren't you? One of us, I mean."

. . . . .

Cuddy shook his head again and scratched at his scalp. Minogue sipped at his mug of tea. Cuddy lit another cigarette. He breathed out the smoke and used the spent match to poke at the other butts in the ashtray. Cuddy was a sergeant in the Special Branch. He had driven in from Limerick just after midnight.

"All right," he said in the middle of another yawn. "Point taken. But this isn't Dublin where help is thirty seconds away."

Minogue pinned him with a glare.

"No offense now," said Cuddy. "Oh no." He placed the cigarette between his lips to free his hands. "But look at it from our point of view."

He began counting on his fingers, pausing to grasp each finger for several moments. "Three ton of stuff from Libya dug up out of the dunes there in near Bracagh over the summer. Semtex. Thirty-odd assault rifles."

He drew on his cigarette to give Minogue pause to look impressed. He feigned an earnestness that Minogue knew was not native to the man.

"And that siege with your man last year, Jesus," he whispered. "Lawlor, the madman on the run for six years. Three solid days and three nights of shooting."

Minogue nodded. Cuddy dug his elbows into the armrests and sloped forward in the chair, one eye half-closed as a shield against the ribbon of smoke rising from his lap.

"None of them come quiet anymore. Can you blame Reilly for using the hardware there?"

Minogue remained unconvinced. Cuddy rallied for more.

"While ago, in Feakle, we got a call there was shots up in a quarry near the town. There was a vanload of us left Limerick and a squad combing the place inside of ninety minutes that night. Nothing, of course. You can't be taking chances."

"But these arms dumps are for the North," Minogue said. "And you know that. You read the same circulars as I do."

Cuddy cocked a bloodshot eye at this inspector down from Dublin.

"Fair enough," he conceded. "Then how come we have a gun in the back of your nephew's car?"

"He had no knowledge of what his pal had in that bag. And you know that."

"With all due respect to you and yours now, your nephew has a mouth on him. It's bad manners to be giving speeches about politics and constitutional rights to Guards who have been shot at."

Minogue weighed a retort but decided to hold back.

"Anyway," Cuddy continued, "the IRA has handed out guns locally, that's plain to see. That's what has us going in hard first time out. Can you blame us, I mean to say?"

Minogue couldn't. He had watched the detectives shambling back to their cars where they now sat while Cuddy held this powwow. Maura had vacated the kitchen, her departure punctuated by the sharp thud of a pot of tea on the table between the two policemen. Minogue had liked what he heard as Maura went back down the hall. She had stood up to her husband and didn't care who heard her tell him to whisht and let the Gardai settle it.

"When did all this happen again?"

"Just around the eleven o'clock mark," replied Cuddy. "One burst of shots — faster than an automatic, awful like what we took away from your nephew's car, the way it was described —"

"Give over with that now," Minogue waded in. "That's Make-My-Day Delahunty's style of management. This national sport of jumping to conclusions's turning into a blood sport."

"The shots came in the windows high up, as if to say they were warning shots. Phone line cut, nice and neat. This fella is kicking up murder. Spillner. He's a big shot. It's a damn sight different than knifing tires and painting slogans on the walls."

"It is that," Minogue allowed.

Cuddy killed the butt conclusively, looking down his nose as though he were putting a fallen housefly out of its misery. He spoke in a monotone now.

"If the IRA is into this kind of a stunt so as to scare off tourist money here, it's news to me. That's all I can say at this stage. It'd get the headlines, let me tell you, and easy enough done too: a few forays at night, a bit of shooting. Millions of pounds frightened out of the country. The likes of yourself or myself might not like some German buying up houses here, but the law is the law and the EC is the religion of the day. We have to chase fellas and kick them around for the sake of some continental you or I wouldn't give the time of day to ordinarily."

Cuddy's face had lapsed into an openly cynical expression. He issued a rueful smile then and scratched the back of his neck. Minogue recalled Spillner smiling, clapping to the music in the pub.

"We wouldn't want to have to consult you in your official capacity if things get out of hand here and some bloody holiday-maker gets himself plugged one night in his cottage. Cottage?" He snorted and threw his head back momentarily. "What am I saying, cottage? Bloody palace he has. You should see it, I'm telling you. 'Vy vould zey doo zis to me?' I heard Spillner saying. Hah. I heard he even speaks a bit of Irish. Sits in the pub soaking up culture. Gas. Him trying to learn Irish, me busy trying to forget mine. They have more respect than we do ourselves, I'll tell you that. Culture and stuff, I mean."

"They're welcome to soak up what they can," said Minogue. "I keep on hearing how we have so much to spare."

"Ah, there's a Clareman talking," said Cuddy. "You Clare crowd have all your high kings and fairies, but it's far from palaces the likes of us in Leitrim were reared. I'll be seeing you."

Minogue congratulated himself on being but one county away in his guess. He had pegged Cuddy for County Longford. Palaces, he thought, and looked around the kitchen again. The old fireplace had been filled in even before he had left the farm for Dublin. As a baby he had been bathed here. Here he had argued with his father, played cards, poured and drunk whiskey over thirty years ago. He recalled the apartment brochures on the kitchen table in his Dublin home. Far from this indeed, he thought.

"Do you want a statement?" he said to Cuddy's back. Cuddy turned with a wry look.

"Ah, no. Thanks. Ye were below in the pub, the three of you, so say no more. We found no one after a night's work, you see. Truth is that Eoin wasn't high up enough on our list. Otherwise we'd have been here in the door on ye at one o'clock this morning."

Minogue followed Cuddy outside. The yard was full of sunlight now. The cold air caught in Minogue's nose and made his eyes water. Mick and Eoin stood by the door to the byre. Cuddy didn't spare them so much as a nod as the two cars left the farmyard, their tires rasping over the patchy cement.

"Black and Tans," Mick hissed.

Minogue's anger propelled him across the yard in long strides.

"Am I one as well, Mick? Am I?"

Mick returned the stare. Eoin shuffled his feet and looked down at his wellies.

"You and your bloody notions," Minogue went on. "Declare to God, you had me driven up the walls years ago. Inside your head must be like, I don't know, the ruin of some old house or something."

"And what have you?" Mick retorted. "Only the company of the likes of those fellas. Up in Dublin, you are — you have no home except up in Dublin. Dublin! Them that turned their chamber pots on the men of 1916 and they marching away to be shot."

Minogue looked away in exasperation. The hedges were dark with the sun low behind them.

"I did as much and more work in this very spot as you did, let me remind you," he muttered then. "I know plenty about knocking a living out of stones and bogs. Them fellas just gone are none to my liking either, but they have this character weakness. We all do, if we're human at all, man."

He stared at his nephew in an effort to get Eoin to look at him. He realized that he had been preaching. He stopped then and his breath tumbling aloft was lit from the sun behind. The endlessly bright morning arching over the farmyard had swiped all his words. He tried to follow that small cloud which was his own spent breath dissipating. Mick was walking stiffly away toward the house.

"They don't want to be blown out of their shoes," Minogue called after his brother, not caring if he was heard. "That's all that's bothering them."

•　　•　　•　　•　　•

Minogue drove into Ennis daydreaming about Santorini. The traffic slowed as he rounded the monument at the Mill Road. He turned by Harmony Row, coasted over the bridge on the River Fergus and drove down Abbey Street to the Old Ground hotel. Ennis sparkled under the sun, black shadow, and glare of shop windows together in the twisting, narrow streets he liked. Pedestrians keen to see a familiar face looked to the passing cars. Knowing none himself, Minogue still lifted his fingers in salute.

With the traffic completely at a standstill now, Minogue rolled down the window. He leaned over and saw a Garda leaning on a car roof ahead, talking in the window. Bareheaded and domestic-looking, the guard had ash-gray hair and a beard that needed attention twice a day. He studied Minogue's card.

"I'm going for a dinner at the Old Ground," said Minogue. "Am I safe in Ennis this morning?"

"Oh, fire away, now," said the Guard and squinted through the glare off Minogue's windscreen. "It's a court case going on to do with the shoot-out there back in July. They're probably breaking for their dinner now anyway. But there's no parking around the courthouse on account of the business."

"Fair enough," said Minogue.

The guard sighed.

"Is it like this in Dublin?"

"Worse. There's no place to park at all."

The guard smiled dryly and tapped on the roof with his fingertips.

"Go ahead now, Inspector."

Minogue counted a half-dozen Garda cars parked in the side streets. He spotted a tactical van immediately with its triplet of antennae and its stubby wire for the telephone link quivering slightly as someone moved around inside the vehicle. The inspector parked and checked his watch. He was twenty minutes early for Crossan. He decided to stroll a roundabout way to the Old Ground.

Alerted by a reflection in a shop window, the inspector turned to find a wigged and gowned lawyer flying, it seemed to him as he studied the billowing robe, across the street toward him. Behind the sharp nose, which made Minoge think of Pinocchio, were bulging thyroid eyes. They made for an expression of intense fright.

"Are you the Inspector Minogue I'm supposed to be meeting?" Crossan called out.

"I am that. How did you know?"

"Ha ha!" Crossan guffawed. "And you the detective! I saw you walking away from a car with a Dublin registration. But sure, you're the spit of your brother!"

Spit, thought Minogue.

"Cut out of him," said Crossan. "Will we mosey on to the Old Ground now?"

Minogue fell into step alongside the barrister. A half-dozen steps from the door of the hotel, Crossan stopped suddenly and wheeled around. He looked up and down the busy street. Minogue imagined the swelling eyes popping out onto the steps, rolling and bouncing down through a Dali Ennis. He dared a quick survey of Crossan's face and noted the blue bristles, each clear in the skin that looked like paper. Definitely an indoor plant. Was he looking for someone or something?

"And you belong to Rossaboe and places west?" Crossan murmured.

Belong? Perhaps he did, the inspector supposed. Thirty years in Dublin had but rubbed him down to bedrock. As weather is to climate.

"Born, bred, and starved there," Minogue admitted. The lawyer smiled briefly, walked to the door of the hotel, and held it open.

A waitress whom Crossan called Maureen led them through the dining room. Yes, she told Minogue, the coffee was freshly brewed.

"You got the envelope then," said Crossan. "The photocopies, like."

Minogue nodded and inspected the cutlery. As regards trappings, the hotel had improved no end, he had to conclude. His last dining adventure here had been nearly six years ago when he had come down to Ennis to bury an uncle on his mother's side. He pondered the possibility of soaking Crossan for a salmon and seafood dish listed for fifteen quid.

"And the, er, thing that Jamesy penned. That epistle? . . ."

"As best I could," said Minogue. "Tended to be repetitive, really."

"Did it make any sense to you?"

"Not a whole lot. Have you had many dealings with mental illness in your job, Counselor?"

Crossan flashed a rueful smile that ended in a frown. The waitress appeared with the wine. Minogue looked around the room as she poured. The dining room was almost full. Businessmen, farmers, and traveling men down for the mart, a few late-in-the-season tourists. A table across from theirs had a reserved sign on it. As he reached for his glass the couple appeared in the doorway.

She looked tall here, he thought. Her hair was actually blonde, her eyes clear and still. She seemed to be brighter and clearer than others in the room, as if she had captured some sharp light all for herself. For an instant, Minogue believed he could smell a faint perfume. Dan Howard stood next to her now. A waitress fussed around them. More faces turned toward the couple.

{ 53 }

"Well, now," he heard Crossan say. The ice was tugging at Minogue's guts now. She had seen them, noted them, he believed.

The tone, a mix of sarcasm and stern humor, brought Minogue to.

"And good day to you, Mr. and Mrs. Howard," Crossan called out.

Dan Howard winked at Crossan. His smile broadened as he walked to Minogue's table. Sheila Howard strolled after him.

"Well, Alo, you're always busy," said Howard. He leaned in and offered his hand to Minogue.

"Parlous times as ever," said Crossan. "Where there's trouble, there's money."

"Hello, Aloysious," said Sheila Howard. She nodded at Minogue.

Minogue's chest was tight but his heart's thump seemed to visibly rock it. Sheila Howard blinked, smiled, and looked from Minogue to Crossan. Minogue tried not to look at her face. He wondered if anyone could see his chest pounding.

"And Mick Minogue's brother, how are you?" he heard Dan Howard asking.

"I'm very well," he managed to say.

"A small world, now, isn't it?" Howard went on. "Are you enjoying your holiday?"

"To be sure," said Minogue.

"Great. I hope you're considering coming back home sometime, are you? We've a lot going on in Clare nowadays."

"In more ways than one," said Crossan.

Howard grinned.

"Time enough," said Minogue.

Howard laughed. An easy, cheery laugh. Disarming, Minogue thought. A favored son, the boy, this Dan Howard seemed.

"Great," said Howard, and rubbed his hands together. He turned to Minogue with a sardonic squint.

"You're sitting next to the best barrister in County Clare, I'll have you know. You know where to find me if you want me, I hope. Drop into the office anytime. Don't mind that crowd up in Dublin."

The Howards returned to their table. Sheila Howard sat down and her husband followed, flapping loose his napkin from the glass. She folded her arms over the mauve cashmere polo-neck that hung loosely from her shoulders. Howard moved his glass to the side of his place setting and smiled at his wife.

Us and them again, thought Minogue: the crowd in Dublin and the country people. Like many another rural TD, Howard championed "his own" against the distant uncomprehending bureaucrats and voters in Dublin. But didn't Howard spend his time in Dublin?

"How do you know Dan?" Crossan repeated.

"Oh. We were in the pub in Portaree. Himself and missus arrived in for some kind of a meeting."

"Indeed," said Crossan with delicate scorn. "The PDDA."

"They live in Ennis, the Howards, do they?" asked Minogue.

"They maintain the residence here," Crossan replied in a nasal drone of nonchalance which Minogue read as his send-up of snobbery. "As well as a *pied-à-terre* in the capital. They dine occasionally here among the patrons of the Old Ground."

"Well, Dan Howard seems to count as a fan of yours," Minogue prodded.

Crossan snorted and sipped at his wine.

"Hah. Do you have fans yourself now, Inspector Minogue? In your line of work, I mean."

Images came to Minogue: a pile of rags in the ditch, what was left after a hit-and-run. And how could you kick a man in the face enough to kill him? Were parts of humanity exempt from evolution?

"Hard to tell, really. But people are relieved when a murderer is caught, if that's what you mean."

Crossan's eyes glistened but remained blank and unblinking. The inspector watched as Crossan's thoughts seemed to return to him. He nodded as though conceding something.

"Oho," said Crossan then, a glint of happy malice in his stare.

The Howards were getting up from their table. Although her face betrayed no signs, Minogue sensed in Sheila Howard an anger held in check. Dan Howard's dimples seemed to have disappeared. The waitress was already darting over to them. Crossan leaned back in his chair and looked out the window onto the street.

"By gor," said Crossan. "Speak of the devil. There's timing for you. The man himself."

Minogue looked out through the curtain onto the street. A bread lorry drove by slowly, revealing in its wake the dog, then the bearded figure and the bag on the footpath beside him. The sun was full on Jamesy Bourke. Minogue watched the waitress persuade the Howards to stay at another table. Dan Howard's practiced, public face regained its affability. He made a joke to the waitress and then looked toward Crossan and Minogue, eyebrows arched, as though to convey a magnanimous patience that Minogue did not understand. Sheila Howard busied herself moving the condiments and flowers around on the table. Dan Howard ran his fingers through his curls once and pointed to something on the menu. Two middle-aged men in suits stopped by the Howards' table and shook hands with Dan Howard. A quip was issued, a joke returned.

Crossan nodded his head in the direction of the window.

"Sometimes Jamesy takes up station outside yours truly's constituency office up the street here. 'The clinic,' as if to say he was looking for a cure, you might say. Our modern version of pagan idolatry."

When Minogue looked out the window again, Jamesy Bourke and his dog were gone. For a reason his mind could not fasten on, the inspector saw the wall where Jamesy Bourke had stood as strangely vacant now, filled with the sun's glare but somehow marked by the absence of the figures, as though a shadow had been left. The waitress snapped open a folding table and laid a tray on it.

Crossan's eyes snapped open and they bored into the inspector's. "Well," he said. "Have you left your bits of rags and your rosaries out by the holy well and done your indulgences?"

Minogue's puzzlement showed.

"Aha. You've lost your religion up in the metropolis. All Souls."

"Ah, I'd forgotten."

"There are no ghosts above in Dublin, I suppose."

Minogue recalled his mother hanging bits of cloth by St. Gobnet's Well amid the statues, the holy pictures, and the flowers. Did Maura now tie pieces of Mick's clothes there to implore a saint no longer a saint in Rome to banish the arthritis seizing more of her husband by the year? Crossan laid his napkin on his knees and leaned in toward the Inspector.

"There's stuff I meant to bring but you hijacked me before I could go to the office and get it. Will you, em, stop by the office with me after? A little postprandial too, maybe?"

Minogue paused in his work of separating his salmon fillet. Did Bourke know that he'd be? . . .

"I will, I suppose," he answered.

Crossan's office was in Bank Place, a terrace of early Victorian houses. His rooms were high-ceilinged, stately, cluttered. Minogue followed him past the secretary's desk, the only businesslike aspect to the place. The long windows, one of the terrace details which more openly aped Georgian, looked down on the street through wrought-iron railings. Some modern devices intruded, Minogue noted, but the fax and photocopier seemed devalued by being half-hidden under papers. A faded rug, its intricate designs formerly blue and probably yellow, took up the floor in the middle of the room. Numbered prints of landscapes covered up one wall.

"I've a secretary," Crossan was saying. As though landing a fish, he lifted a bottle of whiskey out from behind a stack of folders. "But she's only part-time."

Which part of the time, Minogue was tempted to ask: the time she was asleep?

"She's on her honeymoon. In Greece, if you don't mind."

Alerted by the weight of the filling tumbler, Minogue looked up at Crossan. "Whoa, man! Are you trying to do me in?"

Crossan tipped the bottle back up and sat down himself. "Tell me something now. What keeps a man like you going? In your line of work, like."

Minogue couldn't decide whether Crossan was pulling his leg or testing his temper. He looked to the rows of leather-bound books on Crossan's shelves.

"Are you trying to interview me for a job here, is it?"

"Pretend that I was."

"We try to give an accounting for someone murdered." He felt Crossan's eyes drill into him.

"I meant how or why do you stick at it. What drives you?"

"God, what a question. Fairness, I suppose. Especially for the people who are left . . ."

"There's more?"

The inspector looked hard at the lawyer for any hint of a skeptical reception.

"You give something back to the victim, too, even though they're dead. Their dignity, maybe. Now, are these conversational tidbits leading anywhere?"

Crossan sniffed at the remains of his whiskey as though contemptuous of the comfort it offered.

"All right. Jamesy Bourke —"

"Let me ask you something straight out first," said Minogue. "Did you tell Jamesy Bourke that you were getting in touch with me?"

Crossan grinned shyly and nodded his head. It changed his face entirely.

"I must confess that I did. I told him that you were related to a client of mine."

"And the meeting at the hotel?"

"No, no. But I'd lay money that he happened to see the Howards there. It's happened before. Can I get away with that without suggesting that Jamesy is in fact trailing the Howards?"

Minogue studied Crossan's lopsided smile.

"Another preliminary matter there now, counselor. You wangled the participation of various members of my family in setting up this exchange of pleasantries we have current here."

"I believe I did at that. Are you offended?"

Minogue thought of Maura Minogue's laughter, her infectious cheer. "I'm not now."

"Well, I can go on, so. Jamesy Bourke came to my office here a few months back. Frightened the wits out of me, I can tell you. Walked right in that door, so he did, and just stood there. Now remember, this is twelve years or so after he was put away. He's a recovered alcoholic, but he seems to have managed to come out from under that, too. He's on medication for manic-depression. He has episodes where he, er, 'sees things.'"

"You're giving me all the good news first?"

"I want you to know that my eyes are wide open as regards Jamesy Bourke. At any rate, he wanted me to listen to the ideas he had concocted over the years."

"And?"

"Well, I took a look at what there was. There was the summary, the book of evidence. Phoned his counsel at the time, Tighe. Newspaper reports about the trial printed some of the court testimony. Those I copied and stuffed in the envelope for you. I ended up telling Jamesy that I could find nothing that could be construed as legally or procedurally improper in the proceedings of the trial."

Minogue let several seconds pass.

"Well," he said. "That was it, then?"

Crossan snorted but did not smile. He began rubbing his glass around his palm with sudden hasty movements.

"Maybe I should have prefaced that by starting with 'in spite of everything.' You see, Tighe had entered a plea of not guilty because he knew the State's case was circumstantial. But at some point in the second day of the trial, Tighe told me, Jamesy just seemed to give up. Fell apart, Tighe said. Lost his temper on the stand, ranting and raving about witnesses and the Guards. Didn't impress anyone, I can tell you."

"What did Bourke say when you told him that?"

"I think he didn't hear me. I told him he'd have to persuade me or help me by bringing forth new evidence. That was the only way. Shouldn't have opened my mouth there, I thought afterwards, because the next thing is he produces that twenty-page thing, that epistle that I gave you."

"Has it made a difference to you, then?"

"No. I'd have to agree with your reading. Rambling, unreliable. Downright weird. There wasn't one thing I could take from it and seek verification with. It could be used to have him admitted to a psychiatric ward."

"So how come we're? . . . "

Crossan looked at the inspector as though he were deciding whether he would buy something frivolous.

"All I can say is this: I decided that one day — fee or no fee — I'd dig up the whole Bourke thing. The trial, the police investigation. The whole thing. Of course you know about 'one day' — it never comes. But I began to hear more about Jamesy and what he was up to. People see him hanging around the ruin of the house where the fire happened. Talking and shouting to himself as he rambles the roads. I don't want to say that he's following the Howards exactly, but . . . Jamesy seems to be on the high road to a lot of trouble. I think he might go off the deep end."

"So you thought you'd calm him down by telling him you'd do something. I see."

"I wonder if you do," said Crossan quickly. "There's more to it than just feeling sorry for him. I have this feeling that Jamesy didn't get himself a fair trial at all."

"Didn't you just tell me that you had nothing to go on?"

Crossan shifted in his chair and gave the inspector a doleful look.

"There's a strange feel off the material, the records. Sounds terribly professional, I know. But the stuff I saw from the book of evidence putting Jamesy at the fire with the proverbial match in his hand and the proverbial motive pinned to his chest — well, it didn't look that strong to me."

"Maybe Tighe was not as good a barrister as you would have been in his place."

Anger flared in Crossan's eyes but it dissolved and he almost smiled.

"You don't believe that Bourke was guilty, then," said Minogue.

"That's not what I said." Crossan's hand rose from the table and stayed poised in mid-air.

"The investigation, the evidence looked shoddy and put-together. At least from what I saw in summary form, I'd have to admit."

"Come on now, Mr. Crossan. You need to bait your hook, man. The whiskey isn't that good."

Crossan's smile was forced.

"Well, all the work was done by local Guards, for one thing."

Minogue thought of Kilmartin's grim amusement when he recounted the sloppiness of Guards in securing evidence, those arrows in the Chief Inspector's quiver he used when defending his Squad. "Mullocking and bollicking about," Kilmartin called those blunders.

"Maybe the local Gardai had the resources and the competence to do it," said Minogue.

Minogue wondered if Crossan would detect the tongue-in-cheek. The lawyer leaned to one side and took an envelope from under a notepad.

"Interesting you should say that now," he murmured. "That's the same tune they played at the time too. Here, open this up."

Minogue wanted to ask about it but Crossan kept talking.

"Back then I was articling in Limerick. Learning the ropes. Used to come home weekends."

Minogue slid out a photograph and a folded newspaper clipping. Crossan swished more whiskey into their glasses.

"Dan Howard," said Minogue.

"Good for you. You wouldn't know the others, I'll bet."

Minogue squinted at the faces. The snapshot had been taken with a cheap camera and the cyanotic hue of the emulsions reminded Minogue of murder victims. Glare from the flash had whitened a face too close to the lens. Bottles around the room reflected the flash. Red pupils like vampires, a sweaty sheen on the faces. One of the men was playing a guitar backward. Another was holding a bottle out to toast, but the flash had caught him with his eyelids almost completely closed.

Crossan pushed the glass of whiskey at Minogue and poked his finger at one of the faces.

"Come on, try."

Minogue looked again at the long, blonde hair parted in the middle. The girl was smiling, but not in earnest. Her eyes with the eerie pink pupils were looking directly toward the lens.

"Sheila Howard," said Minogue.

"Sheila Hanratty, she was then," Crossan corrected. "Now. See the fella standing up, waving the bottle. The fella with his eyes half closed, looks like he just got hit by lightning."

Minogue looked at the sweaty faces again and shook his head. "Whoever he is, he looks like he's well-on there."

"But can you tell me who he is?"

"No, I can't. I'm from Clare, fair enough, but I don't keep census details in my head."

"He's from your end of the parish."

"So's half the country."

"That's Jamesy Bourke."

Minogue's brain flashed a picture of the bearded man: the dog, the bags of newspapers, the slinging off into the night outside the pub last night. The ghost standing across from the hotel dining room at dinner. Crossan had hinted that Bourke was obsessed with the Howards. The barrister fingered open the clipping, held it out, and put on a haughty air as he read it aloud. Minogue sipped at his whiskey.

"This is the original of one of the pieces I sent you. Christ, the flow of language. My God, man, you can't beat the prose of a reporter on a provincial Irish newspaper. 'While in a state of drunkenness, aggravated by the same narcotic substances bringing ruin to so many young lives, James Bourke killed Jane Clark of Toronto, Ontario, Canada, in an act of manslaughter. . . . In delivering his decision, Justic Sweeney called the case a tragedy but one that has clear lessons for society. The behavior and lifestyle which drink and drugs bring in their wake promote the abandonment of the very values that bind a society together and give it strength. Despite the convicted man's involvement with narcotic substances and a self-admitted drinking problem, and notwithstanding his confession and remorse over what he had done, Justice Sweeney noted, these factors do not diminish decent people's dismay and horror at the death of this young woman, a visitor to our shores. . . .' Will I go on?"

Minogue shook his head. Crossan let go of the clipping. It fell to his lap folded in upon itself. Minogue peered at the snapshot again.

"Typical Sweeney. A spoiled priest, they used to say. Always thought the Bench was a bloody pulpit. Was it merely bad luck that Jamesy Bourke drew the same Sweeney for trial?"

"That's the girl there, the one with the tan?"

Crossan nodded. "Tell me who took the picture, if you can."

"You did," said Minogue.

Crossan smiled briefly.

"So," Minogue resumed with clear exasperation. "Ye were friends."

Crossan puckered his lips and exhaled. He spoke in a subdued tone now.

"We were all friends then. Jane Clark was a breath of fresh air here. She was wild out, but so what? She came to stay a few days and ended up staying the whole summer."

"Longer than that," said Minogue.

"That's right, yes. She had rented that cottage out on the Leckaun Road and she was setting it up to do a bit of pottery. She was here to stay, she said. We used to be slagging her for being a tourist, you know, a blow-in that'd be gone by the autumn. Jamesy was head over heels from the minute he set eyes on her. He wrote her poems. But Jamesy was a tearaway lad, with his music and his poetry, flying around in every pub between here and Ennis. Not cut out for the farming, Jamesy."

Minogue glanced up at Crossan. The lawyer was nodding his head slowly while he bit his lip.

"She's buried out in Canada," Crossan said. "What was left of her after the fire."

The inspector placed his hands on the armrests. Crossan didn't seem to notice the hint.

"The story is that Jamesy set fire to the cottage in the early hours, about one o'clock. After he put a match to it, he sat out by the front door with the remains of a bottle of whiskey in his fist and waited for Jane Clark to run out the door and into his arms. Like a film he had running in his head. Mad drunk."

"Out of his mind," said Minogue. "We're getting to the point here now, I think."

"When she didn't come out, he lost it," Crossan went on. "Started screaming. He had had a big row with her earlier on that evening, on account of her sharing her favors with someone else."

"Yourself?" Minogue tried.

Crossan snorted. "Spare me. No, it was Dan Howard."

Minogue sat back in his chair. He thought of Dan Howard's ready smile.

"Ray Doyle was the sergeant at the time," Crossan continued. "Not the worst, I'd have to say. A bit thick, really. Naughton was the Guard most involved. Tom Naughton. He was the old hand around Rossaboe, a Limerickman. He was also a bollocks of the first order. Naughton was the one who got things done around Rossaboe, really. He was first on the scene that night. Well, Tom Naughton went out of his way to nail James and get him locked up as quick as he could for as long as he could."

"Personal thing with him, was it?"

"Yes. He had it in for Jamesy. Jamesy was always one step ahead of the Guards here as regards any general mischief. Naughton himself was partial to the drink and that was well known. Jamesy was a terrible mimic — to beat the band, really. He'd have us all in stitches in the pub. Naughton hated him. Vindictive type of a man, Naughton. A real bastard."

"We number some in our ranks," Minogue offered after several seconds. "Did Doyle go after any other, em, Bohemians in the area? Such as yourself and Master Howard, like."

"Hah," Crossan sneered. "He'd never go after Dan Howard or myself, for all the mischief we might have been up to. We were gentry after a fashion, safe enough with our wild oats. But Naughton was in a lather over Jamesy Bourke and the carry-on out at the cottage. The attitude with Naughton was that Jane Clark was a one-woman crime wave with a mission to subvert the morals of the whole bloody country. He'd called on the cottage a few times, poking around, but she knew her onions as regards the law, as I recall. Search warrants and what have you. She wasn't afraid of him."

Minogue placed his glass down heavily on the desk at this elbow.

"All right," he said. "Now. One question."

Crossan stared at the inspector.

"Why now?"

Crossan paused before answering. Minogue realized that Crossan had thought about this, had expected it.

"Well. I could start with circumstances. It was when I was talking to Eoin that you came up. He didn't tell me much about you, except that you were up in Dublin these years. Your job, of course. Then there was Jamesy hanging around, haunting the bloody place, standing out there on the footpath looking up at the bloody window. Even when I'm not there he stands around, sometimes for an hour. It's as much as I can do to stop the secretary from calling the Guards when she sees him. It wouldn't surprise me if the Howards, one or the other of them, finally has too much of Jamesy gawking at them."

"Even after you told him the whole thing was a non-starter from a legal point of view?"

"Yep. One day there, a couple of weeks ago, I came back from court and there's Mary in tears. She says he was around. 'Looking at me,' she says. Wants to quit. Thinks Jamesy is out to do what he did to Jane Clark. Very upset. The next time I see Jamesy, by God, I'm annoyed, so I go pelting down the stairs and look him in the eye. What does he tell me? He tells me that his memory is coming back to him better than ever. 'It's all coming back to me,' says he, with his eyes like bloody saucers, sitting there where you're sitting now."

Crossan sat back and let his legs straighten out in front of him.

"He had electroshock after his breakdown and he's been on medication for years."

Minogue felt his own irritation rising again. A dinner of salmon, a glass of whiskey, and Crossan's humor over dinner had seemed bargains at the time.

"His memory, you say."

Crossan waved away Minogue's sarcasm.

"I know, I know. And there's everyone else running around here trying to forget things, building bloody folk-village museums to bury the past by putting it behind glass or something."

Minogue feigned shock.

"Dear God, counselor. A radical?"

"Objection sustained. Anyway. I told him maybe I'd look into it again. And so, between the jigs and the reels, your name came up."

"Thanks very much."

Crossan abashed looked surprisingly vulnerable to Minogue. He looked at his watch. The barrister leaned forward in his chair.

"He told me that he thinks he might have been — get this: *thinks* he might have been — in a car sometime that night. He remembers drinking from a bottle and spilling a bit down his shirt because the car was moving. That never came up at the trial as far as I could ascertain. But how am I to ever know Jamesy hasn't imagined all this?"

"Tell me about it," said Minogue dryly. "What about setting fire to the house? Is he getting his memory back on that too?"

Crossan glared at the inspector. Threads of remorse brushed against Minogue's whiskey-dulled mind.

"Even if you had the full steno transcript of the trial, it wouldn't necessarily help," he said.

Crossan nodded, and ran his fingertips along his neck.

"So, presuming any material evidence is long gone, the only avenues open to you are to go to the people who testified?"

Crossan nodded again. His nails scraping against the bristles filled Minogue's attention with their rasping. He sensed that Crossan was expecting him to say aloud the words that were foremost now, that he had next to nothing — a lost cause. A motorcycle howled by on the street outside.

"'Why now?'" Crossan asked as the noise receded. To Minogue it seemed that the barrister had lost interest. "Christ, I don't know. The time of year, the day that's in it, I don't know. We were friends once, all of us. But now there's none of Jamesy left the way he was. He was destroyed."

"So what do you want me to do?" Minogue asked.

Crossan's face was slack.

"You've already done it; you sat and listened. I can ask no more. You could put it in your file of yarns to tell your pals in the pub after work, I suppose."

The tailflick of sarcasm stung Minogue. He gave Crossan a cool appraisal. What made this barrister tick? He had refused payment from Mick and Maura for Eoin in lieu of something he valued more? For a moment, Minogue saw again the sour glee on Crossan's face at the Howards' embarrassment. Maybe Crossan was trying to make some Guards look stupid too. But what if this marble-eyed lawyer was nothing more than kindhearted, a man however contrary but decent?

"Well, now, Mr. Crossan," Minogue began, puzzled still. "Smart-alecking with me is hardly the best way to . . ."

He let the rest of the sentence die. Crossan set his jaw and jerked up from his chair. Had he just given up?

"Have to go," said Crossan.

Minogue was slow to stand. He felt the exasperation stronger now. It had taken Crossan, a man whose job routinely involved him in flaying Garda witnesses in court, a lot to come to a Guard for help. Was it fair of him to sit here and sell Crossan a line about local Guards being expert murder investigators?

"Well," he began.

Crossan turned. His eyes were straining now. Minogue looked at a print on the wall.

"I don't know now," he muttered, "and I can't make a promise."

"Okay," said Crossan. "That's a start."

CHAPTER 4

"COME ON, DAMN you," he said. His voice was thick.

A band of afternoon sunlight blazed on the wall. Its reflected glow made their skins look tanned. She slipped his jeans over his hips and slid her fingers under the elastic belt of his underpants. He squirmed.

"Jesus," he said in a hoarse whisper. "Don't make me beg."

"Or else?" she said. Sometimes images came to her mind for a moment: she could take his gun, straddle him, and point it in his face. Now! You do it, you do that!

"Or else I'll be well and truly fucked," he said breathlessly. They both laughed.

"And isn't that what you want?"

He groaned, "Don't be such a tease. You're killing me here. Come on."

He closed his eyes and, again, the image of her over him, shoving the gun in his face, came to her. She cupped him in her palm. He whispered something but all she could catch was "do it." His head went from side to side on the pillow. The cheesy smell came to her nostrils, and she watched the skin draw back slightly, the purple orb bud.

"You've never had to wait for anything in your life, have you?" she murmured.

Again she felt it throb and she closed her hand around it. All it is is a muscle, she thought. He pees there; he pulls and scratches himself there. He makes me take it in my mouth, and he thinks I really care or mind or like it or dislike it. Her thumb peeled back the foreskin a little more. And this is what he shoves in me like a stick. Wanting her to say things to him. Dirty boy talk, like the stuff he kept in the van. Often he came with a big fuss before he had managed to get inside her. Well, don't be telling me to do the other stuff first, she had told him. And he was pissed off. She had said no, forgetting that that would only make him do it more.

She thought of the times they did it in the kitchen. Dimly reflected in the glass of the cooker, she witnessed his lust and shock and helplessness. She had known then that she had won something. Dare you. Do it, so, she remembered murmuring to him, turning back to look out the window again. She had seen enough. She heard his breath and believed he was a little frightened as he tugged at his trousers and stumbled into her, panting with those tiny, squeaky sounds, rough. When he asked her, she had told him she wanted it this way.

"I can't wait," he wheezed. "You're a savage, so you are."

I am that, she thought. He opened his eyes and they wandered around her skin, hardly ever looking into her eyes. He had grabbed her at the door and pulled their clothes off. All fingers and shoving, he had pinned her against the wall with his hips. Probing, shoving, his fingers. All he thought of was between her legs. He had pulled her hair there but she didn't cry out. His nails were dirty.

"You like it," he said. "You just don't like to admit it."

She squeezed him and he shivered. Her best friend had shocked her when they were twelve: you can lead any man by his . . . After he had stripped her, he had made her stand in the doorway so he could look at her. Posing the way she had seen in his magazines.

"I saw him take a naggin of whiskey from the cabinet and put it in his pocket," she whispered. "He's in love with the drink as well as the guns."

His frown lasted for several seconds: he hadn't understood.

"He'll screw up on you, you know. It's just a matter of time."

Her thumb sought out the opening again and she pressed down lightly as it pulsed, as if it was a button. Then his face clouded. He spoke in a careful, surprised monotone.

"You fucking bitch. Don't start up on that now."

She held his stare until his face slid into rapture as she bit gently on the tip. He suddenly grabbed her head and pushed her down with both hands. She had guessed he would. He lifted and pushed into her. She felt his tics, the itch in her throat. He'd never understand, she knew. He fell under her and the mattress bobbed with their bodies' weight. She looked up at his face. He was staring at the ceiling, his tongue slowly rubbing along his lower lip. His cheeks were flushed. Later, she knew, he'd tell her to do something and she would do it. It could be the mirror, or the plastic thing, or something really stupid when she couldn't help but laugh out loud. He didn't like that, even when she had told him that it felt stupid.

"Did you like that?" Now his voice was soft.

"Yes," she lied.

He closed his eyes again. Maybe later he'd tell her to go outside in the dark and take her. In that stable, probably. She still had the bruise on her hip. That didn't matter either, she knew.

.   .   .   .   .

"By the way," Minogue yawned. "Thanks."

Kathleen looked back at her husband. They had gone out to walk the fields before teatime. Minogue looked around at the grass and the thinning hedges. The air already had the metallic, lilac hue of evening.

"For what, exactly?"

"For helping to set me up with Crossan."

"I did no such thing."

"In cahoots with Maura, that's clear enough."

Kathleen Minogue pursed her lips as the words of a retort formed on them. She too was looking out over the hedges at the drumlins. The world turning in on itself more every minute, he thought.

"All Maura knew was that Crossan wanted some advice off you. Was that too much to ask?"

"More than that he had on his mind —"

"Well, let's leave the matter there for the time being, can't we?"

They stepped over a stile in the stone wall into a field adjoining the farmyard. The farm dog, a wily and stealthy collie, came out to meet them. Maura was standing by a gate.

"Hello all," she called out. "There was a phone call for you, Matt. From Dublin."

.   .   .   .   .

Minogue was drowsy and dry-throated even before they hit the Dublin Road proper. They had sat around over tea while Minogue became even more impatient and then left.

"Single-vehicle accident," he said to Kathleen. "You know what that means."

"Um," she said.

"That's often code for a drunk driver."

"You never got to talking to Mick or Eoin about the future," she said.

Minogue held his breath to keep himself from issuing a sharp reply.

"Knocked out but he had his belt on. Overnight tonight again."

"Why didn't you phone him at the hospital?"

"Eilis said he didn't want me to know."

"A great way to pass along information."

A sizeable bump shifted Minogue in his seat. His thoughts returned to Bourke. He had tossed Crossan's envelope into the suitcase in a hurry. Bourke was a crackpot, dragging Crossan in with him — all because Crossan felt remorse for doing well out of life while Bourke had not. Christ, there'd be no end to it if he got pulled in.

Kathleen fell to wondering aloud about their son. In his last letter home he had been enthusiastic about a job interview he'd had. Minogue had noted the Americanisms: world-class, leading edge. Dark shapes gathered in the outer orbit of his thoughts as they drove the bypass route out of Portlaoise. They advanced in a relentless phalanx and clutched at him. Caught in no-man's land between Kilmartin and Tynan like a shuttlecock. Kathleen's bloody apartment scheme. Crossan trying to finagle with this Bourke thing. Now Hoey. He had a momentary glimpse of himself in a few years' time, sitting in a pod called an apartment, trying to pen letters to his son in the States, asking to be remembered to Kathy. Or maybe making forays into town to meet Iseult for lunch so that he could borrow some of her brave disdain and shore up his own diminishing life. No garden to rescue each spring, kitchen appliances that worked flawlessly, carpet everywhere. Desperate.

He felt Kathleen's eyes on him as he jerked the wheel and crashed the gears. He had put it off too long, he realized, put it off too long to avoid a real row now. Now there'd be hurt when he'd tell Kathleen that he couldn't face a future like that. His own fault: he had deceived himself into inertia by hoping she'd get tired of the idea. She hadn't, and her stupid husband had played his cards too close to his chest. The remorse pulled at his belly and left him helpless and weak. Later, with the Fiat climbing up onto the grassy plain of the Curragh, he found himself staring into the yellow glow of Dublin as it spread out on the windscreen.

"Please God Seamus is on the mend," he heard Kathleen say. Her steadfast and conciliatory tone betrayed to him that she had been happily thinking about her plans at the same time he had been hoping to avoid them.

.　　.　　.　　.　　.

He came down over the stone wall and landed lightly on the sod. Without the dog he felt uneasy. He stopped and listened again. Could dogs be ghosts, like people? More than once he had caught himself making remarks aloud, waiting for the dog to respond with the gasps, the happy whines and paws Shep had used to converse with her master. He had found himself standing and waiting for the dog to return to his side from the darkness, to bound up to him, to rub against his legs. Once he had even called out to Shep before he realized what he had done.

He knew the gorse-patched hedges, the fields, and the faltering stone walls over which he had come. Here the ground was covered with blackberry bushes dying back before the winter. To the east the lights of Rossaboe were hidden behind the drumlins of these outer edges of the Burren. He grasped his stick tighter and slashed at the brambles while he skirted crumbling sections of wall. He used the stick to steady himself while he stepped through a gap in one wall, over the jumble of rocks mossed over and half-buried under the wild grasses.

He stopped again and stared at the lights of the cottage. Not a breath of air, he thought. He was warm now and he undid the top button of his jacket. The strangeness of the still air and what he was about startled him. Is this what a ghost feels, he wondered. He stood listening, but he heard only the swish of his own blood in his ears, the muffled throbs of his heart. He peered out into the darkness toward the sea but he saw nothing until he turned toward the Galway side of the bay. Far off and slowly came the sweeping beam of a lighthouse. The water shimmered briefly as the light revolved and left the water dark again. My place, he thought, my fields. His mind felt clear now, the way it hadn't felt for years. Had he been asleep these years? The drugs and the routines of prison life had put his mind somewhere beyond reach. Once he recalled watching his own body as three warders hit it. They had even tried to make him do it to himself when he was released: Keep the routines, keep your head down, keep track of the medication. Stay in touch with the social worker. They had made him his own jailer. But no more.

He turned the walking stick around in his palm and swung it at a bramble. The noise of its slash reminded him of a whip. It pleased him. He struck again and again, stopping only when the fear pierced his euphoria. That fear rushed into his mind more often too now, and it left him shaking. He knew the risk he was taking. If they found out . . . But even if they came for him, that couldn't be worse than the torture of not being able to remember, of having something just out of reach. He was certain that something was there, and that remembering would help him reverse the flow of his life since that night.

He had tried to write down more for Crossan as the ideas and pictures came into his mind. Sometimes he had been too excited by the explosions of half-formed images and feelings that had crashed around him. When he looked at what he had written later, he knew that he couldn't show it to Crossan. He couldn't afford to risk turning Crossan off. He had even begun to remember her voice, longer bits of the conversations they'd had. When the voices had first started coming back to him, he had been terrified. He had thought of going back on the pills or going to the social worker and telling him, but after a few nights he had become used to them. After all, the voices were his own — and hers. Their clarity stunned him. Her accent, the expressions she had used, slang and curses they used in Canada, her mocking tone when she slagged him. He had always believed that his agony would be over someday, that he could get back what had been hidden from him, the he could regain the shore of whatever he had been swimming in, floundering in, all these years.

There were other voices too. Those ones had brought back the stabs of fear. Hearing those voices before had brought him trouble, paralysis, agony. Some days he wouldn't leave the house for fear he'd hear the voices and have nowhere to run and lock the door. They'll take everything, one of the voices said. They're afraid of you. They want to put you away again. Dimly he understood that if everything was coming back to him there'd be good and bad, so he might as well get used to it. There was no going back on it. Everything comes around again. This time they'd not get him.

A faint memory rushed up to him then — faces of adults chastising him, warning him as though he were a child. Him screaming and hitting out with all his limbs, trying to bite at the restraining arms alarmingly strong, the straps around him, tightening. He swung harder at the brambles and swore aloud to get back the feeling of hope.

"Bastards," he hissed. "Fuckers! Robbed I was, and ruined!"

His eyes flooded with tears but he kept beating the grass and brambles. "Dirty fucking thieves and bastards, you took everything, my mind even! And you think you can plow away and take more anytime you want!"

He heard his own sobs then as though they were coming from someone else. He wondered if he had said the words aloud. That had happened a lot last night, he remembered, when he wasn't sure whether he had just been thinking or really saying things to himself. Yesterday he had caught a glimpse of himself passing the mirror that hung over the sink. He had stood watching the face for several minutes. His face had felt numb and his cheeks twitched while he stared at the mirror. There's a piece of me, a huge piece of me, missing these years, he had heard a voice say. The face in the mirror had puzzled him at first, but then he had begun to laugh. The laugh had lasted for only a few moments before despair seized him.

He picked his way along the wall toward the cottage. *And I won't listen to him if he tries to tell me that he didn't notice. Or that he can't speak English or something. I won't have any of that fucking bullshit off him, I won't. Seen him too often with that stupid smile on his face, clapping away to the music and blathering away in the German accent. Bastard.* He stopped and again considered going back to the house and waiting for the morning. He could be in Crossan's office first thing. Then maybe even get Minogue to do something about this too. Yes, maybe he should have gone straight over to Minogue and just started talking last night in the pub instead of waiting around in the street and having those three bastards start a row with him. After all, Minogue had stared at him in the pub, recognized him. Crossan must have passed the stuff along after all. Talk to Crossan in the morning, see what had happened with Minogue, see what he would do now.

Have a look at the car first, he decided. Make certain. There'd be some sign on the car. He winced as he remembered the sound of the car hitting Shep. A shriek of tires, a yelp, and the thump that had propelled him out of the chair and onto the road in his stockinged feet. At first he couldn't see more than the taillights of the car because the driver was still standing on the brake pedal. He had shouted and run toward the car, a hundred yards distant, but the brake lights went out, and the other lights too, as the car sped off. He had almost tripped over Shep in the roadway. She was still breathing but her head was at a wrong angle to her body. Her body shuddered and a faint whine escaped the shattered mouth. He thought he saw Shep's eyes roll slowly into her head, but the low rasp of breathing continued while the dog waited for death.

He had stood up from his knees, the night wild and terrifying around him. He ran back a few paces toward the house but changed his mind and ran back to the dog. She was still breathing but there was a low squealing sound that seemed to come from near her. She was trying to move her head. His pants were stuck to his knees with blood. He had felt his own body turn to water and he wailed in anguish when he realized what he must do. He ran to the shed and grasped the spade. He couldn't find the flashlight. Out on the road again, the clammy, cold tar underfoot seemed to hold his feet fast as he stood over the dog, too stricken to move. He aimed for the neck and, with a great shout, brought the spade down. Two blows had been enough and he threw the spade down the road before falling to the pavement himself, slapping his hands on the road while he howled.

He shivered and took a deep breath. The curtains were drawn, but muted light still caught the metal on the car parked by the side of the cottage. He wiped his eyes and walked in a roundabout route past the shrubs and the fallow vegetable garden. Did these people have a dog? How the hell could they have a dog and they doing what they did last night? The car bonnet was wedged under a forsythia growing by a side gate to the cottage. He kept out of the dull glow of light from the windows and moved around the car. D for Germany sticker next to the BMW badge on the boot-lid. Fucking people. Thought they owned the world. Their city money.

Rather than tread on the gravel, he backtracked slowly onto the grass. He stopped to observe a lighted window again. The faint sounds were voices from the television, he realized. He listened intently for a full minute and heard nothing more than the changing tones, the jingles, and the futile enthusiasm of ads. He moved sideways along the doors of the BMW, raised his stick to hold back the forsythia and stooped to get around to the front of the car. Cute fucker, he thought with the anger catching fire in his chest again, trying to hide the damage by shoving the car in the bushes.

A branch escaped along his stick and flicked onto the bonnet. He hunkered down and leaned against the shrubs to see the front of the car proper. While he paused to get his eyes used to the darkness there, he thought about what he should do when he was finally sure that this was the car that had left his dog mangled in the road. Were there other cars in the village or the area with D stickers on them? Maybe Crossan'd give him one of those sympathetic looks and try to fob him off. To hell with Crossan and to hell with these tourists and to hell with Tidy Howard and to hell with Sheila Hanratty and to hell with Minogue.

His fingers found the grille and traced the broken plastic moldings. Cheap hoors, he thought with satisfaction, a fancy car made of plastic. One of the headlights was broken. His fingertips sought out any traces of hair. Branches slid off his stick and lashed his face, but he didn't feel their sting.

He stood, leaned into the bush again, and raised his stick to fend off more of the shrubs. The click he heard then was very different from the scratching which the branches had traced on the bodywork of the car. He looked over the car and froze. He stayed that way for less than one second, for less time than his brain needed to confirm what his eyes sought out so desperately in the shadows, for less time than he could utter a word, for less time than he could will his body to move. An unbearably bright and thunderous flash lit up the side wall of the cottage. Jamesy Bourke catapulted through the forsythia and flopped like a sack of rubbish on the rocks behind.

•   •   •   •   •

The Minogues reached Dublin at half-nine. Kathleen looked up at the bus crammed next to the Fiat while they waited for the traffic light near Portobello Bridge. Minogue fell to staring at the rills of canal water cascading over the lock.

"So that's the story of Jamesy Bourke," he murmured.

He had been surprised at Kathleen asking him about it. Perhaps she felt badly about her part in pushing Crossan at him.

"How was I to know Crossan was going to ask you to get involved in something like that now?"

"How indeed," Minogue grunted. He led the Fiat away from the green light. "Well, he can't be all bad. Trying to ease his conscience is no offense in my book. But Bourke sounds like a real head-case. Still and all, if I ever get the time sometime — maybe — I'll see what's in our files about him."

"I don't want you caught up in any conniving," Kathleen said. "That crowd in Clare are tricky."

Minogue gave her a one-eyed scrutiny. She elbowed him back to attention in time for him to dodge a taxi. The conversation died until they reached Elm Park hospital fifteen minutes later.

"I'd prefer to go up on my own, if you don't —"

"I knew you would. Go on up with you. I'll wait in the foyer and read the magazines or something. Tell Shea I was asking for him."

Minogue tried several times to decipher his wife's mood as he negotiated his way through the wards. Was she still annoyed that he hadn't persuaded Mick and Eoin about something? Hoey was in a private room. The inspector held his breath, tried out a smile, and knocked.

He believed that Hoey had lost weight. He studied the bruise that extended from his eyebrows up to his hairline.

"Does the Killer know?" Hoey asked.

"I don't think so. Not yet."

Hoey's eyes remained fixed. His cracked lips were colorless and dried saliva clung to the corners of his mouth. Minogue sat back in the chair and stared at a purple and green weal that lay smack in the middle of Hoey's forehead. The day had caught up to the inspector. He felt something welling up slowly in his chest. Hoey glanced back into his scrutiny but Minogue ignored the hint. He tried to clear his throat but lapsed into coughing. Minogue looked away.

Hoey's cough subsided. "Won't do much for the looks," he whispered.

"Look, Shea. You were never much of a talker. Isn't it time for a bit of a change?"

Hoey squinted out from his good eye. "What do you think the Killer will make of it?"

"You weren't breathalysed or sampled after they pulled you out of it, so there's nothing formal to trip over. Yet."

"Won't stop Kilmartin."

"You could have talked, Shea. Should have."

"About what?"

"Whatever the hell is bothering you. Here you go, obviously pissed, behind the wheel of a car, and you wreck —"

"It's my business."

Minogue's anger began to uncoil behind his ribs.

"I came up from Clare after I heard from Eilis to see —"

"Ah, fuck it, man! I'm out!"

Hoey sat up, rolled slowly off the bed and began walking stiffly around the room. Except for his shoes he was fully dressed. Minogue noted the streaks of dried blood on his shirt. The compound smells of the hospital began to add to his claustrophobia. He counted to five.

"What do you mean 'out'?"

"Look. The Killer won't have me back anyway. A head-case. I can just see him. I'm sick of the whole bloody caper anyway."

Hoey whirled around to face the inspector, his hands out.

"How the hell did I ever wind up here? That's what I'd like to know."

Minogue sat forward. His joints had turned mushy on him.

"You went on a tear and you ran your bloody car into a wall. It's not the end of the world."

"Not that," Hoey snapped. "The job! How the hell did I end up dealing with the likes of that fucking yob the other night? I mean, it suddenly struck me . . ."

"Nolan?"

"So he's been on your mind too. See? Here I am thinking, will Nolan get bail? Will Nolan do something like this again? Will someone nail him in prison? God Almighty!"

"Forget Noaln. I'm hardly in a mood to be sympathetic now with the crooked humor you're in. You're damn lucky you weren't badly hurt. Or worse: you could've taken someone with you."

Hoey turned away. His hands were fists by his sides. He seemed to be staring out the window into the yellow street-lit haze over the southern suburbs of Dublin.

"Lucky?" he said.

The word came back clearly from the glass to the inspector. Hoey's fists found their way to the windowsill. His body canted stiffly forward until his head touched the glass.

"I knew what I was doing. Or I thought I did. Sure I turned the wheel myself."

Minogue let himself fall back in the chair. He closed his eyes.

CHAPTER 5

Look, Shea. It's half-ten. Kathleen's downstairs. I'd better go down and let her know what's happening."

Hoey gave the inspector a bleak look. His coat had a dark stain across the lapel.

"Sign yourself out, will," Minogue went on. He still felt numbed. "I'll meet you downstairs. Have you any more tests?"

Hoey shook his head and returned to combing his hair in front of the mirror.

"X rays or anything? You weren't concussed, were you?"

"No."

"Pills you need?"

Hoey shrugged. Minogue watched him appraising his own battered face in the mirror. Hoey worked on a stray lick of hair over his ear. Minogue saw his colleague lose a battle to keep his hand from trembling as it remained poised over his head for several moments.

"Okay then?"

Hoey returned Minogue's earnest look in the mirror for a moment before he took a step back and jammed his hands in his pockets.

"Jesus Christ," he spat out. "I look terrible. I feel terrible. I'm not going. I don't know. Can't you leave me alone?"

"You missed a button there. Second one down on your shirt. Come on now, let's go."

Kathleen kept her shock well-hidden, Minogue thought. They walked to the car park.

"Well, Shea," she said as she waited for her husband to unlock the passenger side. "We're right now, aren't we?"

Hoey squinted at the cars in the car park. "Well, Kathleen" he murmured, "to tell you the truth, if I was right, I wouldn't be here."

Kathleen got into the car and gave her husband a look of alarm. Minogue grinned.

"That's the style, Shea," he said. Kathleen's laugh was forced.

Minogue let the Fiat out onto Nutley and aimed it up toward the Bray Road. He began whistling softly between his teeth. Kathleen kept her gaze fixed on the road ahead until they stopped by the lights at Montrose. There she rallied and began working on Hoey's embarrassment. She spoke in a tone of mock reprimand.

"Sure, what's wrong with staying out in Kilmacud awhile? Himself here is at a bit of a loose end. Hang around, can't you, and see that he doesn't make an iijit of himself."

Hoey sat back in his seat and began licking his bottom lip. Minogue eyed him in the mirror.

"Yes," Kathleen went on, "Daithi's room is going a-begging. You might as well . . ."

Minogue sensed the hesitation in her voice. She had almost said that Iseult's room was available too, that Iseult and Pat . . . But that would be to admit aloud what she had yet to admit to herself.

"There's a garden, you know," she went on boldly. "There's transplanting to be done before the winter proper. I must say now that I only like it for walking around in. But you people from the country, I suppose? . . ."

Minogue looked at the dashboard clock. It wasn't too late to phone Kilmartin at home and have a powwow about this. Organize some leave for Hoey, park stuff with Murtagh. He resumed his Handel but hummed instead of whistled. He'd phone Herlighy, the psychiatrist, at home tonight too.

•　　　•　　　•　　　•　　　•

As the evening clouds retreated from the sky over Dublin that night, they took with them some of the yellow nimbus of light that had been reflected from the city below. The air grew colder. Although there was no moon, the summit of Two-Rock Mountain became sharp and purple under the stars. Hoey sat wrapped in an eiderdown by the window. He left the window open a crack with the ashtray next to it. He had taken his pills after the bath, but he did not feel tired. He watched two cats walk along the block wall that separated

Minogues' yard from the neighbors'. A light breeze had the remaining leaves whispering dryly.

Hoey had no handkerchief and, as there were times when he couldn't stop crying, he used a towel to wipe his face. He worried about waking the Minogues and that, ridiculously, made him cry even more than thinking about Aine. He had grown into the habit of imagining her as his wife in future years. How had he done that? When had he started? For long stretches of time that night he was certain there was no future, but then some indistinct, wishful feeling would crawl into his chest.

He shivered and drew the eiderdown tighter. The sky was full of stars and they held his fascination for a long time. He remembered them as a child just being there, company for wonder and excitements like Halloween and Christmas, familiar and near at hand, like a ceiling. Now they seemed impossibly far. As though the sky were no longer a roof over the world but an opening to confusion and indifferent space. The lid had come off his own world, he thought, the roof torn off the house. He thought of light-years, of stars exploded these millions of years but whose light had only lately reached earth. Seeing them in the night sky when they no longer really existed.

His mind moved wearily through memories. They flared and died and flared again around his heart. He craved a drink of neat whiskey, and he panicked at the thought of a future without a drink. The stitches over his eyebrow began to feel hot and his eyes seemed to swell even more. He tried to picture Africa — huts and black people smiling. Kids singing or clapping for their teacher. Aine. How hot would it be? He lay down then. Did they have lions and stuff in Zimbabwe?

.   .   .   .   .

Minogue parked on Dawson Street, and he and Hoey legged it smartly across to Bewley's on Grafton Street. The sky was blue, it was not yet nine o'clock, and Dublin was at its best. Hoey's face drew stares. One child pulled on her mother's arm and pointed at him.

"A bit of everything," Minogue urged the waitress. "We're in from Kilmacud and we're demented with the hunger."

The inspector was obliged to eat most of Hoey's breakfast. Hoey tried a second cup of coffee, lit another cigarette, and waited for Minogue to answer a question he had posed about the psychiatrist, Herlighy.

"Yes, the one I had. Just a chat. He knows Guards. Size him up. Then, if you think he's okay . . ."

Hoey blew a thin stream of smoke out under his lip.

"Don't think that I don't appreciate what you're doing," he murmured.

"And don't you be worrying about the Killer. I'll push him around. He'll be all right. Really."

Hoey gave a snort. The inspector concentrated on his saucer.

"You won't know yourself in a while, I'm telling you, Shea."

Hoey let smoke stream out his nostrils.

"I thought the whole idea was to know yourself better," he muttered. "Or stuff like that."

"No doubt," Minogue shrugged. He chewed on the tail of a fatty rasher while he searched for a rebuttal which might buoy Hoey.

Hoey cleared his throat again and looked warily around the restaurant.

"He'll want to know about the love-life and the da and the ma and the rest of it, no doubt."

"What?"

Hoey's gaze had settled on a table where five women sat smoking and laughing over coffee.

"Herlighy," said Hoey. "The shrink."

"Oh, yes." Minogue felt his body ease back into the chair. "Yes. Probably, I mean. And he may ask you what you want. How you see yourself after this, you know . . ."

Hoey pushed a butt to the rim of the ashtray.

"He didn't push the church at me, you'll be glad to hear," said Minogue.

"Huh," sighed Hoey. "I'm not much on the church and devotions this long time, I can tell you. Even with Aine and the lay missionary thing out beyond in Zimbabwe."

He paused to take a drag on a fresh cigarette.

"We had rows about it. I asked her what the hell the Church could do for people in Africa. Christ, the damage we've done out there already. The white people, I mean. Not to speak of the famines and poverty. Do you want to hear her answer? This'll give you an idea of how it went sour."

Minogue said nothing.

"She said I had seen too much of the bad side of people. In the job. All I know is that I'm not about to be running up to hug the altar rails at this stage."

Minogue was relieved when the talk lapsed. Hoey sat forward in his chair, an elbow on the table, while he stared out at the floor. Minogue recalled people, notably Kilmartin, taking pride in the missionary zeal of the Irish abroad. Television programs on catastrophes in Africa always seemed to interview Irishmen and -women there.

Hoey breathed out heavily.

"Africa," he said, and turned his one good eye back on Minogue. "I read where we're all from Africa. The one mother or something like that."

The inspector thought of the children's swollen bellies he had seen on the poster in Galway city.

"Here, Shea. It'll take you the best part of fifteen minutes to get to his office. I'll be waiting for you at the gates of the National Gallery at twelve."

Hoey rose slowly from the table, patted his pockets for his cigarettes, and then followed a meandering path around tables toward the exit. Minogue followed him, noting the head and shoulders down on Hoey as he threaded through to the doors.

•   •   •   •   •

Kilmartin was cagey. Solicitous and polite, his suspicion masked, he slouched in his chair and waited for a cue from Minogue.

"So there," Minogue said. "He's going to stay with us a few days until this gets sorted out."

"Jesus," said the chief inspector. "He looked a bit shot-at the other day, I must say. I don't mind telling you that I was on the point of taking him aside and . . ."

Minogue fingered change in his pocket and looked out the window of Kilmartin's office. Clouds from the west ran low over the city.

"I'm on holidays, remember. All I want is for Shea not to get trampled on."

"Oi! Don't get on your high horse, mister. You know, and I know, that we can't overlook things like this. I only wish he'd so much as, you know, hinted —"

"Maybe he did and we didn't read it."

"You sound like you're blaming the world and his mother for this. That he was bamboozled, like. More excuses."

Minogue ignored Kilmartin's provocation.

"You'll set up a leave of absence for him, will you?" he said.

Kilmartin's tone turned righteous.

"Course I will," he replied. "We look after our own."

The chief inspector's eyes slid around the room before lighting back on Minogue. He loosened his tie. His hand strayed to his collar and began stroking his neck.

"Think he'll try it again, do you?"

"Try what?"

"He tried to top himself, man. Don't play me for a gobshite here, all right?"

Minogue held his breath. A Guard at the scene had probably let his suspicions slip and the remark had found its way to Kilmartin.

"Won't be the same again, that goes without saying," Kilmartin added.

"What won't be?"

Kilmartin flung a glare at his friend.

"He won't be! Hoey. The fella who is as of this moment hiding behind your bloody skirt!"

Minogue knew he mustn't goad Kilmartin now.

"It's a good thing he won't be the same again," he began. "Who'd want to be the same again? All hemmed in, at the end of his tether. It's out in the open now. Between the people who care about him, I mean."

Kilmartin's eyes took on a glint.

"God, you're the cute hoor. Out in the open is right. That's the trouble! Lamb of Jesus, Matt, I can't have a head-case on staff!"

Minogue clenched his teeth. The chief inspector tapped a cigarette against the packet.

"You took me on, Jimmy. Remember?"

"You never tried to do yourself in, man! You had a lot going for you back then. Never looked back either, if I may be so bold as to remark."

"Shea has a lot going for him."

Kilmartin spoke as though he hadn't heard Minogue.

"Never one to lay his cards on the table, Hoey. I mean, I like him and all the rest of it. He's done great work. But we can't have things jumping out of the woodwork at us. Especially these days."

Kilmartin was still now, his cigarette poised above the box. Minogue cast a glance at his colleague. The chief inspector stood up and stretched. Then he stood back on his heels and scratched across his belly. He had tried to keep his stomach in over the years, but his frame

— his gait, his manner, his words — all mocked the idea of containment.

"The last cases were ugly, to say the least," said Minogue. "Maybe Shea couldn't leave them behind him in the squad room. The pressure —"

"Oi, oi! What's this, mister?" Kilmartin waded in. "A fucking sermon? Don't talk to me about pressure! My insides are like the AA map to pressure! There's surgeons building holiday homes and buying Jags and retiring early with what stress has done to my insides. Hoey doesn't have to answer to the public and those fucking jackals in the media — I do. How many people do you know who could take that kind of pressure?"

Minogue nodded his head and pretended to listen. Kilmartin concluded his peroration and tapped him on the shoulder. The inspector looked through the window at a gap in the clouds. He decided to drive along the seafront by Sandymount on his way home.

Kilmartin grunted and raised a conciliatory arm as if to conjure away the stupidity of those who could never understand him. Minogue knew that his colleague was coming down from his vituperative peak.

"I mean to say, Matt. We're getting it from both sides, man."

Minogue decided it was time to light a fuse.

"Absolutely," he murmured. "Never more important to stick together than now."

"Definitely," Kilmartin declared, and tapped his forehead with his cigarette. "As long as we're 100 percent upstairs. The lift has to go to the top floor in our line of work, Matt, and don't forget it."

Kilmartin lit his cigarette. It was time, Minogue decided.

"By the way. Bumped into Tynan the other day."

Kilmartin turned around one-eyed through the smoke. He stared at his colleague.

"Told me he'd pay us a visit," Minogue added. "To, em, throw a few ideas around."

"You don't say, now. Tell him, if it's not too much trouble, to throw his ideas out the shagging window, would you? They're giving me heartburn."

"I'll see what he has in mind, I suppose, later on sometime."

"Sometime? Jesus Christ, Matty, don't pretend it was the dog that farted! Ever so sly, you drop this in my lap. What the hell does Tynan want? Come on now!"

Minogue shrugged and looked back into Kilmartin's stony glare.

"Wait a minute there, you. Whoa right there. What are you trying to

{ 84 }

tell me? That there's some connection between Hoey making a gobshite out of himself and Tynan's blackguarding? Call a spade a spade, man!"

Minogue looked Kilmartin up and down before reaching into the cache of phrases he had built up over the years to deal with the likes of James Kilmartin. He allowed his eyes to open wide and he spoke in a whisper.

"Good God, Jim, what sort of man do you think I am?"

Kilmartin put his hands up.

"Oh, Christ, will you listen to that? Oi! Don't piss on my shoes and then tell me it's raining. Why did you wait until now to tell me that Tynan's on the prowl our way? Is this what loyalty means to you? That you'll run to Tynan if I don't cover for Hoey here?"

Fully inflated now, the chief inspector disdained further words. He shook his head in disgust as he moved around the office. Minogue wondered if Eilis were recording all this.

"You've know me long enough, bucko," Kilmatin resumed in a low growl. "I'm surprised at you. I eat threats and then I spit them out."

"I sort of thought it'd be nice to, you know, get an idea of what's on Tynan's mind."

Kilmartin spun on his heel.

"What the hell does that mean? Aren't you in here to con me into something for Hoey?"

"You know Tynan's under pressure to disperse us, Jim."

"Thanks for the tip there, Sherlock. Tell me something I don't know. Tynan's top dog, in case you didn't know. He tells us all when to jump. Frigging Tynan. What's his thing, Tynan? Jesus, I still can't get a fix on him. The bastard."

Kilmartin stopped by the window. The two policemen fell to watching this patch of the world.

"Listen, Matt," Kilmartin said at last. "I'm not questioning your motives. You're saying to me keep Hoey aboard or else —"

"— it's not —"

"Shut up. I know what you're saying better than you seem to. I'm saying to you that I'll weigh things in the balance as I decide. Like the quality of the job you do on Tynan."

"What job exactly?"

"You know what I mean. Get Tynan off my back. The Squad's back. Maybe he doesn't believe me when I tell him. You try it. Tell him the

Guards down the country would make a pig's mickey of a murder investigation. Tell him. Show him."

For an instant, Minogue saw Bourke's shadowed face in the sun outside the hotel in Ennis. He watched Kilmartin grinding his cigarette into the ashtray.

"I'm going to look around in the files," he said, and rose from the chair. "Pretend I'm not here."

Minogue didn't need to look away from the riot of sunshine to know that Kilmartin's face was telling him he wished that were indeed so.

$$\cdot \quad \cdot \quad \cdot \quad \cdot \quad \cdot$$

Fifteen minutes later, Kilmartin stopped by Minogue. The inspector stayed on his hunkers by the filing cabinet, ignoring Kilmartin for the most part.

"What are you looking for? I probably know it already."

"Negative, Jimmy. Remember, I'm not here."

Minogue's eyes darted to the thumbed-back folder as his fingers dawdled through the files. He held the folder with his left hand and reached in with his right to turn back the tab.

"Bingo," he whispered.

Kilmartin was lighting a cigarillo. Minogue reached down, loosened the folder from the press of its neighbors and stood up. He kicked the drawer shut while Kilmartin blew gusts of smoke toward the ceiling. Minogue cleared a path through the smoke with his free hand.

"Well, seeing as there's nobody here," said Kilmartin.

Minogue guessed from the forced tone that Kilmartin had probably squeezed out a sneaky fart.

"That's an old file copy, that. Wasn't our work. Divisional HQ file. What are you looking for?"

Minogue leaned against a cabinet and scanned the summary of the judgement. As he did, Kilmartin's bygone fart insinuated itself into his awareness. The inspector swore under his breath, held his breath, and stood.

"Well?" said Kilmartin, and followed Minogue.

The inspector turned on him.

"Honor of God, Jim, don't fart in here at least. Show a bit of mercy, man."

Kilmartin leered around his cigar.

"Tell me what you're up to, so."

"This case here. I just wanted to look over the summary."

"To what end, Mr. Trick-of-the-Loop?"

"Maybe the Tynan one," Minogue murmured. "Eventually. A long shot."

He sat down and flicked slowly through the photocopies. He jotted the names down as he came across them. Dan Howard, Sheila Hanratty, Garda Tom Naughton. Sergeant Raymond Doyle, sergeant in the station in Portaree. The coroner's certificate presented at trial, autopsy performed by Dr. J. Marum of Galway city, author not called.

Kilmartin blew a smoke ring across the desk at Minogue.

"Jimmy, here's a case that we never had a hand in. Not even consultancy that I can see."

Kilmartin blew another ring. "Maybe there wasn't an unlawful killing involved."

Minogue ignored the sarcasm.

"Didn't you hear me telling you that it's an old file copy?" Kilmartin went on. "Wherever it came from was all divisional work. That's before your time here. Ancient history."

"A girl killed in a house fire near Portaree, County Clare. Convicted for manslaughter, received a life sentence —"

"A life sentence? Sounds tough. Are you sure?"

"— James Bourke. No participation by the Squad."

"You said that already. That's back in the time of the Flood, man. A lot of stuff wasn't in place and coordinated back then, as I recall." Another well-formed ring emanated from Kilmartin.

"Common enough then," Minogue went on, "to let the local Guards dispose of a murder case?"

"Christ on Calvary hill, man, don't you be listening to me at all around here? That's what I keep on banging me head against the wall about trying to convince the powers that be, every time the bloody topic of 'decentralization' comes up the shagging pipe from some crank super in frigging Ballygobackward. Things have improved since then, we all know that, but the same thing could conceivably happen in the morning." Kilmartin paused and puffed on his cigar.

"'Conceivably,'" said Minogue.

"Shut up a minute," suggested the chief inspector. "Such was done, that I can say. And several times there was an almighty pig's mickey made of things, let me tell you. Do you remember the case of that young fella killing the married woman, the Shaughnessy thing in Cork? He nearly walked the first day of the trial on account of know-it-alls in Mallow that decided they could handle everything. They made a bollocks of it. Lost half their evidence when some bloody barrister fresh out of school in his robes drove a coach and horses through the exhibits."

Kilmartin perched on the edge of his desk and leaned in over Minogue. "Christ, tell that one to Tynan if he gives you the chance. Don't you remember that one? Jesus wept, man. Some of his exhibits were kept in a drawer along with first-aid stuff, and leftover egg sandwiches. Stuff wasn't even cataloged! And then the fella who attended the PM got sick and left the room for half an hour, bejases, so the defense nearly put it over that the Guards didn't even have consistent control over the bloody corpse to be sure of cause of death! Such a mess! Comical."

"I had a conversation with a barrister below in Ennis —"

"Your time is your own to waste, man. It's a free country."

"— and what he recalled of the thing is true so far. According to him, the whole thing deserves a good scrutiny at the very least."

"A good scrutiny indeed," Kilmartin whinnied. "Sue us, then. The bollocks."

"Sue the Guards in Portaree and in Ennis, you mean."

"But maybe they had an open-and-shut case then. Christ, maybe the local Guards actually got it right for once and someone's taking you for a gom, pal."

"Count in the last ten years the number of murder cases that didn't have our involvement."

"It's not statutory procedure that we invade every town and village in Ireland when there's a murder," said Kilmartin. "I've seen murder cases put to rest with a coroner's inquest. But if you think any case was made a bollocks of, or hushed up . . . Far be it from me, etcetera."

Minogue flipped the folder shut. The pungent staleness of the papers lodged in his nose.

"The fella who was convicted, he's back on the streets. I saw him."

Kilmartin put on a biddable expression.

"Look, now. If you're fishing for prime examples of Guards down the country making iijits of themselves when the Squad is not called in, you should find something more recent to feed Monsignor Tynan with. I'm all for that."

Minogue looked at his watch. Hoey'd be finished by now. He stood up.

"Here, lookit," Kilmartin said brightly. "Are you planning to kill someone below in Clare, yourself? And then close the case in record time to make headlines? Public relations, like? What about the potshots they're taking at the tourist cottages down there?"

"You're a laugh a minute, James," said Minogue, barely listening.

Something remained just outside his grasp as he sat there. Kilmartin issued smoke rings indolently into the squad room. Minogue's eyes began to smart from the smoke that now hovered in layers around him. He looked up at his tormentor and friend. Up, he decided. Out of here to get Shea Hoey. He rose and picked up the file.

"Tell me something. Are the records for sittings of the Central Criminal Court from, say, more than ten years back or so still kept in paper?"

"The books of evidence, yes," Kilmartin declared. "The summaries of judgments, yes. You know yourself that transcripts are typed up in full only if there's an appeal launched — and only then if it's not *ab initio*."

"*Ab initio?*"

"Will I turn that into normal conversation for you? It means you throw the old trial out completely and start from scratch again. That's what it means."

"I didn't know you spoke Latin."

"There's a lot you don't know about me, jack. I could nearly say the whole mass in Latin. Yes I could, by God. Memory is a very odd thing, the way it all comes back to you after I don't know how many years. I remember the whole thing nearabouts. The whole mass."

"I should ask you to say it, so."

"Huh. A lot you'd know about going to mass. I'll tell you this: you could find out a lot more that'd surprise you, if you try to give me the shitty end of the stick with this, this . . . whatever bollocking around you're going to do between Hoey and Tynan."

"I'll bear that in mind now, James." He waved the file at Kilmartin.

"Watch your back, that's my advice," Kilmartin called out. "And keep your eye on the ball."

Did he mean Tynan? Hoey? Crossan? Minogue rolled his eyes at Eilis as he hurried out into the sunlit morning outside.

•   •   •   •   •

Minogue caught sight of Hoey immediately he turned the corner by the National Gallery. He stopped behind a lamp post to observe him. Hoey was leaning against the lip of a water trough set into a monument opposite the Gallery. Sunlight filtered through the branches hanging over the railings of Merrion Square. Very occasionally, a leaf fell to the footpath, unhurried by the passage of the constant traffic on Merrion Row.

Framing Hoey with its tired splendor was a memorial fountain erected two centuries ago to the Duke of Rutland. Dublin's coal-smoke winters had rendered most of the cornice molding and the edges of the pilasters above Hoey indistinct. It had been over a century since either lion's head had spewed water into the troughs. Minogue had been used to seeing down-and-outs lying on the stone benches at the foot of the monument. He watched Hoey watching a couple as they marched arm in arm and kicked at the leaves. His features were tight and drawn as though a wind unknown to others on the same street was blowing dust into his face. The inspector took a deep breath, put on a smile, and skipped across the street. Hoey watched him approach.

Minogue gained the broad footpath, and the stone mass loomed over him. Hoey stood on his cigarette and shoved his hands into his pockets. Minogue glanced up at the monument. Sculpted stone panels that had contained figures in mourning were incomplete. Other sorrowing figures in Roman dress were missing heads; supplicating arms had broken off at the forearms. Noble death in classical relief, Minogue thought. And here's Hoey, a round-shouldered and pasty-faced survivor in a creased coat, looking small and defeated. Minogue's stomach went wormy and the fake smile began to lock his jaw.

Hoey nodded and looked to a passing bus. Minogue nodded back but could think of nothing to say.

"Well," he tried at last. "Let's pick up some stuff from your place and put it in the car. Then we don't have to be chasing wardrobes around the town."

"I don't get it."

"Stay at our place awhile, Shea."

"Well . . ."

He smiled witlessly at Hoey and shrugged. Hoey's suspicious squint lasted several seconds. Minogue looked around at the trees and waited. He thought of Hoey at his desk, tired, smoking while he did the work he was best at, organizing evidence. Tagging, notating, receipting, filing — preserving impeccable chains of evidence for the State case. Minogue worked well with him, believing that, like himself, Hoey could let his thoughts become still when he needed to. Methodical and routine but acutely sensitive to nuances at a scene, Hoey instinctively absorbed details. Minogue knew that his colleague left those details in suspension while he waited and then coaxed the impressions and facts into some trajectory as he felt their gravitational pull stronger. Hoey was sizing him up.

"Come on, Shea. I have the car parked down in Nassau Street."

Hoey began to say something but Minogue was gone. Hoey caught up with him.

"Your man says hello, by the way," Hoey said.

"Herlighy? Great."

Minogue kept striding down Nassau Street. Part of him observed the passing faces, the doors, the signs and traffic, the commonplace mysteries of his city. Its every detail seemed too sharply present in the November sunlight. His mind went to Ennis, Bourke's eyes in shadow outside the Old Ground Hotel. Maybe today Bourke was standing across from Howard's constituency office. Crossan's wryly chiding words about forgetting to do his devotions for All Souls, to hang his cloth by the holy wells for a cure, came to him then: there are no ghosts in Dublin?

"Are you going to see Herlighy again?" he heard himself ask Hoey.

Hoey stopped and lit a cigarette. Minogue watched him exhale and look away down the street.

"I will, I suppose."

"Good. After we get set up in the clothing and toothbrush line, what do you say to going wall-eyed looking at a microfiche?"

Hoey kept his stare on the railings of Trinity College ahead. Minogue recalled that a car bomb had gone off by this part of Trinity's wall, killing seven or eight people. Wasn't one of them a child? The wall and the railings had withstood the blast, but scars remained gouged into the limestone.

"A microfiche of what?"

"Has to do with a thing down in Clare years ago. Newspaper reports. Sort of dabble in the archaeology business a bit. What do you think?"

Hoey's one-eyed gaze wandered past Minogue's. It settled on the far end of the street where sunlight cannonaded out of the mouth of Grafton Street, a golden vision that seemed unattached to the rest of Dublin city.

·   ·   ·   ·   ·

"Ow!"

"What?"

The one with the earring took his thumb out of his mouth.

"That big stone I dropped on me thumb the other day. I don't know if it needs looking at. Ow!"

The driver was about to look over when he saw the figure step out from the hedge.

"Jesus."

In the gloom ahead he saw the cars parked tight in to the hedge. A Guard wearing a reflective waistcoat stepped out into the middle of the road.

"Don't get all panicky," hissed the passenger. "There's nothing we have to worry about."

The driver rolled down the window. To his right he saw movement in a gap in the hedge. There were two men in the ditch. They held submachine pistols close to their sides.

"Howiya," the driver called out. The Guard was young, and he wore a flak jacket under the fluorescent green waistcoat. The driver remembered him from a checkpoint by Rannagh a few days ago. He looked cold.

"Lads," the Guard called out. He stood on tiptoe looking through the open window. "Are ye done for the day?"

"We jacked it in for the day, all right," said the driver. "Had enough battering stones and pouring cement."

"Open up the back and I'll take a look," said the Guard.

"Fire away," said the driver.

Driver and passenger turned in their seats to watch the door swinging up. A plainclothes Guard joined the one in uniform. A flashlight was snapped on.

"Are ye nearly done with it?" the Guard said.

"Another couple of weeks and we'll be out," the driver replied. "A palace entirely."

"Good work being done, is there?"

"Only the best."

The plainclothes Guard seemed to deliberate about going around to the other door. He shrugged and looked in at the two.

"All right, lads."

He drove away from the checkpoint slowly and nodded at the two in the ditch. The evening had already taken over the ditches and hedges. The headlights swept over their faces. They didn't move, but their eyes followed the van until it was past them.

"Whoa, Jesus!" said the passenger and whistled. "They're getting very fucking serious! Did you see the pair in the ditch? Wearing their guns out in the open?"

"Good."

"Good? Oh, right. Yeah. There's that to it. Ow." He put his thumb in his mouth. "Bloody planning permission and all the shagging stones and cement they want in, just to make it look like it belongs here," he mumbled around his thumb.

"The vernacular, they call it," said the driver. "Native materials."

The passenger sniffed.

The driver concentrated on the road ahead. He wondered if there was another checkpoint ahead. They had spent most of the day carrying and sorting stones they needed for the walls of the addition. The stone is local, he thought, the tradesmen are local, and we're being paid by a man from Dusseldorf. And this guy wants his holiday cottage in fucking Ireland to look really Irish.

"He's gone back to Dublin," said the driver.

"Who is?"

"Your man. The uncle."

"So there never was anything to him," said the passenger.

"The undercover thing? Doesn't look like it now, does it? Coincidence."

The passenger began to laugh. The driver looked over.

"What?"

"I was just thinking. The other night. What your man must have done when the bullets started flying. In the window. It's lucky he was in the jacks!"

The passenger slapped his knee.

"Ow. Me thumb!"

•   •   •   •   •

Hoey had fallen asleep without Minogue noticing. The inspector drew into the shopping center and began scouting for a parking spot near to the supermarket. The setting sun crested Two Rock Mountain and flooded the car. Hoey's breathing turned to snores. Minogue looked at the sleeping policeman and wondered if he should wake him. Hoey looked somehow smaller to him. Deltas of blood vessels stood out on his purple eyelids. The face was waxen and his lips were again dry and cracked. He recalled that Hoey had swallowed a pill as they had got into the car. Antidepressant? He levered himself slowly onto the pavement and let his door rest against the latch.

The inspector rubbed his eyes as he trudged toward the entrance to the supermarket. His eyes still stung and ached from the two hours at the microfiche reader. He might have to concede on a matter of vanity, he reflected, and finally go to an ophthalmologist. No more of his errant bragging to Kathleen about having hunter's eyes, that he could see what he wanted to see, when he wanted to see it. Hoey had tried to show an interest during the afternoon, but had gone out for a smoke several times. Twice Minogue had sneaked out to make sure Hoey hadn't fled. From the microfiche he had copied two newspaper reports that hadn't been in Crossan's envelope. He had studied them on the reader and again from the photostats, but he'd still found nothing that went beyond what Crossan had already dug up and copied. He'd had to struggle several times to remind himself of the point: it was what hadn't surfaced that had kept Crossan's interest.

As he entered the supermarket, Minogue felt the task of shopping to be suddenly exhausting. His mind buckled under the weight of relentless details, of shelves full of foods and household cleaners and spices and a frightening number of things you could fill your home with. He reached for a basket and tried gamely to start his task. Some holiday. Milk, he remembered. Bread? Should he have woken Hoey up and at least asked him what foods he liked?

He balanced two bags of groceries in either arm as he headed back to the car. In the ten minutes he had spent in the shop, half the daylight had drained away into a crucible of cooling yellow that glowed above the shopping center. He looked ahead for Hoey's form but couldn't see him against the sunset glare on the windscreen. Minogue laid his bags down by the boot and poked with the key before looking in the back window. Hoey was gone. He clutched the keys and stepped around the passenger side. Dazed, he stared at the empty seat. His thoughts couldn't form. He looked over the rows of cars and squeezed the keys in his palm. He was alert now, with an ache low in his stomach.

The inspector skipped down to the bus stop and searched the faces of a dozen people there. Had a bus come and gone in the last few minutes? No, said a wary teenager. Minogue wanted to run but he didn't know where. Had Hoey gone to a pub? Just run away? If Hoey was on the run from him, he meant business. He stood still and felt the panic take hold of him. Hoey the quiet one, the one who had left no hint of what he was going through, had scarpered. Had he woken up suddenly, stricken by the uselessness of things, his defenses robbed in sleep?

Minogue ran back to the car park and headed for the walkway that led to the center of the shopping center. Maybe Hoey had gone looking for him in the supermarket. Minogue ran by his car and then stopped short. The two bags of groceries were gone. He leaned down and looked in to find Hoey smoking a cigarette, the glow stronger in the gloom as he drew on it. Minogue held his breath, let it out slowly, and sat in behind the wheel. He could not resist a glance at his colleague.

Hoey rolled down the window to let out more smoke.

"Did you forget something?" he asked.

Minogue was still trying to hold his breath. "I did."

"I woke up and I had no fags," Hoey murmured. "I thought I might bump into you beyond." He pointed his cigarette toward the supermarket. "I put the stuff in the backseat."

Minogue tried to breathed normally as he steered out onto the Lower Kilmacud Road.

"Hard to see anything now, but." He heard his inane words again. "One minute it's all right and the next thing you know is that it's night."

Hoey nodded and crooked his arm to squint at his watch. Minogue's heartbeat was slowing now but he could not stop words rushing out of himself.

"The days are getting very short now, yes, they are."

•   •   •   •   •

By nine o'clock, Minogue was both exhausted and uneasy. He was trying not to notice Hoey's fidgeting. Trying so hard, he noticed it all the more. He looked up from the guidebook to Greece. After a long bath, Hoey was halfheartedly watching a documentary on grizzly bears in Canada. Minogue felt trapped in his own house. Kathleen had discovered that the Costigans up the road needed a visit, and she had left Minogue with a furtive glance of commiseration. Hoey had flicked through some of the books Minogue had left near the fireplace, but the one he had settled on lay open on the same page in his lap this last hour. The ads came on. A well-known comedian began singing about shampoo.

"So this Crossan thinks poorly of the whole thing," Hoey murmured.

"Yes. More to the point, how it was gathered."

Minogue ached for a glass of Jamesons. Hoey's constant shifting in his chair — the leg-crossing, the foot tapping air, the hand straying to his nose and mouth, the incessant flicking of ash into the fireplace, the throat-clearing and the swallowing of phlegm — had all accumulated somewhere in Minogue's mind until he himself was jittery. He had read exactly four pages of his book in the last hour, and he was beginning to have trouble hiding his irritation.

"Well, I don't know," said Hoey and yawned. "Kind of hard to get excited about it."

He lit up another cigarette. Minogue counted the butts in the ashtray and divided the number into one hundred, the number of minutes he estimated that they had been sitting here. Still layers of smoke shaped by the light overhead reminded Minogue of the holy pictures of his youth. He slid out of his chair and opened the window a crack.

"Sorry," said Hoey, and began coughing. "I forgot."

"Smoke away, man. It's not as bad as what Jim Kilmartin puts out. Between the cigars and the farts — and then those damned Gitanes of Eilis's."

Hoey gave him a wan smile and rubbed the side of his cigarette around the saucer. He looked around the living room as though assessing the knickknacks and pictures, those weights and anchors of home.

"Did Crossan put any of this down in writing?" Hoey asked. "Any documentation, like?"

"Just Bourke's ramblings on paper. A few copies of newspaper reports."

"You didn't talk to Bourke?"

Minogue shook his head. He joined Hoey in watching a tranquilized grizzly being lifted into a wooden crate and then airlifted, dangling in a net under a helicopter. The nasal tone of the commentator against the bat-bat of the rotors detailed the hopes of the biologists for the grizzly. Minogue wondered what effects Hoey's pills had. He watched as the grizzly's crate came to rest on a small plateau somewhere in the Rockies. Two men entered the picture and began setting up the door of the crate for the bear's release. Minogue's exasperation crested. He thought of a walk of the neighborhood.

"What would you be doing of an evening at home, now, Shea?"

Hoey kept his eyes on the screen. The biologists retreated to safety, ready for the release.

Hoey replied with a cheer which Minogue found disquieting.

"Tell you the truth, I'd probably be in a pub."

The inspector struggled to recover from his own folly. He studied Hoey's profile as the door of the grizzly's crate was opened. Was it the glare from the screen or was there really a dull sheen of sweat on Hoey's forehead? Hoey didn't look keen on a walk. Minogue wanted a bloody drink and couldn't for fear of tempting Hoey: a prisoner in his own home. He picked up his book and tried to read again. The phone trilled twice before he recognized it as a phone at all.

•   •   •   •   •

Crossan screwed the top on the bottle and waited for Minogue to answer. He took a belt of the whiskey and rubbed the glass in a slow semicircle on his desk. An hour ago he had felt that he wouldn't be able to stop himself from puking, but the anger had taken over and had saved him this humiliation and a greater one — being sick in front of two Guards. They'd have it all over the town by teatime that the great Aloysius Crossan had made a gobshite of himself when the going had got tough. He still felt the outrage and shock like acid in every part of his belly. Ahearne and another Guard, along with Tom Igo, the county coroner, had been waiting for him in the morgue of the County Hospital. The body had been brought there just after nine o'clock last night. It was only this morning, after several hours of Gardai trying to find next of kin, that Ahearne had thought of contacting Crossan.

Jamesy Bourke's chest had taken most of the charge, but a scatter of pellets from the blast had lodged in his neck. Like those black spots, Crossan thought numbly, recalling from his youth the warts treated with burning lotion. Bourke's jacket was shredded and soaked in blood. His eyes were still open in shock. One minute Crossan's throat was tight with outrage, and then, with the sheet pulled back, his stomach had fallen, almost taking his control with it. Only anger and will had prevented him from vomiting. He remembered turning to meet the eyes of the Guards, Ahearne and Murphy, defying their expectations. *Yes, I attest that this is the body of James Bourke, known to me personally.* The bitter formality had registered on the faces of the two Guards, and Crossan had walked steadily out of the morgue, knowing that he had seen a hint of shame on both faces. Through the rushing noise and the nausea, Crossan had heard Tim Igo whispering wheezily next to his ear that Bourke had "gone instantly."

Two rings. Where was Minogue? Maybe half-ten was a bit late to be phoning him. What the hell took him back up to Dublin anyway? So he could avoid being bloody-well asked to do something for Bourke. He thought again of Jamesy Bourke's body being lifted from the compost heap as though he, like his dog, had merely to be disposed of. "Gone instantly" — no: Jamesy Bourke had died slowly over the last twelve years.

The phone was picked up at the other end.

"Minogue?"

·   ·   ·   ·   ·

Minogue packed two changes of clothes, extra socks, and a few books in a soft-sided overnight bag and went downstairs to wait for Kathleen. He tried to imagine her reaction. Would she laugh? She'd want him to take up the job of talking to Mick and Eoin again. Hoey had stretched out his legs and was pouring more tea while the ads rolled. Minogue sat scross from him and watched an aging rock star peddle soft drinks.

"Last night," Hoey said.

"Around eight o'clock, he said," replied Minogue. "According to what the Guards told Crossan, this Spillner fella thought that it was the same thing that had happened the night before at another place."

"Was Bourke . . . ?"

"Not at all. He was mooching around the man's car, looking for something."

Hoey drew on a fresh cigarette, blew out smoke, and scratched at the back of his neck. The pop star of forty-five landed improbably on his feet and was surrounded by teenagers who made skilled, jerky motions in a wave around him. He grabbed one of them — a delighted girl — and she hung on to his arm while stars burst behind them.

"Well, I don't want to be . . ."

Hoey left the sentence unfinished and fell to staring at the fireplace. Minogue squirmed and thought of phoning Kilmartin tonight. He looked down at his watch and decided against it. Half-ten. God Almighty, wife of mine hiding out at Costigans' while we sat here like iijits watching rubbish on the box.

"I don't want anything backfiring, Shea," Minogue stated. "I feel bad enough about not having talked to Bourke. I have to go down and find out what happened, at least. But I can't be looking over me shoulder. You know what I'm saying now."

Hoey's puffed eyes remained fixed on the fireplace.

"I might be shaky, but I'm game," he muttered.

"Look, Shea. It mightn't be smart to be getting involved in something like this. At this stage."

Hoey drew hard on his cigarette.

"Did the Squad get a call on it at all yet?"

"Don't know. I'll ask Eilis in the morning. This Spillner fella who shot him was brought to the station. He's been moved to HQ in Ennis since. Crossan told me that he heard that there's someone coming down from the German Embassy to sort it out too."

"Where did he get the shotgun?"

"Well, I'm only going on what Crossan was told. Apparently Spillner brought it with him in the boot of his car on a trip here last summer. Since the trouble below in Clare and Limerick and so forth. The arms finds and the shooting and the foofaraw starting up about the tourists buying up places. Last I saw him he was sitting next to a musician, clapping his hands."

Kathleen opened the hall door. He intercepted her in the hall as she was taking off her coat.

"Guess where I'm going?" He paused and decided. "Where we're going, tomorrow, Shea and myself."

CHAPTER 6

A BAD PATCH of road outside Nenagh jostled Hoey's lolling head against the headrest. He elbowed up slowly and licked his teeth. Minogue looked at his watch. Two and a half hours from Dublin: that was fast.

"Sorry," said Minogue. "But that's Tipperary County Council for you. Did you sleep last night?"

"I did, I think," said Hoey. "Better that the other night, I can tell you. These bloody pills. Stayed up awhile talking to Kathleen. It's too bad she didn't want to come down . . ."

He looked out at the fields. It was midday now and sluggish clouds had moved in from the coast. Minogue had expected rain since Portlaoise.

"Nenagh," Hoey whispered. He stretched and felt his pocket for the orange bottle of pills.

"That's it. We'll be in Ennis before you know it."

The inspector had made several phone calls before leaving Dublin. Kilmartin, still in his kitchen, hadn't argued with him as much as he had expected. Eilis reported that no call had been logged to the Squad yet about Bourke. Minogue had phoned Crossan and arranged to call to his office by dinnertime.

"Look at that," said Hoey.

By a bend in the road Minogue spotted what he took to be a County Council crew working with little vigor to remove slogans spray-painted onto a wall. Hoey turned in his seat as the car passed them.

"EC Robbers Beware. What's that other one? Irish Land for Irish People."

"Maybe they should write their slogans in German or Dutch or whatever," Minogue murmured.

Forty minutes later he was accelerating out the Ennis Road from Limerick.

Ennis had changed, he believed. The town of bright streets and busy shops was now slow, dulled by clouds and stillness. The streets were almost deserted. Not every day can be market day, he tried to reason with himself. That logic didn't gain any ground against his impressions. The air felt heavy. The walls of the buildings seemed to be thicker, their windows turned inward. He reached Bank Place and drew into the curb by Crossan's office. He touched the horn and looked up at the windows along the terrace. Crossan appeared at one and waved once. A minute later, he closed the door behind him, paused to throw on a raincoat and swept down the steps toward the Fiat.

Minogue introduced Hoey.

"Let's go to the Garda station first," said Crossan.

"Have you heard more about Spillner?" Minogue asked.

"Well, I don't know if he got bail yet."

"I'd expect him to be held over for even having the gun," said Minogue.

"Word is that Tom Russell, the super in Clare, has asked Dublin for new commando-type outfits to patrol the place," said Crossan. "The ones trained to eat their children and run through walls with their heads."

Minogue crossed the bridge and turned down the cul-de-sac toward the Garda station. He debated telling Crossan about his run-in with the Special Branch out at the farm but decided against it.

"So Russell and Co. haven't phoned your mob for expertise," Crossan went on. "Maybe he lost your number, do you think?"

Minogue parked behind a black Mercedes. Crossan squinted at the CD plate on the grille.

"Look at the shine off that car, will you," he said. "Blind a beggar, so it would."

A chauffeur stepped around one of the gateposts that formed the entry to the yard of the station and began to study the dowdy Fiat and its passengers.

"A fiver says that's he's down from the German Embassy in Dublin," said Crossan. "Herr Spillner being the big-noise industrialist back in the fatherland."

Minogue plucked the key out of the ignition and nodded at the chauffeur, a well turned out man in his thirties, thickset without looking at all flabby.

"*Guten Tag*," said Crossan. The chauffeur stood with his feet spread and nodded.

The lawyer strode down the short avenue and sprang, it seemed to Minogue, through the architraved door into the public office. A tall Guard with a bony nose and a flushed complexion looked up and greeted Crossan before allowing his eyes to search Hoey's features. God, thought Minogue, Hoey probably looks like a suspect they were bringing to a lockup. The Guard studied Minogue's card for several seconds.

"Are ye expected, now?"

"We're here to see Sergeant Ahearne," said Crossan.

The Guard tugged at his tunic to straighten it under his belt.

"Hold on a minute, yes," he said. "He's on the premises, I believe."

With a shy smile the Guard turned tail and went through a door behind the counter. Two Guards ambled in the door, laughing, from the yard.

"How's Alo?" asked the older one. He had ginger hair and pale, tired eyes still full of humor after the joke he had been exchanging with his mate.

"I've been better," said Crossan.

Ginger-hair smiled at Hoey.

"Did Alo do that to you?"

A Guard in the lighter blue tunic of a superintendent came through the door into the public office. For several moments, Minogue could not grasp what was going on. The superintendent's eyes had been on Minogue's from the moment he had appeared around the door. The two Guards in from patrol stopped abruptly, straightened, and looked from the superintendent to Sergeant Ahearne following. Behind Ahearne came the desk officer who dared a look toward Minogue before looking away. Minogue's thinking still lagged behind his awareness that he had walked into an ambush.

Superintendent Thomas Russell of the County Clare Division of the Garda Siochana was fifty-three years on earth. He retained a full head of crinkly hair that flowed back from a heavily lined forehead. The hair reminded Minogue of a child's drawing of ocean waves. Two unfashionable patches of sideburn hair high on Russell's cheeks hinted at an inflexibility. Vanity, Minogue guessed. Look at me, I am fierce. I can grow hair right up under my eyes. Thick eyebrows couldn't deliver any softer, owlish aspects to this warrior's face. Minogue wondered if Russell's wide face with the thrusting tufts and the incongruously small features looked this impassive as a matter of course.

"Gentlemen," said Russell. "Will you step into this room here?"

The trio were ushered in ahead of Ahearne and Russell. Ahearne, an athlete run to fat after resting on laurels probably twenty years old, but soft on his feet yet, pulled out chairs. Russell nodded as introductions were made. Then he opened with a weak facsimile of humor.

"Well. To find Jim Kilmartin's boys here in Ennis. Who'd have imagined our good fortune?"

Minogue did not mistake the tone. He wondered what Russell being here had to do with the Mercedes bearing CD plates outside.

"I'm acting for the deceased," said Crossan. "I met the inspector socially and I called him for advice. He was acquainted with Bourke."

Russell gave Crossan a blank look.

"Half the county was well acquainted with Jamesy Bourke, I believe," said Russell.

Mingoue looked into the flat face and the tiny eyes that hardly moved.

"This man Spillner shot him the once?" Minogue asked.

"The once, yes," Ahearne replied. "But with two barrels."

"And killed him outright?"

"Very much so," said Ahearne. He shifted slightly in his chair, drawing a squeak from the vinyl as he issued a sympathetic nod.

"How far away from Bourke was he when he —"

Russell raised his hand.

"Inspector. You appear to be launching an investigation here. Sergeant Ahearne is, in point of fact, the investigating officer. He is already in possession of sufficient material to pursue the case to its conclusion."

Minogue looked at Ahearne. The sergeant blinked and rubbed his hands together once.

"That's great," said Minogue.

"We'd like to talk to this Spillner man," said Crossan.

"Ah, Mr. Crossan," Russell said with exaggerated civility. "In what capacity, now?"

"As counsel for Jamesy Bourke."

"He retained you, did he?"

"As a friend, then."

"A friend? With all due respect now, Mr. Crossan," said Russell, leaning in slightly, "this is a delicate enough matter. There's a foreign national involved. There's the possibility of hob-lawyers — no aspirations on your profession, now — trying to make something of this business. The issue of land, I mean. Now, I don't see how you can help the investigation by interviewing Mr. Spillner —"

"*Herr* Spillner," said Crossan.

Russell fixed a stare on the barrister before resuming.

"I don't see how you can help us by interviewing this man. All the expertise and training, well, we have them at hand. The inspector here can assure you of that, of the professionalism and training we have here on the Force."

Russell paused to raise his eyebrows as he looked at Minogue.

"The County Coroner has provided us with a very clear picture of what happened, and what Mr. Spillner has told us accords very closely with that report. It's a tragic event. But the atmosphere in parts of the county, what with hooligans and guns and their heads full of slogans, well . . . I would tend to lay some of the blame at the feet of those people for helping to make things so strained."

He turned to Minogue.

"Are you up on the tensions we are having here in Clare, Inspector? There are people now from fine families getting caught up in this nonsense."

So Russell knew that he was related to Eoin, Minogue thought. He returned Russell's look. The superintendent continued with a poor pretense at being guileless.

"Now, I don't know if it's widely known in Dublin, but we might have a repeat of the Land War on our hands here. Whiteboys and Rapparees they're not. These characters have machine guns, et cetera."

"If he was so close to Bourke, why did he kill him?" Crossan demanded.

Russell jumped at the question.

"This Mr. Spillner has a great command of English, am I right, Sean?"

Ahearne nodded.

"Very good indeed. Very precise account of everything, right down to the times. He was out to the house with us twice and we reenacted the whole thing several times. It's all consistent with what the PM shows."

"'Suggests,' you mean," said Crossan. "Why did he kill Bourke?"

"It was night," said Ahearne. "He didn't know Bourke from Adam. And he thought Bourke had a gun in his fist —"

"A gun?" Crossan echoed.

Ahearne shrugged. "We have an ashplant from beside the house. Spillner says he was certain that Bourke was pointing a rifle at him. So he let fly with the shotgun."

"His defense is that he was in fear of his life?" Crossan spoke with a sharp tone of incredulity.

"It's not for us to be deciding or guessing at what Spillner will or will not claim in his defense," Russell retorted. "But I imagine that will be brought up at an inquest."

"Inquest?" asked Crossan. "Don't you mean trial?"

Russell's expression didn't change but he spoke more softly now.

"You hardly need me to explain the procedures to you, now, Mr. Crossan. We give our reports to the authorities."

Russell paused to let his listeners reflect on the way he said "authorities."

"They'll decide how to proceed on behalf of the State. We have plenty on our plates here in Clare, but we'll proceed in good order."

His eyes left Crossan and they settled again on Minogue. Russell's expression had now changed but faintly. The edges of his mouth rose, in what ordinary citizens might believe was a smile.

"Remember me to Jimmy, won't you, when you go back to Dublin." The superintendent rose from the table. "But tell him that Mayo should stick to the football. Leave the hurling to the experts."

Minogue was surprised to find Russell's hand extended across the table. He shook hands with the superintendent.

"Such as?" Minogue tried.

"Such as Waterford."

Close, Minogue thought. He had guessed Russell's accent as high-hat gloss on Kilkenny.

"Funny, you'd pick them, now," said Minogue. "My money'd be on Clare."

"Safe home to ye, now," said Russell, and turned on his heel.

•　　•　　•　　•　　•

Minogue looked back up the short avenue that led from Abbey Street into Ennis Garda Station. Solid, he thought, almost like a fortress. Gates and a house fit to stop any number of pike-bearing rebels when the gentry had built it as Abbeyfield House, two hundred and fifty years ago.

"Come on, will you," barked Crossan. "Let's not stand here gawking like wallflowers that were stood up on a date. I have work to do."

"Well, the Mercedes is gone," said Hoey.

"I'll bet you Russell kept us there, lecturing, so as this cowboy German could get his bail fixed and have himself whisked away in that bloody Mercedes."

A sudden gust blew grit down the street into Minogue's face. He knew then what he would do. He followed Crossan.

"I'd like to go back in there and annoy that bollocks," the lawyer said. "But where would that get us? A brick wall. Jesus!"

The swollen eyes widened even further, and Minogue took a step back. The sharp, cool air had grayed the barrister's skin and watered his eyes. They reminded Minogue of some picture, one from his children's storybooks.

"Not a damn word about charges, about whether he's to stay in custody," Crossan went on. "Wouldn't surprise me if this Spillner fella is on his way to Shannon Airport this very minute."

"Let's go somewhere and sit down and drink a cup of coffee," said Minogue. "Have a think and a chat. I have a phone call to make."

Crossan blew out smoke and pointed conclusively at the curb.

A blue Ford Sierra with its antenna waving came down the avenue. Russell nodded to them from the passenger seat before the car picked up speed.

"Just happened to be there," said Hoey.

Minogue drew his coat around him and looked up at the brown and gray clouds massed over the town. The River Fergus hissed over a weir, gray itself and flat, its banks lined with blackening leaves.

He studied the roof lines and the windows along Abbey Street.

"Time to stir the pot, I think," he murmured. "Throw in another ingredient. I need a phone."

•   •   •   •   •

Minogue sat next to Crossan and looked at the plate of sandwiches.

"Where's Shea gone?"

"Off to get fags," said Crossan. "Here, what happened to him anyway?"

"He's recuperating from a recent accident."

"Would he need to be irrigating his throat too with a few jars, maybe? I for one certainly feel the need this very minute."

Minogue gave Crossan a lingering look to drive home the hint.

"No. The few jars are definitely not part of the cure," Minogue said, and he bit into a sandwich.

"What's this 'ingredient' you were talking about?"

"I phoned a man I wouldn't ordinarily phone. You may know him. Shorty Hynes."

"Not that bloody ghoul that writes for the *Indo*, is it? The murder-and-mayhem fella? Do you know him?"

The inspector nodded. "I certainly do. He's a royal pain in the arse. He'll do nicely, I imagine."

"Do what?"

"He'll be phoning the Garda Commissioner about this fella Spillner. Why his bail might allow him to hightail it off to Germany courtesy of the German Embassy."

"Oho," Crossan snorted. "Good move there, Guard. The proverbial leak. I didn't think you had it in you. You might as well fill in your request for asylum here in Clare after a stunt like that."

"The public interest the right to know, counselor,"

Minogue took another bite and wondered how long it would take for Kilmartin to phone. Half an hour, he guessed. Hoey returned, tearing the cellophane from a packet of Majors.

"Let's go over what we have, so far," said Minogue. "See where the gaps might be."

He rearranged the photocopies on the table and looked to Crossan.

"Will you start?"

"All right. We have the summary and copies of the book of evidence used to prosecute him."

"Yep," said Minogue. "All I found were copies of two Dublin newspapers' coverage. Nothing new."

"We all know that no appeal launched means no transcript?" Crossan asked.

Minogue nodded. "The full steno record is above in the strong-room in the Criminal Court in Green Street," he said.

"Maybe I'm getting ahead of myself here, but," said Hoey, "why didn't Bourke launch an appeal if the prosecution case was shaky? Didn't his lawyer push him about an appeal, anyway?"

"Well, Jamesy recalled Tighe talking to him about it," said Crossan. "And I talked to Tighe about it. According to him, Jamesy turned it down. 'Why?' I asked him. 'Bourke was a poet, you have to understand, and he had to have his way right to the end,' says Tighe to me."

"What does that mean, the poet thing?" asked Minogue.

"To pay the price maybe," Crossan replied. "Give one's life in lieu, that sort of grand gesture."

"He wanted to be punished for killing his sweetheart, like?" Hoey asked.

The lawyer looked squarely at Hoey.

"A crooked kind of grandeur in this day and age, you're thinking?"

Hoey's mouth hung slightly open. A stream of smoke cascaded slowly over his lower lip as he squinted at the barrister. Crossan took a deep breath, blew it out slowly from puffed cheeks and sat back in his chair.

"Something broke inside Jamesy the first day of the trial," Tighe said. "I believe that. It was like he gave up. And that attitude stayed with him for a long time, he told me."

"Why'd he give up?" Minogue asked. "The second day, you said."

"Okay. Tighe entered the not-guilty plea. The prosecution is going to use circumstantial evidence to put Jamesy there with the matches in his hand and corroboration as regards a motive. State gets up, Tighe told me, and presents witnesses: the Guard, Naughton. Tighe's hands are tied in a sense because Jamesy had blacked out. But Tighe knows what he wants out of the not-guilty; the worst he can get, he figures, is manslaughter. Pucks of diminished responsibility and everything else. So far, so good. Jamesy was very straight with Tighe, said he couldn't remember a damn thing, yes, he was really angry at Jane Clark, et cetera. So Tighe is sailing along nicely until the State gets witnesses talking about Jane Clark. The judge didn't rule many of them out of order, Tighe remembers. He was new to the job and wasn't as full of vinegar as maybe he should have been. To make a long story short, Jamesy Bourke erupts right there in the court."

"He's embarrassed at the information coming out?" Hoey asked.

"Oh, Christ, man, more than that — way more," said Crossan. "'Who was anyone here to judge her . . . bunch of hypocrites . . . always out to get him.' The whole bit. Tighe tries to calm him down but makes a big mistake. He confides to Jamesy that it's fine by him to have comment on Jane Clark's character because that'll help. Provocation, track record, bad influence, hashish — you can make that into anything, really. Jamesy sees red now. He was never the willing fool, he tells Tighe. Furthermore, he tells Tighe that he will — and Tighe remembers the exact words — knock his fucking block off if he has any part in sullying the name of Jane Clark."

Crossan sat back and looked from Minogue to Hoey and back.

"So there he is in open court displaying the personality and behavior a judge and jury scrutinize all the more keenly when there's so much hanging on circumstantial evidence anyway," said Minogue.

"The nail on the head," said Crossan. "From then on, Jamesy gave up on it. So Tighe says."

"So what did Tighe do?" Hoey asked.

"He did his best, I suppose, but maybe he lacked the experience. Maybe Jamesy threw him off track so much that . . . Well, maybe it's in the full trial record that Tighe at least tried to hammer at the Guards or got some leverage out of the postmortem report or something. Tighe actually ended up calling witnesses or cross-examining them as to Jane Clark's mode of living up at the cottage."

"A bit of character assassination in the service of diminishing his guilt," said Minogue.

Crossan almost smiled.

"You kept your ears open in all those trials you've attended, I can tell," he said. "God help you."

"Yeah, well," Hoey began, "how come it's twelve years later and we're talking about this?"

"Your man here" — Crossan nodded at Minogue — "asked me that the other day: 'Why all these years later?' Jamesy began to remember bits of things from that night. He thought it was the electroshock sessions he had after his breakdown that messed up his brain, his mind. Don't forget, he was well and truly gargled the night of the fire. But he did say that he remembered Jane Clark hadn't been drinking all that much that night. Nowhere near drunk enough to pass out."

"How did he know that?" Hoey interrupted. "The way I heard it, he showed up at her place only to see she had the other fella there, Howard. Then they had a row and left. Bourke was away from the cottage two or three hours. Maybe she hit the bottle after he left."

"She wasn't drunk while he was there," said Crossan.

"But she drank plenty," said Minogue. "And had hash too."

"Jamesy told me that he asked her for a joint but she told him it was all gone. And she liked to drink in the pubs, more than at home," said Crossan.

"She could have been lying about the dope," Hoey said.

"Whether or which," Crossan continued, "I half expected this line from ye. I'm not complaining, now. Jamesy told me he remembered her saying she'd see them later on, after they made up."

"That was in the thing he wrote too," Minogue murmured. "But — I have to say this now — after all that time in jail, he'd have time to make up anything. Not even to speak of the mental trouble. He mightn't even have known he was making it up."

Crossan drew in his breath through his teeth.

"You may well be right," he said, "but humor me a little, can't you?"

"All right, so I will," said Minogue, "by changing the subject a little. I haven't yet found any mention of smoke inhalation in the stuff I was able to collect so far. It's almost always that finding that establishes clear cause of death in something like this."

"Right," said Crossan. His face had set into a grim smile. "And I haven't been idle here at all. I've been trying to hunt down a copy of the autopsy performed on Jane. So far all I have is two telephone conversations with a clerk who looks after them. She got shy of me asking all those questions and as much as told me I'd have to put my request in writing — through Dublin, if you don't mind, too. I'd sort of let the matter lie, but I think it's time to hammer away at it again."

Minogue stretched his fingers. Kilmartin should be exploding just about now, he reflected.

"In some respects Jamesy brought his own shovel to dig his grave," Crossan said. He paused to swallow a portion of his sandwich and touched his lips as though to help the bolus descend past his protruding Adam's apple.

"Here, you better take some of these before I have them all gone."

Minogue took a half sandwich. Hoey slid down in his chair and crossed his legs at the ankles.

"Back to this memory thing now," Crossan resumed. "The nervous breakdown probably confused things even more. Jamesy admitted to me that his memory was tatty enough. He also told me that they — the psychiatric staff, he meant — had robbed him of his memory deliberately. With the convulsive therapy and the drugs, he meant."

"Uh-oh, here we go now," said Minogue. "Deliberately for what?"

"I had the selfsame reaction," said Crossan. "Didn't ask him. When I heard him talk that way, I thought it was all a lost cause. If he couldn't recall details I could verify, then I was at bedrock."

"Well, how is it he was able to recall anything at all?" Hoey asked.

"He maintained that things came back to him over the last few years," said Crossan. "He'd had dreams."

Hoey released a mouthful of smoke and watched it travel in a ball toward the ceiling. Minogue's wandering eyes looked up from where they had been browsing, and he became aware of Crossan's anger.

"Look, I know what you're thinking," said Crossan. "Jamesy Bourke is — was — a head-case. Obsessed, paranoid, delusional — the whole bit. He probably had psychotic episodes. I never said I believed his version of things. I told you" — Crossan pointed his finger at Minogue — "that in no way was I sure that a proper verdict had not been delivered. Am I clear on this?"

Hoey looked at Minogue and shrugged. A lounge-boy asked if they wanted more sandwiches. Minogue waved him away.

"Okay," said Minogue. "Let me move on again: the odd accounting of time and who's where the night of the fire. I expected to find a better mention in the book of evidence of the people involved. Of course, if I had the trial transcript proper, maybe I wouldn't be thinking what I'm thinking. But usually the book of evidence has the stuff laid out a lot clearer. You know, a clear run of events, the time, the people. I lit on this probably because I'm oftentimes the one who gets called up by the State and I bring a judge or a jury through the places and the times and the people with the proper prods from counsel."

Crossan was studying the smoke rising from the ashtray. He looked up and nodded once.

"So you saw that too. Look. Think back to that night again. Jamesy Bourke is on the piss in serious fashion and he bowls around to Jane Clark's place. With amorous intent, you can imagine. It's around the nine o'clock mark. A fine summer's evening."

Crossan began stripping the crust from another sandwich.

"In the door he goes, with a great welcome for himself, no doubt. Thereupon he discovers that Jane Clark is, shall we say, in congress with another suitor."

"Dan Howard," said Minogue.

"Yes, the very man. *In flagrante.*"

Minogue noted Crossan's delicate mannerisms. The barrister dropped a long section of crust with a deliberate gesture the inspector read as a sign of distaste.

"Words are exchanged, a row starts. They end up rowing out the back of the cottage. Jane Clark starts laughing at them. So far it's a comedy. She locks the door, throws Dan Howard's clothes out into the yard. Dan Howard collects a few pucks from Jamesy and they give one another the odd dig. Shouting at one another, that class of thing. No major damage being done so far, except to the male ego, maybe."

Crossan paused to take an exploratory bite of his new sandwich.

"Jamesy has cooled down a little. Don't underestimate Dan's ability to talk his way out of trouble, now. Anyway. They both leave for the village with their heads hanging. Yes, they sloother into the village without damaging themselves."

The barrister looked down his nose at the sandwich. Something in the sandwich took his attention and he peered in between the slices of bread.

"Jamesy is by times threatening to beat the shite out of Dan Howard and then by times cursing Jane Clark. In any event, by the time they walk into the village, they're mighty thirsty. Howard has conceded that Jane Clark and himself had a bit of a thing going, 'a fling' as one might say, for several weeks prior. He tells Jamesy that she was, quote, 'only a hoor,' and that, between friends, they should give her the thumbs-down and not fall out over her. Dan Howard and Jamesy repair to the pub. Howard pours oil on the waters by plying Jamesy with drink. They're there until closing time and beyond."

"Where were they drinking?"

"Howard's hotel, the Portaree Inn."

"How did Howard get around? Didn't he have a car?"

"He did, but not that night. It's as well too, I suppose. He was full of drink most of the evening and more or less legless by the end of the night. It was Sheila Hanratty who tracked him down in the pub and put him in the door of his house."

Something in the way Crossan spoke her name released an airy feeling in Minogue's stomach. For an instant he imagined her in sunlight, the light showing up fair hairs on her forearms.

"Didn't she get called to the stand?"

"Yes, she did. She was one of the witnesses brought up to testify to Jane Clark's mode of living as regards drink and carry-on."

"Who called her to the stand, anyhow?"

"Tighe, the lawyer. By this stage he had nothing going for him except to chop down Jamesy's responsibility as best he can. Paint the victim in as bad a light as you can without having judge or counsel call you on it — and avoid offending the jury either — and that can influence the sentencing."

"Was she his girlfriend then?"

"She wasn't really doing a line with Howard. She hung around in her own mousy, demure way."

"Mousy?" Minogue could not keep from saying.

"Oh, I grant you she's no longer mousy," said Crossan. "She had her designs on him. But, sure, so did half the county. Dan was a class of, what would I say in these enlightened times . . ."

"A ladies' man?"

Crossan's grin beamed suddenly and then relapsed into a rueful stare at the patterns in the carpet.

"More like a whoremaster."

"That's a term of some weight," said Minogue. "Even for a lawyer to utter."

"You don't say, now."

"You mean, I take it, that it was all right for Dan Howard to play the field but Jane Clark, she was supposed to go by different rules of conduct?"

"Right," Crossan replied with a clear hint of derision. "You don't need informing on the mores of Catholic Ireland, do you?"

"What did you think of Jane Clark yourself?" Minogue asked.

"Trouble," Crossan answered without hesitation. "A lot of trouble. But she was a very exotic bloom in these parts. Like one of those plants up above on the Burren, something that'd have the botanists drooling over it: how the hell did it get here and how the hell can it grow in the middle of all this . . . Oh sure, tourists come and go, but for one to stay and try and make a home of it around here? She was very talented. But hearing about her and that girl Eilo McInerny colored things a bit even for me. Not because of what they did but because I knew the girl was no match for Jane Clark."

Crossan picked up another corner of sandwich but dropped it abruptly. He curled his lip. "Look, even if she seduced half the village, the parish priest, and the schoolgirls even —"

"Did she?"

"Don't be an iijit. Of course she didn't. But the way the testimony was given and used, it sounded like she was the divil incarnate. What I was saying is that Jane Clark was not the galvanized bitch she is remembered as."

Minogue withdrew into his own muddled thoughts. Crossan poured more coffee. Hoey scratched himself slowly and carefully under his arm. Crossan's long bony forearms escaped his cuffs and his hands move expertly around the cup to grasp the spoon.

"You can actually say 'bisexual' now without having to duck your head," Minogue mused.

"You don't say," Crossan drawled. "This young one, Eilo McInerny — a waif in from Ballygobackwards — eventually said that she had been dragooned into the whole lesbian thing. Seduced."

"You have this McInerny girl's whereabouts, don't you?"

"Just about. It took me time, I can tell you. She went to England right after the trial, but she finally came back. She's working in a hotel below in Tralee. Another casualty we forgot about, I suppose. A lousy enough life she had, skivvying in the hotel and no prospects. I don't doubt but that Dan Howard might have tried knocking on her door by times too. But Tighe got her up on the stand to help hammer home the witch bit. The devil-woman, the man-eater."

Crossan broke off to drink some of his coffee.

"So Tighe did a good hatchet job on Jane Clark, I suppose," Minogue prodded.

"So he thought until the sentencing: a life sentence for a charge of manslaughter. That was the shocker. Sweeney, the judge, had a rep but even Tighe didn't expect Sweeney to hit that hard. That's what I still can't get over, if you want to know."

"What?"

"You'd think one person couldn't have all the bad luck land on them. Or at least poor Jamesy didn't deserve all that went on. Look. He finds out that the one he thinks is his girlfriend, his ticket out of being a lost soul out on a farm in the back end of the bloody Burren, she has other interests. Gets Tighe, brand new barrister on the Legal Aid panel, to defend him. And then, even if he had King Solomon in his corner, he draws bloody Sweeney as the judge for the trial — a notorious one-man morality squad. Maybe it's no wonder Jamesy went under, gave up on the system."

Crossan's eyes were bulging over the rim of his cup when he finished. He steadied it with the fingertips of his left hand and turned to watch as three tourists stepped into the foyer.

"I'm willing to start with this Eilo McInerny," said Minogue. "In Tralee, you said. Have you spoken to her?"

"Matter of fact, I did," said Crossan. "I phoned her a few months back, asked her would she be willing to talk it over, what she remembered of the night and so on."

"How'd she react?"

"Told me I was wasting me time — her time too."

Minogue looked over at Hoey to find him busy trying to scratch out a stain on the knee of his trousers with his thumbnail.

"Let me try with her now, then," said Minogue to Crossan.

"When, like?"

Minogue glanced at Hoey again.

"Today. This afternoon. Whenever. Why not?"

"I'll have to make sure she's still there," said Crossan. "And I'd have to tell her what we're about. That ye're Guards and so on. No shilly-shallying here. Proper disclosure."

Minogue shrugged his concession. A lanky youth with a crew cut sharp over a slack, pimply face appeared in the foyer. Minogue watched the youth seek him out, his eyes shifting from Crossan to Hoey to himself and then settling back on him.

"There's a phone call beyond for a Mr. Minogue, a Guard."

Minogue thanked him and rose.

"I'll tell you what," said Crossan. "I'll try to get in touch with the hotel in Tralee right now. Would you drive down there this afternoon?"

"Sure, I will," said the inspector. He poked Hoey in the shoulder.

"Do you want to talk to the Killer instead?"

Hoey feigned a grin but it was one of aversion. He reached reflexively for his cigarettes. Crossan went in search of a phone. Minogue sloped over to the desk and was directed to a stool by the wall. He sat down and leaned against the wall.

"Yes, Jimmy," he said, and held the phone away from his ear.

"Close, but not close enough."

Minogue elbowed away from the wall with the surprise.

"I wasn't expecting —"

"You have such high regard for journalists like Hynes that you fired him right in my face?"

Minogue tried desperately to gauge the current mood of Garda Commissioner Tynan.

"Ah now, John. Shorty Hynes is like that. I merely passed on some facts to him. He's not my puppet, now."

{ 115 }

"He's a nasty little gawker. What do you think you're doing? You're supposed to be off on your holidays."

"Has Jim Kilmartin been in touch with you?"

"I was in touch with him," said Tynan. "Ask me if it was before or after I received calls from Superintendent Tom Russell and Hynes."

Jesus, I'm sunk, thought Minogue.

"You know Tom Russell, don't you?" Tynan pressed on.

"Yes, I've met him briefly."

"In the recent past?"

Minogue suspected that Tynan's sarcasm was a teasing prelude to tearing his head off.

"Look, John —"

"Look, yourself. Tom Russell wants you out of his hair. I want Tom Russell out of my hair. He says you showed up at the Garda station in Ennis without an invite but with an IRA lawyer."

"Wait a minute. Crossan's not that, he's just a damn good barrister who wins too many down here."

"What are you doing prowling around there teamed up with this lawyer and another Guard on leave? One Seamus Hoey?"

"Give me five minutes — no, three minutes — to explain. Three minutes."

"You had your five minutes and more in Bewley's restaurant the other day. I phoned Kilmartin and told him I'd be speaking with you over this, what can I call it, gatecrashing. He asked if you'd be kind enough to phone him after our conversation. I believe he has something to tell you."

He'd not need to pick up a phone in Dublin for me to hear him, thought Minogue.

"Three minutes, John. Did Hynes give any details?"

"'Details'? All Hynes and his ilk are likely to give me is a migraine."

"But maybe he believes that the Garda Commissioner should know that a man accused of and freely confessing to the shooting death of another man, with the use of a firearm illegally imported into this country, is allowed back to Germany on his bail."

"Is this a recording of a speech you've prepared? Does a journalist think this would be the first time that Justice has left Guards with their jaws hanging? This is news? If Hynes wants to make a thing of it, it's in the Department of Justice and the Courts he should be kicking shins."

"Didn't he tell you anything about the man who was killed, though?" Minogue persisted.

"I didn't give Hynes the chance. I gave him the number for an assistant secretary in Justice."

"It's the fella who was killed. That's what has me here. Listen, about twelve years back . . ."

Minogue's armpits were itching when he finished. Tynan had not tried to interrupt him. Minogue looked down to see that one of his feet was tapping away rapidly with a will of its own.

"You're on holidays, right?" Tynan asked finally.

"Right."

"You're Sean Citizen in Ennis. You're pursuing some research of your own. Right?"

"Right."

"And there's no call for you to be elbowing yourself in to investigate this shooting, pestering people to see autopsy reports, or to hang about the scene. Right?"

Minogue balked.

"Do you hear me?" Tynan's tone was mild enough for Minogue to recognize the impatience. "And Tom Russell and his well-trained Gardai can manage this shooting all the better now that he knows I'm aware of it here. Do you recognize that?"

"Yes," said Minogue. "But —"

"Tom Russell will take care of it. Consider me briefed. As for the other stuff, your hobby there —"

"Look, John, the more I learn about it, the worse it looks. Bad process at the very least. If ever the Murder Squad should have been —"

"Wait, wait," Tynan broke in. "Go ahead and find bad process then. You wouldn't be the first to find it. But just for your own edification now, proceed with your research, but only if it has some basis in fact. I want to know in advance of anything important you expect to dig up. Phone Kilmartin too, by all means, and tell him you are to keep me posted. Point number two is this: I'm wondering if you might get vexed enough if things don't go your way in Ennis to leak some more laments to the likes of Hynes. 'Commissioner and Superintendent try to quash investigation into shooting.' Call Hynes off, man. You went right over the wall with that, now. I don't need to tell you. If you leak again, I'll have you plugged. You made your point. If I see stuff like that in the papers, I'll step out of Russell's way."

Minogue put on his protective coat of indignation.

"Come on now, John. I wouldn't go over anyone's head. Except maybe my own."

"Come on, yourself. I'm saying, don't do it. Last point. I know what your colleague, Seamus Hoey, did or tried to do. I'm saying nothing about it except this: Don't be so sure that you know better than the caring professions.

"You may phone me if you find yourself being crucified, though," Tynan added. "Crucified unjustly, I mean."

"I don't know how to thank you."

"Cut that out, now. Don't spend time trying to think of a way. Phone Kilmartin."

Minogue walked slowly away from the phone. He was too bewildered to feel anything distinctly. One clear idea emerged from the fog. He would not phone Jim Kilmartin without having a lash of whiskey first. He waylaid a lounge-boy and had him bring a small Jamesons to the foyer. He thought of Kilmartin's ugly mood awaiting ignition with a phone call. He tipped the returned lounge-boy, swallowed the whiskey in four gulps, and headed back to the lounge. Hoey had slid far down in his chair in a defensive slouch, fortified as best he could against Crossan's bulbous, straining eyes. Preoccupied, Minogue tripped over Hoey's outstretched legs and staggered a few steps before regaining his balance.

"For want of it," said Crossan.

The inspector's befuddlement gave way suddenly to irritation. Thwarted, he thought, and he couldn't even have a damn drink without having to hide it from Hoey.

"Friend or foe?" Crossan asked. "The phone call?"

"A bit early to tell," Minogue grunted. "I have to make a call. I'll be back in a few minutes."

He returned to the foyer little mollified by the fact that neither Hoey nor Crossan had pressed him on whom he had been talking to. Had his expression told them all they needed to know? Kilmartin's voice was full of the light inflections of whimsy, the sonorous and beguiling range of tones and emphases, of words lingered on, others dropped like petals on water, at once inviting and intimate, one minute wryly direct, dreamily inconclusive the next. Many still mistook such signs from James Kilmartin. Minogue guessed what could follow and it made him more nervous.

"Yes, yes," Kilmartin went on in an eerily lighthearted tone. "I neglected to tell you, you might be interested. That clown in Drimnagh, Nolan. He got bail."

"How? Why? When?"

"Ah, well now, you surely know that there's been so much progress in law reform in the country now, Matt, what with us being real Europeans now and the whole place rotten with consultants and the helping professions and what-have-you. All the fine barristers and social scientists and psychologists we have choking the universities."

"How?"

"Well, now. It appears that this fucking slug, Nolan, is a walking compendium of troubles. Wisha, the poor little scrap. They're after discovering he has a learning disability so he's a class of illiterate, and that, you know, builds up all kinds of trouble. Has a, ahem, poor self-image. He doesn't feel good about himself, I was told. Poor lad has an alcohol problem too."

Minogue had enough.

"All right, Jimmy, all right. I was —"

Kilmartin snapped back with the first show of anger.

"Shut up and listen. I want you to know what you're missing. Poor lad has a gambling syndrome. Worst of all, God help him, he has food allergies —"

"Jimmy —"

"Yes indeed! A walking collection of troubles and tribulations. His food allergies that he didn't know he had must have caused him to kick the other fella, you see. Now why didn't I think of that? I heard of the case in the States where a fella got off because he was demented by a bar of chocolate, but we're obviously way behind here in our grasp of this new psychology. Nolan's *a victim of society*."

The back of Minogue's neck began to ache with tension.

"But as I was saying," Kilmartin resumed in a singsong voice, "I think that I didn't give this place in Greece a fair hearing when you were talking about it."

"I was going to phone you anyway," said Minogue.

"You were on your granny's teeth. Like hell, pal. The more I think of it, Greece is the best place for you. Without a doubt. I hear that the police there need experienced men for mountain work, chasing the runaway goats and sheep. After your few days in Ennis, sure that'll qualify you eminently for that class of demanding work. Gob, you could count the sheep for them too. Oh, and I hear tell there are good-looking sheep there, as well. Why don't you toddle down to Shannon Airport, it's right beside you there, and head for Greece. And take Hoey with you —"

"Leave Shea out of it, Jimmy."

"And take that double-dehydrated, know-it-all, troublemaking bollocks Hynes with you. Where the hell did you get the idea of letting that bastard out of the bottle? That move was well below the waterline, man."

Minogue did not think it wise to tell Kilmartin that he could muzzle Hynes for the moment because he intended to give Hynes exclusive if the Bourke thing came to anything. Then Kilmartin could afford to smile again at seeing Hynes all over the likes of Tom Russell and the supers who wanted Kilmartin's monkeys in their own zoos.

"I can phone the airport for ye, and lay on a plane," Kilmartin was saying.

"Tynan told me to lay off the shooting death here, the one with the German tourist. That I'll do."

"Very big of you. Why didn't you tell him to piss off? He's only the Garda commissioner."

"But the rehash of the Bourke thing still stands. It stinks. I feel bad that I sort of fobbed off the thing when Crossan got to me, and now it's too late. Maybe I can get something out of it —"

"For who? Isn't the man dead now?"

"I plan to talk to the principals in the case, if I can find them."

"Did I tell you that the hearing is gone bad on me?" Kilmartin asked remotely. "Maura says I should have me ears checked. I get a buzzing in me ears at certain times."

"Look, Jimmy. I used Hynes because I had the local nabob, Tom Russell, slam a door in my face here. Hynes phoned Tynan about the German."

The chief inspector's voice turned gravelly.

"A word to the wise now, Hair oil: Tom Russell's a hard man. Russell has his friends and Tynan knows that well. If you play trick-of-the-loop with Tom, he'll nail you. And he'll set the phone lines to Tynan's office burning."

"He already has. He might do it again if he finds out I'm talking to the witnesses and so on."

"Listen," Kilmartin said with a softer urgency. "You started out this thing with some remarks that this lawman fella — what's his name again?"

"Crossan. Alo Crossan."

". . . that Crossan made. If you really want to firm up, why not do the paperwork for an official reopening? I'll phone Sheehan or someone in Justice, if you want. See what the score is. The appeal period is long gone but maybe we can work out a back door to getting the trial record typed up. Then you might see that you're going nowhere."

Minogue was taken aback by this sudden solicitude.

"Well," he hesitated, while he tried to guess Kilmartin's motive. "We don't really have any new evidence to warrant a . . ."

The inspector imagined Kilmartin's smirk.

"Okay, look, Jimmy. My quandary is that I'll have nothing until I talk to the people involved in the case. It's tricky, I admit."

"Tricky, you admit. Hhnn. And if you find the investigation produced the proper conviction?"

"I'll walk away from it, with me head hanging. And I'll buy you a hearing aid."

"Ha, ha, ha," said Kilmartin solemnly. "Very smucking fart, I'm sure. Keep your head, that's what I say to all that. By the way, how's the patient?"

"Progressing."

"Unn-hhh. Florence Nightingale. Off the jar, I hope. That'll be the cure, if you ask me."

"Yes."

"Well, I can tell you're not going to be talking your face off about that particular matter. I have something to tell you now and you'd better mark it well. Monsignor Tynan spared me five minutes of his precious time here on the phone. 'Asked' me to let you alone on this Bourke thing —"

"He did? Well, why didn't you tell me that first?"

"Because I wanted to hear your bloody side. Do you take me for an iijit? Do you think I don't know what Tynan's up to here? Anyway, he phones me. As if he wanted you seconded, bejases. Gave him a soft ball, you know, 'The inspector is on his holidays,' says I. 'That's the whole idea,' he says back to me. Very shagging strange conversation. Tynan did not tell me that he'd be pleased as punch if you dug up any dirt in Tom Russell's field. Do you know why he didn't tell me that? It's because I bloody well know that already!"

"I don't think Tynan's playing politics," said Minogue.

"God, you're the trusting little schoolboy, aren't you?" Kilmartin scoffed with genial scorn. "Sure what do you know? You have your head in the clouds half the time. You don't care who's backstabbing who here. Tom Russell got passed over for Tynan several years ago. He can't stand Tynan!"

"A question, James. Tell me something now, my memory if failing. Is Tom Russell also one of the divisional superintendents asking for the Squad to be dispersed?"

"Ha, ha," said Kilmartin. "You finally woke up! You're a quick learner. Figure it out for yourself, smart arse. Ha, ha, ha!"

There was bounce in Minogue's step as he headed back to the dining room. Hoey was alone at the table.

"What's the word?" said Hoey.

Minogue sat down.

"Well, we still have jobs. Jimmy stepped aside for Tynan, but don't expect an overdose of help and encouragement is about the size of it, I'm afraid."

"Tynan? Where does he fit here?"

Minogue considered his reply.

"Remember the archaeologists going through the Viking rubbish pits down by the city hall?"

Hoey frowned and began playing with coins in his pocket.

"You can tell a lot about what's been kept by what's been swept under the carpet."

Crossan strode across the floor and flopped into his seat.

"I'm not guaranteeing Eilo McInerny will sing, now," he said. "And she sounds cagey enough, but she'll be in the hotel this afternoon."

His eyes had returned to their full, startled appearance. He handed Minogue a piece of paper with a phone number and address of the hotel.

"I told her you were Guards, mind," Crossan warned. "Everything aboveboard. She wasn't too keen, but I think I have her persuaded."

"Did you tell her what happened to Bourke last night?"

"No. Let it be a trump when you deliver the news."

Minogue nodded his appreciation slowly.

"We'll be off this minute," he said. "Before she or anyone else up in Dublin changes their minds."

"What does that mean?" Crossan asked. "About Dublin?"

"It's an inside joke."

"Well. Go easy on her now," said Crossan, and rolled his watch around his wristbone. "I told her that, for Guards, you were all right."

"Don't be worrying, counselor," said Minogue. "We're housebroken."

"I'm serious," Crossan insisted. "It took a lot of persuading. Phone me. Will ye be back in Ennis tonight?"

Minogue doffed an imaginary hat.

"To be sure, your honor," he said.

CHAPTER 7

Mᴜɪɴᴏɢᴜᴇ ᴛᴜʀɴᴇᴅ ᴛʜᴇ Fiat onto O'Connell Street and, within minutes, was accelerating down the Kilrush Road. While he drove he thought back to Crossan's sardonic manner with the photographs, the subtle gibes at the Howards. Other images slid across his mind: a house afire, a man naked, drunk, and terrified. Jamesy Bourke, the bearded spook leaving the pub in Portaree was now a stitched-up carcass. He shivered and tried to shake free of the undertow that could have him spiraling deeper into the grisly images.

"That Killimer ferry will save us an hour each way from Tralee," he said.

"That fella's eyes drill into you," Hoey murmured. "Like a fish or something."

"What do you make of him?"

Hoey rubbed his chin.

"Don't know at all. I'd say he's good at his job for one thing. Can't read him much. Yet, anyway. I'd sleep with one eye open all the same."

The two policemen reached Killimer dock in time to coincide with a sailing to the Limerick side.

"There's timing for you," Hoey said between yawns.

The ramp hummed and ground upright behind the car. Hoey followed the inspector up the steps to the railing and there they fell to staring at the Shannon estuary, wide and gray before them. The tide was coming in and the air was tangy with salt. What had been a slight breeze on shore became buffeting gusts as they left Clare. With the engine throbbing underfoot and his lungs full of the sea air, Minogue watched a jumbo going over, its wheels down for landing at Shannon Airport. Hoey turned to observe the coastline — Limerick or Kerry, Minogue couldn't tell — drift closer to the ferry. His hair tousled in the wind made him look boyish.

"Where do you think that German fella is by now?" asked Hoey.

"I don't want to be thinking of that at the present time," Minogue muttered. He had been thinking of Crossan again. "Let our friends in the Department of Justice be the sitting ducks for Shorty Hynes on that."

Hoey stayed on deck until the ferry docked. They made better time than Minogue had expected through Listowel and into Tralee, where he parked the Fiat in a street next to the hotel. He had decided to try and get Eilo McInerny out of the hotel for a chat in some unobtrusive place. A woman with flaming red hair, an overabundance of perfume, and fine white teeth had a great welcome for Minogue when he approached the desk. Her broad smile faltered a little at Minogue's question.

"I'm not sure Eilo's actually on, now. But sure can't I find out for you?"

She looked at him for an extra few seconds before dispatching a dour adolescent with a white shirt and a slow, reflective manner into the in-nards of the hotel. Minutes passed, the longer for Minogue because the piped music got to him. He caught the redhead's eye, and she smiled with a professional benevolence back at him. He was about to rise and return to the desk when the general factotum reappeared and imparted his news to the receptionist. She frowned momentarily, regained her smile, and beamed at Minogue to beckon him over.

"Well now, she's not here this very minute. But she's supposed to be on shift. I wouldn't be surprised if she just stepped out for a minute. She was expecting you, was she?"

"She was." Familiar strands of doubt worked stronger on him. "Did you see her leave?"

"Oh no. Can't you sit down there and take the weight off your feet? She'll turn up in a minute."

Minogue elbowed onto the desk and mustered his best confidential bluff.

"Do you know now," he whispered, "I'm in a bit of a spot. I'm only passing through and it'd save me a lot of bother if I could find her fairly fast. Do you know where she lives?"

The receptionist took in a breath and smiled. She was in her middle thirties, Minogue guessed, with the robust and hearty manner that even the Irish assumed was natural to redheaded people. Her lingering gaze into Minogue's eyes made him think of country girls at dances long ago, their comfortable dumpling bodies sensual and inviting, a placid mockery in their smiles as they danced. She could probably tell what he did for a living, what food he'd like, how vigorous a lover he might be.

"Do you know now," she whispered, in a subtle mimic of Minogue's fake intimacy. "I don't know her all that well. But, sure, if this is as important as you say, then you'll find her around the corner here. She rents a house there on the terrace. It's next to Nugent's shop. You can't miss it."

She winked at him, and he felt the first itches of a blush starting around his neck. What did she think, that Eilo McInerny and he had a matinee session planned? He sensed her merry eyes on his back as he left. Did the same Eilo McInerny have the reputation of entertaining men?

No one answered the door. Minogue inclined his head closer and knocked again. Then he stood on tiptoe to peer through the patterned amber glass that formed an arch high in the door. He turned the door handle to no avail and then stepped into Nugent's shop. A young woman with dyed black hair hanging down over her eyes was packing a shelf with bags of potato chips.

"Do you know Eileen McInerny who lives next door?" he asked.

"I do."

"Have you seen her lately, in the last half hour or so, I mean?"

She put down the carton. "Well, she works over at the hotel."

"You haven't seen her coming or going this last little while?"

Her face seemed to set itself, as though she now knew that she didn't need to be polite. She pushed back a strand of hair.

"It's important that I see her," Minogue tried. "She was expecting me."

"Well, I don't know now. Her little one, Melanie, came in from school and then I heard the door close about fifteen minutes ago, like someone slammed it. I didn't actually see anyone."

"Someone left the house a quarter of an hour ago?"

She tugged at a lock of hair, twirled it over her ear, and gave Minogue a wary glance. He tried harder to control his impatience.

"It's not trouble at all," he said. "I just need to get in touch with her."

He managed a smile. The girl gave him a feeble, distracted smile in return but backed into the shelves. She twirled some hair quicker now.

Crossan had spoken with Eileen McInerny only an hour and a half ago, Minogue was thinking; her daughter got in from school, maybe after playing with some other kids, and off someone went from the house shortly afterward. She spoke in a low voice without looking over at Minogue.

"Well, Eilo came in. She wanted a packet of fags."

"How long ago?"

Her fingers stopped turning the lock of hair and she darted a look at Minogue.

"Are you a Guard?"

Minogue tried to smile again but immediately knew it was phony.

"Yes, I am. But that's not why I'm calling on Eilo."

"Herself and Melanie are gone down the road there."

"To her car, is it?"

She tugged a lock of hair out until it was inches from her eyes and looked at it.

"It's not the likes of us has cars. Her Melanie walks my little one home. Usually."

A picture of two girls walking home from school hand-in-hand together came to him. It sawed into his chest. Iseult, he thought, she's probably of an age with Iseult.

"We have children all right, but we didn't manage to hold on to their fathers."

She let go of the lock of hair and it uncoiled quickly. He recognized the disdain, the small leavening of humor in her eyes. No matter what he said, he was a Guard. He was far across other chasms from her too: husband and father, middle-class. Detector, pursuer, catcher. Moses down from the bog, via Dublin, full of law and order. How could he persuade her otherwise?

"Do you know where she might be going?" he asked. He watched her pick up another box. How could they look so heavy and they only potato chips, he wondered?

"Where would you be going with a bag in your hand?" she asked as she turned back to the shelf.

On a bloody holiday, he almost growled. She kept packing the shiny plastic packets on the shelves. Steadily the rows of Cheese and Onion, Salt and Vinegar filled. He muttered his thanks and yanked the door, almost pulling a pensioner in on the floor of the shop as he did. He kept the old man upright and asked him where Tralee's bus and train stations were.

· · · · ·

"The one place," he said to Hoey, and turned the wheel sharply in a U-turn. "The buses and trains. She had to wait for the child to show up from school or from her playing."

"What's she running for?"

Minogue shook his head. "Who knows? Bred into her, maybe."

He reversed in the middle of the street, crunched the gears, and shot forward.

"Maybe she has an outstanding on her," Hoey said. "Or maybe she's not a fan of the Gardai."

"Perish the thought."

Minogue braked at the head of a one-way street, deliberated, and turned down, grunting over the wheel. He took out the key and stepped out onto the footpath. A bus revved behind the high wall of the station, punching diesel smoke into the air. Hoey went off to his right. Minogue stepped into the bus and looked down at the faces on each side of the aisle.

"Board at the platform," said the driver. "And a ticket'll come in handy."

"Are there buses or trains gone out in the last little while?" Minogue asked. The driver was a gray-haired Dubliner, with a decade's commerce with culchies in his approach.

"Which one are you hoping to be on?"

"Dublin, say. Or Cork," Minogue asked with more urgency. The driver nodded toward a herd of buses half-hidden by a wall.

"There's a Dublin bus due to hit the trail now, if it's real excitement you're looking for."

Minogue skipped off the bus and jogged around the wall toward the other buses. Clusters of passengers stood near the door to one. Hoey appeared from the ticket office and waved. Minogue surveyed the faces as he headed toward him.

"Dublin," said Hoey. "A woman and a girl with an English accent, chewing gum and blowing bubbles with it. The girl is black."

"What?" said Minogue.

Hoey looked beyond him to the people boarding. "That's what the man said. I dunno."

Minogue realized he didn't even know what Eilo McInerny looked like. She had a bag of some sort and a daughter with her. A black girl? He walked to the end of the shortening queue by the bus door and waited for the last passenger to step into the bus.

"I'm looking for a woman traveling with her daughter. I have a message for her."

The driver gave Minogue an expert scrutiny in the space of three seconds.

"Not on here."

Minogue looked down at the passengers settling in. "Are you sure now?"

The driver arched his eyebrows.

Minogue stepped down and looked about the oil-stained tar macadam of the station yard. A bus wheeled by and Minogue studied the faces in the windows. Hoey was beside him then.

"Come on," said Hoey. Minogue was still a little dazed. Diesel smoke settled in the air around him. Had Eilo McInerny bought tickets to Dublin and then decided to wait for a later bus? Maybe she had forgotten something and had gone back to her place, or to the hotel.

Hoey was breathing hard from his canter back into the yard.

"I took a look down the street the far side of the station," he said. "There's a taxi rank out there but no taxis. A woman carrying a bag's heading off down the street. Come on quick or we might lose them."

Minogue skipped along beside Hoey. "What did she look like?"

"Who cares what she looks like," Hoey said over his shoulder. "There was a girl with her."

The woman was walking hurriedly, but her short legs could not propel her stocky body fast. She stalked on, hand-in-hand with a girl in a school gabardine. The girl's hair-do brought her height to almost a head over her mother. Eilo McInerny knew that the two policemen were closing on her. Resolute, she pressed on, struggling with her suitcase as it clattered against her leg, refusing to look back. Her hand grasped her daughter's tightly and their joined hands waved stiffly in a martial parody. Drops of rain began to spot the pavement.

Hoey caught up with Eilo McInerny. She ignored him and turned the corner sharply. By the time Minogue rounded the corner, Hoey was walking backward next to her, trying to explain something. The girl said something and Hoey looked over to her. The trio slowed and Minogue closed in on them. Eilo McInerny's suitcase banged into a pole and she staggered back a step.

"Wot chew wont wiv moy muvver?" Minogue heard the girl say. Her upper body canted forward as she addressed Hoey. "Loyve ass uloawn, yeou cryeep!"

Hoey, still backpedaling, careered into a rubbish bin bolted waist-high to a bus stop. He staggered away from it, grasping his back and wincing.

"Missus McInerny, wait a minute," Minogue said. "We only want a word with you — nothing more than that." An elderly woman clasped her string bag closer and looked with pursed lips at the group across the street. "We mean no harm!"

He moved around Hoey who was hopping about now holding his back.

"Wait, can't you! My friend here is liable to walk under a bus or something if ye don't let up."

The girl turned and made a face at Minogue.

"Loyve ass alaown!" she shouted.

Her mother tugged sharply at her arm and pulled her farther along the footpath. Hoey's dance was slowing now. The inspector caught a glimpse of Eilo McInerny's face. A short, wide women, she looked tired and determined, her face flushed with exertion.

"We're trying to clear up what happened to Jamesy Bourke, the trial . . . We need your help."

Eilo McInerny locked her gaze straight ahead and tried to move even faster. Her suitcase scraped the doors of parked cars and bumped into a lamppost. With a sudden rip, it was on the pavement. She stopped and looked at the handle still firm in her grip. Her chest rose and fell rapidly. She licked her bottom lip, blinked and then threw the handle with great force across the street where it bounced off the roof of a car and fell to the pavement.

"Let me," said Minogue.

"Fack oaff in don't bovver moy muvver nao mower!" hissed the girl.

Minogue stepped back and looked into the huge eyes of Eilo McInerny's daughter. Great God, he thought, she had that look in her eye that it wouldn't bother her at all to kick a guard in the family jewels. Eilo McInerny wrenched her daughter's hand, reached up with her free hand and gave the girl a clout across the side of her head. The girl raised her hands to her head as she ducked, but her mother hung on.

"Don't be talking like a tramp, you! It doesn't matter who they are or how they provoke you!"

Minogue looked into her face. Eilo McInerny's lips were white with anger, but her face glowed. Nearer forty than thirty, he believed. She wore a white blouse and black skirt under her coat. Work clothes, he guessed. He placed himself out of range of a kick from her daughter and picked up the suitcase in his arms.

"Here's your getaway bag now," he said.

"Give it to me and then push off and leave me alone," said Eilo McInerny.

He heard a Clare accent rooted under the cat's meow into which he understood Londoners extended their O's.

"You could help someone if you'd only talk to us awhile," he tried.

Hoey limped up. Eilo McInerny took the suitcase from Minogue and held it across her chest. Her daughter caught Minogue's eye. She stuck out her tongue at him. "Piss off, copper," she mouthed.

"Leave off that," warned her mother. "Or as true as God I'll hit you a thoose here in the street with everyone looking on, so I will." She looked with open contempt to Minogue.

"This is my daughter Melanie. She's not like this normally. That's all I'm going to tell you."

Melanie McInerny was long-limbed and brown, her perfect teeth framed by pink lips that Minogue considered wondrous. She still wore her school pinafore under the gabardine coat. Left in a hurry, Minogue thought. She was within a few inches of his height. He tried to pin the insolence in her eyes with a forceful civility.

"Hello, Melanie."

"Piss oaff, coppah! Pig!"

"Sacred Heart of Jesus," sighed Eilo McInerny. The suitcase fell with a soft crunch on the footpath. Before Melanie could make a run for it, Eilo McInerny had grabbed her daughter's forearm.

"Not on my account," Minogue protested. "Please. I've been called worse. Even by people who know me. Couldn't we go somewhere and sit down so as tempers can cool?"

Eilo McInerny looked at Minogue, her arms poised. The rain had begun to tell on the concrete now. A passing car's wipers squeaked across its windscreen. The road was greasy. Melanie tried to duck away.

"Yew dzoan't hiv to tork wiv 'em, Mum!"

"And I don't have to listen to you either, you bould strap! I'm martyred with you! The fucking language out of you is a disgrace!"

"We just need to clear up a few things, Mrs. McInerny," Minogue rallied.

Eilo McInerny didn't take her glittering eyes off her daughter.

"There's nothing I can do for you, mister. Leave us be, I tell you."

Melanie was smiling now. The inspector realized that this scene had happened before. Anger betrayed love: sisters more than mother and daughter? Eilo and her daughter were gently rocking now, the younger one trying halfheartedly to free herself. Hoey took a deep breath and rolled his eyes.

"Where were you off to in such a hurry?" asked Minogue.

"What running am I doing? This is a free country."

"Crossan phoned you and said we'd be coming. You said all right. What's changed?"

The rain seemed to make Eilo McInerny relent. She let go of her daughter's arms.

"You bought a ticket to Dublin and then walked out of the station," Minogue added. "But you're off somewhere else on a mad rush. What's the matter?"

"Asking me for help," she scoffed. "Jesus, the ways of the world. The Guards asking me for help. Hah! You must take me for a right iijit." She turned toward her daughter. "Come on, Mel."

"But 'sroiyning, Mum."

"Of course it's raining," snapped her mother. "This is Tralee you're in!"

"It might be that we could clear Jamesy Bourke's name after all these years," said Minogue.

She snorted derisively, and he saw the disbelief cross her face. She wrestled with the suitcase again and staggered down the footpath. She spoke in a withering tone.

"That gom. Me help him? Him and his poems and his drink. He was the same as the rest of them in the end. All after the one thing."

Minogue took up the pursuit again.

"I know it may seem too late to do anything," he began.

"Damn right," said Eilo McInerny.

"Crossan told you how Jamesy died, did he?"

She stopped and turned toward Minogue. Melanie stood by. Her expression suggested to Minogue that she imagined each drop of rain that landed on her smooth, café au lait face might be acid.

"What?"

"He was shot dead the other day."

She frowned and looked down at the pavement as though she had just dropped a coin on it.

"To do with the IRA or something?"

"No. A case of mistaken identity, I suppose you could describe it."

"I'd heard he had a bad run of things in prison," she murmured.

The drops were heavy now, and Minogue felt them plop and burst on his skull. Tralee counted as a place where, like West Clare, one would be thought wise to build a commodious boat and begin rounding up pairs of animals when rain was on the way. Hoey was holding his collar tight under his chin.

"You told Crossan you'd talk to us," Minogue said.

"Mum —" bleated Melanie.

"Be quiet, can't you?" hissed her mother. She looked up warily. "Down from Dublin, are ye?"

"We are. And we have no right to ask you for your time or one iota from you."

Eilo McInerny shot a look into Minogue's eyes.

"I don't need trouble. I'm a lot of years away. Are you going to try and cod me into thinking things've changed since I left?"

Minogue let his bewilderment show.

"You Guards, you do what ye like," she said with quiet disgust. "You're all hand-in-glove with one another. 'You scratch my back' and the rest of it. You're on the inside the likes of me are on the outside. You do what you're bid, by them what bids it."

"Well, I can stand here getting soaked," he said, "or I could try to persuade you otherwise."

CHAPTER 8

"WOT HAPPENED WIV yeou enyway?" Melanie McInerny asked Hoey.

Hoey's arm froze, the cigarette within inches of his lips, and he gave her a startled look. She sucked on the straw again and rolled ice at the bottom of the glass.

"How do you mean?" he asked. He cleared his throat while completing his arm's trip with the cigarette but rested his knuckles against his lips as he coughed.

"Theowse black ooiyes iv yose. Who 'it chew?"

Minogue looke over. Eilo McInerny drank from her vodka. They were sitting in the otherwise deserted lounge of Spring's Kingdom Bar.

"A car accident," Hoey murmured with a hint of affronted pride.

"Yeou shuddn't smoake, should yeou? Dzo yeou jog or anything?"

The surprise was twisted off Hoey's face by another cough.

"Stop giving him the treatment, Mel," said Eilo McInerny. "He's the cop, not you."

"Yeou smoke too, Mum. It's desgasting."

Minogue could only smile. He tried again to reboard the derailed conversation.

"I don't expect you to have a perfect recall of what happened back then."

Eilo McInerny took another drink but she would not get back on track.

"Imagine that," she murmured, the glass poised under her nose. "Shot dead, just like that. By the fella who ran over his dog. The bad luck folleyed him and caught up to him in the end."

"It's a tragedy, to be sure, but can we —"

"Tragedy, is it? What the hell would you or the likes of you know about tragedy?"

Melanie looked over at her mother. "Yeou shuddn't drink nao moahr, Mum."

That was the bottom half of her second drink, Minogue realized. He was already drifting nicely offshore in the lee of one Jamesons. He hoped he wouldn't have to keep pace with her. Hoey looked steadfast enough with his 7-Up.

"She gits loike that," said Melanie with a superior air.

"What?" barked Eilo McInerny, as though returning from a distant place. "What?"

"Shea, you have to get some cigarettes, I daresay," said Minogue. "Melanie, would you be kind enough to direct my friend here to a shop? Maybe you could help him pick a box of chocolates too, a gift I should maybe bring back to relatives. He's not really with it as regards that sort of thing."

Both Hoey and Melanie frowned and stared at Minogue.

"Mum?"

"Go on with you," said Eilo McInerny. "He won't bite you."

Melanie McInerny plodded to the door as though to a firing squad. Her mother watched her go.

"I don't know from one day to the next if I'm doing the right thing with that one," she muttered. Minogue heard less of the English accent now. "I couldn't leave her with Ralph. Ralphie's an iijit. Nice, but he's a slob. It'd be neglect with him. He wouldn't notice her going to the bad. No, I couldn't leave her there with him."

"So you came here to try and make a go of things."

She took a cigarette and toyed with it. "Yes, Mel is a bit of a curiosity about town. It's not a holiday for her anymore, though. She gets fed up. She finds school hard here and the kids here are innocent really. But the nuns are very good to her. Whatever else you can say about the nuns . . ." She lit the cigarette.

"Why did you run today, so?"

She nodded once at the ashtray and pointed her cigarette at Minogue as though locating his head along a gunsight.

"Don't ask me that again or I'll fucking throw that at you."

"Point taken."

"I don't plan on getting burnt like what I had done to me before. Now, can you get that through your thick skull? I have responsibilities. I have enough on me plate with a daughter full of hormones, and me with no man here in Tralee. I do me work and I pay me rent. Why would I be volunteering to be put through the mill again?"

"You had a tough time on the stand back then, I believe," he said.

Her eyes narrowed.

"What do you know about what I went through? You and your 'tragedy' and a big long face on you like a dog fishing for his dinner."

She flicked ash at arm's length toward the ashtray. It fell a foot short.

"You. Ralphie. Howard. James Bourke. Your brains in your trousers. Full of chat and buying drinks and joking. All ye want is a poke. Then ye're gone on to the next one. Do you think for one minute that Jamesy Bourke was different, do you?"

"I didn't say he was a saint."

"A saint," she mimicked. Minogue asked for the same again from the barman.

"When you're a man, you have the power," she went on. "Rich or poor, black or white. And when you're a man that has money in his pocket, or when you have a uniform, the world is your oyster."

"As a matter of fact, my uniform doesn't fit me anymore."

She gave him a scornful grin and waved the cigarette at the ashtray again.

"What about Dan Howard?"

She spoke with little feeling. "Dan Howard is a fucking bastard. And his wife is a jumped-up, money-grubbing bitch. And Tidy Howard, as for that old bags . . ."

She seemed to catch herself then as if she had spotted herself in a mirror.

"You were dragooned into taking the stand."

"I was," she murmured. "I was called as a witness, and I was picked up by the Guards. That prick — Doyle. He was the sergeant in Portaree at the time. Little did I know that I'd be in court to dirty someone else's name."

The barman, a rheumy-eyed man not ten years from retirement, laid down the drinks.

"I had no dinner," she said. "If I have another one of these, I'll be plastered. Have to watch the figure and that too." Minogue watched her poke at the ice and then lick her finger. "There might be a bachelor farmer on the lookout, you never know."

Her smile was brief and it fell away quickly. She took a gulp of the new drink. Minogue looked at his own Jamesons sitting implacably next to him. How could he preach to Shea Hoey about drink? It'd be like Kilmartin delivering advice about etiquette.

"I was told back then that I could help James Bourke get off lighter," she said. "Fool that I was, I didn't think about how it was going to be done. I half felt sorry for him. My mistake. We both know where that got him, don't we?"

"You thought he didn't deserve —?"

"Look," she broke in. "Jamesy and the rest of them were gobshites. But it wasn't entirely his fault. Even I could see that, and me knowing Jane. What was the use of throwing one life away for another? The world is full enough of revenge and killing. What use would locking him up for his life be to anyone? I've been roughly used in my time. I've seen the bad side of people but I've survived and still come out human. When you've been through what I've been through over the years, you don't be so certain, cocked up in your armchair and looking down your nose while you're discussing how people go to the bad. He was too simple for the real world. Too stupid, maybe. The way we all are sometimes, maybe. But you can't live your life like that. You have to wake up sometime."

"You were given the boot," said Minogue.

"You said it," she snapped. "Treated like dirt. Like an iijit. I didn't see it coming."

"What for? Liking Jane Clark?"

"I did, you know." She cast a bitter look at Minogue that caused him to sit still. "Not in the way you people'd like to be thinking it either. Not the way they threw it around in court. Ask yourself how the whole matter came up in that damned courtroom. Go on. You're the cop. Go on, ask me, then."

Minogue took a deliberately slow drink of Jamesons.

"You mean that you and Jane Clark had a relationship?"

"Relationship," she cackled, and coughed. "Where did you get that word? In one of your courses, or off the telly or something?" The coughing took control of her again.

"Go on, say it," she wheezed. "Say the word!"

She sat upright at the front of her chair, trying by her posture to stave off more coughing. Minogue knew he had to meet her gaze, but the effort of looking over to her was almost too much for him.

"Say it," she growled. "I bet you like to think about it. Two women. You're like the rest of them. Come on now, don't let your side down!"

"Jane Clark and you had a love affair of sorts," he said.

There was triumph in her eyes.

"Say it like they kept on saying it that day. Lesbian. Homosexual. Perverse."

The barman looked up from the paper.

"Not all of us are cavemen, you know —"

"'I'm not like the other ones.' Like hell you're not, mister." She drew fiercely on her cigarette.

"There I was, an ignorant skivvy up on the stand, being made to paint a picture of a lesbian for all the learned gentlemen. Guards and reporters and the judge, and the women — they were worse than the men. They looked at me like I was a piece of shite. There are plenty more words for it and I've heard them all, so I have. There I was, in tears, being made to tell people that Jamesy Bourke was provoked by the fact that she was a lesbian as well as a whore. And that she had laughed at him when she was with me, for his efforts at playing the Casanova. Sure with the drink he had every day he wouldn't have been able to get it up with a crane."

"I'm just trying to find out what happened. If she was lesbian, well . . ."

"Hah," she scoffed, and returned the barman's stare. The barman let his eyelids down slightly and returned to penciling in something in the paper.

"Sure, how could she, and she taking up with Dan Howard and Bourke?" she asked. Minogue considered the Jamesons lolling in his glass.

"You're the cop. You tell me how Bourke's lawyer, that weasely looking . . . what was his name?"

"Tighe."

"Yeah, him. How the hell did he get wind of me and her, to get me on the stand and take the oath so that the wide world would know that Jane Clark and myself had put our arms around one another?"

"Dan Howard must have told him."

She squinted through a ribbon of smoke. "You're not as thick as you look."

"Because Dan Howard would have heard it from her," he added. "And in the heat of the row with Bourke, he'd have been doing his best to put Jane Clark down. To persuade Bourke that she wasn't worth fighting over."

"Nice work there, Guard. I'll tell you something, now" — she leaned forward to better deliver the sarcasm — "and it's this. Dan Howard told him — Jamesy Bourke — sure enough. That must have driven Bourke wild. Does Dan Howard end up on the stand for inciting Bourke to go out there and set her house on fire? Does he? He might as well have handed Jamesy Bourke the order and the bloody matches.

"Yes," she continued after a scrutiny of her cigarettes and some part of her palm, "she was like that. She'd tell him straight out. I know that he knew because he'd come by the hotel with his wandering hands, pushing himself against me. Asking me if I'd try out a man for a change. Jamesy Bourke was the same way. Chasing skirts and slobbering over women and pints. God's gifts to women."

"Do you recall Crossan at all?"

"Ah, he was kind of gawky. Tall and skinny, with eyes like Halloween. Nice enough, I suppose, but he wasn't around much. A Protestant, I believe. Sort of aloof, like you'd be careful talking to him. But I remember thinking he sort of followed Howard around a bit. He was never up to the high jinks that Howard'd get up to. Quiet type."

Minogue watched her put out the cigarette. Resignation had crept into her face, her tone. He thought of Crossan for a moment, the glaze on the barrister's eyes when he'd spotted the Howards.

"I wanted a bit of comfort," she muttered. "That was my big sin. I had no mother, you see. She died when I was three, she was hit by a car. My da was useless. I couldn't wait to get away. Never keen on the schooling. Fool that I was, I took up as a chambermaid and general skivvy in the hotel in Portaree. It was all right during the summers. You'd be busy and you'd meet people that'd keep your interest. The winters were the pits. Damn the bit of difference I made at the end of the trial anyway. I got me walking papers. He said he couldn't employ a person of my character. Fucking bastard."

Minogue sat up again.

"Tidy Howard," she muttered. "'Old Dan' some of them called him. I hear he's still alive, in some nursing home after a stroke or something. Another bastard. I hope he rots before he dies."

The barman folded his newspaper noisily. Minogue looked over at him.

"Is that everything you need to know now, Guard?" she asked. "'Cause I don't want to talk to you again."

Minogue could think of nothing to say.

The door squeaked open as Hoey and Melanie McInerny returned.

"He solves muhdahs, Mum. Is nit cryeepy?"

Eilo McInerny looked from Minogue to Hoey.

"We'll hang around here a few minutes," Minogue said to Hoey.

Eilo McInerny labored upright.

"Do what ye like," she said. She pushed her daughter, who tottered with the suitcase ahead of her. "But don't be bothering us again."

The door swung closed. Minogue sat down heavily on the vinyl seat. The scent of tired-out perfume hung in the air.

"That girl is wild out," said Hoey. "A maniac. I can't believe she's thirteen."

Minogue looked down at the remains of his whiskey. A young couple, the beginnings of an after-work crowd, entered the pub.

"Another round, men?" the barman called out.

Minogue gave him a look of manic intensity. "What would we want more drink for? Do you want us to be dragging ourselves out of Tralee with no shoes on our feet? Our pockets hanging out? What kind of a man are you at all? We've been very ably fleeced here already. Where's your telephone?"

The barman maintained his expression of solemn detachment.

"You'll be passing it on yer way out."

·   ·   ·   ·   ·

Minogue yawned and stretched all the way to the ferry dock in Tarbert. They arrived just in time to see the ferry twenty yards offshore, heading away from them. The estuary was at full tide and the Clare shore was softened by a veil of drizzle. Muddy, gray-green swells were beginning to splash against the rocks with more insistence by the minute. He was only now beginning to get the better of the whiskey. He turned the key and tapped at the wiper lever. Hoey was smirking.

"I'm glad to see that one of us is in fine form at least. What has you so chipper?"

"The pair in Tralee," said Hoey. "Ever see anything like them? They're a team, there's no doubt."

"You missed her speaking her mind about the Howards et cetera."

"I'd say she laid it out straight as a die," Hoey said. Minogue looked away into the water. Hoey's voice dropped to a monotone now. "You badly want to show them up here in Clare, don't you? Russell and company."

"I suppose I do, at that," murmured Minogue. "But more than that, I'm going to find out what happened that night. To answer your question, though, it would please me to find out that they had made a mess of the Bourke case, yes."

The smirk returned to Hoey.

"It'd please the Killer more," he murmured. "Here. I have to take a leak after all that 7-Up."

Minogue watched his colleague slouch out into the rain. He gave up trying to see clearly through the windscreen and thought about Jane Clark. She had been a woman with the nerve and the will to set herself up in a foreign country, in rural Clare. She had had experience of the world well beyond whatever Jamesy Bourke or Dan Howard might pretend to. Here was a woman who had slept with the both of them and made iijits of them into the bargain. Her mocking had probably excited Bourke and Howard even more. Howard could have laughed in return, and even encouraged more, but Bourke would have been more touchy. He thought of Kathleen and himself, in the sand dunes in Brittas Bay, frantic, whispering, wrestling. He squirmed in his seat as the desire pulsed through him and ground in his stomach.

She had slept with Eilo McInerny: low score on the inhibition scale. Back with Howard: yes, he might even have enjoyed her mockery. Not Bourke: rooted locally by land, by habit, but fired with the ambition of being a poet, what Kilmartin would describe as a few sandwiches short of a proper picnic. How would Bourke have reacted to her reciting the names of a score of lovers? Was Howard more free and easy or just less involved? Howard might have been the duller man, unimaginative. Son and heir, he could grin and move on to the next. Bourke would have idealized her. Her scorn would have flayed him.

The warmth surged in his belly, stirring his loins. What a land for Bourke to find a woman with a sex drive she wasn't ashamed of. He shifted again. His mouth was dry. He thought of Sheila Howard, and his forehead became suddenly itchy. Did she contain this boyo of a husband? Was she charged with an eroticism in private? A wave of prickly heat settled around the top of his forehead. Damnation, he thought, getting flustered, sitting here swelling up like a teenager. He opened the window and received for his trouble a spray of fine, cold rain. Eilo McInerny's words came back to him. Crossan, aloof: jealous of Howard? Hoey got into the car in a hurry and slammed the door hard against the weather.

"God, it's hot in here," he muttered.

Minogue's mind flared with embarrassment. Had Hoey sensed what feelings had bullied him these last few minutes?

"We need to talk to Dan Howard," said Minogue.

"If he's in town," said Hoey.

Minogue switched on the ignition and batted the stick for the wipers. Was it getting darker, or had the clouds settled lower over the water? A finger's width from the blurred Clare shore, the ferry had embarked on its return trip. The inspector blinked back to the present. The air in the car was stale and damp, full of the smell of Hoey's wet coat, itself redolent of cigarette smoke. Minogue flicked on the wipers again. The ferry was clearer now, halfway, he calculated. He watched it breast the estuary waves, bucking slightly. In the mirror he studied the faces in a car nosing in behind. The subdued-looking children to either side of an infant asleep in the backseat looked out opposite windows. The infant's face was turned awkwardly, mouth agape, and the expression suggested he or she was about to cry. The driver, a farmer with heavy sideburns, wore a dark suit and a look of resignation. From the passenger seat, a woman stared at the water. A funeral?

He looked again to the ferry and saw smaller creases in the waves alongside it. He held his hand on the wiper switch and concentrated on that part of the water.

"Well, I declare," he began to say, "if those aren't porpoises or seals or something. They're following the boat, man!" Hoey turned to stare at the ferry too.

The weight of the afternoon, all its irritations and disappointments, dropped off the inspector's shoulders. Across time and place, beyond time and place, he relived the days he had fished with his uncle off Doonbeg. His uncle had pointed them out as they approached the rowboat. Minogue, eight or nine and afraid, had dropped his rod. Not to worry, his uncle had said. He recalled his uncle's face going blank as he'd looked toward the glistening bodies arcing and slicing the water nearby. Not to worry, they had come to inspect us, that's all. Now the same wonder stirred Minogue, but, he realized, in his own rising exhilaration was envy.

"They're seldom here. Maybe the water is warmer this year, and we don't know it."

The ferry in, the porpoises headed back toward the mouth of the estuary. Minogue waited for three cars to disembark and then drove on. The car with the yawning, somber family followed. The wind drove rain and sea against the boat and the sprays of rain hissed against the windscreen. The inspector stepped out into the water-world and felt the muffled throbbing of the engine rising up through his bones. Waiting on the deck for even a minute meant a thorough drenching. He entered the small waiting cabin under the bridge and had to pull the door hard against the wind. Despite the rain on the windows here, he'd still get a fair view of the porpoises.

Rain lashed the windows harder as the ferry moved away from the dock. Minogue scanned the waters. Five minutes passed but he couldn't find the porpoises again. They were out there somewhere, gleeful and rapturous, he knew. Shudders of waves slapping against the hull passed up through his legs as he stared at the water. Disappointment came to him as a tired ache in his shoulders, with gravity and age winning easily at the end of the gloomy afternoon. He made one last sweep of the waters before stepping out onto the car deck.

Hoey was smoking and listening to traffic news from Dublin. Minogue took a notepad from the glove compartment.

"They're gone," he said. He began writing names on the pad. Hoey watched him but said nothing. Minogue took out photocopied pages from the envelope and glanced down at his own notes in the margins.

"Tom Naughton, the Guard who worked with Doyle, was first on the scene. Maybe we're a bit late for doing anything more today."

Hoey glanced at the clock. Minogue's stomach registered the ferry's yaw.

"Where will we put up, so?" Hoey asked.

"One of the B & Bs out the Clarecastle Road. I thought of my brother's place but . . ."

Another wave thudded against the hull and the air in the car vibrated with the relayed shock. The wind smeared raindrops across the windscreen. The ferry was eased expertly into the Killimer dock, its engine rallying and slowing to negotiate the waves. Minogue felt the faint lateral sway of the boat, drawn by the waves, before it came to rest with a bump. He waved at the man lifting the gates and called out through the slit in the window as he inched the Fiat forward onto the ramp, "Damp."

The man was young, and his face shadowed in the hood of his rainsuit reminded Minogue of a monk. The Fiat hesitated at the bottom of the ramp before beginning the incline up to the Kilrush Road.

"Well, now," said Hoey. "Look ahead there. We're back to civilization here now."

A Garda checkpoint was in place where the short road to the dock met up with the Kilrush Road. Minogue found first gear and approached the two Guards slowly. Rain poured thinly from their hats as they leaned to look in the window.

"Hello now," said one. "Where are ye coming from?"

Minogue had his card out. In his side vision he saw a figure stirring across the back window. He reached up with the card while Hoey tendered his own to the Guard on his side of the car. The inspector looked back and through the streaming window he saw a hooded figure standing to the driver's side, just out of sight of his wing mirror.

The Guard tried not to look surprised as he returned the card.

"Thanks, now," he said.

Minogue guessed that the two Ford Granadas were Emergency Response Units.

"We didn't see ye on the way down," said Minogue. "Around the two o'clock mark."

The Guard shrugged.

"Ah, we do the spot checks for a couple of hours. Move around a lot," he murmured. "Catch them on the move is the idea."

"The West's Awake, The West's Awake," Minogue half sang, half growled.

"You said it," the Guard grinned. "Pass on, now."

"By the way, is head-the-ball behind us from Dublin?" Minogue asked.

The Guard took quick control of his smile but it lived on as a wry cast to his face.

"How well you spotted him now. Was it the cars beyond?"

"As well as where he's standing, with the hardware hanging under his coat. Never thought we'd see Clare so lively, I can tell you."

"Ah, it might blow over . . . sooner or later," said the Guard. The expression on his face reminded Minogue of a farmer guessing on the weather.

"If only they'd stick to painting slogans on the walls."

Minogue wished the sodden Guard good luck and headed for the Ennis road. No shilly-shallying around the bog-roads by Carabane trying to save a few miles either, he determined. Cars the age of his sclerotic Fiat that had started out on such boreens had never reached their destinations.

• • • • •

Save for the streetlights smeared on the black, shiny streets, Ennis was gray and unfamiliar. Minogue parked under Crossan's office window.

"See the score with him," he muttered. "It'll only take a minute. Then we'll go and get a bit of tea or something. Have you any appetite in that line?"

"As a matter of fact," Hoey whispered, "I have a fierce thirst on me."

The despondent urgency in his voice startled Minogue. He looked to Hoey's face and remembered his own whiskeys in Tralee while Hoey had nursed 7-Up. He knocked and made room for Hoey in the meager shelter of the doorway. Crossan flung the door open energetically.

"Yiz are back," he announced. "Come on up."

Minogue felt his mood flattening out with each step as they trudged up the stairs after Crossan.

"Ye'll have a drink," Crossan said.

Minogue struggled with his reply. "None at all thanks. A bit of tea and the prospect of a bed would do wonders to, er, build morale."

"Had a call from Dan Howard," Crossan called out. "Wants to help out with the funeral expenses and what have you. Himself and the missus want to help in any way they can."

"Is Howard in Ennis right now?" Minogue asked.

Crossan nodded. "I told him that I'd call by his house tonight if I could find the time," the lawyer said. He looked toward Hoey. "That eye of yours is going green. Is that a good sign?"

"I don't know," said Hoey.

"I'll go with you," said Minogue.

Crossan hesitated. Rain blew across the window with a sigh.

"Let's eat something for the love of God," said Minogue. "Oh. I need to use the phone here first."

Crossan waved his arm over the phone and Minogue sat forward to reach it. He dialed his home number and watched Crossan shrug into his coat. Why had Crossan hesitated, he wondered? The phone was picked up.

"It's me, Kathleen," he said. "Your present husband. I'm in Ennis. It's raining."

"That's not news to me," she declared. "Tell me what else."

He detailed the sighting of the porpoises from earlier in the day, the trip to Tralee.

"Is Shea Hoey holding up yet?"

Minogue glanced over. Hoey was studying the ceiling, his head resting on the chair-back.

"Yes, or so it looks."

"He's there beside you?"

"That's true."

"I only hope he doesn't do something wild, you know," she went on in a whisper. "Because you might get caught up in it. I got to thinking that, you know, he should be staying up here in Dublin to get his, you know, treatment. I worry about him being next to you. What could happen, I mean."

"You should have seen them. I remember wanting to ride on their backs. Off they went, happy as Larry, I don't doubt, off out to sea. Live with them and never come back home to the farm."

"What? What are you going on about? Those creatures? Be serious now."

Minogue took her advice. Yes, he had enough changes of clothes and was installed in a good B & B. He concluded the chat with a request to his wife to check yesterday's temperature in Athens. When he put down the phone, both Crossan and Hoey were looking at him.

•　　•　　•　　•　　•

Minogue thanked the waitress and started immediately in on the black pudding, a blood sausage favored in rural areas yet. A generous portion, along with the waitress's commiserations about the unsettled weather, accompanied the mixed grill.

"Kathleen asked how we were doing on our, em, hobby."

Hoey grasped a chip with his fingers.

"What did you tell her?"

Much to Minogue's distaste, Hoey kept a cigarette going in the ashtray, taking pulls at it between chips. The long plateglass windows of the Beehive Restaurant were densely freckled with rain. Hardly a car passed on the puddled street.

"I informed her that we had the personnel to do a right good job of it. That's probably a way of saying that we've gotten nowhere yet. But that we might know better tomorrow."

Hoey munched reflectively on a chip.

"That wasn't so big of a whopper," he murmured.

Minogue watched two cars moving slowly down the street. A customer opened the door and Minogue heard the hiss of tires from the Fords. Each car had three men in it, he noted. Light from the restaurant caught the antennae waving by the back windows of the cars. The faces were in shadow until the car drew level with the restaurant. A young man stared in the window and his eyes met Minogue's for several moments. A hard-case from Dublin, the inspector registered: prowling. The face fell back into shadow as the car passed. Hoey's eyes were still fixed on the empty street.

"The cavalry," said Hoey. "It's getting to be like a garrison town."

Minogue worked on his grill but had to leave most of the chips. He dared more coffee but wished he could smoke to blunt its taste.

"Kathleen asked how you were doing."

Hoey rubbed his nose with a knuckle and concentrated on moving the ashtray in a pavane around the Formica. Minogue suspected that his colleague was putting his fingers to work so that his hands would not shake.

"Looked better by the hour, I told her. More or less, like. What I didn't tell her, of course, is that I'm worried about leaving you on your own tonight while I go over to Howard's place with Crossan."

"Well, let me go along with frog-eyes and yourself, so."

"Two Guards off the Murder Squad, Shea? I don't think that'd be a sound move. I want it to be as social as it can be. More will come of it."

"The Clare connection?"

"I suppose. Sorry."

Hoey's fingers slowed, and he rubbed his forehead with his thumb. He and Minogue had booked into a bed and breakfast run by a Mrs. McNamara. She had kept her curiosity in check for the moment, issuing a great welcome for her two guests. She explained the weather to them, told them that there was plenty of hot water, the prospect of a session with melodeons in Davitt's pub, told them there was another bathroom at the back of the house, asked them if they liked a big breakfast, invited them down to the parlor to watch the Miss Ireland beauty contest on the television tonight, recommended visits to the Ailwee Caves and the Folk Village by Bunratty.

The ashtray had begun its segue again. Hoey didn't look up when he spoke.

"Tell Kathleen I'm all right. Considering."

Minogue's mind was drawn to the movement of the ashtray.

"I'll head back to Mrs. McNamara," Hoey added. "Have a wash-up. I'll take a gander at what Miss Ireland's like this year."

Minogue wrenched his eyes away from the mesmerizing movements of the ashtray. He tried to lighten the atmosphere. He remembered the holy water font by Mrs. McNamara's door and the picture of the Sacred Heart reddened by the glowing bulb. Their widespread use and illumination on the island surely landmarked Ireland for sightseeing aliens, he believed.

"If you're watching with Mrs. Mac, I'd stick to the details about charm, personality, and poise, Shea. Rather than dwell on the merely physical, I mean."

Hoey feigned mild amusement.

"I'll be fine," he said. "You can even take a drink or two with Crossan and not feel bad."

"If I'm treating you like an iijit, Shea . . ."

"You're not, it's all right. I just have to decide for myself with this drink thing." Hoey sniffed and slowed the ashtray's dance.

"Us driving around today," he murmured, "it's hard to say. A few times I had the strangest ideas come into my head. It's like I've lost something. Something is over. And I know that I can't go back and get it, whatever 'it' is. Never. But I'm kind of glad of it."

Hoey let go of the ashtray abruptly and pushed it into the middle of the table. Immobile, it seemed to draw his attention even more. He snapped open his packet of cigarettes, lit one, and stared at the spotted, violet window.

"Do ye want anything else?" asked the waitress.

"No, thanks," said Minogue.

He watched her load up with plates and head back for the counter. Hoey's face eased, as though he had just understood a subtle joke. He nodded toward the window.

"I was looking at that window when we came in. For a few minutes I didn't realize that the fella in the window was me. Did that ever happen to you?"

Minogue nodded.

"You are who you are," Hoey said. "Hardly news now, is it? I'm not proud of what I did. I'm not ashamed of it either. But it's me, and I'm here. That's it. That's all of it."

Hoey's face had cleared of lines. He returned to gazing at the window as though it were a lush landscape where he could see forever.

"If Herlighy heard that, he'd sign me in somewhere, I'll bet you."

Minogue held fast to his wish not to interrupt.

"Look at you, though," Hoey went on. "Nothing seems to knock you down."

"I have Kathleen and the children, Shea. And I do enjoy being around Jimmy and the others —"

Hoey waved away Minogue's words with a tired, knowing grin.

"Yeah, yeah. The Killer looks out every day of his life to see how he can look good and have people think he's the bees' knees."

"He's a good leader, Shea. Has to crack the whip sometimes. But he leaves us plenty of room."

"He'll turf me out. That's the kind of room he'll give me."

"He will not," Minogue retorted. He met Hoey's eyes. "I won't let him. And that's that."

Hoey's eyes lost their piercing intent after several moments and slipped back to the window.

CHAPTER 9

Y‌OU'RE RIGHT! Jesus!"

"I told you, see?"

He let the van coast by the restaurant, his foot on the clutch.

"Who's the one with him? He looks like he was in a row."

"Never saw him before. Here, do you think he's an informer who got the shite beat out of himself at the station or something?"

The driver took a deep breath.

"There. I told you he was down here undercover. He's Clare, so he wouldn't stick out."

"Shut up a minute!"

"Well, how come he's back, then?"

"James Bourke getting shot, maybe."

He turned the van into Cornmarket and stopped. The wipers began to squeak on the window.

"No, it isn't! It's because of the fucking German the other night! They're sending in a spy —"

"Jases, get some sense, would you!"

"Well, what's your bloody explanation then?"

"I don't know," he murmured, "I just don't know."

"I'm *telling* you! It's too much of a coincidence." The passenger began squeezing his thumb again. He held it up to the windscreen. The street-light showed the nail black.

"It'll fall off and a new one'll grow under it," he murmured.

"Maybe we can find out more about him," said the driver. "I'll phone and ask."

His passenger gave a scornful whinny.

"Run to that bollocks? Christ, us doing all the work and taking the risks. What's he going to tell us, for fuck's sakes? To go and hide?"

The driver was too tired to get angry. His passenger stuck his thumb in his mouth.

"Come on and we'll go for a pint," he grunted around the thumb.

"No, I'm going to go home and phone. Where will you be later on?"

"Up in O'Loughlin's. Miss Ireland's on tonight."

The driver looked over into the shadows where his friend sat.

"That's as near as you'll get, is it?"

· · · · ·

Minogue left Hoey at Mrs. McNamara's door. The rain seemed to have eased off. The television glowed behind the curtains in the parlor. Mrs. McNamara might well drag Hoey away to watch Miss Ireland while she poured tea into him. There she could pry at leisure and not be rushed into indiscreet questions.

The inspector felt the weariness return to his shoulders. He fought free of a belch from deep in his diaphragm and grimaced at the greasy aftertaste. He let the Fiat coast lumpishly through the narrow streets before he drew it next to the curb by Crossan's office. He honked once and saw the light being extinguished. The lawyer came down the steps two at a time.

"Such a night," said Crossan with a hiss. "We'll be drowned. Go out the Gort Road. I'll give you the billy when we get near to the Howards."

A mile outside town, Crossan jabbed a finger toward two stone piers. The gates had been drawn back. The house was out of sight of the road. Minogue turned onto the avenue and felt the Fiat sink slightly into the pebbled drive. The swish of the stones under the tires made him think of the steel-hooped broughams of the gentry cutting lines in gravel raked daily by servants. The headlights swept over old trees, rhododendrons, and a white metal railing that led to the front of the house. Minogue parked by a white Audi and stepped out. The rain had let up but the gardens and grounds around the house seemed to be waiting for more. Sounds persisted: drips and pats, the gurgling of a gutter close by, the wet hiss of a car passing on the road below the house. The earth released smells of damp, decaying leaves.

The Howards' residence was two stories over a high cellar that could be entered through a door under the steps. Tall windows to both sides of the front steps formed oblongs of yellow on the face of the white house. Flower beds of turned sod with rose bushes recently cut back fronted the house. White wrought-iron chairs surrounded an elaborate table on a bed of cut stone to the side of the house. A lorry's air brakes squealed on the road. Crossan slammed his door hard, a gesture whose intent Minogue was not sure of. His toes sank back into the pebbles as he trudged toward the steps, making him lean forward to gain some momentum.

"Grand spot," he tried on Crossan.

"The White House," grunted the lawyer.

Minogue gained the foot of the steps and looked back. The light of Ennis twinkled between the trees.

"Don't feel you need to doff your cap here and you in from the wilds of Rossaboe," said Crossan, skipping up the steps. Halfway up the flight he paused and scraped his sole on the edge of the step.

"Jesus," he muttered.

Minogue strained his eyes. After a few seconds he could see the spots on the steps.

"Watch out," said the lawyer, still scraping. "The slugs are out after the rain."

Crossan reached the top of the steps and hit the bell with his fist. Minogue decided against voicing the gibe that came to his mind: a lawyer in a hurry to knock on a door could only mean someone's misfortune. Minogue was halfway up the steps when Sheila Howard opened the door. She watched him ascend and Minogue felt as if he were floating up. He tried to keep his breathing regular by using his nose alone, but the breath came in whistles. He became acutely aware of the condition he was in. His hair and shoulders were still damp from stepping in and out of cars and houses and pubs. Hoey's cigarettes, the smell of the Fiat. Have to get a new car, damn it. He wished he had bathed and shaved and done his hair and brought fancy clothes with him down from Dublin, changed his shoes at least . . .

"Aloysious," he heard her say. "And . . . the inspector."

Crossan's voice was a bark of forced humor.

"But, sure, let him in anyway, will you?"

Minogue's impressions collided with the thoughts and feelings welling up inside. He stood in the doorway feeling like an unkempt supplicant. A scent of flowers wafted out from the interior. She stood aside near Crossan and waved Minogue in. He swallowed, glanced, and nodded at Sheila Howard before walking into the hallway.

"I'll take your coats here," she said, and closed the door. Minogue wished she wouldn't. A stairway curved up to a landing overhead. Polished wooden floors ran through the hallway and then disappeared under what the inspector took to be a Persian carpet covering much of the floor of the front room to his left. Track lighting bathed the hall but the peach-colored walls softened its glare.

"Miserable old day, isn't it?" said Sheila Howard. Minogue pivoted around and stole a glance at her back. Her hair was tied up in a loose ponytail and her jeans were faded. He guessed her pastel red polo-neck was lamb's wool. As she stretched into the cloakroom, Minogue looked down to see her bare heels stand out of her shoes. Crossan had made no reply to her. Minogue felt that he should fill the vacuum.

"Par for the course, I suppose," he said.

"Are you a golfer?"

"Well, no, in actual fact."

"Golf is for iijits, Sheila," Crossan interrupted. "Hell is full to the brim of golf courses. Saving your husband and all that. I know he only bought his clubs to play with the tourists out in Lahinch."

Steps sounded softly and Dan Howard appeared in a doorway to the right. He took off his glasses with a smile, folded the newspaper, and plugged it under his arm.

"Come in, can't ye," he said. He reached out for Minogue's hand.

The inspector sat in a heavily upholstered chair by the fire and made a quick survey of the room. High ceilings and long windows gave him a sense of comfortable spaciousness. Elaborately flowered plasterwork radiated from the center of the ceiling, over an unlit chandelier. The antique furniture, few of the pieces with a shiny finish, suggested elegance without appearance lavish. Minogue's amateur but wary eye recognized one of the paintings as a Paul Henry. The only clear concession to ego, he thought, was a writing bureau with elaborate inlay placed strategically by the window. At least it was covered in papers. Howard sat forward on the edge of a high-backed sofa.

"Something to wet your whistles, men?"

"Glass of Paddy," said Crossan. "Nothing tricky, now."

"Any Irish," Minogue said. "Jamesons if it's easy to hand."

"I'll get it," said Sheila Howard. She walked to a cabinet and turned a key. Minogue spotted a wide array of bottles. She took tumblers from behind another door and began pouring whiskey. Then she took a small, ornate pail and left the room. Ice, Minogue realized.

Howard spoke as though responding to a question that no one had asked. "The time of year, all right."

He ran his fingers back through his hair once and yawned. Minogue found more comfort in the chair and his nervousness began to ease. He looked at the turf burning vigorously in the fireplace.

"Do you mean there's an election coming?" asked Crossan. "Or with Captain Moonlight and his raiders out in the hills?"

Minogue decided that Crossan's tone was a way of keeping an edge on conversation with people he knew. Howard fobbed off the sarcasm with a flick of his head.

"I meant the weather and the season that's in it," he said.

"Ye're well in out of the weather here," Crossan said. "A glass of whiskey, a turf fire, and all, begob. Ye're truly a man of the people, Dan Howard. Where's your high hat and your shillelagh, but?"

Sheila Howard returned with the ice pail and a jug of water. Minogue looked up at her in the doorway and felt his belly tighten again. She rubbed her hip against the door to close it.

"What's that about an election?" she asked.

"Alo's fishing," Howard said. He winked at Minogue. "But the bait is old."

"Alo" from Howard, "Aloysious" with its full burden of ironic grandeur from Sheila Howard. The fancier name to keep Howard at bay, Minogue reflected. She placed the ice and water on the cabinet while she plucked one of a nest of tables from next to the sofa. The phone rang in the hall. She held her hand up before her husband rose.

"The Chief?" Crossan asked. "A summons to higher office in Dublin?"

"Hardly," Howard answered easily. "More likely someone who thinks I can diddle the Revenue Commissioners for income tax or get their road tarred again."

Sheila Howard closed the door to the hall. Crossan pursued Howard with the pushy mischief that Minogue knew was playing to the gallery.

"And can't you do it, so?"

"Ah, now, Alo, that class of thievery is well beyond a TD. For that you'd need the services of a barrister."

Crossan guffawed and his eyelids slid down a little. He sipped from his glass.

"Damn fine, I'd have to say," he said, and smacked his lips. "The duty-free always tastes better."

Howard looked sympathetically to Minogue.

"Familiarity breeds . . . and the rest of it."

"With the exception of being married to the right person, I imagine," Minogue offered.

"Making a virtue out of a necessity there," scoffed Crossan.

"Aren't you going to tie the knot yourself one of these days, Alo?" Howard asked.

Minogue found himself liking Dan Howard's easy retorts.

"Tie the noose, you mean" answered Crossan. "Or the yoke, maybe." He nodded and held the tumbler against his chin as though considering sage advice.

"So as the women of Clare can sleep easier," Howard observed. "Or at least forget their daydreaming and attend to their louts of husbands."

Minogue smiled. Crossan seemed to take the repartee in his stride. It must be a friendship of sorts. Rivalry? Crossan put on a melancholy expression.

"Ah but sure, how would we bring up the children?"

Howard laughed and rested his head on the sofa-back. An older joke shared, Minogue believed. Howard rubbed at his eyes with thumb and forefinger and then looked at Minogue.

"Alo digs with the other foot, I suppose you know," he said.

Minogue remembered Eilo McInerny's mention of it and nodded.

"Hence the expression 'footless' in relation to the amount of drink needed on this island," said Crossan in a dry tone. "When we want to get beyond considerations of religion. Or lack thereof."

Howard stayed with the quickening pace of the exchange. "Are you lapsed, is it, Alo?"

Crossan's expression turned grave and mischievous. "More in the nature of prolapsed," he murmured. "Herniated, you might say, from carrying such a heavy burden . . . Hiberniated, I suppose you'd say."

Howard chortled and looked at the inspector.

"I used to spend a lot of time and effort persuading Alo that he wasn't an outsider. Then I realized he was milking me for my inherited faults."

"Such as?" Minogue asked.

"Oh, you know. Having a pet Protestant, that sort of thing. We're quite sophisticated here as regards the psychology, you know."

"For being townies," Crossan qualified.

"Maybe not as down-and-out cute as the people of west Clare proper," said Howard. "Rossaboe people, now, they're cute hoors."

So he knows me and mine, thought Minogue. He yielded to the polite dig that Howard had used to place him so that he could allow it to boomerang back to Howard with more velocity.

"Cuter still after living in Dublin awhile," he said.

Crossan spoke as though addressing a jury timid of him.

"Aha, yes. Well, I'd have to admit that being a God-fearing Protestant born, bred, and starved here in Clare has its moments. Oh, yes. The urgency of the task of survival came to my mind as a newborn in the crib. 'Litigate!' the Lord bade me. 'You'll never want for a crust among such a disputatious people.'"

The inspector joined in Howard's laughter.

"There are said to be poor Protestants in Ireland," Crossan was saying, and he sniffed at the rim of his tumbler. "Silk knickers and no breakfast. A romantic might consider that being an outsider."

"Was that how you found your niche looking after the outsiders and vagabonds in matters criminal?" Howard goaded.

"If I do me job right, they don't become criminals, Your Honor," Crossan shot back.

"Alo's a ticket," said Howard to Minogue.

From the hall the inspector heard Sheila Howard's tone as she spoke into the phone. The fire and the whiskey had warmed his bones and driven away the creaking dampness that had been with him all day. Crossan finished his drink and let the ice cubes fall back to the bottom of his tumbler.

"Well, now. In the course of conversation, I explained Jamesy Bourke to this Guard here. Well, the best I could . . . So when Jamesy was shot and killed, I phoned his nibs here to see what the Dublin Guards might think."

Howard listened with a frown of concern and nodded occasionally.

"And the answer is — nothing," Crossan went on. "The Guards here are handling the matter themselves. We had this fact confirmed this very afternoon when we bumped into none other than Superintendent Tom Russell below at the station here in Ennis."

Howard folded his arms.

"That kind of procedure or jurisdiction is reminiscent of another episode in Jamesy Bourke's life," Crossan murmured. He paused when the door opened and Sheila Howard entered the room.

"Sorry," she said. She sat sideways on the sofa next to her husband. Minogue noticed that she had no drink yet. Howard scratched his scalp.

"Yes, well, the poor divil is at rest now," he added.

Sheila Howard had picked up on the changed atmosphere, Minogue noted. She sat very still, her expression unchanged. Crossan did not conceal his cynicism now.

"The light of heaven to him."

"His people have a plot above the old church ground in Portaree," Howard said. "I think we can see him put with them there."

Crossan started to say something but stopped. Sheila Howard glanced at him and looked away.

"Jamesy cut himself off from people so," Howard added, and stared at the fire.

"Someone will show up," said Crossan. "Where there's a will, there's a relative."

No one spoke for several seconds. Minogue had a momentary mental snapshot of these four people, all preoccupied with their own thoughts, sitting here in a comfortable room with the night thick about the house. He recalled the slugs on the steps, the dripping undergrowth alive with creatures making their move as the rain had allowed them.

"God, how things turn out," said Howard at last.

"This Spillner fella is well-to-do," Crossan growled. "There was a big, black Merc, with an embassy plate on it, waiting outside the station and we going in there this afternoon. We fell to wondering if the same man is now back in Germany?"

"And is he?" Sheila Howard asked.

"We don't know for sure if he's gone or not," Minogue answered.

"Well, I believe I can find out," said Howard.

Sheila Howard bobbed back in the sofa as her husband stood. Howard headed for the hallway and closed the door behind himself.

"Is Dan thinking of footing the bill for Jamesy's funeral?" Crossan asked her.

"Until someone comes up with a better plan," she replied.

Minogue let his eyes travel about the room. The colors muted by the light kept the room looking warm. Peach now, Minogue saw, perhaps ochre in daylight, and a definite orange, but none of these colors deadening. Waylaid by his own tiredness and lulled by the whiskey and the warmth of the fire, Minogue was slow to pick up on Crossan's stare at Sheila Howard.

The barrister spoke in a tone of strained politeness.

"And how are your horses?"

"They're all well, thank you," she replied. "They were asking for you."

Minogue almost laughed.

"They have grand names, as I recall," Crossan continued, still serious.

"Another drink?" she asked. "Oh, but that ice is a shambles already. I'll be back in a minute."

As she closed the door, Minogue heard Dan Howard saying thanks very much, Sean, say no more. He watched Crossan's eyes lose their intensity, slip out of focus, and turn flat as he stared at the fire.

"Why are you taking digs at her?"

"It's a ritual," Crossan replied dully. He didn't look up from the fire. "Don't fret over it."

"Work out your digs some other time then. We don't want to be raising dust when we need to get something from the Howards."

Crossan gave a mirthless snort. "You think it's sour grapes with me, Guard? I like horses, don't get me wrong. I'm a horse-protestant, am I not? It's in my blood."

"Beggars ride to hell. We need their good will here, so back off with the smart-aleck stuff."

Dan Howard returned to the sofa, frowning. Minogue felt suddenly irritated when the thought came to him: Had Crossan a sizeable chip on his shoulder? Was he here less to discover what had happened to Jamesy Bourke or Jane Clark than to embarrass the Howards? Self-absorbed and intent on his own battles, was Crossan's judgment warped by some humiliation he had suffered at the hands of the Howards or their like? "Horse-protestant": witty in context here, derisory everywhere else.

"You were right," said Howard. "That man was put on a plane today." He shrugged. "I don't know what to make of it. I suppose that bail conditions allowed him to leave for Germany."

Minogue decided it was time to change trains or, at the very least, to get on board. He sat forward in his chair.

"I think I should tell you, Mr. Howard —"

"Dan."

"— Dan, that I'm not here tonight to discuss that case exactly. To be candid now, I have no jurisdiction at all in the matter. I am interested in an event that happened a long time ago. In relation to Jamesy Bourke and Jane Clark."

"Oh, I believe that I knew what you were here for now," said Howard. "A man of my calling has to be aware of things that are being associated with his name." He smiled wanly at Minogue and looked over at Crossan. "You know what I'm saying, like . . ."

The inspector nodded. Dan Howard could pick up the phone day or night and check up on him. He might have already done just that.

"Some peculiar things happened in that case. Or, should I say, didn't happen."

Howard blinked and sat back. Crossan's eyes stayed fixed on the fire as Minogue resumed.

"Now, it's not that the case is reopened, no. As a matter of fact, I'm on me holidays." Howard's expression changed into a look of puzzled humor. "I thought I'd just look into it. Satisfy myself that the case was merely, how can I put it, a little more full of . . . Well, I'd better be careful with a brace of lawyers in the same room. Let's call them episodic incongruities that mark the proceedings of law. I want to be sure that justice has been rendered."

Howard smiled broadly as he leaned over to whisper to Crossan.

"Where did you find him, Alo?"

"Fell out of a bloody dictionary, by the sounds of that," came the barrister's droning reply.

Howard turned to Minogue again.

"I can tell you've had a lot of truck with the legal profession. Go ahead, now."

Sheila Howard returned with more ice. She left a scent in her wake as she passed the inspector. Flowery with cloves in it somewhere, he thought. As though all other sounds in the room were silenced and all other movements were stilled, Minogue heard the movement of her jeans rubbing while she walked. A gust rattled the window frame. Unsettled, Minogue tried to keep easing out his thoughts as though they were a net issuing over the thwarts of a boat. Her face turned to the window brought Minogue a confused memory of portraits in the National Gallery. He realized with near alarm that he couldn't seem to stop himself from staring at her. As though aware of this, she hesitated before sitting down. Dan Howard was waiting for him to resume. Crossan was lost in the glowing fire, his fingers driven into his resting chin. Minogue sought out Howard's eyes to bring himself back. "Now I don't want to be asking you things that'd, you know," Minogue began, "bring up old, em . . ."

"Resentments," said Crossan unexpectedly.

"You mean about Jane Clark," Howard said. "Oh, you needn't be worrying there. We testified at the trial, Sheila and I. A lot of things came out."

Minogue dared a glance at Sheila Howard.

"If you don't mind, then . . ."

Her forehead lifted and she nodded at him.

"Well, let me go directly to the matter. Forensic evidence. I was much taken aback to discover, for example, that there were no statements from the county coroner in the book of evidence used in the trial. As to how Jane Clark met her death exactly, I mean. If she was asphyxiated from smoke inhalation, for example, or died as a result of burns, or from injuries resulting from the collapse of the roof during the fire. Her remains were recovered from the bedroom. That suggests she was asleep and was overcome by smoke or fumes before being able to make the effort to escape the fire."

Minogue paused and glanced from face to face.

"But in the heel of the reel, I suppose, there have been cases where people who are sober have gone to bed and a fire starts, and they are indeed overcome by the smoke quite rapidly. Such that they, em, perish in the fire. Now what I'm coming to is this: In what condition was Jane Clark when you left the cottage that evening?"

Howard looked to his wife and then to his hands before looking back to Minogue.

"Do you know," he began in a quiet voice, "it's a bad thing to talk about someone who's dead and them not able to speak for themselves. Bred into us never to speak ill of the dead, no matter who, isn't it? That night . . . well, hardly a day goes by that I don't think of it or some part of it." He released a long breath which whistled through his nose.

"Jane Clark had a lot of drink that night," he went on, his voice firmer. "I did too. So did Jamesy." He began rubbing his knuckles and changing hands in the slow, measured rhythm Minogue associated with men who worked outdoors.

"She could hold a lot of drink as long as it was whiskey, of all things. She kept whiskey in the house and I know that she took a drop of it even when she was on her own."

"How did you know, now?"

"Well, there were times I'd go by and she'd be working on something. She did a bit of pottery — she had a wheel but no kiln. She was keen on setting up a darkroom. She had a plan to do a big coffee-table book on the ancient sites around Clare. It was the Burren she came to see. She'd often have a glass by her. Not a lot, now."

"Would you describe her as a heavy drinker?"

"I don't know," Howard replied. "It didn't stop her doing her work. She had worked a lot on her own back in Canada, doing graphic art and designing and the like. She had decided to go around the world but ended up here. Days on end she was up on the Burren. High up on the rocks, now, where there's nothing but the birds, I suppose."

Howard looked down at his empty glass.

"I thought they were all like that over in the States or Canada. The way you'd see them on telly, like — martinis and cocktails and that for their dinner. She was much the same person with a few drinks on as without, that I remember. She had the same . . . manner about her, I suppose you'd say."

"Meaning she had the same appetites," said Crossan, his eyes still on the embers.

Anger flared on Howard's face, and it surprised Minogue.

"Alo, there are some things —" Howard began in a sharp tone, but he let the rest of his words go.

"That night," Minogue persisted, "that night, she was not, can I say, terrible drunk?"

"I'd have to tell you that I had a lot of drink taken and I don't like drinking on my own so . . ."

"So you poured a few for her."

Howard nodded.

"And did she keep up with you?"

"She did."

"Were you drunk and you leaving her house that night?"

"I was half cut, as they say."

"Can you hold your drink, then?"

"I can, I suppose," said Howard, as though resigned to losing an argument. "I had plenty of practice. But look now."

He paused and laid his hand over one of his wife's beside him on the sofa.

"I don't want you leaving here thinking she was a tramp or that. And there are things that I'd prefer we talked about on our own, you as a Guard, I mean, and myself."

"Excuse me now if I'm bringing back . . ."

"Well, it's never over," Sheila Howard said. "Really, like."

Minogue could not decide if her tone leaned more toward exasperation or pity.

"I was there at the trial, yes, and I heard everything. So don't hold back on my account. Would you like tea?"

"Yes, please," said Minogue. Crossan sat up as she left and sat forward, elbows on his knees, and rubbed at his eyes. Minogue had read Sheila Howard's restless coming-and-goings for ice and tea as signs of her nervousness about their conversation. Maybe it was Crossan who was annoying her the most with his digs.

"How did you get out to her cottage that evening?" he asked her husband.

"I walked out. Sure it was only a mile or so out the road. A Clare mile, to be sure, but it was no great bother. A fine evening. I thought that she'd come in to the village with me after, for a few scoops and for the music. There were sessions with local box-players and a bit of set-dancing. She liked that."

"Had you no car?"

"Yes, I did. But I had loaned it to Sheila. She was gone to Galway city for the day."

So Sheila Hanratty had known him well enough to get a loan of his car, Minogue thought.

"You and Jamesy left her place, so . . ."

"Yes, Jamesy came in without so much as a knock. Barges in the door with a great welcome for himself and there we were. He had a bottle under his arm. Only it was full, he would have broken it over my head, I don't doubt."

"Ye proceeded to have a row," Minogue led on.

"We did just that, yes."

The inspector heard in Howard's tone embarrassment and impatience now.

"Not a pretty sight, as you can imagine. I'm trying to get me various articles of clothing on and Jamesy is working himself up to —"

"A volcanic fit of anger," said Crossan with a sober expression.

Howard glanced over at the barrister and nodded as if to register the lawyer's immaculate work of disguising the sarcasm.

"To add to my, em . . ."

"Predicament," said Crossan.

"Predicament. Thanks, Alo. Jane seemed to find something funny about the whole thing. After she got over the initial fright, of course —"

"She was frightened of Jamesy Bourke?" Minogue interjected.

"No. Just the surprise factor, you might say. She turfed us out. While I was busy avoiding Jamesy's digs and kicks, she took my stuff and threw it out the door. Quite the spectacle. Anyway. I managed to get out of the house and Jamesy stayed awhile giving out to her. There was plenty of shouting and roaring between them."

"What did he say to her?" Minogue asked.

"He called her names for the most part. And he called me names too, of course. Bad language basically."

Minogue looked to Crossan's face. The mask was beginning to slip. An eyebrow fought to control the smile Minogue was sure had been building for several minutes now.

"Threats?" Minogue asked in a low voice, still watching Crossan.

"No. Name-calling. No threats or the like that I heard."

"He called her names," Minogue repeated.

Howard nodded.

"Would you care to enumerate any of the things he said about her? Or you, for that matter?"

"I wouldn't really," said Howard in a strained voice. "There was nothing you or I haven't heard before. To the effect that she was a whore and suchlike."

"No threats," Minogue repeated. "Didn't say anything about future meetings or looking forward or revenge? That class of thing?"

"No. He came out after me then and she locked the door. I heard her turn the latch and slide a bolt . . . Jamesy had boots on. I got a few pucks and I gave him a few. But by then I had me stuff on and I was able to go."

"What did he do then?"

"He tried to get back in the house. But of course he couldn't. More shouting and roaring."

"Could you hear what he was saying this time? How far away were you?"

"Well, I had hightailed it out to the road. I was caught between two stools really. I didn't want him getting into the house for fear he'd hurt her. Then again, I didn't want to be so close that he'd get ahold of me. I hung around near the gate."

"You heard him shouting."

"I did. He gave up pretty quick and out he came onto the road. He opened the bottle and took a big wallop of whiskey. He saw me and started up again but he didn't run the greatest. I headed back to the village, trying to talk him down a bit. I was glad to get him out and away from the house. I offered him a few drinks but he wouldn't at first. But between the exertions and what have you, maybe we sobered up a little because when we got to the village he said all right."

"How did you calm him down?" Minogue probed.

Howard rubbed his ear and studied the mantelpiece.

"Well, for one thing, I didn't try to make an iijit of him. I told him that she was different from us, I remember that."

"How do you mean?"

"That she didn't have the same upbringing. That she would do what she liked, sort of."

"Sexually?"

"Yes, she had told me that she had had plenty of, you know . . ."

"Lovers," said Crossan.

"That he shouldn't feel bad about it; that it was nothing personal."

"Nothing personal," Minogue echoed.

Howard nodded. "What I meant was that *I* didn't take it personally, like, and that he shouldn't. People were entitled to live their lives the way they thought was proper, and just because we were from the back of beyond in County Clare . . ."

Minogue said nothing. Crossan's hand strayed to his Adam's apple. Minogue heard his fingertips seeking out bristles.

"Basically I was trying to make him see that he shouldn't take it so much to heart. That we should be friends despite it. Despite her, I mean."

Crossan's baleful gaze remained fixed on Dan Howard. Noting Crossan's stillness, Minogue felt something brush around his thoughts. Was this Crossan's idea of fun? He took up the thread again.

"So ye went drinking then. Did he continue to talk about her?"

"Awhile, yes. He was mighty annoyed at her and he was still sour on me, even after a few rounds of drink. But I couldn't get mad at him, even when he was trying to give me a box in the teeth."

"How do you mean?"

"Not to be shooting meself in the foot here," Howard whispered, and looked up from the fire at Minogue with a sad and faintly amused look. "And me a self-respecting, tax-paying TD —"

"Spare us the speech, can't you," Crossan broke in. "If it's a revelation you're about to land on us, you won't lose votes from the present company over it."

"Nor gain them either, I suppose, Alo," Howard added. He gave a quick smile before continuing.

"Well, it wasn't hard to feel sorry for Jamesy. He had all his eggs in the one basket, you could say. Jamesy was convinced that she was his and that the pair of them could set up shop, her with her pottery and her photography gallery and him with his plays and poems. And that they'd travel the world."

"Did he tell you that himself?" Minogue feinted.

"He didn't." Minogue heard Howard breathe out slowly. "She did."

"I remember wondering if and when she'd run out of patience with him — or all of us, for that matter — and she'd let him have it. Lower the boom on him, maybe pack her bags and bale out."

"Do you mean she led him on?"

Howard took a deep breath and held it in with his shoulders. Then he let it out and sagged back into the sofa.

"Maybe she did. It's not for me to say. Jamesy wanted everything, you see. For all his wild ways, the same Jamesy was far from, what can I say, frivolous about her. Jane wanted to flit around and to dabble and to experiment. She had a lot of experience of men. She did things and said things that surprised me. I mean, at the time, I thought I knew a lot, but I had never met a woman who was so . . ."

"Assertive," said Crossan.

"Come on now, Alo," Howard snorted and sat up again. "You can do better than that. You knew her too. She wasn't a man-eater, no. That wouldn't be fair to say that of her, now."

"I think," Crossan said momentously, "that perhaps she was so exciting because she gave the impression that she could do what she liked. She wasn't stuck to the land. She was a free spirit."

Howard smiled with a tired look and he held two fingers to his forehead in mock salute. "There you have it," he said. "Bachelor wisdom that can't be beat."

"But you had plenty of eggs," Minogue said. "Or do I mean baskets?"

"Baskets," said Crossan.

"Whereas Jamesy Bourke had but the one. Or thought he had."

Howard nodded, serious again. "At the time, yes," he murmured.

Minogue struggled to keep up a momentum whose direction he couldn't determine.

"What did ye talk about in the pub, though?"

"Well, a lot of it was about Jane Clark," Howard said wearily. "There were other lads there too, and I was hoping we could get Jamesy off the subject of you-know-what or you-know-who. There was crack and music and plenty of drink. I remember him talking to me about some poetry and a plan he had to go to the States for a while so he could make money to live on."

More details came to Howard, but none of them sparked Minogue to intervene. While Howard talked and Crossan stared into the fire, Minogue's eyes strayed to the windows. From his earliest days in school, the inspector had realized that he was a better listener when he wasn't intent on the talk. As though, by looking to the side, one could see a star better, Minogue had come to depend on this faculty of understanding without the effort of listening closely, this keen reverie. The window facing away from the town was a panel of violet where the absolute country night pressed on the glass.

Howard's voice stopped and then resumed. Minogue listened, heard, and waited, but he allowed his inner eye to leave through the window. He imagined the ghostly heights of the Burren. The names on the huddles of houses and villages came to him: Carron and Gortleca, Kilshanny and Rinnamona. Reciting their names within gave him an odd pleasure. He tried to list more villages from memory but the names drifted away. Ruins of fort, village, and church: Corcomroe Abbey, he remembered, Holy Mary of the Fertile Rock. Those scarred terraces crowning the landscape above Ailee Cave that had caused Kathleen to stare at them that day they had the puncture on the way to the farm. Howard continued.

Sheila Howard was backing in the door with a tray of tea things and a plate of biscuits. Howard sat forward in the sofa and began rubbing his hands together. He stopped after several moments and looked at his hands with a frown as if they were new to him. Crossan coughed and crossed his legs.

"This may sound corny," said Howard. "But I will always regret to my dying day that I pushed drink at Jamesy that night. I thought it would . . ."

"Incapacitate him?" Minogue prodded. "Settle him down?"

Howard's voice fell lower to a monotone.

"I suppose."

He watched his wife sit down beside him as though it were for the first time.

Minogue said thanks to Sheila Howard. He was keenly aware of her in the room, near to him. Was she still annoyed? He was relieved that he had gained some control over himself. Still, he felt the restlessness return as a sag somewhere in his chest, the heat at his collar. At least he wasn't sitting here glowing like a beetroot, flustered and dripping from the jowls, he thought with sour gratitude. She shoved the plate across the table toward him and he saw that her hands were big. There was no daintiness about her nails. Some surprise twisted at his mind: she wasn't a bird in a gilded cage.

"We talked about anything and everything," Howard was saying. Minogue watched him pour tea for his wife. "The way two lads who are drunk can talk."

"Huh," said Crossan.

"What kind of order was he in by the time you left the pub?" asked Minogue.

"Drunk."

"Was he on his feet at least?"

"Barely," said Howard. "To tell you the truth, I wasn't paying much attention at that stage myself."

"Tell me," said the inspector in a tone he hoped didn't sound too urgent, "did Bourke leave the pub very annoyed at her yet?"

Howard shrugged and then sat very still. A frown came to his face.

"I couldn't honestly tell you now. I seem to remember him saying things at some point during the night, but I can't tell you when, I just know it was in the pub, that that was how they are over there."

"'They' meaning Canadians, is it?" Minogue asked.

"Canadians, Americans, I suppose," Howard murmured.

Minogue stirred his tea without allowing the spoon to touch the inside of the cup.

"Did he tell you that he might try to make up with Jane Clark that night?"

Crossan had moved in to the table. Howard reflexively pushed a cup and saucer toward him.

"I'm trying to remember, now," said Howard.

"He did," said Sheila Howard.

Minogue hid his surprise.

"I forgot, Mrs. Howard," he said. "You met up with them late in the evening."

"That's right. I came in late from Galway. And I stopped in at the hotel to listen to a bit of music and see the girls before heading home."

"Yes," said her husband, "there was a mighty session on that night. Tourists all over the place. The weather was good, strange to say."

"The place was packed, all right," Sheila Howard added.

"Strange how you remember things when you get reminders, even a word or two," said Howard. He shook his head slowly before sipping at his tea. Minogue noticed Crossan poised with his own cup. He was struck by Crossan's alertness as the lawyer eyed Dan Howard.

"That's it," Howard said then. "St. John's Eve, do you know it?"

"The midsummer's night," replied Minogue. "Yes."

Howard sipped more tea and looked into the fire.

"The bonfires and everything," he murmured. "They don't do it so much nowadays."

Minogue turned to Sheila Howard.

"May I ask you something, Mrs. Howard?"

His voice sounded small in the room. The inspector swallowed and glanced at her eyes.

"You may indeed," she replied.

Minogue was struck again by her poise and stillness. Mona Lisa — Mona Sheila . . . Minogue's gargoyle flung an image at his brittle composure: *Sheela-na-gig*. An image of those pagan carvings and statues of women came to Minogue. These statues of women and goddesses, with their knees up and their fingers tugging the lips of their vulvas apart, were widely regarded as grotesque and had been quarantined to the back rooms of the National Museum in Dublin.

"Were you aware . . ." He struggled through the question and swallowed again. "Were you aware that night of what had gone on out at Jane Clark's house?"

"Yes," she answered. "I became aware of it."

The formality struck Minogue: "became aware." A rebuke to him for a phrase that did not belong in this chat, in her home? A phrase used in law, in court. He looked over to Crossan and again doubt came to him.

"The girls had heard about it," she went on. "And you know what that would mean in town. It was no doubt the way Jamesy was acting that got them wondering. Word travels fast, especially inside a pub."

He looked over at Howard.

"Well, I don't doubt that I let something slip," Howard said. "With everyone coming and going in the pub and all the chatting and what have you. And sure once one knew, they'd all know in a matter of minutes. There was a funny side to it, I'd have to admit. Before what happened later, I mean."

"You were part of a crowd?" Minogue asked Sheila Howard.

She nodded. "The way girls hang around together. Our mothers told us to hunt in packs."

Kathleen had issued the very same admonitions to Iseult. Did every Irish parent have the same script? He gathered his thoughts to frame the next question.

"Do you recall if Bourke himself was teased about what had happened back at the cottage, if he had his sensitivities tested on the matter by people in the pub that night?"

It was Dan Howard who answered.

"Well, people tend to slag a lot. It's a pastime of sorts, and that's common knowledge." He rubbed his chin and looked at a landscape print on the wall as though he believed it held the words and knowledge he needed.

"I didn't slag him at all and I'll tell you why: I didn't want a puck from him. Even while he was drunk, he could still rear up on you and throw shapes. We were out in the street around half twelve or so."

"Your people owned the pub, didn't they?" Minogue interrupted. Howard frowned.

"Yes, yes. My father did. I mean, he still does, yes. . . . Oh, I see what you mean. We didn't live over the pub at all, oh no. Our house was out the Ennis Road. We had a man living over the pub. We hung around on the street awhile, a few of us. It was a warm night."

"Jamesy went his own way," Sheila Howard said.

"You were there?" asked Minogue.

"Yes, I hung around. I wasn't tired really. But I went off home myself a little later."

"After she drove me home," Howard added.

Minogue began to draw detail out of the fog. "Ah, the car."

"I had loaned the Mini to Sheila, remember?" said Howard. "She was gone to Galway for the day."

Minogue put on his sage and satisfied expression to cloak his rambling thoughts. Were the Howards daring him to put pointed questions — policelike "were you aware"s — to them in their own house? He felt Crossan's eyes on him and he looked over. The lawyer's eyes were not at full bore, but his expression was both expectant and mocking as he hooded his eyes slightly to signal Minogue. The inspector looked away, baffled. Something was going on here that escaped him. He bargained for time by reaching for the teapot. Howard took some turf from a basket, placed it on the fire, and sat back with a sigh.

Was this Crossan's moment of spiteful triumph, having finagled a Garda Inspector into Howard's home to embarrass the TD and his wife? Doubt clawed at Minogue.

"Yes," said Howard, "I retired in disarray that night. Sheila poured me into the car and left me at home."

Minogue decided to brazen his way out of his predicament.

"Did you offer a lift to Bourke?"

"No, I didn't," Sheila Howard replied. "I wish to God that I had. I wish that Dan or someone had shoved him into the car."

"Now," said Dan Howard. "We've been over that a thousand times. Don't be taking it upon yourself."

"I know, I know." She cut him short and looked to Crossan. He returned her level, appraising look.

"I wouldn't have been safe in the car with Jamesy." She looked down at the teapot. "I'll get more tea."

Crossan sat back and crossed his legs.

"Just between us men," he murmured. "Jamesy had a tendency to be mauling girls."

"Rough, in any sense?" Minogue asked. "If they weren't interested, like?"

"Not to the extent that you seem to be implying," said Howard.

"Well," said Crossan from his slouch. "The training in the law stood you in good stead with that one."

Howard let out a breath.

"I'm sorry. I grew up overnight after that. I don't mind admitting what I was like before that either. There was privilege and money in my family and I could do as I pleased, really. I didn't have to look forward to buckling down to the farming like Jamesy would have had to. But I can tell you this." Howard paused and looked up with a pained expression. "I can't go around full of remorse about it the rest of my life. Yes, Jamesy saw in her the love of his life and all the rest of it. But I was hail-fellow-well-met, playing the field. It's not my fault that Jamesy was the way he was, God rest him."

"Thank you for being so candid," Minogue said. "Rely upon this being a confidential matter between us."

Howard nodded and looked to the fresh sods of turf beginning to catch fire.

"If only she had come down to the pub that night," he murmured, "and got rip-roaring drunk with us, things might have been much different. She wouldn't open the door to him at that hour of the morning, and, sure, why should she? Sick of the pair of us, I've no doubt."

Minogue asked where a bathroom might be and excused himself. He stopped in the hall and looked into the greenhouse kitchen. Terra-cotta tiles, dried flowers, real wood panels, and all the wizard devices. Here was something he had seen only in the color supplements of the English Sunday papers. He had tried to persuade Kathleen that such kitchens existed only in showrooms and advertisements but here was proof otherwise. He heard a kettle purr stronger and a paper turn — Sheila Howard was there, he realized, and he moved off.

He switched on the light in the toilet. Blue water in a green porcelain toilet startled him. For that moment before he recognized modernity, he imagined some disease in a household member. He remembered that Kilmartin's new home in Killiney harbored the same gentility. Tired, tired, he thought. No toys underfoot. A damn fine house, the inspector decided. And the Howards seemed to be polished, accomplished people, with none of that gombeen smugness he had expected. They seemed well-used to one another and even intimate in ways he felt were sincere. He could not imagine them having a screaming row. There was the touch of the resting champion to Dan Howard at home here, the certainty of his return to dynamism and diligence tomorrow. Parliamentarian and businessman, Howard gave Minogue the impression of one who advanced steadily and relentlessly on some goal.

He flushed the toilet and stared at his face in the mirror. Howard's no mere base charmer, he thought. He had that air of durability, a man you could dependably expect to be there in twenty years, higher in the constellation of public life. Maybe shaking hands with one of these plain-suited, smiling Japanese billionaires, both togged out in hard hats as the sod is turned for a factory to manufacture whats-its in Portaree or Ennis or Gortaboher.

There was nothing providential about Sheila Hanratty's success either. She gave Minogue the same sense of diligence and control as did her husband. Tolerating Crossan, knowing that he knew that she and her husband could outlast him, she went her own way. Were they going to remain childless, Minogue wondered with sudden pity? Maybe a shared sadness there had given them their composure and solidarity?

He draped the towel carefully on the rail. There on the wall to his left was a print, a scene of stones and grasses topped by the orb of a golden sun. He squinted at the print close up, but found no place that he recognized exactly. Then he thought of that warm evening twelve years ago, young men and women, not yet out of their careless years. A summer's night with music spilling out into the night-street from the open doors and windows of the pub. The Portaree Inn, or Howard's Hotel as Minogue had known it in his youth, had been uninspiring enough, but Tidy Howard had seen his chance and he had plumbed, nailed, illuminated, and painted his way into presenting what tourists might imagine a traditional country inn could or should have looked like.

Minogue recalled the stone walls of the Portaree Inn shiny with coats of polyurethane, the light from brass lamps, their luster factory-aged, glistening on the stone. Locals who had laughed laughed no more. Their sons found work building houses and fixing roads, pouring drink for visitors. Commerce in high gear had pounced on Portaree, and a population that had known only episodic bursts of comfort in the form of work for non-inheriting children leaped at the opportunities. Minogue had himself observed the prospering village on his many forays to his home county over the years. The disingenuity of the "traditional" being hawked in the Portaree Inn — the Inn and the Out of it, Mick still called it — and the ingenuity of Tidy Howard, by now a figure of stature in more ways than one, had impressed Minogue. He had returned to Dublin after those holidays unable or unwilling to join in his brother's disparagement. Mick had carried on the farm and forced emigration was unknown to him, Minogue reasoned. Why be ashamed of wanting prosperity?

He shook himself out of his wonderings and left the bathroom. In the hall he heard Crossan's characteristic rapid-fire tones barked out behind the living-room door. He stopped by the closed door and swept his fingers over the top of his fly for the third time, again to make certain that he had zipped it and would not make a complete iijit of himself in front of Sheila Howard. He look about the hallway again. The staircase spindles were clear-lacquered over a cherry-colored varnish and the mahogany handrail curved as the staircase ascended. The hall door was a generous width, heavy between slim windows to both sides . . .

Minogue stopped his hand turning the knob and looked more intently toward one of the windows flanking the door. Gone, whatever it had been. A cat or a dog out by the cars? He let go of the door handle and stepped across to the window. He stared at the pebbled drive where his Fiat was parked, stubby and down-at-heel next to the Audi. Light from above the hall door outside did little more than confirm the shapes of the cars and outline the low hedges nearby. But someone was out there.

His fingertips began to tingle and he held his breath. His mind could not fasten on anything beyond his own quickening heartbeat now. He stepped back from the window but kept his eyes on the narrow strip of glass. Half-formed images tore through his mind: the muzzle of a gun firing, the sense that the world in smithereens had been thrown at impossible speeds into the air, the bomb's shock waves pounding his eardrums, the windscreen coming in at him like a lace tablecloth. His mouth turned chalky with the memory of his own near-fatal greeting from death. Sourness burned low in his throat and he heard his breath come out in a tight sigh.

He grasped the door handle, turned it sharply, and stepped through the doorway. Crossan said all right to Howard who said the day after tomorrow and I was already in touch with Father O'Loughlin and he knew the Bourkes years ago . . . Eyes turned toward the inspector and stayed on him. The broad window to his left, that graceful opening to the night outside that had pleased him before, now issued a silent shriek of alarm. Ice gathered in his chest.

"What is it?" someone said, a man's voice.

Minogue looked: Howard. The window remained in his side vision.

"What's wrong?" Crossan asked.

Minogue's thoughts returned. Damn: he had walked by the phone in the hall. Go back?

"I'm not certain now," he began. He tried to clear his throat. "I'm not sure now, but I think I saw someone outside."

Howard's eyes snapped into an intense stare.

"Does there be anyone around here at night?" Minogue asked.

"No," said Howard.

The inspector reached over to the strings and began pulling the curtains closed. Howard catapulted up from the sofa and grasped Sheila Howard's arm. Crossan stood to a crouch.

"We'd do well to stay low," Minogue whispered, and he sank to his knees. He put his hands out on the floor. He remembered playing horsey with Daithi and Iseult twenty years previouosly.

"Aren't we being kind of stu —" Crossan began.

"No!" snapped Minogue. The Howards were now on all fours and Crossan was kneeling.

"The phone —" Minogue started to say when the curtains danced. An instant later, even before he heard the chat-chat-chat of automatic fire, pieces of glass batted and tore at the curtains before cascading onto the floor. More tears appeared in the curtain and it danced quicker, as though being whacked by invisible hands. Minogue felt his cheek against the wood floor. A part of his mind not swept away in panic wondered about ricochets. He opened his eyes and saw the spots being punched across the ceiling. Fragments of cornice and plaster flew in the air and dust swirled under the ceiling light. Then it was dark. Minogue heard a lampshade being flung against the wall. Small, sharp things rained down on him. Wood splintered and he heard the window frame chirrup before it disintegrated. Minogue clenched his eyelids tight then against the maelstrom of dust and minute flying shards and he began to wriggle toward the doorway. Through his knees and elbows he felt the dull percussive thump of bullets as they hit the walls and were stopped by the stone bulk within the plaster.

Several seconds passed before he realized that the shooting had stopped. The remains of the ceiling light kept swinging wildly in the lull. The torn curtains settled slowly against the windowsill. Odd fragments of glass and plaster fell at intervals, making Minogue's heart leap each time. He steeled himself for the shooting to resume, for footsteps coming up the steps or running through the kitchen. He rubbed knuckles in his eye sockets and opened his eyes cautiously. Light from the hall sliced into the clouds of dust. He looked up at the wire of the ceiling light still swinging, the frayed curtains. Suddenly his body tensed: he heard running steps on the gravel outside.

They were going away from the house. As the sound of the footsteps receded, he began to hear gasps nearby. The fire glowed in the grate still, its yellow glow widened but dulled by the slowly falling dust. The room was now eerily calm.

"Are ye there?" Minogue whispered. An engine coughed down on the road and he listened intently, hoping that he could at least tell if it was a six- or four-cylinder or something.

"I think so," Howard answered.

"Yes," said Sheila Howard.

The engine didn't catch on the first turn of the key. When it did, the driver let out the clutch immediately and the tires bit in, leaving a rasping hiss as they scrambled for traction on the wet road.

"Is there anyone hurt?" Minogue hissed. No one answered.

"Alo!" Howard called out.

"Oh, don't worry about me," Crossan replied before coughing. He elbowed up from the floor. "This isn't my house at all," he spluttered and coughed again.

"We'll get out of here right away," Minogue said. "They may have left something behind that could do damage."

Like figures in a dream, the Howards, with Crossan following, scurried like monkeys to the door.

"Stay well down still," Minogue warned. He reached up from his crouch and switched off the hall light, then hurried the shambling, hopping figures toward the kitchen and the rear of the house.

CHAPTER 10

RUSSELL SHOWED UP an hour after the first Gardai from Ennis, and a half hour after two carloads of Guards from the Emergency Response Units. A half-dozen squad cars, an ambulance, and several vans now clogged the road by the gates. Minogue watched the superintendent slide out of his seat and listen while a sergeant briefed him. Minogue was sitting in the passenger seat of a squad car, the Howards in the back. Crossan, the last to be interviewed, was in a nearby squad car. Minogue had noticed that the ERU Guards didn't mix much with the uniformed Guards. The former had at least covered their guns after inspecting the house. Minogue looked down at the Elastoplast on the back of his hand. The air in the car was too hot now and he turned down the blower.

He spoke over his shoulder to the Howards.

"Are ye warm enough in the back?"

Sheila Howard was leaning into her husband and he had his arm around her shoulders. Dan Howard touched his forehead where a small, fine piece of glass had been expertly removed by an ambulance attendant.

"We are," said Howard in a whisper.

The interior light of the Toyota accentuated Howard's pallor. His curls were grayed lighter in parts by dust from the pulverized plaster. Minogue turned around. His elbows rubbed at the cloth of his jacket and reminded him that he had rubbed raw spots there from his movement across the floor during the fusillade. Sheila Howard's eyes were small and fixed on the headrest in front of her.

"Are they here yet?" Howard asked.

The bomb squad, he means, Minogue realized. He edged closer to the windscreen to be rid of the glare from inside the car and squinted at the house. His Fiat and the Audi seemed like sleeping, animate threats. He still couldn't believe that his own geriatric, baby-blue Fiat — a mobile part of his and Kathleen's home, full of receipts five years old, tinfoil from chocolate bars (Kathleen still liked Whole Nut, he recalled lazily), hairpins, screws and nuts, faded maps, and ancient paper handkerchiefs used and unused — all this, and now his car might harbor sudden death. He shivered in spite of the heat.

"I don't think so," he said to Howard.

The driver's door opened and Russell, strangely chaste in civvies, got in.

"Evening, Dan, missus," said the superintendent before he slammed the door against the damp air. "Don't be worrying now, I'm not about to drive off."

The Howards didn't seem to notice the humor.

"And the man himself," said Russell nodding to Minogue. "Alo Crossan's the fourth one?"

"Yes," said Minogue.

"Let's see Alo stand up in court and defend these gangsters now, after we catch them," Russell said. "See if tonight's work has given Alo a bit of insight into his clientele." He turned away from Minogue as best he could under the wheel and addressed the Howards.

"Sure ye wouldn't like to stop in at the 'ospital, just in case?"

Howard shook his head. Minogue watched Russell's eyes make a study of the Howards for competence, shock.

"We're going to wait for a bit of daylight to have a look at the cars," Russell went on. "We can get new sensors down from Dublin that might save us putting a few dents in the vehicles. Have ye a place to go tonight?"

"Well," Howard mumbled, and glanced at his wife.

"We'll have the Guards with ye night and day, that goes without saying," said Russell.

"All right," said Howard. "I mean, thanks."

"We found casings — spent ammunition, that is to say — out in the driveway," Russell said mildly. "It looks as if someone fired a submachine gun."

Again Russell looked the Howards over as if to assess their suitability for a task. Howard merely nodded.

"Have ye had any, ah, inkling, that this might happen?"

{ 177 }

"No," answered Howard. "I didn't think I'd be considered a . . ." He looked down at his wife. Target, Minogue finished the sentence within.

"Can I have a word with you outside a minute?" he asked Russell.

Russell seemed to consider granting a favor, then stepped out before the inspector. He met Minogue at the front of the Toyota and took a peppermint from his pocket. He dropped it onto his tongue, eyeing Minogue all the while.

"They're a bit out of it," said Minogue.

"And you're not?"

"Less so, I'm thinking. I tend to get the jitters later on."

"You've been under fire before, so," said Russell with heartless levity. "Dublin's full of excitement, they say."

Minogue put on a tight, insincere smile.

"Dull enough, compared to here."

Russell maneuvered the peppermint to his back teeth and bit it decisively.

"What were you up to with the Howards tonight? Aside from ducking bullets, like."

"Exchanging pleasantries and noting interior decorating tips to relay them to my wife."

"Huh. You and Alo Crossan. The Liberator."

Minogue reflected for a moment on Russell's cynical nickname for the lawyer. The Liberator, Daniel O'Connell, champion of Catholic Emancipation a hundred and fifty years ago, had seen his monster rallies eclipsed by the tactics of gelignite and guns. The superintendent's small eyes bored into him while the jaws worked at crushing the last pieces of lozenge.

"Crossan has given himself the mission in life of setting defendants free on the streets, gangsters that should be kept under lock and key. *Ad infinitum*," Russell said, grinding his teeth in final farewell to the peppermint.

"That's Latin," he added. He kept his blank stare locked onto Minogue's eyes.

"Who?" said Minogue, adverting to grammar. Russell ignored or misread Minogue's pedantry. He thumbed another lozenge into his mouth.

"Maybe even the likes of the boyos that did the work tonight," Russell said. "Wouldn't that look good on his gravestone: 'Shot by his clients'?" Minogue looked away from the superintendent to the arrival of a Hiace van.

"I think that Mr. Crossan plans to be around and working for quite a while," he murmured.

"Lie down with a dog . . ."

Russell let the proverb find its own way home in Minogue's mind.

"Have you people in mind for this shooting?" Minogue asked.

"Course we have. We'll be knocking on doors all over the county tonight. Will that put a dent in your holidays?"

Minogue considered the Howards' plight again. Howard did double-duty as a prosperous member of the new Ireland, a man of land and commerce as well as a parliamentary figure. He was an ideal target. Would the Howards ever feel safe in their house again?

"It'll put dents in a lot of holidays."

"You may well be right," Russell allowed. His crinkly hair, backlit by the headlights, glistened with a covering of fine rain.

"There could be jobs and factories lost on the head of this. Speaking of heads, now. Preliminary investigations" — he paused to sniff the air and survey the scene before him — "preliminary investigations tend to suggest that the job done there tonight on this fine house was fairly, can I say, 'fine-tuned.' The shooters went high. 'They needn't have ducked,' Sergeant Hanrahan inside tells me."

Minogue resisted the inclination to retaliate. He watched Russell lob another peppermint into his mouth.

"Rank amateurs tend to down high-flying birds when they pull triggers," the inspector said.

"Are you suggesting that this was attempted murder, so?"

"You decide that. After all, I'm on me holidays."

"You're hardly the kind of tourist that these gangsters had in mind of frightening now, I'd say," said Russell. "And by the way: you can have the tourism thing and still keep people on the land, to my way of thinking. People's livelihoods depend on the tourists, even tourists down from Dublin."

"You don't say, now. I was born and reared on a small farm. I've a brother who wouldn't be in the farming today if he hadn't been able to pick up a few fields over the years. There are families who can't bid down a man from Hamburg or Rotterdam."

"Not Dan Howard," said Russell, moving his lozenge around. "You're gone out of farming longer than you were ever in it. Parnell is history, O'Connell is history, and de Valera's history —"

"With O'Leary in the grave," Minogue interrupted.

"Who's O'Leary?"

"I can tell you that his politics didn't tend to the shopkeeper's side of the ballot."

"Look," said Russell as if he were concluding a deal that could shortly go sour. "Howard's popular. He had a good majority the last election. His father put Portaree and West Clare on the map. Anyway. You got nothing clear on the fella in the garden or whatever, did you?"

Minogue shook his head. The image of the flitting, shadowy figure upended his musing. "A shadow, really. I didn't even know if there was a mask."

"One car?"

"Yes. I'm fairly sure there was a driver waiting. One door slammed after the shooting. The car took off sharpish."

Russell crunched the lozenge and nodded toward the house.

"Looks like the job done on that holiday cottage. Might have hurt someone . . . by accident." Minogue tended to agree so he said nothing. The other possibility, quickly dismissed, was that a novice had pulled the trigger, not compensating for the upward jog of the barrel as the gun fired.

"Well, whether or which," said Russell. "We'll look into a few nests to see if some birds were home tonight. Each and every one of them. Cuckoos included." Minogue believed Russell meant Eoin Minogue.

"How's your German coming along?"

He was pleased to have his effect displayed immediately.

"How do you mean?"

"Someone is going to need fluent German for —"

"I get it, I get it," Russell snapped. "Don't you be fretting over that matter."

The superintendent made to head over toward a huddle of plain-clothes Gardai gathering around a van, but he stopped suddenly and glared at Minogue.

"Here," said Russell, "a word in your ear. I know more about you than you may think. Kilmartin wouldn't have you on board if you weren't good either. But you're too long out of County Clare to be up to the likes of Alo Crossan. I hope for your sake that you don't find yourself up the Suwahnee River with shite all over you, and then trying to tell me that Crossan told you this and Crossan told you that. 'Cause

Crossan may take you out for a long walk and that could easy bring you down the far side of the street from me. Alo Crossan could buy and sell the best brains in the country for shrewdness. If he makes an iijit of you, that makes an iijit of me and my men here . . . being as we're on the same side."

The superintendent nodded once, suggesting to the inspector that he was taking his own advice seriously. Then he pointed a finger at Minogue.

"Play by the rules here, Minogue." Minogue watched him walk away and then sat in the car.

"I think it might be a wise move to sort out alternative sleeping quarters for the next little while," he said.

Sheila Howard nodded.

"If we can get a lift we'll go into town and stay at the Old Ground," said Howard.

"You'll have a lift, all right. You'll have two armed detectives with ye," Minogue murmured. "Better get used to them. You'll have them awhile."

The inspector stepped out of the car again and went looking for a Guard to drive them into Ennis. The Guard, a prematurely bald smoker who rubbed at his nose a lot, was surly and tense. He grunted at Crossan as the barrister got into the Nissan. The drizzle haloed lights over the town as the two cars negotiated the roundabout coming into Ennis proper.

"Sun tomorrow but colder, I hear," said Minogue.

"Unk," said the detective. Minogue gave up. He realized that this Guard was probably anticipating a sleepless night by the Howards' door. Hoey or not, car or no car, delayed shock awaiting or not, Minogue decided that he was going to stop at a pub, walk back to the B & B and get a bath out of Mrs. McNamara's plumbing. He would not tell Hoey about this until the morning.

"Let me off at a good pub, can't you," he said to the detective.

"Good move," said Crossan.

"Ennis is full of pubs," said the detective.

"Well, don't trouble yourself on my account," Crossan said sharply. "Let me out at the Old Ground and I'll fend for myself."

The car stopped. Minogue watched the Howards getting out of the other squad car. Sheila Howard still looked blank as the detectives shepherded her in the door but her husband seemed to be coming through the dazed state. He waved shyly toward Minogue.

•   •   •   •   •

The drizzle seemed to be gone, but Minogue held out his hands to be certain. Beside him the O'Connell monument rose into the night. He walked alongside Crossan to Considine's pub. Chance cars moved sluggishly in the narrow street, whispering by the two men.

"I'll have the one with you," Crossan said.

The lawyer pushed the narrow door open. They took two stools at the bar where a half-dozen patrons idled. Considine's was one of the few pubs left in Ennis that still purveyed all manner of goods, from wellington boots to tea, flypaper to rashers, custard powder to sardines, as well as selling drink. A coal fire glowed in the grate, a color television glowed on the counter. When Miss Monaghan walked confidently onto the Miss Ireland stage in Dublin, Minogue almost expected her to walk out onto the counter.

An elderly woman with very thick lenses and a face like a kitten emerged from a door to the kitchen.

"Mr. Crossan," she murmured, and gave Minogue a nod. "A little inclement tonight."

"The prospect of better, ma'am" replied Crossan.

"That's the style,' said Mrs. Considine. She pushed back her glasses and grinned. Her brown teeth were all her own, Minogue saw, but they were small and feral.

"And how are ye all tonight anyhow?" she said as she sought out whiskey glasses.

Her greeting had that gentle, heartfelt tone that Minogue associated with talk at wakes, or when mentioning someone on whom great misfortune had fallen.

"Not bad," replied Crossan. "Considering."

"Paddy, the same as his honor here?" said Mrs. Considine to Minogue.

"Jamesons, instead, please."

Minogue watched Mrs. Considine's arthritic fingers manipulate the glasses and he wondered how Hoey was. He and Hoey had adjoining rooms at Mrs. McNamara's. Would Hoey be prowling about in the night? Would Tynan or Kilmartin have heard about the episode yet? God, he thought, if they put his name in the paper reporting the shooting, Kathleen'd be down dragging him out of Ennis by the neck. What could a man do?

They retired to a bench by the fire. Crossan nodded at the customers and they returned to their contemplative drinking, pretending to carry on with their conversation while watching Miss Monaghan and eavesdropping on what Mr. Crossan might have to say to his companion.

"There'll be no other mischief, I hope," said Crossan. "With the cars, I mean."

Mischief, Minogue thought. Flicking a gun to automatic and holding the trigger. He had a fleeting image of the boot-lid of his benighted Fiat popping up with the force of the small charge he expected the bomb squad would employ. Would the insurance pay for it? "Act of God"? "Civil unrest"?

"I'd as soon they find out for sure come the morning," Minogue murmured. The Jamesons scorched this throat.

"Be the laugh of the year if the Guards find whoever did this and I end up being hired to defend 'em."

"So thinks Tom Russell too," said Minogue.

"Tom Russell can shag off," said Crossan. "He'll eat humble pie soon enough. I'm not about to be put off now, no matter what. What about yourself?"

"Well, I sort of thought we could sort things out a bit over a breakfast tomorrow morning. You and me. Shea. Maybe it's a good time to call in on Naughton in Limerick. If I have a car at all, that is."

Crossan's eyelids drooped slightly over the eyeballs but this did little to relieve the intensity of his gaze at the television.

"The Howards with their bodyguards. By God, it's like Sicily or somewhere. Latin America . . ."

Minogue too looked over at the television.

"Turn it up, Mrs. C," said one of the customers, an old man with his hat resting on the back of his head, his thumbs in his braces where they were buttoned to his trousers. "And we'll listen to the girls."

"An occasion of sin, Tom Quinn," murmured Mrs. Considine. "Young ones walking around with hardly a stitch on them. They'll catch pneumonia, the half of them. Sure there's not a pick of fat on any of them, the poor things."

"Yerra, 'tis not fat we want, missus," said Quinn, unencumbered by the dentures he had made a habit of taking out and placing in his pocket each evening as he entered the pub. "The doctors are always tellin' us that fat is bad for us and that's no lie, now."

Mrs. Considine turned up the sound. The audience in Dublin clapped; the camera swung away and up to reveal platforms of flickering lights and starbursts of spotlights. Another camera rushed in on Miss Monaghan's mother and father who were being emotional in the audience. A ruddy-faced man still in his overcoat placed his empty pint glass on the counter with a crisp tap.

"Is our one up yet?" he demanded softly. "She's from Corofin, you know. Dwyers. Bofey Dwyers, the funeral director in Corofin. I have money put aside with Bofey for when the time comes. So as I won't be a burden."

"God, you were always the careful man, Florrie," said Mrs. Considine. "That's very thoughtful of you, to be sure."

Florrie took the compliment in his stride and continued looking solemnly at the television.

"You know not the day nor the hour," he said. Mrs. Considine sighed as she drew a new pint of stout for him.

"You're right, Florrie, you're right. But you don't look that close to the wood to me."

The camera sprang on a bikini-clad Miss Cork.

"Suffering Jesus that died on the cross," Quinn marveled.

The compère asked Miss Cork if she liked farming. She giggled and said she loved the outdoors.

"I'm not so keen on the farming myself," muttered Florrie.

Two young men entered the pub. One had reddened eyes and a smirk. Minogue, haggard, nodded at them and wondered if everyone looked familiar to him in County Clare. Both men ordered lager, and they took up watching Miss Cork giggling and shifting about on her high heels. Minogue wondered if Iseult had already stormed into RTE to throttle the producers of this sexist tripe. The patrons of Mrs. Considine's select bar warmed to the sparkling personality, poise, and deportment of Miss Cork. Minogue noted that her collarbones were very prominent and that, despite her large breasts, she looked underfed.

Bourke had thus been left very high and very far from dry, on the street after midnight, free to indulge his own bitterness. Abandoned, left to his fate? Minogue tried to imagine it: drunk — swaying, by all accounts — and alone on the street. What was Bourke feeling as he saw the

car drive away, the streets empty? Despair? Fury? Dan Howard was being driven home while James Bourke was left kicking his heels there on
the side of the street, pockets empty, drunk. Did Bourke feel used,
bought off? Howard could always call on money or help or comfort.
Bourke had had nowhere to turn. Naughton, Minogue thought, the
first Garda reported on the scene. Perhaps he could help Minogue see
where he was drifting, help him to a mooring at which he could tie up
the impressions and facts he was still unable to link. How drunk was
Howard? How drunk was Bourke? Too drunk to walk?

"Which one is she?" asked one of the newly arrived. His fogged eyes
suggested to the inspector that he had visited other pubs tonight.

"Can't you tell she's Cork the way she rolls her R's?" said the sage and
observant Florrie.

"Arra, man, that's only the high heels what does that," scoffed another.

Miss Donegal followed, arriving to accolades. She began talking effu-
sively of her interest in travel. Minogue turned to Crossan and wondered if he himself looked half as washed out as the barrister did.

"Tell me something," he said in a low voice to the barrister. "Is there a
part of you that likes to see the Howards haunted?"

"Haunted? What are you on about?"

"Bourke. The fire, the trial. Howard's the big banana here now."

Crossan kept his gaze on the television.

"What difference would it make to the facts of what we're about?"

Minogue wasted no time on delicacy.

"So you are."

"I must say," Crossan enunciated with care, "that there is a part of me
that's turned off by the pair of them."

"We shall so agree then."

"You don't understand. I don't envy Dan Howard or Sheila Howard. I
just think that Dan Howard inherited his due with Jamesy Bourke. And
I did poorly by Jamesy when he was alive. There's cause and effect at
work somewhere in the back of it all, even if I can't shine a light on it
for you. Do you know what I mean?"

Crossan leaned forward and rested his forearms on his knees, all the
while keeping his eyes on the screen.

"Let me hazard a guess now. You think you're listening to a sour fart
elbowing up to forty, with life passing me by, no family or kin, is it? A

misplaced sense of responsibility or something? Crank, maybe, huh? No, maybe it's more like you're seeing someone who wants to buy off his conscience."

"You're giving me a lot of choices, I'd have to say."

"Let me try a few more on you. Maybe I was starstruck by Sheila Hanratty? Hah. I was never so. But you're right in one suspicion which you haven't mentioned. I don't vote in Dan Howard's direction."

"Probably one of your best kept secrets, counselor. But there's something you're holding back."

"Tell me, so."

"If I could, I would."

"About me personally or about the Bourke thing?"

"Why separate them?"

Crossan guffawed loud enough for all eyes to turn from Miss Donegal's spotted bikini.

"As true as God, Minogue, you're a ticket. I think you're trying to see how far you can push me. Is it that you want to see me rear up at you?"

"I'm going along with you still because I will find out what happened to Jane Clark and Jamesy Bourke with or without your help. I want you to know that. I also want you to know that I'm doing it for my own reasons. I want you to know that if you've kept stuff back from me I'll crease you."

Crossan's smile lingered, diminished.

"A very genteel way of issuing threats . . . What's turned you so sour on me?"

Miss Donegal said that she'd like to say hello to her family in Gortahork, her sister in Glenties who was due to have a baby any day now, and all her friends in the Department of Finance in Dublin Castle. Lovely teeth, Minogue observed. The compère, his thinning hair expertly and sharply scalloped, blown, and sprayed toward his forehead like an unstable Roman emperor, invited her to go ahead.

"Well?" Crossan prodded.

"Well, indeed," Minogue grunted. "I'm trained to be suspicious. Don't take it personally."

Crossan's smile had dropped off his face and a look of resentment took its place. Minogue shivered and finished his whiskey. He realized that his body was aching. Images of the shooting, the curtains dancing, came to him and his stomach tightened. Miss Donegal waved. High heels and a winning manner, he thought.

"Nine tomorrow," he said. "See what we can salvage."

He wished Miss Donegal a silent goodnight — she was leaving the stage — and he stepped out into the night. Muddle-headed, shivering occasionally, Minogue took deep breaths. He wondered when the real effects of the episode at the Howards tonight would take hold of him and frighten him as it should. Crossan's face stayed with him. Weariness flowed over him in waves and the images came to him quicker: Sheila Howard's face, the light from the hallway radiating through the dust from the shattered plaster as it eddied out of the doorway. A moment of panic stopped Minogue as he thought of the bullets streaming in the window, ricocheting, tearing into his body. He knew, now that he was alone, he could not avert his thoughts about it. His knees felt watery and the cold air found his neck. He clasped his collar shut against his neck and his body gave one long shudder. A car passed the mouth of the street. Better get somewhere warm, get into bed, he realized.

The door to Considine's pub opened and Minogue watched one of the late arrivals look up and down the street. The man paused and raised a hand to his hair. He glanced at Minogue and their eyes met momentarily. Then he crossed to the other footpath and searched both ends of the street. Minogue stepped out, walking briskly and woodenly toward Mrs. McNamara's Bed and Breakfast.

·   ·   ·   ·   ·

Mrs. Mac related that Hoey had gone to bed an hour ago. She had almost finished one sock and was still as keen and bright-eyed knitting as she had been nearly four hours earlier.

"God, you look perished," she said. "Are you coming down with a cold, is it? I have powder and aspirin inside if you want."

"Thank you, no. Was Shea looking for me or anything like that?" Minogue asked.

"No, he wasn't. I thought he wanted to go out awhile, on account he looked a bit restless . . ." She paused to gather a stitch, smiled, and went on. "He had a cup of tea and a read of the paper. He said he wasn't really up to being himself lately."

She looked up suddenly.

"Are ye related, by any chance?"

Bewildered, Minogue almost smiled. Had she read something into them, some caretaker or parental thing? Clare people had indeed cornered the market on intuition.

"We watched a bit of Miss Ireland," Mrs. McNamara went on. "He fancied Miss Donegal to win."

"Same as myself," Minogue blurted out. Mrs. McNamara gave him a knowing smile.

"So you saw a bit of the talent where you were?"

"I left after Miss Donegal. She seemed very nice."

Mrs. McNamara smiled at the sock taking shape. "I recall her ankles being a weak spot."

Minogue shrugged.

"Ye mightn't notice, being men, but thick ankles have a habit of making a girl look very flat on her feet. Not to speak, you'll excuse me saying this now, of a girl having legs like a table. It's the diet down the country, I maintain. The fat tends to settle."

Minogue vaguely recalled an adage about Irishwomen having a unique dispensation from God to wear their legs upside down.

"Well. Miss Kerry walked away with it in the end," Mrs. McNamara sighed.

Her tongue moved around her lips as she negotiated a difficult part of the sock. She approached the toe now and Minogue watched her draw out the needle.

"Good for you," he said. She drew her tongue in and squinted at the television.

"But she had a tan on her that came out of a bottle," she declared. "How would she come by such a burn honestly in Kerry, I ask you? It's a cod."

"I suppose," Minogue allowed. "I'll be off now and good night."

"Ye must be very tired. What with all the work ye're doing?"

Minogue gave her a broad, fake grin.

"Do you know," she went on. "A woman down the street was telling me — now she does be around the town a lot more than myself — there's a lot of Guards in the town. Well, so she says, but she's very quick to pick up on things, don't you know."

Minogue said that he did know what Mrs. McNamara meant about other people. He paused by the door.

"I wonder if there's something going on here in town now."

He rested his hand on the door handle.

"Ennis is always full of life, as I recall," he said.

Mrs. McNamara looked up with a little mischief in her eye. "You know where you are. Down the hall, like."

• • • • •

The porpoises were smiling as they talked. He knew what they were saying without the need to hear their words. They surrounded him and he wondered if he should swim back to the surface to take a breath. But it was windy and raining there. Far cozier here. How could they talk underwater? Stay here if you like, one of them, he didn't know which one, told him. Why would you want to go back? It's better here.

It was neither light nor dark; the water was neither warm nor cold. The water must be clear because he could see anything he wanted. How far can we go before we have to turn back, he wanted to know. Look where we are now, he was told. Without any effort, he was able to stand in the water and look at the cliffs. I wanted to come here, I know, he said, but not like this. I must go home. That's all right, but you'd be foolish to want that, one told him. You can't keep me here if I don't want to stay. In an instant he was in the Shannon. Watch for nets, they said, but he couldn't see them anymore. Come back to the ocean and . . .

He was over the water now, clear of it, still, and he knew that wings had grown on his shoulders. Hoey was sitting on the rocks, staring out to sea. His feet were bare and his trousers were rolled up to his knees. I don't know, said Hoey. What was the question? Eilo McInerny was searching for seashells and periwinkles in the pools between rocks covered in seaweed. Her daughter stood next to her. Naked and unconcerned, she was brushing her hair. See, said Hoey, still staring at the swells of the retreating tide. Although it was Hoey, he knew, it wasn't Hoey's face. It was the face of that stranger again, the one with the mustache. In the air now. I'll fall. No. There was the fire. The stone walls were patterned like a child's puzzle, a maze. Help little Jane find her way home. He knew the way and he hovered over the blazing cottage. The man was screaming and his body was blackened. How can I see and it dark, he wondered, but he didn't care.

He looked through the burning thatch and the woman was there. Her body was white, untouched by the inferno. She lay on the floor, her eyes still and calm, looking up at him. It was Sheila Howard. This, she said. He looked away and the people had come. They leaned on the walls and

{ 189 }

watched the fire. The whole town is here, the whole county, he knew. The crowd was gathered in a perfect circle about the fire. He felt the heat on his wings and he wished for the ocean again. The faces turned up to the sky and he knew them all. Now you know, the porpoises said. I don't, he said.

·　　　·　　　·　　　·　　　·

He focused on a corner of the room. The bedroom was full of a milky light, soft shadows. No Kathleen? I'm in Ennis. Fragments of his dream came and left his mind. The unfamiliar smells of the house drew his thoughts away. He realized that he had slept deeply. Was that a radio on somewhere? He was stiff. It was half-past seven.

In the parlor, Hoey looked up from the *Clare Champion* and did a quick examination of the inspector's face.

"How's Shea?" said Minogue.

"Middling to good."

"I was about to knock," said Mrs. McNamara from the kitchen. She came through moments later, carrying a tray with steaming scones and tea.

"Are ye sure ye won't have a proper breakfast, a fry? I have rashers in the fridge."

"Thanks, no, Mrs. McNamara."

Minogue let the smell of brewing tea soothe him. Mrs. McNamara retreated to the kitchen.

"Did you have a good night?" he asked Hoey.

There had been no light under Hoey's door last night, he recalled. He had dithered over checking on him, but he had fallen into sleep himself while thinking about it.

"I did."

The inspector rubbed at his eyes. Hoey did look rested, less cautious. Mrs. Mac returned with jam.

"Did ye see outside?" she asked. Fog dense as smoke, still and white, had covered Ennis overnight.

"I did," said Minogue.

"You can't see twenty feet in front of your nose now," she said. "It must have got warm in the night."

She left with a warning to eat all the bread and scones. Minogue slumped into the chair as the door closed behind her.

"You look a bit shook," said Hoey. "Did you overdo it a bit last night?"

"Did I what? Wait'll I tell you what came my way last night." The memory of the swirling dust, the thumps as the bullets hit the walls made Minogue shudder.

"Miss Kerry?" said Hoey.

Minogue thought of the porpoises, the crowds watching the house on fire. He heard himself begin to tell Hoey about last night. He saw Hoey's jaw drop and his face take on the lines and arches of incredulity. He wondered how his own words came out with so little effort from his thoughts. It was only when Hoey, agog, jarred his own cup into his saucer and spilled tea that Minogue realized the effect his story was having on him.

"Yes," he murmured, and shivered again.

"Jesus." Hoey sat taut over the table now. "You're joking me. Why didn't you wake me up or something?"

"For what?"

"So's I could, you know . . ."

Minogue shrugged.

"Is there any follow-up on it yet?"

The inspector shook his head. "I'm going to get the car now. I hope it's still in one piece."

Hoey narrowed his eyes and flicked a glance at the closed door.

"Wait a minute, here," he said. "Do we really need to get caught up in some shooting match here in Ennis? Do we? This sort of says to me that it's time to pull back. For the moment, at any rate."

Minogue did a quick calculation of Hoey's words, his tone.

"With those Response Units foostering around, like," Hoey added. "It's like waiting for something to blow up."

Minogue didn't want to argue with a Hoey who this morning looked almost robust compared to how Minogue himself felt. He dodged Hoey's eyes.

"Well. I'll have a wash and a shave and we'll mosey on over to the hotel for now."

• • • • •

An unmarked Garda car materialized out of the fog, a creature with lights for eyes. Faces turned to look at Minogue as the car purred alongside. A face on the passenger side nodded at Minogue, and the car pulled in ahead of the two policemen.

"Who're these fellas?" asked Hoey.

The far end of the street disappeared into the fog. Through the muffled whiteness Minogue heard the sounds of Ennis — clanging aluminum kegs as they were slung empty onto the brewery lorries from the doors of pubs, the shutters being rolled up on shops, the dull thumping of a hammer on metal somewhere close by — being carried on all around them.

"Cuddy, from Limerick. Special Branch. I met him down at the brother's farm and I down visiting."

"How's the man?" said Cuddy.

"Better met than the last time, I'm thinking," said Minogue. Cuddy gave a wan smile and nodded at Hoey.

"Shea Hoey," said Minogue. "Works with me."

"Are ye official here?"

"No, we're not. But there seems to be an oversupply of Guards who are."

A squeaky transmission erupted from a radio in the car. The driver turned it down.

"Were ye in town here last night?" asked Cuddy.

"Matter of fact, we were."

Cuddy looked down the street before confiding more.

"We're going to keep up the pressure. Something has to give, I just know it."

He looked up under his eyebrows at Minogue as if daring him to recall aloud the episode at the farm. The inspector looked beyond the policeman at the shroud of fog.

"Good luck," he said to Cuddy.

The car slid down the street ahead of them before being swallowed up in the whiteness.

Alo Crossan was not yet in the dining room, but the Howards were. So were two detectives — replacements for the ones Minogue had traveled with last night. Their eyes were on Minogue and Hoey from the moment they appeared in the door of the dining room. One of the detectives stood and the other kicked his chair back slightly with a coiled, careful nudge of his leg, Minogue noticed, as he laid his hands in his lap. His jacket came open as he leaned forward in his chair.

Howard waved, his mouth full.

"They're Guards," he struggled to say around the food. "Don't worry."

The Howards wore the same clothes he had seen them in last night.

Minogue wondered if he himself could ever get away with such dereliction and still look well-dressed. Howard, with his shirt open two buttons, unshaven, looked genially rakish. Sheila Howard looked relaxed and curious. Something in the couple's appearance startled the inspector. He felt the beginnings of a blush as he approached them. They looked to him like a couple full and languid after a night of lovemaking. Howard made an elaborate swallow.

". . . absolutely refused to eat a breakfast above in a hotel room," he said. Minogue felt Sheila Howard's eyes on him.

"Yes, yes," the inspector replied, working clumsily around an image of Sheila Howard's body. He glanced at her by way of greeting. The detective sat down and the other sat back in his chair with a nod.

"Howarya," one said to Hoey.

Dan Howard waved his arm at two vacant chairs. "Join us, can't you?"

"Thanks, but we're expecting company." Minogue looked at his watch. It was ten minutes before nine.

"How are you now?" asked Minogue.

Howard exchanged looks with his wife.

"Could be better," he said. "But sure, considering the alternatives . . . Yourself?"

"I've been worse," Minogue avoided. "Any news from the house?"

Howard sat up and crossed his ankles.

"Yes, there is, and it's not bad at all. There was nothing in the cars. And there's nothing else suspicious about the house itself. So there."

"Was that your yoke up at the house?" one of the detectives asked. "The blue one?"

Minogue glanced over at the boxer's nose, the untidy mustache.

"Yep. Is it in one piece?"

"For the most part. Sure, that wasn't a new car anyhow."

"That Fiat was and is a damn fine car," said Minogue. "What did they do to it?"

"They wheeled up a big shield. First they shook the car, then they drilled the lock on the boot —"

"They drilled out me lock?"

"The robot did."

"With the video camera next to it," the other detective piped in. "That's it. Never saw the likes of it in action. It was great."

His partner nodded, sharing in an accomplishment he had had no part in. Minogue sat down heavily next to Hoey. A waitress approached. Minogue looked to the window: no Jamesy Bourke standing vigil across the street ever again, he thought. At least the fog was beginning to lift. The waitress picked at a button on her blouse.

"I dunno," said Minogue. "Coffee for a start, I suppose."

Dan Howard rose from the table and cocked an eye at the inspector. Me? Minogue fingered his chest. Howard nodded in the direction of the foyer.

"I'll be back in a minute."

Hoey shifted in his chair and reached for his cigarettes. The hardcase with the mustache accompanied Howard to the foyer.

"I have to make me confession," Howard said to him. "You wouldn't want to listen in on my sins, would you, but?"

The detective backed away a couple of paces. Howard's amused expression lingered as he made a quick search of Minogue's face.

"A word out of earshot of Sheila, if you don't mind," Howard began. "I woke up shaking this morning, I can tell you. But not that shook that I couldn't see that the thing last night wasn't about murdering anybody." He paused and smiled. "What do you think, yourself?"

Minogue studied the smile.

"I'm inclined to agree with you."

"Publicity, I put it down to," said Howard. "Brazen, cocky. A half-arsed effort to be like the War of Independence, making the country ungovernable."

"I thought the parliamentarians and public service were well on the way to achieving that already."

Howard chortled.

"You still have your wits about you anyway. But I'm sure part of the plan might be to have the likes of me close shop and hide up in Dublin."

"Which you may do? . . ."

"Hide, no," Howard murmured. "Stay there awhile, yes. I was going to go up for a few weeks to finish off the sitting anyway. There are bills coming up for final reading and . . . Well, you know, the hazards of public office, I suppose."

"Going back up to Dublin?"

Howard smiled. "Not that alone. No. I meant shootings. I imagine that Alo wouldn't be so keen on this side of public life, any more than I am myself."

Said so easily, it took Minogue several seconds to realize that the remark had carried a charge of something else. What had he missed?

"As to? . . ."

Howard looked at some point on Minogue's forehead.

"You know that Alo has his own plans for public office, I take it."

The inspector felt his cobwebby, morning mind awaken with a sharp stab. He looked again to Howard's face but all he met with was the fixed look, a stare both sardonic and intent.

"What are you saying?"

"I'm saying that Alo will be running for something. I wondered if you knew. Yes, County Council, I hear. Fine man that he is, Alo may not have considered the kinds of attention we received last night. Very effective way to get national attention, firing off gunshots in the window of the local TD's house."

Howard folded his arms and leaned against the wall.

"I'm sure someone will be happy to take the credit for last night soon enough. They'll not be frightening me out of office, I can tell you."

Minogue thought of Crossan and felt his resentment grow suddenly large. The detective with the mustache crossed the foyer toward them just as a young man in a leather jacket came through the door of the hotel. Howard's smile turned into a grin.

"Thanks be to the hand of God" he murmured. "Tom Neilon from *The Clare Champion*. The press is here — we're saved. I'll see you again?"

Minogue stood aside and studied the carpet. His thoughts staggered around, colliding into one another. Was Crossan having him on all this while? He trudged back to the table. Crossan had arrived and was talking to a wary Hoey about horse-racing, something Minogue had never heard Hoey show an interest in before. The lawyer seemed to pick up on Minogue's mood.

"Trouble?" asked Crossan.

Minogue sat down on the edge of the chair and looked beyond Crossan's shoulder to Sheila Howard. To an innocent eye, she was looking through a newspaper, but Minogue noted her attention directed in her side vision toward his table.

"That was a hell of a thing last night," said Hoey to Crossan.

"Don't be talking, man," said Crossan. "It was wild."

"It's hard to imagine that whoever was doing the shooting was actually meaning to kill anybody," Minogue said in a low voice.

"How does it change things for us?" Crossan said. "That's what we need to decide this morning."

The inspector felt the resentment turn to anger as he turned to Crossan.

"There's something I just heard which may change our approach, counselor. Dan Howard said something to me that I wish I'd known before now. Concerns you, counselor. Or should I say councillor?"

Minogue gave Crossan the full weight of his stare which, along with the calm tone and expression, had unnerved even the likes of Kilmartin. A screen seemed to come over Crossan's eyes and his eyelids relaxed a little. He looked down his nose at Minogue.

"Go ahead, Guard," he said. "And don't stint yourself either."

"You are interested, involved, planning, intending — whatever — to run for some public office, something in the line of politics, aren't you?"

Crossan spoke with lighthearted whimsy. "Well, I thought I might take a run at being a town councillor here in Ennis." He arched his eyebrows. "Do you think I'd be right for the job, now?"

"If you're planning to waltz into public office by dragging people through the mud or, perish the thought, playing trick-of-the-loop with me, I can tell you that —"

"That I'd be the equal of any of the blackguards in politics at the moment?"

Hoey folded his arms and studied the sugar bowl.

"That you'd be a damn sight worse than them," Minogue retorted. "You won't be making a monkey out of me en route either, mister."

Crossan's eyes locked on Minogue's.

"That's a very harsh judgement, Your Worship. Rest assured I'll be launching an immediate appeal."

"That's nothing to what will happen if I find out that you've been codding me here."

"Don't be such a gobshite, Minogue!"

The inspector leaned forward in his chair.

"Don't you be stupid, counselor," he retorted. "If I think that you inveigled us down here or concocted bits of information to suit your own ends, all as a way to run the Howards into the ditch because you have some grudges —"

"Hah! You must be the right gobshite entirely! Do you think I'm interested in making you look stupid while Dan Howard gets dirt on him, is that it?"

"Declare your interest then," Minogue growled.

"I belong to no party. No faction, no jobs-for-the-boys, no back-scratchers! No fat-arse gombeens! What I would like to do, you probably wouldn't understand. But for the record, I plan to go for election to Ennis town council. That way, I can get houses built for poor iijits so that they won't end up breaking-and-entering and robbing and beating the shite out of one another, and then sloothering up to my door bothering me. I want to be put out of business. So there."

Crossan leaned in over the table and pushed aside cups and saucers. Hoey blew smoke out the side of his mouth and blinked at the inspector. Sheila Howard glanced over as did the detective at the table next to her. Crossan waited until she had returned to her newspaper and then he spoke behind his hands.

"They're trying to derail you with this case —"

"This is not 'a case,'" Minogue snapped. "And, for that matter, it wouldn't take much this morning, with you trying to hang some class of a Chappaquiddick around Howard's neck."

"Don't walk away from it now," said Crossan.

"What are we walking away from? Except for finding out that people did stupid things. Guards included."

Crossan pointed at the table as if explaining a route on a map.

"Lookit," he said, "Jamesy Bourke is dead. Whatever life he had before that was torn away from him by the State. Jane Clark went back to where she came from little more than a bucketful of cinders."

"And you want to tar-and-feather the Howards and a few Guards on the head of it?" Minogue asked.

"Are you going to ignore what we've discussed? Bourke's trial?" Crossan raised his hands. "Can you? Do you think for one minute that I'd sit here telling you this if I didn't believe in what I was doing?" He looked to Hoey as though he were a judge considering an appeal.

"Don't look at me," Hoey murmured. "I'm from Galway."

Crossan turned his attention back to Minogue again. He spat out the words in a harsh whisper.

"You're backing away from your own instincts. Covering for your pals beyond in the Garda station. For all I heard about you, Minogue, now I know you're a quitter."

"Oh, so you did some research, did you, before you put out the bait?"

"Yes, I did — I freely admit it. It was too good a thing to pass up when your nephew hired me. I began to think you weren't the common-or-garden cop so then I thought well, this must be meant to happen. The fates had turned kind to Jamesy for once in his bloody existence!" Crossan sat back, his eyes still blazing.

"But what I had underestimated was the degree to which Guards will cover up for one another."

"I do not," said Minogue. "So shut up throwing things at me. I have enough lumps on me head from pulling down things off high shelves, things I didn't know were so damned heavy and awkward when I got the notion to take a look at them."

"What is it, then?" Crossan pursued him. "Is it frightened you are after last night?"

"I think differently about the Howards after last night." Minogue heard the defensive tone in his own voice. "So I don't much like you sitting in their house, slashing away at them, in however clever a manner."

"Hah," Crossan growled, and sat back with an expression of disbelief. His eyes widened in glee and he glared at Minogue.

"You like her nibs, do you?" He nodded toward Sheila Howard but kept his eyes on Minogue. "And the heroic Dan standing steadfast here in outlaw country and won't be intimidated? Our Clare Camelot, by Christ!"

Minogue said nothing but returned Crossan's look with the policeman's neutral observation of a specimen.

"Heroes, is it?" Crossan went on. "Well, you wouldn't be the first to fall under her spell, so you wouldn't. Dan the man owes half his success to her. Twice the man he'll ever be. He has the charm and the rest of it but she's the backbone of the operation. Make no mistake, Minogue. The Howards are going places. 'She'll drive Dan to the Park,' they say here. And that's his supporters saying that behind their hands, too."

A cease-fire arrived in the form of the waitress who began unloading plates. Hoey might be right, the inspector reflected. Get the hell out of the way of whatever was going to happen in the wake of last night's shooting. Leave County Clare to the brick-faced gymnasts and ditch-crawlers with their submachine pistols and their souped-up, prowling Granadas.

"Don't be rehashing public house gossip about the Howards to me," Minogue murmured. "The Howards can do what they want."

Crossan slouched back in his chair and joined his fingertips under his nose. Now, looking over at Minogue, his searching eyes seemed monstrous. Minogue looked away in exasperation toward the window. For a split second he saw the tall, bearded Bourke and his dog at the wall across the street. He shook his head and blinked. His nerves were more rattled than he had realized. When Crossan spoke again, his voice had taken on the scornful, challenging tone of the courtroom.

"So tell me what you want to tell me then, and get it over with."

Minogue let him hang for several seconds. The same Bourke screaming in his dream last night, the circle of faces gathered around the blazing cottage.

"I want to eat my breakfast," he said.

Crossan rounded on him.

"So you've been put off by Dan Howard putting a flea in your ear then? Or is it because her nibs has put stars in your eyes?"

There were small trembling shapes in front of Minogue's eyes when he looked away from the window at Crossan. His chest was swollen with the anger and his arms tingled. Hoey divined his anger and sat forward, closer to the lawyer, staring across at his colleague's face. Crossan looked away momentarily, then returned to the inspector's reddening face. Crossan dropped his knife and fork on the table and reached into his jacket pocket. He drew out an envelope and dropped it in front of Minogue's plate.

"What's this?" he asked. "More snapshots?"

Crossan didn't reply.

Minogue flicked it over and saw that it was addressed to himself. He fingered through a hole in the flap and tore open the letter. The page was a photocopy of what looked like a bill.

"There are two names on there that you'll recognize," said Crossan. "I didn't anticipate having to give you this so soon, but I'm not going to sit here and fight a losing battle with the pair of ye."

Minogue read the name Thomas J. Naughton. Hoey wiped his fingers on the serviette. Minogue handed him the paper.

"That's a dividend statement for Naughton. He's a shareholder in that outfit. Dalcais."

"What's Dalcais?"

"Dalcais owns four hotels, one folk village, and a castle where the Yanks sit down to medieval banquets after they are carted off the jumbos down in Shannon."

"Put things together then," Minogue said to Crossan. "Let me hear it from you."

"I'm giving you this to catch Naughton on the hop. He might just clam up on you. Naughton was the first Guard to the fire that night, remember. Ask me who owns 53 percent of Dalcais."

"The Howards."

"Not bad," said Crossan.

"Why didn't you tell me this last week?"

"Because I didn't need to and you didn't need to know either. It'd prejudice matters."

"My God, man, I didn't know you had such delicate nerves," said Minogue. "No more shenanigans. What the hell else have you up your sleeve?"

"I admit that I need ye here to shake up the place. That's my strategy here. Ye're Guards, ye're down from Dublin. We need to shake up the box and see what falls out —"

"Give us a bit of plain English, man," Minogue cut in.

"I told you that I couldn't find anything in the trial records that'd help Jamesy. And I'm not optimistic that anything can come from a full transcript of the trial either. My only real chance is to put a bit of pressure on people and see what happens."

"Damn-all will happen except buckets of trouble if you're playing us for iijits," said Minogue.

"You want a token and you got it," Crossan resumed in a scoffing tone. "How did I get it and copy it? I tracked down the firm that handles Naughton's stuff — his will and deeds and the rest of it. I paid a clerk by the name of Margaret Hickey a hundred quid to get me anything on Naughton. Christ, man, that's the damn prejudice I'm talking about! To hell with Naughton and the rest of them — it's myself I'm throwing to the wolves here!"

Minogue glared one-eyed at the lawyer.

"Now. Are ye still in, or what?"

"What are you going to do if and when you have to tell anyone how you came by this?" asked Minogue.

"Do you really need to ask me that? You're the Garda inspector. The quiet fella here in the corner is taking it all in too. My goose is well and truly cooked now. I have no other tricks for ye. So what do ye say?"

Minogue poured lukewarm coffee from the jug and tried to think.

The most he could do was dither. Crossan had taken a big risk handing him this paper and telling him in front of Hoey what he had done. And yet it could lead into another cul-de-sac. Wasn't Naughton entitled to buy and sell any damned shares he wanted? Couldn't he sink his money into any investment he might have heard about during his years in Ennis? Like nuns, teachers, and publicans, Guards were notoriously cute with their money.

Minogue looked at the photocopy again.

"How long has he been receiving dividends?"

Crossan shook his head. "I could find out but I'd be digging me grave deeper. Listen. I was looking for where to put some pressure. Any weak point. Naughton had the name of being an alcoholic, but he had it well under wraps. Didn't you ever meet an alcoholic that kept at it for years and years, hail-fellow-well-met? Could do his job and turn up every day but had his bottle hidden above the cistern in the jacks, hah?"

To his side Hoey blinked and froze. Minogue nodded.

"Well, Naughton was one but he didn't drink all his money by the looks of that. It's not a fortune by any means, but it'd pad out a pension into real comfort. I'm still waiting for your answer."

Minogue glanced at Hoey.

"We'll proceed with Naughton in Limerick this morning," he said.

Crossan's face seemed to lift as Hoey's frown descended. The barrister flipped his wrist over and drew his cuff back from his watch.

"It'll take you until dinnertime if you go to Limerick right now. I even have Naughton's address here. Find out from him —"

"What do you think we should be finding?" Hoey asked.

"Ah, for Christ's sake, don't you start in on me now!" Crossan snapped. "Have ye forgotten everything we've talked about?"

Minogue repeated Hoey's question. "What do you think we should be finding?"

Crossan spoke in a controlled, even tone.

"Garda incompetence. New evidence. Changes in testimony. Gaps in testimony. Inconsistencies in testimony. Don't tell me that you decided to spend your off-time down here only because I put you up to it!"

"You're right, I won't," said Minogue.

Crossan looked at his watch again and drew in a breath.

"When do you think you'll get back from Limerick? I mean, how long do you think you'll be? . . ."

Minogue was rubbing his eyes slowly and distractedly. He kept it up for a half-minute before he paused, opened his eyes, and looked at Hoey.

"As long as it takes, counselor," he said.

Crossan bounded up from his chair, plucked the photocopy from the table, and launched his lanky body toward the foyer.

"I'll phone a taxi for ye this very minute," Minogue heard him say.

$$\bullet \quad \bullet \quad \bullet \quad \bullet$$

"What a tricky bastard," said Hoey.

Minogue shrugged. His anger was gone now.

"Well, a point in his favor has to be the way he's put himself out with the Dalcais stuff," Minogue offered. "But I just wish to God he had told us about his plans before Dan Howard told me."

"Very tricky people down this part of the country," said Hoey. "Still don't trust him as much as . . ."

A yawn stole the rest of Hoey's words. Minogue's Fiat leaned into a bend on the dual carriageway that skirted Shannon Airport. The fog had given way to a blue sky. The sun was hard and bright on the windscreen of Minogue's car. A jet passed low overhead, its shadow racing across the fields inland.

"No rest for the wicked," said Hoey, and returned to looking out the window.

Minogue turned the mirror down until he saw the boot-lid bouncing against the rope he had been given to tie it down. His thoughts went to Naughton, and he recalled Naughton's growl when he had phoned with a wrong-number yarn. Naughton was sixty-six. Still going strong, was Crossan's arch description. Not bad for a drunkard, in other words. He thought of Hoey then. The inspector's misgivings broke free of their leash and tumbled into words.

"Shea, it just occurred to me that I may have drawn you into a big pile of . . ."

"What?"

Minogue tried to put some order on the words.

"I wonder if maybe I'm doing something very, very stupid indeed here." The words dried up. His mind returned to the porpoises as the suburbs of Limerick joined up with the road. He imagined them smirking as they turned from the starlit harbors of the west of Ireland out to sea.

"Look, Shea, I know you're far from keen at this stage. I could leave you off at the train station as long as you promise me —"

Startled, Hoey looked over at Minogue. The inspector braked hard for a traffic light by the Gaelic Athletic grounds. They were a mile yet from the Sarsfield Bridge into Limerick.

"I mean, it's nothing to me basically," Minogue went on, "I can take it, but you —"

"I have my career to consider?"

"Well . . ."

"Well, what?" said Hoey.

Minogue started off from the light but forgot that he had left the car in third. The Fiat staggered and stalled.

"I don't want to pull you down with me," Minogue muttered.

Hoey began to laugh. He tried to stop but he couldn't.

CHAPTER II

MINOGUE KNOCKED and inclined his head to the door. Naughton's house was at the end of a terrace. Heavy curtains hung from the one window next to the door. The window wells were freshly painted with a thick cream gloss and the two upper windows had double-glazed aluminium frames. Minogue stepped back and looked at the upstairs window. Hoey was standing in the sunshine at the end of the terrace. The door opened abruptly and Minogue turned to face a tall man with a full head of white hair brushed back over a pink face. Two clear and piercing blue eyes stared into Minogue's. A light scent of shaving soap and brilliantine came to the inspector, followed by house smells of tea and a fry. Naughton had said something but Minogue hadn't heard. He had been watching the harelip scar as Naughton had uttered the words.

"Hello there, now," said Naughton again.

He was wide and big and his hands hung low alongside his thighs. There was something of the giant about him, Minogue thought, like those ex-RIC men he had known. The physical size of those precursors of the Gardai had been adduced to be one of the prime drivers of law enforcement until the guerilla warfare of the War of Independence had swept away any grudging respect accorded them.

"Good day to you now, Mr. Naughton," he began. "I'm Matt Minogue, a Guard . . ."

Naughton's eyes were on Hoey now, who had sidled down to stand beside Minogue.

". . . and this is my colleague, Seamus Hoey."

Naughton folded his arms. Minogue looked at the bulk straining the jumper. A bit of a pot on him but by no means gone to seed. A bachelor, a retired Guard, who still wore a collar and tie under his jumper.

"Well, I haven't met ye before," said Naughton. He looked up and down the terrace. "Are yiz here on some kind of business?"

"We're down from Ennis —"

"Are ye attached to Ennis Station?"

"No, we're not actually —"

"So where are yiz from then?"

Minogue paused and glanced at the old woman passing on the footpath behind them.

"Good morning, now, Mr. Naughton," she crowed.

"Isn't it now," said Naughton.

Minogue looked beyond Naughton into the house.

"Come in, I suppose," said Naughton. "Come in."

The front room was a musty parlor, spotlessly clean and unused. The inspector sat on a hard-sprung sofa and looked around the room. There were photographs of men in Guard's uniforms of thirty years ago, one of an old woman with the face of a mischievous child, bunched in a smile. The fireplace had been fitted with a gas-burning unit complete with bogus glowing coals. A nest of tables squatted under the window. Between two cumbersome chairs stood a buffet with glass doors over a series of drawers.

"Ye'll have something?" said Naughton.

He rubbed the back of his huge right hand with the thumb of his left. Minogue associated the gesture with big men who could never lose a teenage awkwardness about their size.

"Ah, no, you're all right there, thanks," said Minogue.

"Are yiz sure now? A smathan, even."

The inspector shook his head and stole a glance at Naughton's face again as he made to sit down. If this was what recourse to alcohol in a big way did, Minogue wondered, then maybe there was something to be said for it. But no. Something about Naughton put the inspector in mind of a bull elephant, a creature who might go suddenly, felled by a massive stroke, crashing to the ground.

"From Ennis, you say now," said Naughton. He sat forward, elbows on his knees, a massive hand clasped around the knuckles of the other.

"Yes."

Minogue tried to put on a friendly face, but he continued to be distracted by details. The soapy smell from a face meticulously shaved, the faint smell of shoe polish, the razor nick by Naughton's ear, the outline of the braces that the retired Guard still attached to his trousers. A life of habit, a man who liked and needed routines.

"But yiz are not Ennis."

"We work in Dublin."

"God help yiz, so."

Minogue tried again to smile.

"It's gone desperate in Dublin, I believe," said Naughton. "Not safe to walk the streets, they say."

"I suppose," said Minogue. "But sure troubles can come anywhere. The divil has his own guide, as they say."

"'Tis true for you. Tell me, are you a sergeant?"

"I'm an inspector, in actual fact. They kicked me upstairs to be rid of me."

Naughton issued a skeptical, knowing wink.

"I came down on a visit to my relations this little while back," Minogue said. "And I, er, ran into a man above in Ennis. He told me a few things about events back, now, a good number of years back . . ."

"Who?"

"Aloysious Crossan."

Naughton scratched the back of his head.

"I knew him," he muttered. "He's a big name in the law. Is he still at it?"

Minogue nodded. "To great effect too, I believe."

"Hah," scoffed Naughton. "He was mighty sharp with his mouth as I recall. But he had the name of being good for them that needed it."

He sniffed and gave Minogue a grin with no warmth in it.

"You know yourself," he said.

Minogue raised his eyebrows.

"His clients," said Naughton, his hands working over one another. "He hires himself out to scuts."

"I've heard that said," said Minogue.

"If and he was a woman, he'd be a prostitute," Naughton added. He glanced down at his own hands. Like a boxer listening to a pep talk, Minogue thought, a horse of a man. "But sure you wouldn't know these days, with the homos and what have you, would you? Anything goes, nowadays."

The blue eyes that came up from the stilled hands had a glaze of satisfied amusement. Minogue's eyes were drawn to the wiry white hairs, like pigs' bristles standing out by Naughton's collar.

"He is a Protestant, all right," said Minogue. "But you probably knew that."

"Prostitute, I said."

Minogue feigned relief. "Oh. That's not so bad. I thought you said Protestant."

With no movement that Minogue could detect, the face had become blank and hard.

"What do yiz want?" he said.

Minogue thought about the house afire in his dream, himself weirdly aerial over the blaze, with the sea black under the stars and the porpoises racing out to sea.

"How much did you have to drink the night of the fire?"

"What fire? What are you talking about?"

"Jane Clark. Jamesy Bourke. Dan Howard. You."

"Fuck off. Inspector or no inspector, you're nothing to me. Get out of here."

"Or you'll call the police?"

"Fuck off outa my house."

"Where was she when you got to the house?"

Naughton's hands reached for the armrests.

"Where was she?"

Naughton propelled himself up. Hoey also stood. The inspector raised a hand toward Hoey.

"Take yourself up and outa my house this minute."

"Phone. Go ahead," said Minogue, and concentrated on the sunlit window.

He wondered if Naughton would take a swipe at him. He leaned slightly to his left, away from the giant. Naughton clumped by him and walked down the hall. Hoey cleared his throat and rattled his cigarette box in his pocket.

"Are you sure you want to go at him like this?"

"Head first, Shea," Minogue whispered. "No other way at this stage. If he's a drinker, got to shake him. And Eilo McInerny got it hard from Naughton too. Man's a bully, Shea. We're going after him."

"We could get run out of the place and get nothing," said Hoey. "Except maybe a thick ear."

Minogue reconsidered his strategy for a moment. Shock treatment for a drinker might backfire. Who would Naughton phone? A minute passed. Hoey shrugged, took out his cigarettes, and lit one. He made a halfhearted survey of the room for an ashtray. Minogue watched him all the while, listening for Naughton's voice.

"You're in the pink, anyway," Minogue murmured. "Excepting for those lungs of yours."

Hoey took the cigarette out of his mouth and eyed Minogue, the fag poised in his hand.

"It's the excitement. Never a dull —"

Minogue knew immediately that it was glass, and he was first out the parlor door. The door to the back room was closed. He opened it and looked down to the tiny kitchen where Naughton was stooping. The rest of the room was taken up with a table, television, and dresser. A red-faced Naughton stood up. The smell of whiskey reached Minogue and he looked down at the shattered bottle, the pool by Naughton's feet.

"Get to hell out of this house," said Naughton in a growl, "or I won't be responsible for what happens to you."

"Who will you be responsible to?"

"Fucking smart-arse. Get out to hell!"

"You can't hide in a bottle, Guard," said Minogue.

"Who the hell are you to be coming around here, without a by-your-leave? You come marching in here, without any notice —"

"What do you need notice of?"

"If you had've phoned or let a man know there was an inquiry . . ."

Hoey's smoke stung Minogue's eyes.

"You march in here with accusations . . . By God, I'm going to have you drummed out. You'll be in court over this, so help me." Naughton's hands turned into fists.

"Easy does it, now," murmured Hoey.

"Who are you, you pasty-faced iijit? No wonder you have two black eyes. I'll have you thrown out of your job too, so I will."

Minogue looked at the chairs tucked in under the table.

"Why don't we just sit down like civilized human beings for a few minutes? And discuss the matter in a calm, gentlemanly manner."

"Ye're not in that category," Naughton called out. "By Christ, I'm glad I never had to meet the likes of yiz on the force. We were aboveboard and dacent in my time."

He reached out suddenly and pointed at Minogue. Hoey stepped back.

"We didn't take our orders from maggots like Alo Crossan. The shite-hawk. Hah, look at ye! Hook, line, and sinker, bejases! He's got you codded. It's sorry for you I should be."

"You said in testimony that Jamesy Bourke was falling-down drunk when you got to the cottage. That the whole place was an inferno."

"Do you know what a thatched roof is?" Naughton sneered.

"But you were there when the fire was put out. And you were the first policeman in the door."

"What if I was?"

"Where did you find her?"

"What difference does it make to you where she was?" Naughton's voice rose. "She was gone to glory by then."

"You were drinking that night, weren't you, like the way you did and the way you still do," said Minogue.

Naughton pushed away from the sink with his backside and came at Minogue. Hoey had anticipated it, but Naughton took him in his rush toward the inspector. The three fell across the table and Minogue felt Naughton's boozy breath rush out over his face. Hoey wriggled to the side, extricated himself, and rolled off the edge of the table. Naughton was trying to clamber up on the table fully. His hand found Minogue's throat and squeezed. Minogue yelped and tried to raise his arm but Naughton pinned it with his own. Hoey shouted at Naughton and grabbed him by the shoulders. Naughton kicked at Hoey who groaned as he tottered away, falling over a chair. Minogue's eyes began to bulge and the grip on his throat turned to a stabbing pain. Naughton was wheezing and muttering under his breath. Minogue tried with his arm again but all he could do was thump Naughton on the head. Dimly he heard Hoey scrambling to get up. Naughton's feral eyes darted over to Hoey and Minogue took his chance. He chopped with his free hand down inside Naughton's elbow. Before the giant could straighten his arm again, Minogue's head shot up and butted him. Naughton reared back with a grunt and fell groaning from the table. Minogue elbowed up slowly, the crack still resonating in his head.

"Jesus," he heard Hoey say. He watched his colleague pull himself up crookedly, holding his crotch. Minogue gulped in air and rubbed his throat.

"Are you all right?" he said to Hoey.

"He kicked me in the nuts!" Hoey wheezed. "Me. A Guard did that to me!"

"Retired Guard," said Minogue, still trying to catch his breath. He looked down at Naughton, who was holding his head and muttering. Hoey suddenly kicked at Naughton.

"Shea!"

Hoey glared back at the inspector. "If and he gets up and tries that on me again, I'll give him what-ho!" said Hoey."A fuckin' oul' hooligan."

"Get outa my house," Naughton whispered hoarsely from below. The stench of whiskey nauseated Minogue now. He beckoned to Hoey.

"Come on," he said.

"This is only the start, whatever your name is," said Naughton sitting up. "Yiz don't know the trouble yiz are in."

Minogue inclined an arm and Naughton took it.

"Sit yourself down now, Guard," said Minogue. "We've had our spat and handed out our clouts."

"You've more coming to you," snapped Naughton. "The fat's in the fire on you now. And you the big knob down from Dublin with your gutty moves like that!"

"What do you call kicking a Guard in the balls?"

"I was attacked!" shouted Naughton, but then grimaced and held his head. "And then your man here pulls that low stunt like that. The Ringsend kiss, by Christ!"

"Trying to choke the life out of me isn't a great way to tell me what happened to Jane Clark," said Minogue. Naughton groaned again and closed his eyes with a pain.

"There's nothing to tell, you gobshite. Ask the man who killed her."

Hoey still looked angry. Minogue nodded to a chair. Hoey sat with a delicate motion.

"I'm only sorry I didn't get the chance to do exactly that," said Minogue.

"What the hell does that mean?"

"Jamesy Bourke got killed the other night. That's what it means."

Naughton looked up in pained disbelief. Hoey was almost hovering over the seat. Wheezing, Naughton clawed his way up off his knees, righted a chair, and sat into it. Minogue plugged in the kettle and stepped back over the glass on the floor.

"Go 'way. You're trying to cod me. Jamesy Bourke?"

"He was shot dead the other night. Yes, he was," Minogue replied. "A

German who thought he was shooting an IRA man with a gun in his fist. We haven't been driving all over the west of Ireland here for the sole purpose of trying to cod you. What about some tea or something and a proper civilized conversation?"

"Fuck the tea so and give me something proper," said Naughton.

"So. Who called the station that night?"

The hulking man's tone turned suddenly gentle. He rubbed slowly at his head and his expression changed into something Minogue would later recall as a smile.

"Have you been digging into this a long time?"

"Awhile."

"And what did yiz find?"

That faint smile held fast at the corners of Naughton's mouth. His hand came away from the red swelling over his eye and, as though it were independent of him, began to massage his neck. He looked out the small window to the roof of what might have been an outdoor privy. A battered-looking ginger cat walked languorously across the corrugated surface, its shadow black on the sunlit gray. Minogue looked at Naughton's hand stroking the bristling neck. People paid a lot of money for haircuts like Naughton's these days, he thought.

"Did yiz meet up with Dan Howard at all?" murmured Naughton. The cat stretched and turned its eyes away from the sun.

"Yes, I did," replied Minogue.

"Our homegrown statesman," said Naughton to the window.

"He doesn't claim to be," said the inspector.

Naughton wheeled on his heels from the window.

"'He doesn't claim to be.' What do you know? Dan Howard's a fuck-ing child!"

Minogue felt an instinctive anger. To be young and unstamped with adult knowing was for Naughton contemptible.

"Nothing to his da, by Jesus," Naughton went on. "But sure look at the da now. He's like a cabbage or something, lying in the bed. Fed with a tube, like he's being watered. Hah. I hear that Sheila Howard visits him more than does Dan himself. What does that tell you?"

"Have you seen Tidy Howard since he had the stroke?"

Naughton fixed a look on Minogue. There was condescension in it, hostility too. The kettle began to sigh and give low cracking sounds as the element began to disperse and move the water within.

"Mind your own fucking business."

"Who phoned the station that night?"

Naughton made a pitying smile.

"Dan Howard's not a man at all. Oh, he can talk the best you ever heard, along with the rest of them. But, sure, what's talk? He can smile and play the game, and I don't doubt that he'll get elected again."

Naughton returned to rubbing his swollen eyebrow. Thwarted yet in his efforts to come to grips with this man, Minogue still sensed something to the side of Naughton's contempt.

"Dan Howard doesn't know what made him," Nuaghton murmured. "That's why he'll never be the man his father was." He looked sideways at Hoey before glaring at Minogue.

"I don't know about you but this pal of yours here, I can tell. Soft, like the rest of 'em his age. Complaining about getting a tap in the bollocks. But you" — Naughton closed one eye and squinted at the inspector — "one minute you're all business and the next minute you're asking for tea? Maybe you're a fuckin' head-case or a good one gone soft yourself. No balls, hah?"

To Minogue, Naughton seemed to be both deflated and made even more monstrous at the same time. Maybe he had had his morning gargle and by now the drink had set free the impulses and thoughts of a bachelor too long unshackled from the daily routines of being a Guard.

"You didn't know Bridie Howard. How could you?" Naughton went on in a monotone. "She should have gone to the nuns the way she wanted to before she up and married a man like Tidy Howard. A dried-up bitch and I don't care if she's gone these twenty years. If she'd a been a woman and a wife proper, sure who knows how things would have turned out? She made a baby out of little Dan, so she did. I sometimes thought it was revenge she was after for having had to dirty herself, by God, to get up the pole in the first place. God help her, she's dead."

Naughton licked his lips and snorted.

"It's not natural for a man to marry someone who spent every night with her skinny legs turned around one another like a hawthorn bush inside a nightdress made of feckin' chain mail. With her back to the wall and her rosary beads in her hands . . ."

It was Hoey who asked the question Minogue had framed in his own mind.

"How do you know all this?"

Naughton made no reply, but his eyes slipped out of focus.

Minogue recalled Eilo McInerny's account of Tidy and his cronies gathering in the pub after closing time for a few jars while she had to make sandwiches for them.

"You never married yourself," he said to Naughton. Naughton's eyelids almost closed.

"Keep your fucking nose out of my private life. What would you know about anything? I looked after me mother and five brothers and sisters, so I did. Living in this very house. I put a sister through nursing in London. And I liked my job, by God."

"You'd have known everyone in town, then."

"Damn right, I did. I knew the Bourkes better than they knew themselves, some a them." Naughton paused and pointed a finger at his head.

"Wild out, the lot of them. Wasters and madmen. Only the mother was there, they'd be all in jail or in some mental hospital. You say Bourke's after getting himself killed? Well, I could have told you something like that'd happen to him. I could have told you that twenty years ago."

"So Bourke was completely to blame for the death of Jane Clark."

Naughton flicked away Minogue's words with a snap of his fingers. Hoey stood up.

"What the hell would you like to tell me next?" Naughton was almost shouting now. 'Death by misadventure'? You fucking iijit! Or that Bourke should have been given five years for manslaughter? That it was an accident? Don't you be starting with this mollycoddle stuff the social workers are full of, that Arthur Guinness did it, or the Pope of Rome." He pointed at Minogue.

"Let me tell you something, Mr. Know-It-All." Tiny gobs of spittle flew out from Naughton's lips into the sunlight.

"I'll tell you what *really* killed that one. She did it herself! Yes, she did. She was a whore. That bitch. She had more rides than a bike. There was nothing she wouldn't do, no poor iijit she wouldn't drag into her web. The more I heard about her, the worse it got."

"What sort of things do you mean?"

The kettle was almost boiled now. Naughton's reply came in a savage whisper.

"She fucked half the parish." His eyebrows went up and he gave a bark of laughter. "For free too."

Naughton sank into the chair and shook his head at his own humor.

He enjoyed it the more because neither Minogue nor Hoey was smiling. The inspector studied Naughton's changed face and guessed that he'd go for the drink again any minute now. He glanced down at the mess on the floor and then returned Hoey's anxious stare for a moment.

"You seem to remember that night well, then," said Minogue.

The amusement stayed in Naughton's eyes but he said nothing. He looked out the window and let his face slide into a slack mask of indifference.

"You think you're going to find out something worth finding out if you poke away at this long enough, don't you?"

Minogue shrugged. "I'm trying to fill in gaps in what we know about that night."

"I thought you knew everything, smart-arse. I was out in the car that night. I saw the fire a long ways off."

"No one phoned you?"

Naughton looked away and rubbed at his forehead. Then he looked back at the inspector, frowning as if he were looking at a child who had been warned off mischief but had promptly done it again.

"Did Crossan put you up to this? Christ, Crossan's pot-boy, you are. Hah. Send a Guard to bait a Guard, is that it? How much is he paying you? You turn against your own, is it, and run with the likes of Crossan?"

Minogue didn't answer. Hoey was still standing next to the window. Naughton laid his palms on his knees and slowly stood upright. Halfway up he grasped his forehead, making Hoey recoil in anticipation. The contempt slid off Naughton's face.

"Jesus, it's like the kick of a donkey I got," he whispered. "You can have your tea. I'm due a smathan."

He walked carefully to the dresser and opened it. From behind a dinner plate he took out a half-bottle of clear liquid and unscrewed the top. He drank from the bottle, paused, and took another mouthful.

"There, we're right," he whispered hoarsely. "A fella should always start the day with holy water."

He probably had caches of drink all over his house, Minogue guessed. Poteen gave off little smell. He probably had a cheap and ready supply of it, and his breath wouldn't reek of shop whiskey.

"Tell me about Dalcais," said Minogue.

Naughton stood still and blinked once, slowly.

"You have shares in it. The Howards' company. Have you forgotten, maybe?"

"Oh, I'm only now beginning to see what kind of a man you are." Naughton spoke in a gentle voice. "You won't be happy until . . ."

He closed his eyes and gave himself over to swallowing the poteen until he had drained the bottle. When he opened his eyes again, they were watery. His bellows of laughter rolled about the house. Suddenly they stopped and Naughton rubbed his wet eyes slowly before looking down into the empty bottle. He looked at the policemen with a melancholy amusement.

"So there, Lord Muck down from Dublin."

The steady, watery eyes rested on some point on the wall behind Minogue and he sensed the words waiting to be said, the doubts warring in Naughton's mind. Naughton rubbed at his chin and a faint smile flickered around his lips. A bashful expression crossed his face and lifted his eyebrows, taking years off the crusty face.

"There, what?" Minogue asked.

Naughton's face darkened suddenly with anger.

"I know what you're looking for," he hissed. "You want to know if I did me job that night. Me sworn job as a Guard. I'll tell you how I handled that night's work, mister — like I always did me job, that's how," he snarled. "I did it well. I did right by God and man. And that's more than many are doing these days."

Naughton sniffed, covered one nostril with his thumb, and then looked at the floor by his feet as though surveying a place to spit. Minogue made another foray.

"You saw a fire and you drove over?" said Minogue.

Naughton spoke vaguely as though he had moved on to other thoughts. "That's it."

"Where was Doyle, the sergeant? When did he get to the house?"

Naughton leaned back against the edge of the countertop. A plume of steam came from the boiling kettle behind his shoulders.

"You saw Bourke at the house," Minogue went on. Naughton's eyes slipped out of focus.

"Like a monkey with fleas," he murmured. "Leaping about, he was."

"There was no one in the car with you? Out from town, I mean?"

Naughton didn't answer but stared at the empty bottle.

"Did you know Eilo McInerny — she worked at Howard's hotel?"

"A fat kind of a girl with big agricultural ankles," Naughton muttered. "She's another one."

"Another what?"

Naughton ignored the question.

"She's another what?" Minogue asked louder.

"Another fly in that one's trap," Naughton said. "Sleeping with her. Whatever they do with one another. Fucking animals. What am I saying, animals? Animals don't do that."

"Eilo McInerny doesn't have fond memories of Portaree, the way she was treated," said Minogue.

Naughton looked up at the inspector. "How was she treated, so, if you know so much?"

"Drummed out," replied Minogue. He heard the indignation rising in his own voice. "Kicked out of her job. No family to go home to. Turfed out."

Naughton rose to his full height and let his arms down by his side. He left Minogue a look of easy contempt and turned to the kettle.

"She did better out of it than she deserved, let me tell you," he said into the steam.

He flicked off the socket switch and reached for a teapot sitting next to a plastic bowl in which a head of cabbage was soaking. Minogue waited for Naughton to turn around. He considered this hulk's life here amid the stale world of boiled cabbage and whiskey, porridge and ironing, the stacks of newspapers in a home that reminded Minogue of a guard room. Naughton made the tea slowly, moving with deliberate care.

"Here, I'll get the cups."

Naughton spoke in a tone so soft that Minogue was startled. The inspector had been meeting men like Naughton all his life: Kilmartin himself, the Mayo colossus minor to Naughton but filled with a like mix — the cynical exuberance at another's folly, then the disarming, implacable loyalty to those he had become close to. Policemen trusted policemen and few others. That was part and parcel of the job, Minogue understood. But many Guards were immured in their distrust of people, and Minogue had moved beyond feeling sorry for them.

He watched Naughton, so light on his feet now, his movements dexterous and measured as he took down good china cups and saucers. Naughton balanced them expertly while he drew out milk from the fridge and then stepped daintily around the pieces of the broken bottle.

For a moment Minogue believed that he caught a glimpse of what could have been a fussy parent, a man who would like to cook for his wife or children. Did Naughton drink to escape these things or to indulge them, he wondered.

"There, now" said Naughton, "we're right. Oh, spoons," and he turned on his heel.

"Most of us are retired by now, I daresay," he went on. "It's a lot different since I walked out the door here one fine morning, with my letter in my fist and my new suit in my case and the ma waving. Then in the train to Templemore."

He paused, his hand in the drawer, and turned toward the two wary policemen with a boyish smile.

"God, but they were great days." His eyes lost their sharp contact with Minogue's then. "The most of 'em. But the people now, they hardly have a pick of respect for the law. It's the sex thing and" — he looked sheepishly down at the shattered bottle — "of course, the human frailties, as my mother would say."

He nodded his head conclusively and bit his lower lip. How much of a burden had that harelip been to him, Minogue wondered. Branded for life, made him hostile to any softness in himself? Shamed him with girls? Left him angry at a world whose imagined recoil from his features had closed him off from others?

"My father, and him dying above in St. Lukes in Dublin — God, I hate that bloody town, I wish we had've sold it to the British — my father told me that God always sends the devil to test everyone that's born into the world. The devil can take any shape at all. It might even be somebody who sits next to you in school. Or a woman. Or something that happens in your work. To test you and remind you to be vigilant, be on your guard, like. Do you believe that?"

Lessened by long exposure now, the whiskey smell had given way to the smell of drawing tea. The sweet, strong aroma took Minogue's thoughts for several seconds. Home. Morning, breakfast in bed. Talk, night. The blue sky framed in the window seemed to beckon him to hope. To test you, he heard Naughton's words again. He saw Sheila Howard's face but he felt no shame now. Hoey sat very still. Naughton let the small bundle of spoons free from his fingers onto the table.

"I do," said Minogue. "I know what you mean."

The spell of immobility in the room was broken now. Naughton's words yet unreleased began to exert a stronger force on the inspector. Hope came as a dull excitement in his stomach. *Naughton knows something*, he tried to tell Hoey with his eyes. *Wait*. Naughton grinned again at some recollection.

"It's up to God in the end," he whispered, and spread the spoons on the table. "But do you know what the hard thing is? I bet you don't. I can nearly tell in a man's face if he knows this . . ."

"What is it?"

"God doesn't care. He doesn't, you know. I found that out too late. If there is a God, well, He doesn't care. And what sort of a God is that, then?"

He turned back to the open drawer and took out folded dishcloths. Minogue looked to the sky again. A diesel lorry droned by on the street, its exhaust echo resonating in the window. Naughton flipped open the bundle of cloths, sighed, and lifted the revolver up, clasping and unclasping it as if to test its weight.

Minogue saw the object imperfectly in his side vision. He turned his head, already startled. Hoey pushed back his chair and grasped the tabletop. Naughton swallowed and cocked the hammer. The scratch and click of the metal banished any doubt from the policemen's minds. Naughton tried to smile but Minogue saw that he couldn't. The inspector felt nothing. The world had stopped. Waiting. Somewhere Minogue heard a voice telling him that there was nothing he could do. Something in him struggled against this and tried to resurrect his reflexes, but his body didn't move. Naughton's whole attention was on the gun. His eyes were fixed on it as though it had appeared by sleight of hand, a conjuror practicing, proud of his skill.

"Jesus Christ," Minogue heard from far off. It was Hoey. Seamus Hoey's arm came up, his fingers splayed open, a look of terror twisting his face.

"So do your duty, boys," Naughton whispered. "And I'll do mine."

He lifted the gun up and shoved the muzzle under his chin. His hand wavered but he redirected the gun back, shoved it under his jawbone tighter, and worked his finger inside the guard. Then he yanked the trigger.

CHAPTER 12

"WHICH OF YOU, er, puked, lads?"

The sergeant was a slight man named Ward who wore an expensive English raincoat and a paisley tie. Minogue had been thinking of those few seconds after Naughton had dropped to the floor. The shock waves of the report in the air, the sound itself reverberating in the room and then, long after that, echoing in Minogue's thoughts. The puff of smoke dissipated slowly. It reached Minogue's nostrils and stung while the shouts and the gunshot continued to roar in his ears. Hoey groaned softly and held his face before drawing his hands down his cheeks. Spots of blood had been slapped on the ceiling and upper part of the wall. Several of the spots had begun to drip but then stopped, several inches down the wall. Minogue looked up again at the black spot, darker than the others, where the bullet had gone after it had exited Naughton's head.

"Was it yourself, em, Matt?"

Minogue shook his head and looked around the parlor. He didn't give much thought as to why Ward asked. Was it to appear exacting and professional or to taunt him while he had the chance? An ambulance blocked the window onto the street. Occasionally a head peeped around the window frame, its owner squeezing into the space left by the ambulance on the footpath. Several times Minogue heard a man's voice telling someone to keep moving.

When the echo of the gunshot had died away, Minogue thought he had heard a sigh escape Naughton, but it was not so. For several moments the blood seemed to be the only thing that had any life there. Minogue remembered standing up weakly, dizzy even, looking for a path to the phone that would keep him out of the growing pool that spread out on the floor beneath Naughton, advancing in its own time out and down, beyond his twisted legs toward the table. Hoey said something and then began vomiting, the stream hitting the floor with force, but he stayed on his feet as he backed away. Minogue, still too bewildered to be shocked, had the sense that something had come into the room and that it was still there, a force or presence that suggested to him that it was perusing the situation, lingering even, to see if there was more it should do or effect. How the hell had Naughton come by a gun?

Hoey had trouble with his matches. His lips, clenched around the cigarette, were a pastel purple slash on a parchment-colored face. Ward turned his attention to Minogue again.

"Are you sure you can . . . Now, I'm not suggesting that you're not up to it, or that you can't, no, no . . ."

Ward continued this unsolicited argument with himself, and he touched the bridge of his nose as if to demur.

"After all, ye're the ones with the expertise and all —"

"I can do it," Minogue said. "Shea can too, I imagine. Right?"

"What?" said Hoey blankly, his attention suddenly stolen by the match he had at last managed to light.

"Manage," said Minogue. "Carry on, like."

"Off to see her nibs?" Hoey asked. "Eilo? . . ."

"Well," said Ward, "I have to tell ye now — and don't get me wrong — but my advice is, well, leave things alone for the time being. Can't ye get back to your business soon enough?"

Minogue looked at Hoey. "It might be better if we were to get to her before she gets news of this here, em . . ."

"Incident," said Ward.

"If we stop to think about things at all, we might never get going again," he said. "That's about the size of it."

"I know what you're saying, but ye're here as, well, not as investigating officers, more like . . . well . . ."

Minogue saw Hoey shiver once and lick his lower lip with a raspy, dry tongue.

"We'll stay with it, I'm thinking."

Ward shrugged and left.

"All right, Shea?" Minogue whispered.

Hoey looked up bleakly, ready to refuse. Exasperation and weariness took over his face and he closed his eyes. He pursed his lips and looked out the parlor window as the ambulance drove off the curb. Minogue could almost hear his fretting thoughts. Hoey stood and walked out the door, banging his shoulder as he crossed the threshold. Ward stood by the hall door writing in his notebook. Minogue gave him a card.

"I gave one to the first Guard. Long nose, tall . . ."

"Dempsey."

"Thanks. I'll call you later." Ward started to say something and Minogue stopped, ready for the warning or anger he had been expecting. Did you drive an old man to this?

"There's no way in the world we thought he was going to do it," Minogue declared.

"And you don't know why he? . . . You really don't know?"

Minogue shook his head.

"Maybe I should have picked up on the way he was talking after the row." Ward frowned.

"I was too busy trying to figure out what he was saying. He had drink on him. I hadn't a clue in the wide world he'd come up with a gun, I can tell you."

Ward's deep breath suggested to Minogue a conscious effort to keep his temper in check.

"Okay, okay. Just . . ."

"I will," said Minogue.

Hoey was already sitting in the passenger seat. A faint smell of vomit clung to his clothes. He didn't look Minogue in the eye.

"We didn't do it, Shea," Minogue repeated. "Do you hear me? *He* did it. He wasn't in control of himself, for that matter."

Hoey said nothing.

"Like it or not, it means something to us. You know what he said. We need to follow up on it. What he told us, like."

"So what's the plan now?" Hoey's voice was sharp. "Where can we go to do more damage?"

"'She did better out of it than she deserved.' Do you remember him saying that?"

Hoey looked at his watch and rolled down the window. He blew smoke out and let his arm dangle over the door.

"She kept something to herself that she could have — should have — told us —"

"Why the hell should Eilo McInerny tell us anything?" Hoey snapped. "What good would it do her? Screw up her life again?"

Minogue knew enough to say nothing.

"I mean to say," Hoey's voice rose and he flicked the cigarette long after any ash had fallen. "Who in their right mind would talk to us? All we bring is —"

"We didn't kill him, Shea. You've got to understand that —"

"All for what? Christ Almighty, we're the kiss of death around here."

"What Naughton said tells me that we really don't know what happened that night. Naughton did. Or at least he knew something, and what he knew was important enough — to him at least — that he wasn't going to tell us."

Hoey drew on his cigarette.

"How can we walk away from it?" Minogue asked.

Hoey's eye was smarting from the smoke when he looked at his tormentor. Again he looked at his watch, but Minogue knew it was a gesture. Tralee would take an hour and a half.

.   .   .   .   .

"Take the back, then," Minogue said.

Hoey slammed the passenger door hard. Minogue strode in the door of the Central Hotel. His heart began to beat faster. He dodged a somnolent lounge-boy who tacked across his path.

The receptionist's perfume met Minogue ten feet ahead of her desk.

"Oh, hello," she smiled, and put down the telephone. "You're back. Would you be —"

Minogue flattened his hands on the counter and leaned in over it.

"Eilo McInerny. Where is she?"

The receptionist's smile faded, rallied, and faded even faster when she met Minogue's eyes. She screwed on the lid of the nail polish.

"Well, now, let me think."

"Is she working now?"

"Well, if she's in . . . this is the afternoon . . . she'd be somewhere near the dining room, probably, helping set it up for —"

Minogue strode to the French doors and opened them. A teenaged girl with short dyed hair stopped setting a table and looked over at him. He didn't stop to close the door but said Eilo McInerny's name to the waitress. The girl stepped back and nodded toward a swing door behind a counter at the back of the dining room. He kept moving and pushed open the door. In the kitchen now, he saw a white tunic move between a countertop and hanging pots that obscured the face.

"Is Eilo McInerny here?" he said, rounding the counter.

Under the lopsided chef's hat, which reminded Minogue of a wayward cartoon rabbit, was a watery-eyed man in his forties. The chef's eyes darted toward a stained, stainless-steel cabinet next to a collection of buckets. He stepped out into Minogue's path.

"Who's asking?"

"A Guard, that's who. Step aside, Mister."

He heard a movement next to the buckets, and he skipped around the cabinet. Eilo McInerny was on her feet, her magazine on the floor. She stepped on her cigarette and brushed at her skirt. For a few seconds her eyes continued to betray her fright. Minogue spotted the tumbler, half-hidden by the door of the cabinet that had been held open to hide a chair.

"You again. I never expected to see you back."

Minogue came to a sharp stop and stared hard at her.

"Matter of fact, I told you and what's the other one, the pasty-faced silent type with the black eyes, get lost and leave me alone."

Minogue looked over his shoulder at the chef and then back at Eilo McInerny.

"I was talking to someone that used to know you. Back in Portaree. In the old days."

"Fuck off with yourself," she said.

"I want to pass on to you what he told us," Minogue continued.

She threw her head back but she couldn't shake free of what her darting eyes told the inspector.

"Go to hell. I don't have to do anything." Drinking, Minogue decided, but that wouldn't stop him.

"We can have this out in front of your fella here, Mr. Cordon Bleu, or —"

"He's not my fella."

"Or we can call for a squad car and do the job right."

"You're talking shite," she scoffed. "Take it away with you."

"Naughton. Garda Tom Naughton. You remember him, don't you?"

Eilo McInerny shifted on her feet and folded her arms. Her eyes narrowed.

"Let's talk somewhere," said Minogue.

"There's a crowd coming in from an office for a retirement do."

Minogue returned the chef's gaze.

"Come on, Eilo, before I have to have you hauled out of here."

She shook her head once and made for a door by a set of sinks.

"I'll be back in good time, Tom," she said.

"No hurry," said the chef. His limp, glistening eyes followed Minogue. Hoey opened the door as she put out her hand.

"Jesus," she started, and stepped back on Minogue's toe. "Where the hell did you come out of? You look wicked."

"Don't worry about it," Hoey muttered. They followed him to a door that led into an alley.

"Any fags?" she asked. "I left mine back in the kitchen."

Minogue opened the passenger door of the Fiat first, turned the ignition. Hoey extended his packet and she plucked one before she sat in the car. She coughed with the first drag of the Major and her shudders and gasps shook the car. Minogue adjusted the heater.

"Christ," she wheezed. "No wonder you're so skinny. Coffin nails."

She looked contemptuously at her cigarette and took another drag on it. Minogue leaned against his door and turned to her.

"You sold us a pup the last time, Eilo. Now I want to hear the bits you left out. No messing either."

"What the hell can I tell you except what I done already?"

"Smarten yourself up, Eilo. I'm not codding." Minogue waved away the smoke billowing from her cigarette. He saw the look of worry pass across her face before she recovered the pout. She looked out the window.

"You're not codding," she murmured.

"Tom Naughton said you did better out of Portaree than you deserved. What did he mean?"

"Ask him, why don't you?" she muttered.

Hoey cleared his throat before he spoke. "Tom Naughton blew his own brains out not four hours ago. Right in the middle of talking to us."

She looked away from the window to Hoey and blinked.

"So we're not in the humor of playing games here now," said Minogue. "You'll appreciate."

His words seemed to have no effect on her. She stared right through Hoey.

"Look, Eilo, this is what he told me. I'm not going to hold anything back. You have to know we're not trying to trap you into anything or play off what you say against anyone else."

She let the smoke out of the corners of her lips, like white paint poured into a slow eddy of water.

"You knew Naughton, didn't you?"

"Yeah. I knew him, all right."

She had spoken in a voice so soft that, for a moment, Minogue wondered if she were the same woman he had confronted not five minutes ago. He knew that she believed them now because her eyes shone with hatred and joy.

"Everything comes to them that wait," she murmured.

"What do you mean?"

She ignored Hoey's question. "I always heard that and I believed it, too. I prayed for that to happen a thousand times. Everything comes around again."

She let out a mouthful of smoke but, like a waterfall reversed, she snorted it back into her nose. Then she blew out the smoke. The ferocity slid away off her eyes and her gaze dropped to the dashboard.

"So Naughton did for himself, did he," she muttered. "Well, by Jesus, there's a cure for everything."

"You got something out of your time in Portaree," said Minogue.

"You fucking iijit!" she lashed out suddenly. "I got heartache and misery!"

"And what did Naughton have to do with that?"

"He was like the rest of them, only worse. He was the Guard. He should have been on my side."

"In what?" Hoey asked.

"He knew I was telling the truth. With that dirty smirk on his face."

"He knew what?"

"He knew what they were like, Tidy Howard and the rest of them. Oul' goats like him. Hah. Tidy towns and clean streets. There's a joke like you never heard before, mister. They all sat and talked with one another too, I can tell you. Nudge, nudge, wink, wink. Tidy and Doyle and Naughton, sitting in the parlor after they had cleared the shop. 'Eilo! Make up a bit of something! Eilo! Run up a sandwich for the Guards here now!' One o'clock in the morning sometimes, can you credit that? Sure Howard had them in his pocket —"

"Wait a minute," said Minogue. "What do —"

"Ah, you're not that much of a thick, are you? The Guards'd come by the odd night to make sure we weren't serving drink after hours. They'd make a big fuss about clearing the pub and the rest of it. Then they'd go behind the counter and start up gargling themselves. Tidy knew what nights they'd be in, so for every one night they'd show up, there'd be weeks and weeks of him pouring drinks up to twelve o'clock."

"That's the size of it then?"

"Do you think he'd tell me what games he was playing, is it?" she shot back at Minogue. She looked away and her glare softened.

"'Eilo! Run up a bit of something!' Hah. And Naughton laughing all the while. He had dirty eyes." She darted a look back at Minogue then.

"I asked a nurse I met in London once about strokes, after I heard about Tidy collapsing. She told me that the mind can be working fine and well, but that the body could be paralyzed. Just think, that oul' bollocks trapped inside his own body. The price of him, I say."

As though ashamed of her feelings, she looked down at her hands. Hoey was about to say something, but Minogue flicked his head at him. They waited.

"When I got to the hotel first, there's Tidy telling me he'd look after me like a father. What kind of a father would do that though? But what did I know? All I knew was that I could lose me job and he could make up stories about me. I'd never get a reference off him. That's what Naughton said. The bastard."

"What happened?" Hoey asked.

She looked up under her eyebrows and Minogue believed she was about to launch herself at one or both of them. Her words issued out in a purr.

"None of your fucking business, you whey-faced iijit."

"You have your own life now, Eilo," Minogue argued. "You won. So help us out and don't be throwing things at us."

"I won?" she almost laughed. The contempt froze on her face but her eyes ran up and down Minogue, the disbelief plain. He noticed for the first time that she had bags under her eyes — how had he missed that before?

A teenager with the back of his head shaved and a long piece flowing down from the crown freewheeled by, no hands, on a bike painted fluorescent pink. Minogue looked at Hoey. The silvery film of fatigue and suspicion was clear on his colleague's eyes. Blotches of color by Hoey's nostrils gave him the look of a child in from the cold weather.

"Tidy Howard took me . . . had me," she said.

"He . . . ?"

"Yes, he did," she whispered. "He took me and he dragged me and he pulled at me — and he choked me. Then he was on top of me. I couldn't move. I wasn't always this, what'll I say . . ."

"Comfortable?" Minogue tried.

"Jesus," she almost smiled. "You're the sweet-tongued bastard. Anyway. A big heavy pig of a man and his false teeth coming loose — I could feel them pressed onto my teeth, I remember. My lips were bleeding. Pushing on me. I thought I'd faint. I couldn't breathe. I stopped fighting 'cause I thought I wouldn't make it out from under him. That's the truth." She puffed out a ball of smoke and blinked.

"And when you tried to . . . ?"

"They were in cahoots. Drinking 'til all hours. They next day there's the oul' bastard on the front page of *The Clare Champion*, shaking hands with some German that was opening a knitwear factory."

"You told Naughton what had happened?"

"I did. And what an iijit I was to go and do a thing like that." She paused. "When I think of it . . ." She took a long drag from the cigarette, grimaced, and cast about for an ashtray.

"Fire it out the window, can't you?" said Minogue. She looked down over her shoulder at the inspector.

She rolled down the window and flicked the butt expertly across the street. Minogue was surprised at the distance she achieved with such economical effort. She turned to him with a piercing look.

"So what are you going to do now? What can you do? Naughton's dead, so you tell me. Tidy Howard is up in the nursing home with his plot bought and his box picked out and ready. There's nothing left. So what are you two after?"

"What did Naughton mean about you doing well out of it?"

"Fuck Naughton," she hissed. "I'll tell you what Naughton said to me. I'm sure ye'd like to hear. You want to hear the dirt, don't ye? So you can tell your pals back up in Dublin one night and ye having a few jars. I'm only sorry I don't have a few pictures to show ye."

"It's not like —"

"Don't give me lectures about what it is and isn't like? This is all the help Naughton was to me: 'Did someone ride you right?' was what he said to me. 'Did he ride you straight and did you get cured?' says he. Fucking worm. And him a Guard."

Minogue kept his eyes on the Fiat insignia on the horn. An urge to lean on the horn and hold it came to his hands.

"Only sorry he didn't have a go himself," she whispered. "He knew everything. I'm sure Tidy Howard told him, and them sniggering and drinking."

"Knew what?" Hoey asked.

"About me. About Jane Clark. Her and me. That's what he meant about 'straight,' you thick. With a man, like. Here. Give us one of those Majors."

Hoey held out the packet opened already. She didn't light it but studied it instead, as though it were a weapon.

"So what did you get out of this, then?" asked Hoey. "It doesn't make much sense."

"I knew things," she murmured. "I knew about Jane and what she was doing. But she told too. She was like that. She wasn't afraid of anything. She laughed in their faces. 'What century do you think you're in?' she'd say. That's what she was like. And I liked that about her. She could say things that I'd . . ."

She shook her head as though trying to dislodge a bee caught in her hair and reached across to thump in the cigarette lighter.

"Does this part of your limo work?" she asked.

"Wait and see," said Minogue. "But listen, you lost me there."

"Ah! Dan Howard and Jane. Jamesy Bourke and Jane. She told me. She kind of saw it like a big adventure and a bit of a comedy too. Oh, Christ, but she'd have me in stitches. 'You can learn all you want about Irish history and civilization when you have one of them burrowing away at you' she told me. The things they said to her when they were, you know . . . close." The lighter popped out.

"She really had one over on them. And I don't know if they ever knew it, Jamesy or Dan. Dan" — she blew out a vast quantity of smoke, the first work on a fresh cigarette — "what a gobshite. Dan, only Dan. Curly wee Dan. Hah. He'd get up on a table if the tablecloth looked enough like a skirt, so he would."

"But what did you get out of this?" Minogue tried again. "What did Naughton mean?"

"Did you get in the wrong queue when God was handing out the brains or what? Do you honestly think that Naughton would do away with himself over some revelation like this, a parlormaid like yours truly here, that no one cared enough to believe?"

She taunted Minogue with a wide-eyed stare. The inspector didn't try to hide his exasperation now.

"Look, Eilo. Stop mullocking about here, like a good woman. We're trying to do the right thing. What did she have over these people, Jane Clark?"

"The right thing? Huh. What the hell use is it for me to tell you? It's all done with."

The inspector rubbed at his stinging eyes. His battered Fiat was full of smoke, and he had a pain over his eyes that wasn't going away and would probably get worse. He was homesick for the ordinariness of his home, his wife, his adopted city. He wanted to be sitting in front of the fire with a glass of whiskey and errant thoughts. He had traveled the roads of west Clare more in this last week — and for what? It came to him with the sudden force of a truth he had hidden from wilfully, that the Hoey he had dragged along, that the faded, greenish-colored snapshots of Jane Clark, that the dreams of that familiar stranger, and his own claustrophobic premonitions about Kathleen's apartment plans were part of one story, a story he couldn't make sense of. It didn't matter how, he knew. What mattered was his own obstinate will to see this through. Still, he was angry.

He was out of the car quickly, the Tralee air rushing into his lungs. The force of the door slamming rocked the Fiat and it squeaked on its shocks. The sea, he thought while he waited for his anger to ebb, and the porpoises. Their domain the water, their senses beyond what we could imagine — the very core of the earth itself guiding them, or the stars, perhaps, the squeals of their kind as they surfaced and dived, surfaced and dived.

"Shit," he said.

The roof of the car was cold under his palms. He spread his hands wider. Cigarette smoke issued out thinly from Eilo McInerny's window.

"What the hell got into him?" he heard her say. "He should get a grip on himself or something."

People, he almost shouted — humans. Images flew through his mind. Fire in the night and the stone walls reaching for the sea in darkness.

"He's fed up with being taken for an iijit," he heard Hoey reply. "He doesn't get like this very often, I can tell you."

Hoey said something else to her but in a tone too low for the inspector to make out the words. Minogue turned and leaned back against the window, folding his arms. Overhead a dozen seagulls hovered white against the sky. The sunlight was brass on the side of the street. Naughton was in the morgue and his house was sealed. The bang reverberated in Minogue's mind again and he shuddered. The gun Naughton had used on its way to the laboratory in Dublin, thence to Moran, the Gardai's resident ballistics expert. Would Moran be able to put parentage on the gun, link it to others? Ward, the detective who had interviewed him for a half hour, had asked him twice if he had suspected that Naughton had had a gun. Stupid question. If Matt Minogue had so much as wondered whether Naughton had had a gun somewhere, he'd never have gone near the damned house. Where did he get the gun?

"Oi," he heard. He sat back into the Fiat.

"I have me job to go to," Eilo McInerny said. "Mel'll be home from school. I have to phone her and give out to her about her homework." She paused to take a last pull on the cigarette.

"Then I'll go back to Tom and Bridie and Maureen above in the hotel, and I'll serve up a dinner to a crowd of people. Me feet will be hanging off me when I get home. But I'll go to the bank tomorrow and put a bit of money aside for a trip to London. It's for Mel. I promised her we'd go sometime." She turned up the cigarette and studied the smoke rising from the tip.

"And I might just stay up late and have a few jars with Tom." She looked at Minogue. "And I might have a bit of fun. The Russian hands and the Roman fingers, you know?"

Minogue stared back into her eyes. People, he thought. It's a fallen world, there's no doubt.

"And then I'll go home. And that'll be that. Naughton's dead, and Jamesy Bourke's dead, and if I wait long enough, by Jesus, the rest of 'em will fall into their graves too. Or get shoved into them. But I'll sleep and eat and have rows with Mel and Tom. I'll see all of them down, that crowd. Do you hear me?"

Minogue was caught between respect for her tenacity and dismay at her bitterness.

"All too well," he said.

"Well, because you're not a gobshite Guard — at least not according to your pal here —"

Both Minogue and Eilo McInerny looked over at Hoey. The detective examined his nails. His hands were trembling again, Minogue saw. He stared at Hoey's forehead, willing him to look up.

"— who tells me you're different, to the extent that you're having rows with even the Guards in Ennis about Jamesy Bourke. Now that is something. And now I hear from him here that you're ready to move heaven and hell to get at what happened to Jane." Her eyes stayed on Hoey. He glanced at Minogue and looked out the window. "The oddest pair I've ever come across," she murmured. "Ye remind me of some story I heard and I was in school — I forget it now. Some fool and his pal going around the country looking to fix things. Making iijits of themselves, it turned out. And me the iijit here too now, about to be taken in by ye. It's the right fool I am, God help me, and I'll never be cured of it."

"Look here," said Minogue. "We're not out to cod anyone."

She seemed not to have heard him. A smile began to form at the sides of her mouth. "After all I've been through . . . It must be the look of your man's face here." She turned to Minogue and her eyes narrowed. "Well, I'll tell you a few things now. So listen. Gimme another one of those Majors. You. Shea. What's-your-name."

Eilo McInerny hammered in the cigarette lighter and settled back into the seat with a sigh. She concentrated on the lighter knob, her hand poised for it to pop out.

"You know how I was treated on the stand when I was called," she began. "I was working that night. Saw Howard and Bourke getting plastered and the rest of it. But there's one thing that never came up at the trial and I kept it to myself until after." The lighter popped and she grasped it.

"I remember" — she paused, speaking through the smoke — "I remember thinking to myself that I could keep it up my sleeve. I thought of it as my ticket out of there." Her eye watered from the smoke and she rubbed at it with a soft clicking sound.

"I went up to the bitch and I told her what I'd heard and what I'd seen, with her and Tidy Howard having the row that night. I let her think what she liked, that I had heard what they had been rowing about. She said nothing, just looked at me like I was some class of a lower form of life. That was her way, of course." Into Minogue's mind shot the image of Sheila Howard's face.

"Yeah," she murmured between her teeth. "Looked down her nose at me. Said nothing. But I knew there was something fishy going on. The next day, ould Tidy takes me aside and asks me if I had ever thought of

{ 231 }

bettering myself. Whatever the hell that meant. Would I try London, says he. He'd pay my way and give me the address of a landlady, as well as some money to get me started in digs there and so on. I'd think about it, says I." She coughed and shifted around in the seat.

"Next day, a Guard — Doyle — came by and told me that I'd be asked to be a witness at the trial because Jamesy Bourke was after being charged. I was to stay around because the trial'd come up within a few months. Sure enough, it did. Like an iijit, I thought I'd just be asked about what I saw in the pub that night. But I walked into an ambush. And you know the rest. I came back to the hotel in a flood of tears — raging mad, I was too, and frightened. Then in came this fella, you probably don't know him — a kind of a do-for, a crony of Howard — and he says the dirtiest things. About me, about Jane Clark. Says he doesn't want to walk the same streets of the same village where I live."

"Who was he?" Hoey asked.

"A lug. He came into the bar a fair bit. Duignan . . . Day — God, it goes to show you that I can't remember —"

"Deegan?" said Minogue. "Big, running to fat?"

"Deegan, yes. I hardly knew him. He did odd jobs and he rented farm-land from the Howards, I heard. So there it was: Get out of town. After your man Deegan had gone, in comes Tidy himself, with an envelope of money and an address. ''Twould be better for all concerned,' says he. Liar. Bastard. Pig. There was a thousand quid in the envelope. I couldn't believe it. I was always sure that it was me saying what I said to her ladyship got me the ticket out."

·　　·　　·　　·　　·

His headache was gone. He kept his eyes on Eilo McInerny's broad back as she trudged up the steps into the hotel. Minogue imagined her body in a rococo painting of a goddess reclining in a glade. With her hand on the door, she looked back at the two policemen before flicking the cigarette over the roof of the Fiat. Hoey waved tentatively and let his hand drop into his lap.

"You told her what had happened to you?"

Hoey nodded.

"Why?"

Hoey rubbed at the side of his nose. "She's been through a lot. I sort of thought that she needed to know that we're not per — well, I mean, that we were all looking for a cure for something. That I was, I mean."

"We," said Minogue. "You were right the first time."

Hoey raised a hand as if to make a point but let it drop again.

"If only Tidy Howard could —" he began.

Minogue shook his head.

"What I want to know is whether Dan Howard knew anything about all this."

"He must," said Hoey. "He's married to the woman, for God's sake. Married people don't keep secrets, like."

Minogue laughed aloud.

"What's so funny?"

"The bit about married people."

Hoey's tone suggested irritation as well as embarrassment. "Well, that's the way it's supposed to be, isn't it?"

Minogue started up the Fiat to distract himself from laughing again. Hoey lit another cigarette, coughed, and rolled down the window. A lorry towing a trailer full of pigs stopped next to the car. Their trotters scrambling on the wood, their squeals and the smell of pig shit made Hoey roll up the window again. The lorry moved off slowly. Minogue drove around the corner and switched off the engine.

"What's the matter?" said Hoey.

"Have to think out loud for a minute. That night: Eilo's working and she sees Dan Howard and James Bourke drunk in the bar. She remarks to herself that there's a lot of drink in front of Bourke. Later on she remembers seeing Shelia Hanratty and her friends. Then Eilo's off about the place, 'working' — which means she went out to a storehouse for smoke and a drink from a bottle of vodka she kept out there. She sees Sheila Hanratty come across the yard after Tidy Howard and they're arguing. Naturally she hides. She doesn't hear what they're squabbling about but she's surprised that Sheila Hanratty should be shouting at Dan Howard's father."

"But she does hear one thing that Tidy shouts at her: 'You live your life, I'll live mine.'"

"And some bad language from the both of them. Surprised her to hear Sheila Hanratty like that. Had the name of being well-reared."

"Right. Sheila Hanratty walks off in a huff. Eilo is able to get out of her hidey-hole, and she goes back in to help clear the bar. She follows Sheila Hanratty."

Hoey nodded.

"And the same Sheila Hanratty goes through the bar and straight out the door onto the street." Minogue looked to Hoey for comment but his colleague merely considered the tip of his cigarette.

"This is half-ten, now," Minogue went on. "There's another hour before the pub closes. Come closing time, Eilo sees that she's back, and she's in a buzz around the boyos up at the bar. The same boyos are well and truly pissed by this time. Pretty soon afterwards they're out on the street and Sheila Hanaratty drives Dan home."

"Right," murmured Hoey. "The Howards didn't live above the place."

"Here's my question: If Dan Howard can't leg it the half-mile or so back to his house, how can Jamesy Bourke walk as far as Jane Clark's cottage? If Bourke is as far gone as Dan Howard, don't you know."

"I don't know," Hoey offered. "Nobody knows. Bourke himself didn't know."

"Back away from that for a minute. How do we know that Sheila Hanratty actually went anywhere after her kerfuffle with Tidy Howard? Eilo says she saw her go out the door. Just assumed she got into the car. But she might have driven around the corner and come back to the bar directly. She might have gone to get something in the car. Her handbag or something. Then again, she might have been upset or the like, and needed . . ."

The thought of Sheila Howard distraught over something, using bad language, gave Minogue a feeling of faint but not unpleasant aversion.

"She might have come back in a matter of minutes. Eilo mightn't have seen her until later," Hoey was saying.

"Yes." Minogue was still mired in his sliding thoughts.

"Then again," Hoey added with unmistakable irony, "it'd be nice to know where she actually did go, and for how long."

Minogue awakened to Hoey's mood and glanced across at him.

"Yes and no, Shea. There's Crossan taking digs at the Howards. I'm far from satisfied that Crossan is as pure as the driven snow here. He may be the happier man to see Dan Howard and Sheila Howard with plenty of mud on them."

"You're lumping Eilo McInerny in there too?"

"It struck me that there'd be a certain, what can I call it, a certain relish that Eilo'd enjoy if the Howards, Sheila Howard included, got in the way of scandal."

"You think she's a muckraker?"

"That's not what I said. I'm saying that she could put a cast on her recollections. I'm wondering . . . I'm wondering exactly what Crossan told her the times he was talking to her recently. Maybe Crossan sort of enlisted her — not outright hired her, I mean, but —"

"Crossan? You don't believe her, then."

"I'm saying that she might be embellishing. She didn't actually hear the conversation between Tidy Howard and Sheila Hanratty. And she didn't actually see her drive off, much less where."

"All right," said Hoey. He blew out under his upper lip. "All right. But she didn't claim to have seen or heard everything."

The afternoon sun was just above the rooftops now, and the copper hint of evening was already on the streets. The sun had warmed the car's interior and brought up the smell of cigarette ash even stronger. Hoey had become more fidgety.

"Crossan," said Hoey. "You've got him in your sights, haven't you?"

Minogue nodded.

"Back to the money thing, then," Hoey tried. "She says that Tidy Howard gave her money for the train and then for digs over in London. A lot of money. Maybe because he had her on his conscience?"

"Take-it-or-leave-it type of deal?" said Minogue.

"Right. He rapes her and then later he kicks her out after throwing a bit of money at her. But the way she talks about him, it wasn't in character for him to give a damn about that sort of thing. Why did he wait until after that night to talk her into going away?"

"Bears out her version of why she got the money, all right."

"Yeah. The main reason was that she knew that something was going on that night," said Hoey. He sat forward and began counting on his fingers. "Look. She sees Tidy Howard and Sheila Hanratty having some kind of row. Sheila storms out, obviously not getting the answer she wants. She goes somewhere. When Eilo sees her again, she's back in the bar looking a lot less glamorous than the first time she appeared. We have to go after her. Sheila Howard."

Minogue took a deep breath and looked at his watch. "With what?"

"Naughton got paid off —"

"Can't prove a damn thing now, and you know it."

Minogue's shirt collar began to irritate his neck. The sun came around the door pillar. There was a glint in Hoey's eyes and his fingers moved the cigarette around quickly.

"Ask Mr. and Mrs. Howard," he growled. "Round two. This time put the squeeze on 'em."

Minogue longed for a cup of coffee, to be alone for a while. A vague apprehension had taken the place of the emptiness, itself part of the leftovers of shock. Hoey scratched his bottom lip with his thumbnail. The inspector slid deeper into his seat and looked down the street.

The afternoon light had stretched the shadows across the street. They had begun their relentless ascent on the buildings to the western side. Soon the roofs, the aerials, and the chimneys would take the glare all to themselves and the street below would fall into darker shadow. Gold and bronze had already taken fire in several windows. Minogue watched a mother pushing her pram toward the car. Her face was set firm as if she had just had news that disappointed her. She stopped the pram and called out to a boy crying on the footpath behind her. The boy stood staunchly with his face contorted.

"All right so, bye-bye," the woman called out.

She was too tired to be really angry, Minogue believed. The child continued crying and pivoted toward a parked car. He began fingering a door handle, tracing patterns in the dust on the door panels. His Halloween costume had held together well, the inspector noted. The cloak's high collar suggested Dracula but perhaps he was mistaking it for Superman or Batman. Would this stubborn child insist on wearing his hero's clothes night and day until they fell off in flitters?

"I'll layve you here in the street, so I will, if and you don't come on!" the mother shouted. She had rested one hand on her hip, the other staying the handle of the pram.

"All right, then! Bye-bye." The child wailed and sat down heavily.

"I'm going!" said the mother. She turned and pushed the pram.

Minogue watched her staged resolution and he wondered how far she'd walk before she turned for another ultimatum. Some vague feeling rustled in his chest. The child howled *wait, Mommy, wait.* The mother walked by the Fiat and glanced in at the two detectives. Reflected sun from a window was on her face as she turned. The glare caught every line, the cast of her mouth, her eyelashes. *Wait, Mommy, wait,* cried the child, but he stayed on the footpath.

"I'll do no waiting! Get up off the ground this instant and hurry on with you, you bold boy!"

The threat of abandonment worked. The child tried to swallow his cries and rose to his feet. Boys, thought Minogue, and remembered Daithi's infant temper — a lot more work than girls. Little pleased with her victory, the mother had more conditions.

"And no more whining out of you!" she warned.

"I'd say she's something, that one," murmured Hoey.

"With the pram?"

"No, Sheila Howard."

The surprise worked its way down to his stomach. Hoey's mind was off on its own course. He was giving his colleague and nominal boss a cool survey. Minogue started the car hastily enough to grind the starter motor. He gritted his teeth, tightened his seatbelt, and busied himself dickering with the controls for the choke and then the heater. Up the Listowel Road and on to Tarbert and the ferry to Clare; meet with Crossan, see if he had anything new; try not to take a swipe at him. Try not to have a row with Hoey en route either. He took a deep breath and released it. Hoey was still eyeing him when he turned to check for traffic. The inspector trod heavily on the brake pedal.

"What the hell are you looking at?" he growled at Hoey.

Hoey said nothing, but he kept looking at him. Minogue searched his colleague's face. Hoey's expression reminded him of one of those benchmarks of marriage, a high-water mark, when one partner looks at the other in the wake of a thoughtless hurt. He disengaged the clutch.

"What's up with you, Shea? Quit giving me the treatment."

"What's up with you, you mean."

"This is not a good time to be playing games with me. You've got something on your mind? Do you resent being dragged up and down the country, is that it? Well, if that's the case, all you need do is —"

"What the hell use is it to me to say something to a man with his fingers stuck in his ears?"

Minogue understood that something had lurched out into his path like an inescapable drunkard weaving toward him on the footpath, mirroring his efforts to sidestep him. He had defended the Howards to Crossan, a man who knew them far better than he, Minogue, did. Now he was annoyed that he had to defend them again to Hoey. He, Minogue, had turned away from something, but part of him — that part of him that over the years had become his real intelligence — had been trying to make itself known to him.

"It was just you and Crossan the other night. Going to see her," Hoey said. "I wondered why you didn't ask me along."

"I didn't want two Guards, Shea. It'd change the atmos —"

He saw her in jeans then and the Fiat seemed to get unbearably warm. Sudden heat prickled under his armpits and by his ears. Her blonde hair, her head turning in the lamplight, the swell of her breasts under the sweater. His heart kept up its tattoo and he knew that it was futile to try and disguise the color rising in his face. He looked away down the street and switched off the engine. The car rolled back half a foot and the tires bounced dully on the curb. The street ahead was a striped and jumbled shadow play, glare adjoining gloom under a sky already lightening at the edges. He didn't bother to look at his watch. An hour and they'd need headlights. It'd be dark and them getting into Ennis. What the hell would he say to Sheila Howard?

Hoey looked away down the street before taking out a cigarette. The mother with the pram and the laggard infant were crossing the street in the middle distance. She yanked on the child's arm as Hoey tapped a fresh cigarette on his knee and led it to his lips. There it rested for several seconds. Then he gently plucked the cigarette out again. His dry lips stuck to the filter. He replaced the cigarette carefully in the packet and then nudged his colleague. It was a gesture of intimacy that startled Minogue.

"What's the big hurry back up to Ennis anyway?" said Hoey. "I'll stand you a mug of something."

Minogue nodded and kept his eyes on the opening of the street where the mother, pram, and child had disappeared. Swallowed up, he thought, as they turned the corner. He wanted them to return but he didn't know why. The anticipation he felt while staring at the corner made him alert again. His body felt flabby and loose in the seat. His eyes ached and he rubbed at them. The more he rubbed, the more colors appeared. He thought of his brother's family sequestered on the farm with the night about to come down over their fields, the bleak heights of the Burren that rose around the farm given over to winter again. He stopped rubbing his eyes but held his eyelids closed and watched the wash of red and yellow, the dark blotches spreading. Still as the land might look, there were squad cars parked on sidestreets, Guards sitting by phones waiting: a shooting, a suspect on the move again, a vehicle approaching . . . For a moment, Minogue was hovering over it all again, as in that dream. Fire blazed up from the thatch, the screaming Bourke, the firelight dancing on the stone walls.

"Well, what do you say?"

Like the yarns he had heard as a child about travelers falling into the underworld, he had fallen through a hole somewhere, he saw then. There the pookas and fairies still held sway, marshaling spells and riddles to entrap the arrogant who had inherited the upper world. *Great God, what an iijit I am still.* Decades in Dublin, cute from years of dodging traffic and chancers, criminals and superiors, later content in interior victories. Almost educated, he liked to think. Now he saw that his judgement had gone out the window. Sheila Howard, thinking about her half the day. Hoey had been sitting next to him to witness his blunders. Upside down, reversed: measures confounded, rules obscured. Humiliation grasped at his guts and held. *God, what an iijit.* Hoey opened his door gently and waited. Minogue looked over at the open door but didn't see anything. He felt he was nearing the surface now, but he was still pursued by images and words. Iseult's hunger for life, her scorn keeping her keen; Daithi working toward an immigrant life in the States; Kathleen's steadfast love, her patience and indulgence. Kilmartin pausing in mid-oratory, face framed by anxious cynicism. The porpoises alongside the boat, carefree taunts from their world.

"She's probably up in Dublin by now," he heard himself mutter.

"What?" asked Hoey, and bent down to look in the car.

"She's up in Dublin with Dan Howard, I imagine."

He rubbed his eyes again. His eyelashes clung together when he stopped. When he tugged his eyelids open, there was still no sign of the Superman who had been dragged into oblivion by his mother. The shadows seemed deeper now.

"I'll phone the Killer," he said.

Hoey nodded.

"But Shea." Hoey bent down again. "When we get back to Ennis, when we walk in the door of Crossan's office . . ." Again the words disappeared, despite his wish to sound resolute.

"We'll tell him what we know," Hoey said quietly.

"Yes, I know. But as for speculating, that's not really on, okay?"

"Look," said Hoey, and he looked down the street. "There's an eating-house down there. Maybe they'll have something there."

Minogue tumbled wearily out onto the path.

CHAPTER 13

HAD HE SLEPT? Jesus Christ. Minogue's heart gave a leap, and he grasped the steering wheel tighter. He stared toward the limit of the headlight beam and flicked it on to full. A red band of sky that bled into honey was alongside them, whipped by passing trees. Branches wrung from the trees by last month's gales still lay in ditches, their white stumps catching the headlights. How had he got this far on automatic pilot? Hoey was half-slumped, half-curled into his seat. Minogue had seen his eyelids batting occasionally. Where the hell were they now? As if on cue, a sign to Kilmihill lit up on the curb ahead. Another twenty minutes to Ennis, so. Closer to the sign he made out the white paint on the wall underneath: BRITS OUT NOW. He slowed and decided that the clumsy picture drawn on the wall was a rendition of an M-16. The paint had dribbled down, like white blood, the inspector thought. The Fiat's lights followed the bend, straightened, and dropped the slogan into the night again.

He remembered coming over the bog roads from the ferry, the bootlid rising and falling, snapping against the string that had slackened. The River Shannon had been silver as the ferry nosed out into the estuary toward Clare. He remembered the salmon light from the west reaching out to cover the water too, and he had looked for the fins and backs on the water. Ten minutes of strained searching over the water had yielded nothing more than disappointment. The two cups of coffee in Tralee had kept him going until they drove up the ramp on the Clare shore. Minogue was perplexed by the strange fusion of relief and foreboding he felt as they hit the back road toward Ennis.

A half-dozen cars trailed an articulated lorry driving against them. Their lights burned into Minogue's gritty eyes. Hoey blew out a cloud of smoke. He seemed little concerned with concealing his sarcasm.

"Any more dispatches from HQ?"

"No," replied Minogue. "He said he'd locate the Howards for us. I'll phone in the morning to find out from him."

"You didn't go into any detail about how we're getting on, though?"

"No. I don't know how we're getting on, that's why."

"And being the man he is, he's waiting to see what comes of it," said Hoey. "At a safe distance, of course."

Minogue detoured around by Market Street, drove by the Friary, and parked outside the Garda Station.

"Let's check if there are any, em, breakthroughs here," Minogue said to Hoey's unspoken question. Hoey followed the inspector through the towering gate pillars.

"Whoa," said Minogue, slowing. "Look at them."

Two vans with Dublin registrations were parked on a tarred island in front of the station door. Orange glare from quartz lights over the avenue fell on a car that Minogue and Hoey recognized.

Ahearne, the sergeant, came through the doorway behind the counter and said hello to Minogue. He was in civvies, brown corduroy jeans, and a hand-knit beige jumper over his blue uniform shirt.

"And how are ye?" he whispered.

"A bit on the tired side."

"Aha." Ahearne's eyes went from Minogue to Hoey and back.

"We were passing so we just dropped in to see what headway there was with this incident last night," said Minogue. "Over at the Howards'."

"Oh, that business," said Ahearne. Now Minogue was sure that Ahearne was buying time.

"Yes. The shooting thing," Minogue repeated.

"Terrible, to be sure, wasn't it?" said Ahearne. "Well, I'm not very well up on that at all, being as I'm —"

Through the doorway at speed came Superintendent Russell. His eyes were on Minogue's the moment his head appeared around the swinging door. Minogue felt his throat constrict. The light in the room seemed to become a little dimmer. Russell came to an abrupt stop by the counter in front of Minogue.

"Thanks, D.J.," said Russell.

Ahearne had to work his way around the now firmly planted superintendent. Minogue sheltered in a slow official monotone.

"We came in to find out if there was progress in the investigation of last night's shooting at the Howards' house."

The door to the public office had stopped swinging but Minogue believed that someone was right behind the door, listening.

"I was in touch with the commissioner some hours ago," said Russell. He paused to press his tongue against his front teeth. "And I tried to impress upon him that you two should be hauled back to Dublin and put in front of a Disciplinary Tribunal."

"*Quam celerime?*" asked Minogue.

The sarcasm from Russell was labored. "I beg your pardon?"

"How soon would you like us to go?"

Russell drew a finger up from his side with a motion that reminded Minogue of a cowboy drawing a gun. He jabbed his finger in the direction of Minogue's heart.

"Yesterday. That would have left Tom Naughton alive."

Hoey shuffled his feet. Minogue wanted to tell him to stop.

"I don't know what yous fellas learn by way of technique in your line of work," Russell continued, his finger still aimed at Minogue's chest. "I heard ye could be rough enough if the job had to get done. But, by Jesus" — he directed the finger up to Minogue's shoulders now — "harassing a retired Guard to the point of doing what he did, or what you say he did —"

"Where did he get the pistol?"

"Shut up, Guard," Russell snapped and he leaned over the counter. "Dirty work, bucko, that's what that was. Very dirty work. I can tell you that if I had the full authority, I'd have you two in a cell here or in Tralee or somewhere and then kicked off back up to Dublin to face the music. That way, you'd cause no more havoc here!"

Minogue studied the red-faced Superintendent. The corrugated, wiry hair stayed in place. Like steel wool, he thought, stapled to his head. The furrowed brow like someone had scraped across it with their nails many years ago, the eyes set back in his head, tiny and fierce. Minogue's eyes moved purposely and impudently down from the superintendent's face. Four-button cardigan bought in a shop, a sports shirt that cost a lot.

"Where did Naughton get the gun?" he asked.

Russell slapped his hand on the countertop. "We'll find out in due course — not that it's any damn concern of yours! You're bloody lucky he didn't turn the thing on you."

He began waving his finger in an indeterminate pattern that Minogue believed could be an ellipse.

"If and when I find out how you pressured him into doing what he did — if indeed he did it and you're to be believed about it — I'll personally see to it that you two go to the wall for it. Pension and all, by God."

"No word on the shooting at the Howards'?" asked Minogue.

"No, there isn't any word of the shooting at the Howards' last night," Russell mimicked. The front door opening behind Minogue left Russell's lips shaped with what he was ready to hurl at the duo. Minogue turned to see the four men filing in. Guards, detectives, they returned Minogue's nod. Russell took a deep breath and waved at the swing door behind him.

"Go on ahead in, lads," he said between his teeth.

More detectives, Minogue thought. Russell here after hours, called in from his home — for what? Were they expecting an operation tonight? Russell looked down his shoulder as the last of the foursome went through the doorway. Then he looked back at Minogue.

"I'm told ye're not conducting an investigation but merely 'an inquiry.'"

Sounds like Tynan's sophistry, Minogue thought. It had probably enraged Russell. The superintendent's finger went back to its wavering survey of Minogue's chest.

"I've let it be known that if ye two get in our way here, I won't be responsible for you." His finger swiveled across to Hoey but the eyes stayed on Minogue's.

"Here's my advice: get to hell out of here. I mean Ennis, Clare, and the west of Ireland in general. If you have any legitimate reasons for being here with your 'inquiries,' then they have to wait. We have work to do that's a damn sight more important. Got that?"

Minogue took a step back and put his hands in his coat pockets. Strategic withdrawal as opposed to retreat. He watched Russell pitch a peppermint into his mouth from a considerable distance. Some trick, he thought. Big mouth?

"And another thing," Russell called out. "I'm going to find out what you did. Then I'm coming after you. This is exactly the kind of fiasco

I've spent years trying to persuade three commissioners — soon it'll be four — that we need to avoid. Dublin doesn't rule the roost, Mister. You tell 'em that up there: Those days are long gone. And tell Kilmartin too."

"Tell the crowd sitting around the back office in that meeting we dragged you out of too," said Minogue with an edge in his voice.

Russell hammered the counter before waving them toward the door.

"At least they're proper professionals! They know what they're up against!"

·   ·   ·   ·   ·

"The beef's nice," said the waitress. "They don't overcook it like a lot of places do. Hardly a pick of fat to it."

Minogue sat down opposite, looking a lot less annoyed. Hoey fiddled with his fork, trying to trap his knife between the tines.

"We're expecting another one in a few minutes," said the inspector. He looked up sideways at her. "Put me down for the fish."

"Something light," said Hoey. "An omelette with nothing in it maybe."

The waitress penciled it in, smiled, and turned on her heel.

"Do you think Russell is trying to cover for Naughton or someone else?"

"I doubt it," replied the inspector. "It's more a case of look-after-our-own, to my way of thinking. Until he knows the facts of what happened down in Naughton's place, he'll be full of —"

Hoey shivered and dropped the fork.

"God," he hissed, and shivered again. "Just remembering it now gives me the willies. I don't know now if I can face up to a dinner . . ."

Minogue wondered when the shock would return to him in full. Would he wake up in the early hours, his own heart hammering, the pistol shot echoing in his ears, the awful liquid thud as the bullet tore into Naughton?

Again he considered phoning Tynan. Tell him what, exactly? Something stinks, John. Tynan's subtle communication by not communicating struck him again. If Inspector Matthew Minogue were actually to phone him, the Garda commissioner might well be obliged to recall Minogue ex officio to Dublin. Russell had probably leveled warnings at Tynan that the commissioner could no longer fend off. Tynan had obviously not passed anything on to Kilmartin — yet, at any rate — because the said chief inspector did not seem at all aware of Naughton's suicide.

But this was different now, Minogue knew as he looked across the almost empty dining room. Guards of any stripe did not like to hear of one of their own killing himself, especially a retired one who was being interviewed by other Guards skilled at driving a man into a corner. Even Jimmy Kilmartin might have to stay on the sidelines if Russell went on a rampage over it.

"You're sure she didn't mention anything about a row with Tidy Howard that night?" Hoey asked. "Or that she had left the pub either, in the car —"

"Just let me talk to her first," Minogue murmured. "Hear what she says. Then we can alibi her or look for corroboration."

Hoey looked away and took a long drag on his cigarette.

"You're shielding her from someone, aren't you?" he said then. "Crossan, is it?"

Minogue blinked. He was ready with a retort about Hoey himself being shielded from Kilmartin when he spotted Crossan tramping across the dining-room carpet toward them. A relieved Minogue glanced at his colleague. Hoey's stare stayed on the inspector until Minogue looked away again to Crossan.

•　　•　　•　　•　　•

He pushed home the padlock on the cottage door, tested it, and walked to the van. He was bone weary. They'd be finished this job in three weeks but he already planned to pad out the bill with a few days' dossing. Plenty of money in Germany. The bastard'd never get tradesmen like him for twice his pay back in frigging Germany anyway. Nearly pitch-dark already, God. The radio was on in the van.

"Did you pack the blades and the masonry bits?" he called out.

"What?"

"The saw and masonry bits?"

"Yep. Are we right?"

An ad for holiday getaways in Spain came on the radio. He clambered in and pulled the door behind him. The driver wriggled in the seat and started up the van. Get away from all this crap. Spain'd be nice. Take her too, do it in the water. Swimming and drinking and eating right. The lust hovering in his belly met with the misgivings sliding down his chest. She was getting out of hand: nearly running the show.

He looked across at his friend. Him, this, the dirt caked under his nails, the slogging away renovating this cottage for a German. And then to have people tell you that you were lucky to have a bloody job! Germany, he thought, and a little hope flared. Maybe. Drop everything, just walk away from it all and get a job over there. Be nobody there for a while. Tell nobody, just pack up one morning and go. No more worrying, holding back. No more watching and waiting. When was the money supposed to be rolling in anyway? You have to be patient, he was being told all the time, the insurance business takes time. Your clientele has to know that you're serious. What about all the fucking Guards crawling all over the county this last while, he had protested. Be more careful, plan better, and go at it, came the answer. They need to know that the cops can't protect them, so they'll have to strike a bargain in the end. The money'll come in soon . . . Hah.

"You're buying," said the driver. The van wallowed at the end of the laneway.

"Aren't you?"

"Amn't I what?" The driver shifted in the seat and sat up from the chair-back.

"It's your turn to buy the jar now."

He didn't answer but looked out into the night instead. Christ, the place had been emptied by emigration and famine, and now the rich wanted to take their holidays here. Culture, for God's sakes — you can't eat culture. They had money and they wanted culture: We have no money, just loads of culture. Sick joke. And he wanted receipts for every damn thing, this bloody German. He'd be flying into Shannon for the afternoon at the end of next week, coming to the cottage to inspect the work too. Suspicious, complaining. What effect would the Spillner thing have on them? They never just tell you that you did a good job. No thanks, just pay. Flying in for the afternoon, being driven up by a chauffeur probably.

The driver sat upright over the wheel and squirmed a little as he whistled to a tune on the radio.

"What are you doing? Is it fleas you have?"

"Ah, no. Are you buying or aren't you?"

"Think of something else instead of the drink, can't you?"

"Wouldn't mind a ride, so . . ." The driver looked over knowingly and squirmed again.

"It must be fleas you have."

"It's my insurance policy."

"What in the name of Jases are you talking about?"

"Well, I'm not going to be a sitting duck —"

The passenger suddenly understood. He lunged across and shoved his hand under the back of the driver's jacket.

"Here! Fuck off, Ciarán! I'm driving!"

He felt it but the driver sat back and pinned his hand against the seat.

"Stop, can't you, or the van'll be in the ditch!"

He leaned over with his other hand and levered the driver forward. As he did, he grasped the pistol and yanked it out of the driver's belt. He held it and ran his thumb toward the safety.

"You stupid, fucking iijit!"

"Gimme! Come on!" His voice was just short of a roar.

"You think this is going to help? Is this fucking cowboys and Indians you're playing here or something?"

"Gimme, it's mine!" The van was slowing. The driver held out his hand for the gun.

"Some kind of a fucking film you saw, is it? Jesus Christ, Finbarr! The place is rotten with fucking Guards and you're walking around with a —"

"I'm not going to be caught with me pants down! I'm never going without a fight! Give it back, it's my decision!"

"It's not even your fucking gun, any more than it's mine, you gob-shite! He got this out of a dump along with the other stuff. We're not supposed to have it —"

"It's us that's doing the dirty work! Don't mind him! We're the ones putting our arses on the line! And what do we have to show for it? Nothing! Fuck-all, that's what! So don't tell me how to carry on!"

The passenger laid the pistol on the floor and covered it with news-paper. To his astonishment, his anger had vanished. In its place was an overpowering feeling that he had lost something. It brought an ache of regret and hope to his chest. The driver picked up on the change in his friend and he returned his hand to the wheel.

"Come on now, let's not be bickering," he murmured. "We have to look out for one another, hah? Come on, now. We've always done it, haven't we? It's me and you, Ciarán."

It was a sorrow he hadn't felt since childhood, that sense of injustice and things going irretrievably astray that caused the passenger's eyes to sting. What was the point, he thought. He couldn't fight this. Spain. He knew then that tomorrow he'd be thinking about it all again. Maybe even Germany, work a few years away from all this, get a stake, and buy a house back home. He thought about her then and that familiar turbulence began in his stomach. What would she do?

"Well?" said the driver.

"Shut up awhile, can't you?" he mumbled. "And just fucking drive."

· · · · ·

"That's right," said Minogue, and reached for his cup.

"Up in Dublin," Crossan added.

"That's how it looks," said the inspector. He adopted a patient tone that he hoped the barrister would decode.

"So when I find out where, I'll be talking to her."

Hoey dropped a depleted ice cube into his mouth and crunched it.

"You'll let me know, so," said Crossan.

"You may rely on it," said Minogue with a heavier emphasis.

"Is there going to be an internal Garda investigation about Naughton?"

"We're back off to Dublin tomorrow," said Minogue. "Until I find out what Sheila Howard tells me this time around, I don't know about any internal investigation."

"But what Naughton told you about the fire suggests there was some kind of colllusion going on," said Crossan.

Minogue laid down his cup with a solid thud. "Collusion isn't a term we should be throwing around here now."

"Yet, you mean," Crossan tossed in. "Step back a minute and look at what we have. Fact: Eilo McInerny was paid money to leave Ireland. Fact: We cannot account for key people the night of the fire. Fact: Naughton had a nice fat pad to his pension. Fact: Naughton knew plenty about that night, more than he was willing to tell you. Fact: Naughton killed himself out of some sense of duty or loyalty," — he paused and looked from Minogue to Hoey — "to someone or something. It's time to raise dust here, I say. Make it official. Time for your 'inquiry' to grow up into a proper investigation."

Hoey looked up at the ceiling and blew smoke toward a lampshade.

"I think we need to talk to her first." Minogue realized that his words had betrayed something. "I mean that I need to assess how, er, Eilo McInerny's allegations may affect the situation and so on."

"Aha," Crossan barked. "Allegations. We have allegators now, do we? Maybe we're getting somewhere now."

Trapped, Minogue floundered further. He heard his words sound an ignominious retreat into the formal, public language of a policeman. He did not look at Hoey as he spoke.

"I don't need to remind you that this is a delicate matter. We're obliged to respect the parties' rights. Things must remain as allegations —"

"Naughton blew his brains out," said Crossan.

"— while we sift through what's to be had in the line of information —"

"Are you or aren't you going to press for a full investigation when you confer with your, em, colleagues?"

Minogue took a few seconds to absorb Crossan's sarcasm.

"I give my word that I — we'll — keep you as fully informed as we possibly can."

He waited for another dig from the lawyer but none came. Crossan's gaze lingered on him, but then he swept it away. The waitress timed a visit to coincide with the truce.

"No, thanks," Minogue said, and held his hand over the glass. "Put it all on the one bill, if you please."

"I can't be bought off," said Crossan. His voice had lost its edge, the inspector noted. "But that's not to say that you shouldn't try again with other blandishments."

Mingoue decided it was time for a Parthian shot.

"You can return the favor if you carry an election sometime in the future, counselor. Only as long as it's won fair and square."

"Oh, the sting off that," said Crossan, regaining some vigor. "Dublin hasn't softened your tongue as regards digs."

The drowsiness was heavy across Minogue's chest now, cocooning and holding him fast in the chair in Ennis, County Clare. The curtains were drawn in the dining room. Half-seven. Should he have tried to drive back to Dublin instead of sitting to a dinner with Crossan? All the lawyer had done was to grill him about why he wasn't doing what Crossan himself thought needed done. Even Hoey was looking askance at his judgment. If he closed his eyes, he'd nod off, he believed.

"You'll be in touch," said the lawyer.

· · · · ·

The smell of a fry woke Minogue. His whole body ached. He felt as if he were anchored to the bed, like Gulliver pinned. Is this what a stroke does, he wondered, and thought of Tidy Howard. The mattress was too soft, and he had rolled into a hollow where he had been boiled by a heavy eiderdown into a state of sweaty, aching immobility. Ten to nine, he saw on his watch. And he had worried that he was too wound up to sleep.

He struggled to sit up in bed. A fragment of a dream slid by him before he could see it clearly: a fire, he knew, but . . . He rubbed at his eyes for a full minute. Then he picked up his watch again and strapped it on. He had slept for eleven hours. He remembered that Mrs. McNamara had kept him talking through the news when Hoey and he had come in last night. He had phoned Kathleen, he recalled, and had done a good job of editing out the greater part of the day's proceedings.

He drew the curtains back a little. For a moment he wondered if he were still asleep and dreaming. As his eyes became used to the light he could make out the looming forms in the fog beyond Mrs. McNamara's tidy, wet garden. He dressed and packed his bag. At least he'd get to steal into Bewley's in Dublin today. He knocked on Hoey's door but there was no answer. He opened the door to find Hoey's bed made. His toothbrush, several packets of Majors, and pieces of folded paper were on a dressing table. One of them was an airmail envelope with jagged paper by the opened flap. He closed the door and headed for the parlor. Mrs. McNamara's head inclined out the kitchen door to intercept him.

"Come in," she called out. "I thought I heard someone stirring."

"Hello, Missus. Is there any sign of the other lad?"

"Oh, Seamus?" she beamed. Mrs. McNamara was holding a spatula aslant across her chest. "He's gone out, so he is."

Minogue followed her into the kitchen. A stirring in a chair by the Aga drew his eyes to an elfin figure sitting next to the range. The old woman looked out over her hands, which rested on the handle of a blackthorn walking stick, and issued a myopic smile. Were there more dwarfs hiding about the house? He turned to greet the old woman.

"Good day to you, Ma'am"

"And yourself, now," she croaked back.

The inspector turned back to Mrs. Mac.

"Excuse me now, but did he say where he was going?"

"He went out to get sausages. Such a memory I have, I didn't have a sausage in the house and he offered to go out."

Maybe gone AWOL to get a bloody half-bottle of whiskey or something. He turned to head back to the hallway.

"Ah, sit down, can't you? He'll be back in a minute." Mrs. McNamara's voice began to go up. "Sure he's only gone a few minutes." She pushed Minogue toward the old woman. Maybe he'd pushed Hoey too hard or something?

"Mrs. Moran here comes by of a morning," Mrs. McNamara went on in a louder voice. "Don't you, Mamie? And we have a cup of tea and a chat so as we catch up on the news about town."

The seated elf must be in the high eighties, Minogue decided.

"Don't trouble yourself to get up, now," he muttered. He leaned down to grasp her bony fingers. Her skin reminded him of boiled chicken skin slipping over the bone.

"If and I don't give it a try," she answered back with a shrill, mewing voice, "I mightn't be able to get up when I'd be needing to."

Her denture slipped as she smiled up at the policeman. Minogue readied himself to catch her.

"Matt Minogue, Missus. How do you do?"

His hands had ideas of their own. They stayed up, waiting for her to totter. She did not. She sat back with a sigh and the blackthorn wavered in front of her again.

"Yerra, there's no good in grousing," she shouted at Minogue. "And that's a fact."

Now Minogue knew why Hoey had gone on an errand so readily. Mrs. McNamara shouted and waved the spatula at the window.

"Please God, we'll get a bit of sun before dinnertime, Mamie."

"Please God," echoed Mrs. Moran, and she shuddered. She clasped her blackthorn and, to Minogue's consternation, licked the tip of her nose. How long a tongue did the woman have? Mrs. McNamara turned from the cooker.

"Matt is a Guard, Mamie," she roared. "He's here on a holiday. Lot of excitement in town," Mrs. McNamara went on. "You heard someone took potshots at the Howards' house, Mamie?"

Mrs. McNamara swiveled around with her eyes wide and gave the inspector a conspiratorial smile.

"Merciful hour," said Mrs. Moran. "Imagine that!"

She gave several spasms, which Minogue suspected were poorly governed shrugs, and her dentures came into play again.

"The times that we're living in. 'Tis like The Troubles again."

"If I might use the telephone?" asked Minogue.

"Oh, fire away, can't you?" Mrs. McNamara shouted over the spitting rashers. "But ye'll not leave here without a proper breakfast."

Minogue backed away toward the door.

"Very good of you."

He phoned the Squad office number and waited. Murtagh answered with a fluid delivery of the "Investigation-Section-may-I-help-you" that Kilmartin had directed the people-friendly detectives to answer inquiries with. Partnership, PR, the Human Face were some of the terms Kilmartin had relayed back from meetings with senior Gardai. Serving the public. Eilis had a varied repertoire but she sometimes recited her user-friendly incantation. Such was the charge of sarcasm Kilmartin had noted in her tone one day that he directed her to return to her former delivery of "Yes?" or "Murder Squad."

"Where are you now?" Kilmartin barked.

"I'm in Ennis."

"Hah. Signs on you'd be in the thick of it, you chancer. Ennis is a hot part of the country today. Did you know that, bucko?"

"You hardly mean the weather."

"Damn right I don't, How's Hoey?"

"He's gone out to buy sausages. We slept it out. We were up and down the west of Ireland yesterday."

"I wouldn't mind being in your boots if that's all you were doing. Have you come up with anything?"

Kilmartin had heard nothing of Naughton, Minogue believed. He considered his answer but came up with the truth instead.

"I don't know, James. But something stinks."

"Ho, ho, mister. I don't want to know about it. Save your problems for Monsignor Tynan. He's the one who shanghaied you into this caper, pal."

Minogue ran his finger along the top of the phone. Hoey opened the front door and stepped in. Minogue nodded at him and mouthed Kilmartin's name. Hoey blinked, shrugged, and headed for the kitchen.

"Well, it's a mixed bag, really," Minogue said to Kilmartin. "I'll tell you when we get back up to town. We'll be off within the hour."

"All right. Here, I got a call from that bollocks Hynes. Asking when you were due back in Dublin. Have you something going with him? I hope to God for your sake you don't. Because if you do . . ."

"All right."

"What does 'all right' mean?"

"It means, mind your own business, James."

"Oh, tough talk now, is it? You're the right hoodlum and you on the phone. Come up here and say it to my face. I dare you."

"I need the Howards' address in Dublin."

"Take your time, there. Are all your little deals going sour?"

"The address, man. Stop fighting with me."

"Oh, too busy to talk, are we? Don't be so stuck-up. I say you're right to get out of this in one piece. Leave Tynan swing. Leave them to their maneuvers down in Clare. Stay out of the way. Did you know there's a big operation on to flush out the Libyan stuff that's buried around Clare?"

"Hard to miss it," said Minogue. "The Howards' address."

"The Howards. What are they up in Dublin for? I found out, bejases, that the Branch has men by the house out behind Leeson Street. Someone let fly at their house in Ennis, I find out. Did you hear anything about that?"

"Yes, I did."

"And you didn't tell me? Well, Christ, man, keep well out of the way of flying shite."

"Your advice is well taken, James. Give me the address. Now."

Kilmartin gave him the telephone number first and told him to okay it with Special Branch before going for a visit.

"All right. I'll be seeing you."

"Is that it? You're not going to sneak off to the airport and head for that sanatorium place, what do you call it, on the sly?"

"Santorini. S-A-N-T —"

"Whoa, boy! Christ, you're in a royal snit this morning. Just tell me that you're not keeping something up your sleeve here. Fair and square now, Matt. I scratch your back and all the rest of it, hah?"

Mrs. McNamara came from the kitchen with a laden tray. She smiled at Minogue and toed open the door to the dining room. Hoey followed her and nodded at the inspector.

"I was talking to the Guard who was first to the house that night, Tom Naughton. He's retired a few years now, in Limerick."

"When that young one, the Canadian, was killed?"

"Yes. The fire."

"What did he have to tell you, so?"

Minogue heard the gunshot again, and he swallowed.

"Well, Shea and myself were talking to him and, well . . ."

"Well, what? You're holding out on me. You found something, didn't you? What about this Naughton fella?"

"Well, he pulled a gun out of a drawer and he shot himself."

"He what? What did you say?" Kilmartin shouted. "He what?"

"He killed himself. I'll tell you when I get back —"

"Wait a shagging minute! Don't just land this on me and —"

·   ·   ·   ·   ·

Hoey had an appetite. He finished Minogue's bread and poured more tea.

"You dropped the phone on him," Hoey murmured again. "He'll be dug out of you for that."

Minogue studied his lukewarm tea and nodded.

"I don't doubt it," said Minogue.

"I'm going to phone the Howards and set up a meeting. Then I'll settle up with Mrs. Mac here and we're off up the road to civilization."

Hoey saluted him with a full cup of tea and looked out through the window at the foggy shroud over the Clarecastle Road. Minogue returned to the hall and opened his notebook to the Howards' number.

·   ·   ·   ·   ·

The embossed wallpaper had had several coats of paint. The inspector studied the pattern and traced his fingertips over its curlicues and ridges. Mrs. Mac kept her house well, he reflected. Parts of the pattern had been flattened and further smoothed by the coats of paint. He could not make out the pattern completely with his eyes but his fingers picked it up as they moved across the wallpaper. He dug a fingernail into a rise in the paper but it failed to pierce it. He stopped and looked down at the phone as if he knew it was about to ring. After a halfminute of staring, the phone still did not ring. Mrs. McNamara came out the kitchen door.

Mrs. Howard, did you visit Jane Clark at her house the night of the fire? Did you, upon hearing of the incident with your husband, take it upon yourself to have words with Deborah Jane Clark? Did you not drive away from the pub, go to her cottage, and then return to the pub less than a half an hour later? Why did you not tell us that you had left the pub that night?

"You're in good order are you?"

"I am, thanks. I reversed the charges, like the other call."

"Great, so."

Mrs. McNamara smiled and entered the dining room. Hoey stepped into the hallway after her. His look to the inspector was an appeal to get him out of the clutches of Mrs. McNamara.

"Let's get out of here," said Hoey. "Hit the road."

"Sheila Howard is still in Ennis."

Hoey frowned and blew smoke out the side of his mouth.

"I phoned their place in Dublin, talked to Dan Howard. He told me she decided at the last minute to stay and get the place fixed up. She had to farm out the two horses to be looked after while they're away."

"I want to see her on my own," Minogue said.

Hoey tossed his packet of cigarettes into the air and caught it with a limp palm. "You're going to ask her where she went during the time she left the pub," he said. "Aren't you?"

"Of course I am."

Hoey looked at the frosted glass on the front door and threw the packet into the air again. He grasped it on its descent with a firm hand.

"You're the boss."

"Give me an hour, hour and a half. I'll pick you up in front of here."

Hoey nodded. He let a mouthful of air balloon his lips before he let it out with a soft pop. "You're clear on what you want from her, right?"

"How many more times are you going to ask me?"

Hoey pursed his lips and nodded again, as if he were resigned to the score now that he had heard the final whistle.

"So I'll meet you here outside the gate about eleven. Did you check to see if she's in the house?"

"The phone's still out from last night."

CHAPTER 14

Mɪɴᴏɢᴜᴇ ᴅʀᴏᴠᴇ slowly. The fog seemed thicker outside town. Trees and houses materialized and then slipped back into the whiteness as he passed them. Fields were swallowed up a hundred feet beyond the roadside walls.

He could not see the Howards' house from the gate. He stuffed the Fiat into a spot by the gates and turned off the engine. He was standing outside before he wondered what the hell he was parking there for. He shook his head at his own confusion. Was it a subconscious thing, not wishing to bring the poor Fiat back to the scene of its despoiling in front of the Howards' house? Embarrassment at driving this wreck, full of uxorious litter? He unlocked the door and prepared to get in but then decided to leave the damn car where it was. Perhaps, he reflected as he locked the door again, it was vestigial caution after seeing the police cars and vans swarming around the gates the other night, wisely left outside until the Fiat had been probed for booby traps. A walk up the avenue would give him another chance to clear his head anyway. He looked into the window of the Fiat, ran his comb over the top of his head, and set off up the avenue.

The trees and bushes seemed to move as they came to him from the fog. The house appeared first as a darker patch, gray, then as the outlines of roof and corner. A Hiace van was parked by the steps.

C. LOUGHNANE

HOME REPAIRS, RESTORATION, AND RENOVATIONS

WE'RE NOT HAPPY UNTIL YOU ARE

He walked past the van. He saw no workmen about but a stepladder was next to the window. Minogue stood and studied the damaged plaster around the window opening. The frame was still attached and there were shards of glass in the flower bed below the window. He remembered the whacks as bullets hit the wall. He looked closer and detected the deeper points to the centers of the scooped-out gouges in the plaster. A breeze caught his coat and moved it across his legs. He shivered. Did Sheila Howard have her own car? The damp air seemed luminous now. Minogue's eyes ached when he looked up at the sky. What approach would he use? *Mrs. Howard, I was just mulling over our chat and . . .*

The steps seemed steeper. He grasped the brass doorknocker but the door moved slightly. He let down the knocker and pushed at the door with his fingertips. On the latch to let the workmen come and go? Maybe she had done what she had to do with the bloody horses, or whatever she had stayed for, and she was on the high road to Dublin already. Iijit. He saw his own bulbous face reflected onionlike on the doorknocker as he took his hand away. Better knock. He passed a hand over his hair. Something suggested to him that knocking or calling out here was vulgar, disturbing. He went for the knocker again and heard a short cry from inside the house. His hand stopped inches from the knocker but his other hand pushed the door a few inches back into the hall. A radio announcer issued news indistinctly from somewhere in the house. An ad jingle started up.

"Go on," he heard a man's voice say. Taunting, urgent, whisper and hiss together. The inspector put one foot on the threshold.

"Do it, can't you?" said the man. "Like we do. Come on!"

"Leave me be," Sheila Howard said. "I don't want that. Not today."

"Ah, Jesus, don't be worrying!" The man's voice rose. "You like it," said the man, less pleading now. "Don't play Lady Muck on me! I know how you like it. Tell me now. Go on, tell me!"

Minogue's feet were leading him across the hall. His mind had gone away. The radio ad ended and a bubbly host announced a top hit from the charts while the music started up. The man's voice had a warning tone to it now.

"Are you too good for me today, is it?"

Her voice strained and wavered as though she were exerting herself in some chore. "Not now," she said. "Not here. I can't."

"Prince Charming ran away, so what are you fluttering on about?" He sounded breathless now. The words slowed as though he was concentrating on something else.

"He's having his ride up there. It's your turn. Come on."

"Stop it Ciarán! Take the stuff and go. We'll meet later on."

"Give me a little souvenir, can't you?" His voice fell to a low growl. Minogue heard a grunt.

"No," she said.

Minogue's stomach was tight now and his shoulders felt as though they were sinking down along his sides. He knew something, and he was losing a battle that he didn't remember starting to fight. Better say something, he thought, but his hand pushed at the door anyway. The opening door fanned the scents to him and he knew he needn't fight any longer. Along with those of sweat and the secret, scented clefts, he made out the musky smell. She saw him in the doorway but the man astride her kept pushing his hips into her. She stared at Minogue without fear or surprise. The inspector himself felt no shock. Although he could not take his eyes from hers, he saw and understood all he needed to. Her blouse open, naked from the waist down with one of her legs lying on the arm of the sofa. Her jeans were on the floor by the coffee table and black knickers lay next to them. The man's pants still clung to his ankles. He pushed faster, gasping, and began to mutter. Her eyes were flat and dull but they stayed on the inspector. She began to move under her partner's thrusts. Doesn't she care at all, Minogue wondered? The man's buttocks squeezed as he pushed hard into her.

"Now," he hissed. "Tell me. You bitch! You fucking bitch!"

He grasped her neck and rose up over her. Her legs moved limply with every thrust he made. They were tanned, Minogue saw. Her eyes grew larger and turned to her partner. One side of her blouse fell away. Her breast shook as he began to buck.

"Tell me now," he groaned, and looked down toward her belly. "Tell me, fuck you!"

Her eyes darted from her partner back to Minogue. The man's head turned suddenly. A concentrated, brutal rapture contorted his face. His face was red. He kept his hands on her neck. Dark hair, strands of it hanging over his eyes. Hadn't shaved for a couple of days. Late twenties. Ciarán. Minogue remembered the face: one of the two men who had lurched into the pub that night he and Crossan were trying to steady their nerves after the shooting.

Embarrassment won out over his curiosity and Minogue stepped back. The ugliness of what the man's hands were about stopped his retreat and he stared into the eyes again. The man frowned and began to let himself down. Minogue couldn't take his eyes from her now. With her partner reaching for his pants, she drew her legs together and tugged at her blouse. Her face was flushed and, while her eyes seemed bright, they retained the dull stare. Like a painting he half remembered, Minogue took in Sheila Howard's body as she rested on one elbow, her brown legs one over the other.

The words of the tune on the radio, a familiar ballad, kept coming into his thoughts. Without taking his eyes from hers, Minogue could make out the patch of dark hair that stopped halfway to her navel. Some distant disappointment in her look began to work on the inspector and he began to feel the dismay and desire flood into him. Her body seemed carelessly thrown there, as if it were something she had little use for anymore. But that couldn't be, he realized. Her body did not fit with this man's lust. A slob: how could she? No coy or whorish scorn in her expression. Unconcerned, as if all had been lost some time ago and there was no place to begin trying to explain. How could she? *How could anyone, you gobshite? You know people and what they can do. Are you blind or just stupid? Romance. Do you think people are angels? Wishing your life away. Don't you know anything?*

The inspector's words came out in a whisper. "I'll wait."

The radio went to ads again. Sheila Howard's partner had now turned his back. He was working his trousers up. Ciarán somebody. The air in the room was suddenly overpowering: pungent bleachy mix of genitals, the cheesy stench of the man's socks, his cigarette smell. A picture of him pushing into her flashed into Minogue's mind again. For the first time, he felt angry. Is this what she wanted? *You know she did. You know it.* "*We can meet later on.*" *Didn't you hear her? She doesn't care.* The man she had called Ciarán glared at Minogue and flicked his hair back from over his eyes. His sleeve brushed Minogue's as he walked by, hopping slightly to right the sit of his trousers. Minogue smelled sour sweat from his clothes as he passed.

"Well," came the lilting sarcasm in a man's voice from the hall.

"It's all right," Ciarán grunted.

Minogue headed out after him.

"Go back, can't you, go back," Ciarán hissed, and waved his hands.

"You came up short, did you?" the voice taunted. "Here, maybe I should have a go —"

"Fuckin' move!" Minogue heard Ciarán reply.

The inspector reached the doorway and saw him push another man back toward the kitchen. The drinking pal from the night before at the pub, he noted. A stricken look came into the second man's face and his bloodshot eyes bulged. Minogue's eye was drawn to the stud in the man's earlobe. He smelled whiskey-breath now.

"Who the fu . . . How did he . . . ?" and his mouth stayed open

They know me, thought Minogue. Sheila Howard's interrupted lover, who Minogue wanted to believe was not her proper lover, at least not in the way he imagined lovers, pushed the other man again.

"'Cause you were pissing around, drinking in the fucking kitchen," he whispered fiercely. The man's eyes were still on Minogue. "So go and do your fucking job!"

The inspector decided to wait on the steps outside. He wanted to take this Ciarán aside and give him a going-over. At the same time he knew how absurd that was. As Minogue turned, the man with the earring stumbled and fell backward. He swore as he fell, landed first on his backside and then turned on his forearm to stop himself rolling back feet-up.

"Stop fucking pushing," he grunted as he came to rest. Minogue gave him a contemptuous glance and the man started to get up.

The gun clattered onto the floor from under his jacket. It lay there, still, while the three men looked at it. Minogue held his breath and looked from the gun up to Ciarán and then to the other man. For several seconds, the inspector could not get beyond bewilderment. Were these two lesser species of Special Branch assigned to guard Mrs. Howard? He imagined tumbrels clicking into place somewhere in the back of his addled mind. His heart seemed to be soaring into his throat. He heard a soft slap of elastic clicking over the sound of an ad for fertilizer. Sheila Howard putting her knickers on again, a part of his mind registered.

"Look what you've gone and done now, you fuck —" said the one with the earring.

"Are you Branch —" Minogue started to ask.

Ciarán dropped to the floor. In one smooth movement, he had the pistol up and the barrel of the automatic drawn back.

"It's done now, so shut up," he said. The panic on the man's face had frozen Minogue's thoughts.

"You stupid, lazy fucking —" Ciarán began.

"I didn't *hear* him!" shouted the one with the earring. Minogue continued to stare at him. His entire face was red now and his mustache seemed to quiver. Locks of curly hair stood out over his ears.

"You with the stupid radio on —"

"He didn't drive up! I woulda heard him!" He turned to Minogue. "You walked or something, didn't you?"

Ciarán waved the gun from side to side at Minogue and moved to the foot of the stairs. Minogue felt the door near him and his body almost leaned toward it.

"See!" cried the other. "He's after sneaking up! Close the fucking door! There's probably a mob of them around the house! Jesus! It's a fucking trap, Ciarán! We've been set up!"

Ciarán's eyes turned frantic and his fingers flexing and grasping the grip of the automatic took Minogue's thoughts. The inspector felt his legs begin to quiver. Were they both drunk? How could he buy time?

"It's a fucking setup! They knew all along!"

All along? They knew who he was? How?

"Did you?" asked Ciarán in a soft voice. The other man closed the hall door.

Minogue's instincts had already begun to size up the pair. Ciarán with the gun didn't look drunk. He acted with a natural authority. The one with the earring had been drinking, hence an unknown. Better Ciarán to have the gun? What could he play on, appeal to? They knew he was a Guard. He had seen their faces. If he tried to fool them into believing there really were Guards surrounding the house . . . Sheila Howard stood in the doorway to the living room. Minogue lost track of his calculations and thoughts. He felt himself falling into panic. He looked into Ciarán's eyes.

"Well, did you?" said Ciarán.

Minogue sensed with a dull, awful certainty that this Ciarán was the most dangerous. When this fella acted, there'd be no warning. Details in the hall pressed in on him. Furniture polish, the picture frames, the stupid music from a stupid DJ in Dublin who couldn't imagine Minogue's terror here.

"There is! We're fucked!" hissed the other. "I'm telling you! It was this bastard —!"

He threw a sudden punch at Minogue. The inspector tried to dodge it but the blow glanced off his cheek. He tottered to the wall off-balance, bumping against Ciarán on the way. The shock woke something in him and he came back from the wall in a crouch, his head still roaring from the impact.

"Stop it," he heard Sheila Howard shouting. "Don't, don't!"

Minogue took Ciarán down sideways and chopped at him with his elbow as it met his stomach. The gun fell to the floor and sour breath whooshed out over Minogue's face. He rolled over the downed Ciarán and looked around the floor for the gun.

"Don't!" Sheila Howard shrieked.

Minogue tried to claw himself up but stopped when he saw the gun pointing directly into his eye, the wide-eyed face behind it and the stud glittering to the side of his head. Ciarán began to wriggle beside him and Minogue looked down. As he did, he heard Sheila Howard's shriek again. The hall turned white and disappeared into the glare. In the whiteness and pain and noise, he felt himself falling. Terror and anger overwhelmed him. Kathleen, he thought, I shouldn't have.

·   ·   ·   ·   ·

Jiggling, dull and constant noise, squeaks. Someone spoke far away. Pain — awful pain he could not endure. His cheek was pressed down on a rag smelling of paint. If things would only stop. He was on his chest. He felt the van's tires clip the innumerable cuts in the tarred road, slap the bigger holes, and then bounce over the corrugated bumps the moving bog had pressed up from below.

Alive, he thought. He turned his head slightly and sent flashes of pain across his eyes. Minogue groaned. The van bobbed and rose to the top of its springs before it dropped back, swaying and shuddering.

"Slow down," said a man's voice. "We've enough on our plate. Don't dump us all in the ditch." The van slowed and Minogue opened his eyes again. Sheila Howard was leaning against a wheel-well, looking down at him. Her expression told him nothing.

"Your man's back with us," said a voice from the front.

Minogue recognized Ciarán's voice now. The van braked hard then, and Minogue slid forward. Sheila Howard fell over and rolled into the back of the bench seat. Minogue yelped as pain shot through his neck. Her hand came to rest inches from his face. The van leaned hard to one side. Minogue felt the tires dig into the tar macadam. He heard the start of the ripping scratch that presaged a skid proper and braced himself, but the van righted itself with a sudden bob. Minogue rolled over and gritted his teeth against the flashes of pain.

"Jesus Christ!" Ciarán shouted. "Can you do nothing right today? Are you trying to fucking kill us?"

Minogue's eyes seemed to swell. The van began to climb and Minogue opened his eyelids slightly. The gray shapes of boulders slid back into the fog in the wake of the van. Minogue opened his eyelids a little more. The side of his face on which he had been lying still felt numb. He held the back of his neck and pushed up on one elbow.

"Hey!"

Minogue looked up. Ciarán was leaning over the seat-back.

"Lie down."

The pain was now like a weight on his neck and shoulders. Sheila Howard had settled back against the wheel-well but she was looking out the back window of the van. Ciarán still had his arm over the seat.

"Who else from your mob are here in Ennis?" Ciarán asked.

Minogue focused on him with difficulty. He began to say something but nothing came out. He tried to swallow.

"I don't know what you mean," he managed to croak. Ciarán's eyes narrowed.

"Your mob," he said, louder. "Your pals. Guards. Whatever outfit you belong to. Undercover mob."

Minogue wondered if he dared lift his arm to look at this watch. What would Hoey think when he didn't show?

"Are you deaf?" shouted the driver. That one, Minogue thought, as he heard the tone of a braggart keen to look tough, the one who had been drinking in the kitchen while his pal and Sheila Howard were . . .

"I don't have a mob. I'm down on a holiday."

"Liar," said the driver. "This is your second trip. And you have another fella with you. The one with the black eyes."

"What were you snooping around for?" Ciarán resumed. "What are you looking for?"

Minogue said nothing. The pain dulled his vision but he stared at Sheila Howard. He thought of her straddled on the sofa, this Ciarán rising and falling over her.

"You're an undercover type," said Ciarán. "Who's your boss?"

"I'm me own boss."

Ciarán sprang up, his knees on the seat, and let his arms down over the back of the seat. Minogue looked over at him. The pistol dangled from his hand but the inspector saw the finger on the guard.

"Don't play the fucking smart-arse with me," Ciarán growled and waved the gun. "Who sent you? What do you know about us?"

Us, Minogue thought. He tried to calculate what he should say.

"He's down from Dublin —" Sheila Howard said.

"Jesus, we know that." Ciarán waved the gun again. "The Murder Squad. That's a cover for something. What're you really here for?"

These two had streeled into Considine's pub after he and Crossan had been there ten minutes. Did Crossan? . . . Minogue's thoughts were snapped away by fear then. For several moments his body merely registered the squeaks and the tires' whirr as the van traveled over the Burren road. Across his fogged mind images flared and disappeared back into his confusion: Had Crossan known?

"Ah, to hell with it," said Ciarán. The van jiggled on a series of bumps. Ciarán pressed the pistol against the seat-back to steady himself.

"Look. It's in your own interest . . ." He stopped, still searching for something in Minogue's eyes.

"Fuck it," he snapped. His face seemed to close up. "It's your own lookout if you want to be an iijit."

Minogue watched as Ciarán's eyes went to Sheila Howard. She looked back at him and then returned to the window, her head and upper body swaying as the van took the turns. Minogue believed Ciarán had wanted some sign from her. He moved one hand down the wrist of the other. His watch was gone. Its loss shocked him and surprised him, bringing back the fear. There was something expert about taking his watch, he thought. Planning. He thought of making a break for the door and tumbling out onto the road, hoping for the best. Sit up a little and wait until they passed a house so that Ciarán would hesitate to use a gun. Forget the fact that houses were few and far between here. Minogue moved an elbow under himself and prepared to push his body up in stages. Just then the van slowed and left the tarred road. It wallowed bumpily and slowed as the driver eased it up a laneway. Bushes scraped along the panels once. The van turned sharply and stopped.

"Stay down on the floor," said Ciarán. The driver switched off the engine. Minogue's confusion was burned away. Terror took its place. The insistent knowledge came back still stronger. Knowing what he knew, they would not let him go.

Hoey closed the newspaper and looked at the man behind the counter of Hogan's newsagents. Should he tell him? He felt like laughing, it was so bloody ridiculous. Wait until he showed it to Minogue. He looked at his watch. A half an hour yet.

"That's wicked fog. You wouldn't want to be out on the roads this morning, by God."

He had gone to see *Out of Africa* with Aine and found the landscape behind Meryl Streep's and Robert Redford's faces contrary to what he had imagined Africa was like. Did you think it was all monkeys swinging, like in the zoo, she had gibed. Children with swollen bellies swaying in front of the camera, he had thought. People always unfortunate, winds whipping sandstorms over what had been grass, gaunt scarecrows carrying stick-limbed babies in the heat and dust. But that wasn't a true picture, Aine had told him. You mean millions are not dying? No: the culture, the ruin that white people had brought to Africa. Slavery, colonialism, apartheid. Didn't he know that our ancestor was probably an African, Eve?

"But sure, it'll probably clear off when we get a breeze."

Aine had gotten her last inoculation that afternoon, he remembered. She had showed him the needle mark: the cholera can be bad, she had said. There had better not be any Robert Redford types hanging around out there now, with or without the clap. The images from the picture receded as the memory of their row that same evening came to him. He felt a leakage of something cold into his chest and stomach. He didn't want to think about it but he couldn't help it.

If you'd only wait and give me time, I could get a leave and go with you. You're joking me, you haven't even been out of Ireland on a holiday, Shea. And, anyway, what could you do there? You're a Guard. They want teachers and what-have-you, not more men in uniform. I could visit. I'll write and let you know, Shea. Maybe I need to be on my own for a while, a change of scene. For what? That's none of your business in actual fact. I need to stretch me legs and do new things. There's more to me than being a teacher, you know. There's more to me than being a cop, too. You've changed, Shea. You really have. Over the last two or three years. I haven't changed enough for you, by the sound of things. Don't get like that, you're like a spoiled child. I'm the way I am, I've always been different and you knew that. You never complained about that before. You used to say you liked that even. Look, Shea, let's not fight. We're two grown people. Things change, that's all I'm saying.

Hoey opened the paper again. It was still there.

"Are you down from Dublin?"

Hoey was reading today's copy of the *Irish Independent.* On page four, the features page, was a full-page article on Irish people working for charity organizations in Africa. Aine, her arms around two black kids smiling shyly, was herself grinning back into the camera. "Aine Healey, a teacher on leave from her job in Dublin, has made fast friends with these two youngsters in rural Zimbabwe."

Hoey looked up from the paper. "How much is the *Indo*?"

Mr. Hogan looked over the rim of his glasses at Hoey.

"Same price as in Dublin. Have you it all read?"

"It was the one page I was looking over again," said Hoey. He laid a pound coin next to Hogan's cup of tea. "See her? I know her."

Hogan squinted at the picture. "Africa, begob. She's helping them out in Africa. That's great." He looked up to Hoey and smiled.

"That's the Irish for you. Where there's trouble and famine, that's where we go. We had it so bad ourselves with the Great Hunger, we'd never walk away from people in need. It's in the genes, man. It's the way we are — that's what I say."

Hoey took his change and stumbled back out into the shrouded town of Ennis. He stopped in a doorway and read it again. "They need us and they're terrific kids. They really want to be in school. . . . Yes, it took time to adjust but I fell in love with the people. They really need us. . . . They have taught me so much. . . . Oh, sure, I miss Ireland but not as much as I . . ."

Hoey's eyes began to sting. He stuffed the paper under his arm and searched his pocket for hankies. His chest began to heave and he couldn't stop it. He had no hankies but he wouldn't go back into the shop in this state. Were the pubs open? *Fuck!* His shoulder scraped the wall as he fingered his eyes. He began to look at the shop fronts, hoping to see a pub. He stepped out into the street to see better. The car grew out of the fog behind him. Hoey heard the squeak of brakes and looked around. The antennae were still waving as it started up again. Hoey looked down into the car. The face was familiar. Cuddy rolled down the window.

"Howarya, there," he said. "Minogue's pal, aren't you? Wouldn't mistake you for anyone else with the eyes there."

Hoey registered the attempt at humor with a nod.

"Are you lost?" Cuddy asked. The squad car began to move off slowly.

"No," said Hoey. "No, I'm not really."

"Tell Minogue I was asking for him," said Cuddy.

·   ·   ·   ·   ·

"All right, now," came Ciarán's voice from the open door. Minogue elbowed up and squinted against the light in the doorway. Though overcast now, the light seemed intense. The fog had retired further. He put up a hand to shield his eyes. Pain swept up to a knot behind his eyes.

"Out you come," said Ciarán. The doorway framed Ciarán and Sheila Howard. Behind them in the fog loomed scraggy evergreens. Like so many cottages in west Clare, it was secreted in a sheltering grove of trees and bushes. Overgrown grasses lay in dense, saturated clumps by the door. Minogue looked from the gun to Ciarán's face.

"Hurry up!"

Minogue stood dizzily on an overgrown laneway. Another surge reached the back of his head and he wondered if he might fall over. Sheila Howard had walked around to the front of the van and she stood there looking away. He took a step forward and felt the world tilting. Builder's rubble, loose stones, and disassembled scaffolding lay in heaps next to the house. Ciarán grabbed Minogue's collar and pushed him forward. Minogue fought off the urge to turn or run. He hadn't a clue where they were. He guessed afternoon but he could not make out where the sun was. His eyes hurt. Run for it? He faked a stumble and fell to the ground. Ciarán stood over him, pointing the pistol.

"No funny moves," he said. He took a step back and motioned Minogue to get up. Minogue's mind tried to work on his location again: up the Coast Road, near Lisdoon? Above Fanore?

"Get up!"

The driver came around the side of the van, straining with the weight of a box he was carrying. Seeing Minogue half up, he stopped and stared. The box slipped from his grasp and clattered onto the laneway. The driver swore and hopped about, his hands on one knee. Ciarán turned his head.

"Just leave it!" he shouted. "Leave it until we're ready." He turned to Minogue who was on one knee now. "And you, get up!"

A new slate roof had been put on the house and an extension had been added to the side. The stone walls had been carefully mortared and fitted to meet with the older building. Ciarán shoved Minogue toward the door.

"In the door there."

Dread paralyzed Minogue. The doorway was a black hole. The horror of being entombed routed him to the spot. Ciarán grasped his collar again and pushed. Minogue raised his hand to prevent himself from falling. His hand slapped onto the door before he braced himself against the jamb.

"Get in the fucking door," Ciarán growled, and pushed again. Better to fight, to run. Ciarán jabbed the gun hard under Minogue's ribs, driving him headlong into the dim interior.

•   •   •   •   •

Was it four o'clock? Five? The darkness was unnerving him more and more. The boards covering the small window had been secured with crosspieces jammed and nailed into the old frames. He had heard some kind of cloth being thrown down on the outside of the door. Once he almost cried out, when the image of the house being set on fire wouldn't go away. He strained for minutes on end to smell any smoke. He had tried to persuade himself — and it had mostly worked — that the cloth was to keep any light from coming in under the door. Still, he could not banish the image that flickered in his mind and detonated the panic in his chest without warning: flames raging through the house, swallowing it, him trapped here as the burning roof came down. *Stop imagining. Think.* Would Hoey have alerted Kilmartin?

His body seemed to be soaking up cold from the cement floor. He felt it taking over his limbs, working at the flesh around his waist. He had tried to get out to pee but nothing had come of it. Pee in the corner, he had been told through the door. There had been coming and going, he knew, because he had heard the scrape of a piece of wood that had slipped under the front door when he had entered the house. He shivered again and the spasm ran right up to his chin, making his teeth chatter. His nostrils had become inured to the damp odor of the cement and dust. He was not hungry but he wanted something — a cigarette, even. He drew up his knees again. Something about Ciarán especially chilled him. Along with the anger there was some weariness or resignation that showed in his eyes. Did Ciarán believe that he couldn't let him walk? Ciarán and whatever-his-name — Finbarr. Were they IRA or some splinter group? And how did Sheila Howard get herself mixed up with these two? Her legs, he thought, her empty eyes on his. The same woman he had seen and watched in the dining room of the Old Ground, in her home. Crossan? Minogue stared into the darkness and whispered the name aloud.

.   .   .   .   .

Hoey wheeled around and glared at Crossan. The two men stood at the foot of the steps leading up to the front door of the Howards'. Hoey had been down to Minogue's car. No keys, locked. No clue as to where Minogue might be. At least there were no bloodstains. He and Crossan had been through the yard, into the coach house and sheds, out into the fields. Sheila Howard's car was in the garage. Nothing else. He glared at the lawyer.

"This window," said Hoey. "Come on, give me a leg up."

"Aren't you overreacting again?"

In lieu of an answer, Hoey sprang up on the lawyer's cupped hands. Crossan grunted and his shoes sank deeper into the mud as Hoey stood upright. Hoey's feet moved up to the lawyer's shoulders.

"Guard tramples on well-respected barrister en route to criminal offense," Crossan whispered as he grimaced. Hoey tapped in the remaining pieces of glass from the shattered frame.

"Accessories are supposed to help," said Hoey. "So shut up."

"Break and enter," wheezed Crossan beneath him. "I'm a goner now, to be sure."

Hoey ground his heels into Crossan's meager shoulders as he toed up and scrambled in the window. He was satisfied with the grunt of pain the barrister issued. He stood in the room and surveyed the floor by his feet first.

"What's the story, then?" Crossan called out.

"Wait and I'll open the front door."

Hoey headed for the hall and opened the hall door. Crossan trudged up the steps, rubbing at his shoulders. Hoey spotted the phone and lifted it.

"Shite, it's still not fixed," he said, and slammed it down.

"At least someone's made a start on fixing up the place," said Crossan.

He began using his nails to get mud from his coat. Hoey walked up and down the hall, checking the kitchen and dining room.

"It's not as bad as I thought it'd be," Crossan murmured.

"What isn't?"

"The damage. The shooting. If you'd been here, you'd have thought the place was coming down around your ears."

Hoey sprang up the stairs, calling out the inspector's name. Crossan heard him opening doors and swearing. Then Hoey came down the stairs fast. He stopped on the last step, frowning at the floor.

"They might have gone somewhere for a chat," Crossan tried. Hoey snapped his head up and eyed the barrister. Instead of the retort the lawyer expected, Hoey skipped down the steps onto the pebbled driveway and began walking fast down the avenue.

· · · · ·

He had been thinking of Eamonn. Black head of hair the day he was born, eyelids tight over his eyes. The small coffin. Beyond knowing that Eamonn had been a baby, he could not remember his son's face. The three photos they had of him were not clear: one of Kathleen standing by the crib, the baby cradled but his face invisible; Eamonn asleep in the pram in the back garden, long before the shrubs and trees had grown there; Minogue's mother holding and displaying her grandson to the camera two days before Eamonn had died. Countless times he had scrutinized the photographs asking himself if there was anything different about the child that he should have been alert to. Something different from the start, Kathleen had maintained over the years after Iseult was born — that bold, spoiled, raucous miracle.

· · · · ·

Eamonn's face under the teddy bear: his first thought, as the room exploded around him, the terror and awareness of death in the room changing everything, had been that Eamonn had suffocated. The quiet in the house, dawn, the stillness that brought him from bed and across the hall, knowing something was amiss. Though the infant's hands were cold, Minogue believed that Eamonn had died just before dawn. He recalled wanting his own death for relief from the pain.

He swung his hands over his head and clenched his eyes tight. There must be a way out of this. He stopped stretching: a car outside? He put his ear to the wall. Couldn't tell. He scraped his fingertips hard over his face then but his mind had allowed the words out already — kidnap, hostage. He stopped and stared into the darkness: were they going to kill him? The darkness, the cold, all immediate things fell away. To his surprise, he did not free-fall into panic. His thoughts became clear instead. He began to go through the possibilities. They could hold him until they were safe away. But were they well enough in with whatever groups they belonged to to be handed passports, money, and plane tickets? Not likely. These were local men and, if they were heart-and-soul IRA or affiliates, they'd want to be on home ground, not hanging around shopping malls in Cleveland or Cologne waiting five years for things to die down.

Kill him? No: they'd try to deal their way out. But they'd get seven to ten for possession of the guns alone. Add to that kidnaping, assault. . . .

He traced the lump and the split skin on his head again. His nausea had gone and, except for any sudden move of his head, the ache was manageable. He pushed his knuckles into his eyesockets and tried to think again. Make some strategy or some fall-back position. Lie, talk . . .

Over the water came the breeze, rippling the surface, wave- and trough-like. The sea-skin stretched, swelled again, and drew toward the rocks. Still it seemed to move nowhere. Sea-wrack drifted, sank, and rose again. The fish searched below and then fled among the rocks. There they were, the shapes moving so fast, turning, moiling, streaming cascades of bubbles behind, revolving in rapture. As the image faded, he rose slowly to his feet. Still he couldn't focus on a plan. Where did she fit? Why would she — Something had been going on all around him, Minogue knew, and he had finally stumbled in, clumsy and stupid. He had let his instincts carry him and had even dragged Hoey along. And, in the end, none of this mattered. All past the beyond reach now. No going back. The best of intentions — what did they matter anymore?

An electric jolt ran up his whole body when he heard the steps. They were coming for him. Suddenly frantic, he tried to put the words together for argument. Where the hell was Hoey? Someone was working at the lock. He backed away into a corner. Stand firm anyway, he thought. Run at the door? If there was any chance at all.

The light blinded him. Could it be just those two lousy light bulbs? He squinted through his eyelashes. A flashlight beam ran over his face and chest. He wanted to say something.

"Just fucking well do it, Shea!" Kilmartin roared. "Don't start up on that again or I'll walk on you."

"Well, I can't just sit here like an iijit for a few hours —"

"You can do it and you're going to do it because I'm shagging ordering you to do it! Do not leave the station. Do you hear me?"

Hoey bit back his reply. It wouldn't help Minogue for him to fuck Kilmartin from a height on the phone here. The Killer could work things over the phone for now, get the personnel and the search started right away.

"Are you listening?" Kilmartin asked again.

"Yeah."

"You last saw him at ten, right? And his car is still parked out at the house, the Howards' place."

"So is the woman's, Mrs. Howard. She had a Renault parked in a garage in the yard."

"Where's this fuckin' lawman? Crosbie."

"Crossan. He's here."

"If Matty has been diddled in any way by this little shite Crosbie, so help me, I'll fuckin' burst him. Crosbie, Crossan, whatever the hell his name is. You tell him that, do you hear?"

Hoey surveyed the listless barrister across the table.

"Okay."

"Is Russell there yet?"

"Haven't seen him come in." Hoey was suddenly weary. "Let me ask. He might have come in and I didn't notice."

He put his palm over the receiver and asked Ahearne. The sergeant shook his head, looked at his watch, blinked, and returned to chewing the inside of his upper lip.

"No. Not yet."

"Keep this line open. Sit by the phone. Anyone puts their hand near it, give 'em a puck in the snot. Hard. I'll phone the Branch again."

While he waited, Hoey returned to scraping the remains of a round sticker from a desktop in Ennis police station. Drops of sweat itched in his armpits and on his forehead. He could be back in five minutes from a pub. He scraped harder, oblivious to the sticky detritus collecting under his nails. Guards continued to come and go in the station. Hoey and Crossan had been called in but once to detail what Minogue and they had been doing. Hoey had noted the Emergency Response Unit men checking their pistols in the hallway.

Ahearne was standing by the table, holding a mug.

"No," said Hoey. "Thanks."

Ahearne laid down the mug, glanced from Hoey to Crossan and sat down slowly with a sigh. Two Guards in plainclothes walked in from the yard and stopped by Ahearne.

"Within the half-hour," Ahearne said to them. The two trudged off to the main office.

"Have you picked anyone up yet?" Hoey asked.

Ahearne shook his head. Hoey checked his watch. Kilmartin had told Hoey that he'd be at Ennis Garda station within the hour.

"There's always the chance it might turn out to be a false alarm," Crossan said.

"Shut up," said Hoey.

Crossan considered retaliating but he found that Ahearne was staring at him. The sergeant's usual expression of detached politeness had been replaced by a hard, empty look. Hoey had relayed Kilmartin's threat to Crossan verbatim, unalloyed by sympathy or parody. Hoey had then told him that what Kilmartin might leave intact of him, he, Hoey, a man of modest mien who had given the barrister the appearance of being a cautious, repressed man, as best indifferent to him, would take apart.

"They came back to take the Howards and your man happened to be there at exactly the wrong time," said Ahearne.

Hoey maintained his stare out the window.

"They probably wanted Dan," Ahearne tried again. "Bold and brazen of 'em to come back the next day to do it, I say. Exactly the last time and place anyone'd expect to try and lift Dan —"

"What for?" said Crossan.

Ahearne shrugged. "Well, I'm not up on that. But they'd want to drive some kind of a deal, I imagine."

"How did they know that Mrs. Howard was staying put in the house?" Hoey asked. "They'd hardly expect the Howards to stay put in the house after the shooting."

"And a deal for what?" Crossan probed further.

"Well, I don't know," said Ahearne quickly, as though fending off an accusation. "That's what we're waiting to hear, seems to me."

Hoey turned from the window and looked at Ahearne for a moment.

"Someone had started repairs to the windows anyway," said Ahearne. "They're still trying to reach Dan Howard in Dublin to get the name of whoever was hired to fix the place. Maybe they saw something."

Kilmartin came through the doorway, followed by Russell. Hoey stepped smartly to the side of the door and suffered Kilmartin's sharp, interrogative stare for several moments. Kilmartin nodded at Ahearne, who stood. He spoke in a low voice.

"Are you Crosbie?"

The barrister rose slowly from his chair. Russell stood next to Kilmartin and stared at Crossan too.

"You, mister" — Kilmartin jabbed a finger in the air separating him from the lawyer — "you had better have some big, fat rabbits in your hat. Because, by Christ, we're letting everything off the leash here. If and we can't find rabbits to run down, we'll eat anything that looks like a fuckin' weasel!"

Crossan studied the bulk of James Kilmartin, recently disgorged from a helicopter onto the pad at Ennis County Hospital.

"Tell me now," said the barrister, "did you gallop all the way down from Dublin in a pack or on your own?"

Kilmartin's attention seemed suddenly taken up with a particle of undigested food caught on the tip of his tongue. His tongue scraped his teeth several times as if to flush out any more pieces of food still hiding in his dentures. When he spoke, it was in the gentle and intimate tone the chief inspector reserved for his better threats.

"Listen, head-the-ball. If and you don't cooperate 200 percent with us here" — the chief inspector paused and took a piece of something from his tongue with his thumbnail; he looked down his nose at it as though puzzled at its provenance, flicked it away, and looked back into Crossan's glazed, bulging eyes — "I'll personally give you such a fucking belt that they'll stop you for speeding above in Portlaoise."

Kilmartin turned on his heel and headed for Russell's office. Russell pursed his lips and looked out bleakly under his corrugated brow at Crossan.

"That's merely a figure of speech, Mr. Crossan," he murmured, and followed Kilmartin.

The chief inspector couldn't or wouldn't sit. Russell closed the door behind him and watched Kilmartin as he stood by the window rolling on the balls of his feet.

"Minogue has a mouth on him," said Russell.

Kilmartin's reply came in a restrained monotone. "Well I know it, Tom. And I told him often enough. Sure, don't I have to put up with it every day myself?"

"Didn't help him much here, I can tell you. Matter of fact, I tore into him for it."

Kilmartin nearly lost it then.

"I know, Tom, I know," he said as he drew in a breath. "He has that knack. Definitely, yes, I'd have to agree with you 100 percent on that."

"Is that a job requirement for your mob or that class of thing?"

Kilmartin's teeth were set tight.

"He's Clare, Tom," murmured the chief inspector. "He came by the sharp tongue honest enough."

Russell weighed Kilmartin's anger before he looked away to his desk.

"Well, he's after pissing in the wrong pot today, Jim."

Kilmartin whirled around and strode to the door.

"Wait until we have all the units —"

"I can't fucking wait," Kilmartin hissed. He slapped the door with the heel of his hand. "He's out there somewhere. I was never a man to sit around like a dog by the fire."

Russell hurried out after him. Kilmartin waved at Hoey.

"Drive us, D.J.," Russell called out to Ahearne. "We can work from the car."

CHAPTER 15

THE SMALL, choking black space around his face had become his world. Minogue tried counting his heartbeats to control his claustrophobia. His face felt swollen from the heat, and the musty, mildewed smell of the sack still stung his nostrils. He knew he was facing the wall and that there was a rickety back to the chair he had been tied to. Three men, he knew from their voices, the two from the van and a third he sensed was an older man. He tried to breathe more shallowly. The twine around his wrists was thin and sharp and he worried about the circulation in his hands. His body ached as he tried to sense some movement in the air around him. It was the voice of the third man, this newly arrived stranger, that took Minogue's concentration. He knew that the man was using a clumsy but effective disguise to muffle his voice. A cloth or a towel, he guessed. Amateur or expert? He couldn't decide. His skin prickled in anticipation when he heard someone getting up from a chair behind him.

"You're not giving us much to work with," came the muffled voice. "I'm after telling you that you need to do a job a work here. It's up to you."

Country accent, Minogue could tell. Clare?

"You have the solution, but there's not much time."

Minogue felt he should say something.

"A solution?"

"Yes, a solution. Get to work persuading us."

For a moment, Minogue wanted to shout back that there was nothing he could tell them, that they were stupid to imagine he could.

"Well? Do you think we're fucking iijits here, then?"

Though the man hadn't raised his voice, Minogue felt some shock of familiarity. It was less the swearing than a tone of voice he had heard before.

"I was down here on account of a family matter. My brother's family had —"

"Your brother, hah? And the son, no doubt. A right pair, they are. But sure, at least their hearts are in the right place. What brought you down the second time then?"

"When I heard about Bourke being shot —"

"Ah, don't be trying to pull the wool over my eyes with some cock-and-bull story about this fucking thing, whatever it was. You were down here on dirty work —"

"I came down to see about Bourke. Doesn't anybody care that he got shot out the back of —"

"What the hell do you care one way or another?" came Ciarán's voice. "You took up with this Bourke thing as a cover for doing your spying and sneaking around. What was your mission here?"

Minogue coughed and the twine cut into his wrists.

". . . this shite about you crusading down here, you and Crossan . . ."

He strained forward coughing and his chest tightened with the spasms.

Was this a ploy to make him believe that Crossan was in the clear? The stranger's tone was less contemptuous now.

". . . so stop being a fucking yob. You've worked up a speech and a story that you think is going to work. Guards are like that, aren't they? You think everybody else is stupid." The voice came closer. Minogue stiffened as he heard shoes squeak.

"Ah, but I shouldn't be so hard on you," the voice resumed. "You tried. But there comes a point when a man has to look out for himself. So let's get down to business before we run out of time."

Minogue sat very still now.

"Right. You're an inspector in the Guards. You work for the Technical Bureau, whatever that is —"

"The Murder Squad is one of —"

"Start with the Howards now. You were nosing around there this morning. What brought you there?"

Clare accent for sure, Minogue decided, but he could tell no more.

"I wanted to talk to Mrs. Howard."

"About what?"

"Other details from the night of that fire, when Jane Clark —"

Something shrieked on the floor and Minogue instinctively ducked his head.

"I told you he was a —!" shouted Ciarán.

"It's the truth," Minogue protested.

"Fuck you and your lies!" Ciarán shouted. "You're scouting around for us! Waiting to pounce! You and a whole posse of cops and Branchmen and God knows what else! Aren't you?"

A shiver ran up Minogue's chest and seemed to light with a small piercing shock on his nipples. He waited for the stranger to calm them down a bit. The voice was no longer muffled when it whispered into his ear.

"I'm coming back in ten minutes, and I may have to do for you. It might be quick, and it might be slow. It all depends on you. You're quick enough with the wit when you want to be, but this is not the time or the place for smart remarks. Think hard now, mister policeman. I'll be back. If you're still at this codology, it's be all over."

Minogue heard the footsteps cross the room. The others seemed to be leaving too.

"Leave the bag on him," said the stranger. "Get him used to the dark."

Minutes passed. Fear blurred his mind and he lost track of time. When the door scraped, Minogue's heart leaped. The absurd plea almost came out in words: That wasn't ten minutes . . . They had given up on him, they were going to just kill him because they were losing control of the situation and the time.

"Who's there? Who is it?"

He strained again to hear any movement. The ends of his fingers began to tingle.

"Who's —" A choking sob erupted behind his tongue and his voice broke.

"Ah," came her voice. "You're good and scared now, aren't you?"

Her footsteps behind him, slow.

"You'd better tell them, you know."

Minogue realized that his eyes were wide open. His heart was thudding as if it were outside his body. He couldn't utter a word.

"Do you hear me? Tell them. What's the use of trying to keep it in? What's it worth now?"

"But there's nothing I can tell them," he gasped. "I've told the truth and they don't seem to —"

"Don't play that again now," she said with a faint snort that he read as impatience. "Tell them."

"I can't — there's nothing."

He heard her move to his right side. Her voice dropped to a whisper.

"Tell me then. It was me you wanted, wasn't it?"

The panic blocked his words again.

"Come on. Stupid, you're not. I could tell that right away —"

"People think I know what's happening around here, that's what's so —"

"They sent you because you're *from* here. You're an insider. Come on now, don't be wasting time. They're serious out there. They're waiting for a lead from you —"

"'We,' you mean, don't you?" he managed to say.

Sheila Howard made no reply.

"It was Crossan persuaded me that the Jane Clark case stank —"

"Look. Do you think that time is on your side here? That you can buy time? That they'll forget about you or something? They'll have to decide about you pretty soon."

"'They'?" Minogue risked. "You should know. You're in cahoots with them. They treat you like dirt. Why would you want to —"

"Oh, shut up about that, would you? He wasn't like this. It's all eaten away at him, this whole thing, and he forgets sometimes. That's how he . . .

"Oh what the hell would you understand?" she whispered. "Just shut up talking about that! Can't you see? You're the one in trouble. Start acting like you know it. What did Naughton tell you?"

The name caught Minogue off-guard.

"Well? What did he tell you?"

"He told me several things. He told me that your husband is a fool, for one thing. Then he told me that nobody called the station the night of the fire. I tried to get him to explain but he got into a dander. He took a few swipes at me and Shea —"

"That's just it! You brought more Guards into this. What for?"

Minogue's mind reeled. Where could he begin to explain?

"You're holding something back. What brought you up to the house this morning?"

"You didn't tell me that you'd left the pub in a huff after some row with Dan Howard's father."

"After some row. Oh, Christ, what do you know? What do you think happened that night, then?"

His panic had begun to ease and he realized that talking was giving him back some of his composure. He thought of lying to her but his words came out before he had calculated his reply.

"I think you took the car out to her cottage and you had it out with Jane Clark."

"Had it out?" Toying with him.

"Argued, fought. I don't know."

"Do you think I killed her?"

He knew by her voice that she was half smiling.

"I don't know. She might have been in your way. I really don't know."

"God, you're stupid. At the same time as being smart." Her mood had changed again, he realized.

"Not like Romeo out there?"

She slapped him across the face before he could sense her anger.

"You bastard. Peeping Tom. You think I didn't see you gawking?"

Something in him was satisfied to have had this effect on her. He had his head down and away, waiting another blow. Nothing came.

"So they sent you in to work your spell on me," he said.

"One last chance," she replied, calm again. "They mean what they say. When they come back —"

"They'll have to figure out what to do about you too —" His words were choked off by a coughing fit. "At least let me breathe so as I can talk," he wheezed, and lapsed into another fit of coughing.

Suddenly the sack was off. The cold air of the room fell on his skin. He blinked and took in great mouthfuls of air. A lightbulb on a long cord hung from a nail in the wall. Its glare stung at his eyes and he shut them tight again.

She began to walk slowly around the room and he followed her through a slit in his eyelids. She stopped and leaned against the wall facing him. Her hair was loose and hung out from her inclined head. In her right hand was an automatic pistol.

"Do you really think it's worth it?" she whispered.

He tried to say something but it was a hoarse whistle that ended somewhere near his teeth. He tried to clear his throat.

"They're not going to stop at this," he croaked.

"Don't be stupid," she scoffed. "I'm a hostage."

He stared into the shadows where her eyes were. "You think they trust you so much, they'll let you witness? . . ."

He couldn't bring himself to finish the sentence. She shifted her weight onto her other leg.

"Christ. You really don't have a clue, do you?"

He looked down to where her finger was rubbing against the outer rim of the trigger-guard.

"Let me tell you something now," she went on. "You put most of the bits together and I have the feeling you could probably sort it out in the end. There was something about you that sort of . . . I told them too, that you could be a problem. But if you did get to the stage of putting bits together, you'd be in a lot of . . . trouble."

"Why?"

"Because you'd have opened the door on something more important, that's why. And you still want me to believe that you walked into the whole thing blind?"

He felt that something was rolling toward him, a wave about to crest and lift him high.

"Do you really want to know what happened?" she asked in a soft voice. "Do you?"

She shook her face clear of hair and leaned her shoulder against the wall again. Her head seemed to be shaking a little, he believed. In the space between them, Minogue dazedly took in her anger. She held her breath behind her teeth as she spoke.

"I went to Galway that day because I had an appointment. A doctor's appointment. Why did I go to Galway? Because I didn't want anyone knowing my business around here. The doctor, a man of course, Coughlan, he had a kind of a wart on his nose and it got redder. I remember looking at it and thinking that he had seen me staring at it and maybe he was mad at me for doing that. He told me I had an infection. As if I didn't know. Looked at me like I was a tramp. Asks 'Do you have more than one boyfriend, Miss Hanratty?'" She returned Minogue's stare.

"You know what I'm talking about, don't you?" she murmured.

Though her hair had fallen down again and her eyes had returned into the shadow, the inspector could make out the points of reflected light in her pupils.

"I think so," he said.

"'The tourists, Miss Hanratty?' he says. 'You have to be careful, now, and avoid contact until this is cleared up,' and 'Why did you wait until now?' As if I had answers for him."

She flicked her hair back again and looked away. The gun moved in small arcs as she talked, as if she needed it for balance.

"I knew there was something wrong because I had a lot of pain. Dan, of course. Idiot. So I finally wanted to know. You can guess, Guard, can't you?"

"Jane Clark?"

She nodded, as if considering a point in an abstract discussion that had gone on too long.

"I didn't know what to do." She paused and took a deep breath, her chin down on her chest.

"I knew I wanted to tell her that she had left her mark. I shouldn't have waited. But that's human nature, isn't it? Everyone wants to go to heaven but no one wants to die. I sort of knew that Dan had been seeing her —"

"But if you tried to have it out with him about it, he'd have left you out in the cold?"

"Dan didn't care. That's just the way he is. He does what he wants. There are some things he cares about. I don't doubt but that he has you fooled to the hilt too."

She stared at him for several seconds.

"How many kids have you got?" she asked.

"Two. We had a boy earlier but he died. For a long time, we thought he was our last chance."

"Well, she took a lot of my future with her when she went," she resumed, as if she hadn't heard him. "I came back to the village late and I went straight to the hotel bar. I wanted to have it out with Dan but sure when I got there he was twisted drunk. And I couldn't drag him away."

"You collared Tidy Howard and gave him a piece of your mind instead?"

"You're damned right I did," she snapped. "And of course his attitude was, what do you want me to do about it? Messing around like that was 'immoral' says he. And him chasing chambermaids! Well, I left that hotel raging. Yes, I drove out. And she was still up. She answered the door. She wasn't drunk, I know that. Not then. She might have taken a few drinks after I left. But I think she knew that there was something wrong, maybe the look on my face. We had a row. She didn't just sit there and listen, I can tell you. There came a point that she laughed at something I said, something to do with tourists. I hit her. With my hands. She was strong, but I was really mad. I threw things around and . . . Well, she said then that she was going to call the Guards. She had no phone, of course. I had taken a few lumps out of her, some scratches and that. It wasn't that serious to my mind. After all, I was the one who had been wronged. I got in the car and drove off. I sort of believed her about the Guards. I was still mad, but on my way back I started getting worried."

Minogue looked up from the waving gun. She seemed to realize that he had been observing some part of her that she wasn't in control of, and her eyes narrowed. Her stare moved away from him.

"I came back to the hotel and I told Tidy Howard what had happened. I told him — I was still mad, you see — that I wanted to kill her. Jane Clark, like. He was staring at me like I had just landed off Mars. And I told him that when his darlin' boy woke up in the morning and could hear, I was going to give him a right going-over too. And him looking at me and staring at me, and a smile starts to come across his face. I took a slap at him but he caught my arm. He was a big block of a man. And him laughing . . . He said to me, he said, 'Don't worry your little head, girleen.' I remember him saying that. He told me to get myself fixed up with whatever it took, to go to Dublin if I wanted, and he would pay for it. I was taken aback, I can tell you. The same Tidy Howard who had made little of me the first time. He didn't know any more than I knew at the time that the scar tissue would stop me from — Well, I remember him saying, and him laughing and holding my wrists, looking into my eyes: 'Don't beat the poor boy. Marry him!' Laughing. He thought it was funny. That's the kind of man he is . . . he was."

Her eyes had glazed over now.

"I know this much," she whispered, "that if I had had this with me that night, I would have killed them all. Right then and there. But I was very shook. And when I could think straight, I decided that I'd look out for myself in the long run and do my best. Yes. But I was full sure I'd find some treatment that'd work but . . ."

Minogue's fear had given way to bafflement.

"You just had a row with her?"

"Tidy had it in his head to do something about all this that night," she said. "He knew all the Guards. Naughton was his man more than anyone. Naughton'd give him the nod if the Guards were going to come around at closing time. But Tidy didn't get the Guards that night, not until later. He sent someone else out, then and there, to put a fright into Jane Clark so as she'd pack up and run. Instead of her going to the Guards the following morning, like."

"Who did he send?"

"Well, he got carried away. The way she talked to him — she had a sharp tongue on her, everyone knew, and she wasn't afraid of much." Her voice dropped back to a whisper.

"He got carried away and he wanted to . . . you know. Because she was a whore. She hit him with something and he hit her. Knocked her out. I wasn't there, I only heard later. And it looked bad, he said. There was blood coming out of her nose. He came back to the hotel and told Tidy. That's when Naughton came into the picture."

"Whose idea was it to dump Jamesy Bourke at the cottage, then?"

Her eyes crept back to meet Minogue's.

"Naughton's. Bourke was a thorn in everyone's side around there. As for Jane Clark, Naughton didn't give a damn."

Naughton had covered for them all, then, Minogue thought. Dan Howard, wayward, hapless, spoiled, drunk; Sheila Hanratty, determined to make a husband of him; the man Tidy Howard had sent to bully Jane Clark. He did not feel the cold anymore. His hands still tingled but the cord seemed to have lost its bite. He tried to squeeze his hands into fists but they felt swollen and weak. There were so many questions he wanted to put to her but his concentration was being stolen by his hands, his cramped knees. He stared at the wall and let his gaze slide down to the floor. His head felt unbearably heavy now. Thirsty, weak. How many were involved? Did Dan Howard know? He must. Had Naughton set the place on fire?

"Well, that's all past," she said. "No going back now."

"Look," he whispered. "You know this can't work."

She frowned.

"Keeping me here. A hostage or whatever. Those other fellas don't know it, but I think you do. They're all washed up now. They've screwed up royally. You let them shoot up the house — while you're in it, even — so's we'd all be scared off or something. But you couldn't carry on whatever it is you're doing without one of them making a mess of something —"

"Me!" she hissed, and bent down, her face inches from Minogue's. He saw her chest heaving like his own, smelled her musky scent. "Me? I've screwed up? That's what really galls me! My husband is screwing around in Dublin, playing the fucking statesman and I'm the one that's screwed up?"

Minogue recoiled from her, pushing the chair up off its front legs. She pointed the gun at the ceiling.

"Look," she said. "Even his own bloody father knew that my husband was a good-for-nothing waster. He got me to marry Dan because he thought I could put some backbone into him. And I worked and I worked and I worked at it! I prayed for him, for us, for damn near everybody. I tried everything — surgery in London, even. I went to New York to a specialist. I lived on bloody herbs and yogurt for six months. Then I find out it's too late."

She lowered her arm and poked his chest with the gun. He held his breath. The light in the room dimmed and discolored.

"And I even got over all that, so I did," she whispered. "And I came back and I got on with life. I played the part. It was bred into me to be loyal, to try no matter what. That's how we are. We know life is hard and you have to fight. Christ, we're millionaires now, did you know that? Dan has money stashed away in France and in the States. 'Slush funds.' The ones he told me about anyway."

She gave a mirthless laugh and brushed away her hair with her free hand.

"The tourists are swarming in. He'll get reelected, business is booming. Everything's rosy. All I have to do is shut up and enjoy it. And all the while he's sleeping with every bitch he can find."

Minogue pushed back further on the back legs of the chair. She jabbed hard into his chest with the gun again. The place she struck stayed numb. Jesus, he thought, his chest was about to burst, she could go off the deep end and take him with her. Beyond his terror he realized that he didn't know her at all. She hated her husband, that was obvious. Or did she merely scorn him, hating something or someone beyond and including Dan Howard? This was her revenge, to get in with these half-wit gangsters?

She drew herself up to standing again.

"The Howards," she muttered. "I'm not a Howard, I'm a Hanratty. My father died and I was eleven. He worked digging ditches for the County Council all his life. It wore him down because he was intelligent and he could see another life for himself. He had a heart attack before he was fifty years of age. Died of worrying. He wanted us in school and getting good jobs. But there was something he never really understood, even though he said it a lot." She paused, looked down at the pistol and frowned.

"I found out late enough too," she murmured. "If you have it, you'll get it. That's how life is. And it's no good thinking and hoping otherwise. It's cruel. Nothing has to be fair and equal. The Howards do well and they don't deserve to. But the rest of us, no matter what . . ."

She looked at Minogue again with a doleful, momentary smile. She walked away from him then, slowly and delicately, like a dancer rehearsing moves in her mind. Hearing her footfalls behind him brought the fear back to him: She was leaving him to the others. She started to pace up and down the room behind him.

"You must be good at your job. Me coming in here trying to get you to talk, and it ends up with me doing all the talking."

"What about your husband — ?"

She laughed lightly. "What about him? 'Does your husband know?' Is that what you meant to say? Does my husband know that Ciarán and Finbarr will get paid good money for fixing up the damage they did? Does my husband know crates of guns and ammunition and more were moving in and out of the house for the last eighteen months?"

She tucked the pistol into her jeans and let her sweatshirt fall over the grip.

"Does my husband know that I know he's hopping in and out of bed with those ones in Dublin? Well now, inspector down from Dublin, my husband doesn't know. He knows fuck-all. That's how much he knows."

She looked down at him and resumed with a lilt in her voice.

"But I'll tell you who does know. I'll tell you who knows everything. Tidy Howard knows. He could tell you things. But he never will. He'll go to his grave with everything he knows and it'll be buried with him. And that's just fine by me."

She gave a little shrug as if weighing a decision.

"He knows because I tell him everything. It's my way of thanking him. I visit him and I talk to him and I tell him the news. He always wanted the news. 'Give us the news now,' he'd always say in the old days. 'If you haven't any, make up a bit.' Well, I don't make up anything. I give him the facts. I tell him how Ciarán has me every way he wants in the back of his van. I think that my father-in-law is the type of man who'd be keen to hear about stuff like that. He certainly used to, and that's no lie."

Something squirmed in Minogue's belly. He tried to swallow but couldn't. He saw Ciarán scrabbling and shoving at her, then the paralyzed, wasting shell limp in bed, unable to talk or scream while his daughter-in-law sat next to him, chatting dutifully.

"Oh, yes," she went on, "I tell him everything because I know he's discreet. He won't tell anyone. I tell him the fun we have making a monkey out of Dan. I think he likes to hear my news too because I can see in his eyes that he knows what I'm saying. And I know he's glad to see me because there are tears in his eyes when I get up to go. Yes, with his eyes popping out of his head like they'll burst. Tragic, isn't it? I hear the staff say that regularly. The tragic part . . ."

Had he recognized some of this power in her, he wondered. Her reserve that day as she walked into the Old Ground hotel, her coolness at home, pouring tea and putting up with Crossan. But there was a desperation too, he saw now, in her courting danger, a recklessness that would unnerve even those she ran with.

She stood away from the wall and flexed her fingers.

"Ciarán says that what works is if you start at the feet and work your way up every minute or so."

Minogue struggled for control until he was sure the screams inside could be heard by her. "Sooner or later," he gasped, "you'll make a slip —"

She started to smile but it seemed to be too much for her to finish. Her face fell a little. Her eyes lost interest and an empty look took over her face.

"You've had your chance," she whispered.

With her retreating footsteps the terror swooped down on him again. While she had been here there was some hope at least. The bottom of the door screeched as it caught and dragged fragments of cement across the floor. He looked over his shoulder toward the door.

"No," she said, and she yanked at the door again. It jammed halfway.

"Fucking stupid bastard!" said Ciarán. "Stupid! Time's up."

"You heard him," Sheila Howard said in a dead voice. "He's sticking to it. He says he —"

"Ah, he says! He's a Guard!" said Ciarán.

Then the other man's voice again, this time without any disguise. He spoke in a drawl, as though weather prospects were being guessed. "He's a Guard, all right. Ye certainly got that part correct. Is the stuff all out of the van, by the way?"

The gentle sarcasm, the local accent worked on Minogue's thoughts.

"Yeah. It all fit handy enough in the boot," said another man's voice. Finbarr, thought Minogue.

"Thanks," said the stranger. "A nice job of work. Good."

"Well, how were we supposed to know he'd be hanging around the house this morning?" Ciarán erupted again.

"True for you there." The sarcasm was gone from the voice now. "True for you, boy. You'd never have expected it."

Seconds of silence followed. They're deciding, Minogue thought. No one wants to say it out loud. Footsteps shuffled, a sigh.

"It's late," said the stranger. "Too late really. Come on in now and we'll pay our respects to your man inside. Leave that down on the bench like a good man, Finbarr, for fear you'll drop it again and it'll take the toes off someone. This is my job now."

Minogue heard a low growl, as if he was clearing his throat, rising in his own chest. His own animal terror, his body's need for any movement. He stifled the cry and jogged the chair once, twice, until he had a view of the door. Through the slit between door and jamb, a shadow passed. There was a clump as something heavy was laid on the bench. A choked-off murmur escaped from Minogue. Good God, he thought, his body was acting on its own — it knows something. His mind was gone.

"I don't think he really has anything —" Sheila Howard said.

"Don't be worrying yourself, Mrs. Howard. You don't have to do a thing now."

"Don't keep calling her that!" Ciarán's voice rose. "For Christ's sake, you're always taking digs at her —"

"Sorry, Ciary. Don't fuss yourself now. It's just that me and her nibs go back a good number of years." Minogue sat very still: a good number of years?

"Come on now, let's not be arguing. We can fix the rest up later."

"I'm staying here," said Sheila Howard.

"Ah, come on now," said the stranger. "We're all in it together. It's a lesson for everyone, now."

Minogue heard his own breath rush out of his nostrils. His heart was thumping in a cold, empty place. The door screeched open across the pebbles. Deegan stopped and looked at him.

"Jesus Christ," said Deegan. "Who took the bag off him?"

"He couldn't breathe enough to even talk, so I —"

"You fucking what?"

"Leave her alone!" came Ciarán's rising voice. "What difference does it make now?"

Deegan wandered slowly back into the doorway. He shook his head and looked up from the floor. He looked at Minogue with cold, moist eyes, an automatic pistol in his left hand. Ciarán stepped in the doorway behind him, his face sullen, followed by Sheila Howard. She wouldn't look at Minogue. Her eyelashes batted rapidly and her hand went to her hair. Finbarr shambled in and stood next to Ciarán, his eyes downcast too. With his head tilted slightly and his distracted gaze returned to the floor, Deegan waited for the three to come to a standstill.

"It's yourself that's in it, then," he said.

"You'll be caught," Minogue whispered. "All of you."

Deegan didn't seem to hear him. He shuffled forward.

"You've only yourself to blame," he said. His leather soles crunched pieces of mortar. A vise had fastened about Minogue's ribs. He wondered if he would be able to stop himself from crying out.

"From what I heard, it was our Mrs. Howard doing all the talking in here. Did she tell you everything you wanted to know, now?" They had sent her all right, and they had sat listening.

"Except who killed Jane Clark," said Minogue.

Deegan's eyes suddenly twinkled, and he smiled broadly.

"Well now, can't you figure that out yourself?"

By the tone, the menacing humor, Minogue knew. He stared into the folds of flesh in which Deegan's eyes were almost completely hidden now. "You did it."

Deegan made a mock curtsy but his eyes stayed on the inspector's.

"At your service, Your Honor. Oh, the Howards are no different from any other of the well-to-do. They always need someone to do the dirty work. Well, there was a lot of money spent that night, let me tell you. And they're still paying for it. Amn't I right, Mrs. Howard?"

"Shut up with that 'Mrs. Howard' stuff!" Ciarán shouted. "I'm about sick and tired of it."

Deegan put on a surprised expression and peered around at Ciarán.

"You're right, Ciarán," he sighed. "Begging your pardon and all."

He turned back to the inspector. Something about Minogue's face brought the smile back to Deegan's.

"After that night, sure, we had Naughton in the bag too. The way things worked out . . . Two for the price of one, you might say. We had plenty on our Tom after that night, so we did. So our Tom did his bit afterwards too — not saying he didn't do well out of us. He did. And by us, I don't mean the Howard clan."

Naughton's gun, Minogue thought. Had Deegan given him the gun?

"Well, I hear they caught up with poor Tom the other day," Deegan went on. "And he blew his brains out? He always said he'd do that if and when they came for him. I didn't set much store by that. The drink talking, say I. But that's why he wanted the gun, I suppose, for when they came after him. His own, I mean — the Guards." Deegan shook his head again and chuckled softly.

"The poor divil," he added. He gave Minogue the stage wink that the inspector remembered from their meeting at the pub. "Ah, but his heart was in the right place."

Ciarán snorted and started to say something but bit back his words and folded his arms again. Over his thudding heartbeat, Minogue still heard Ciarán's angry breaths in his nostrils.

"Take it nice and easy there, Ciarán," Deegan murmured. "Sure the man has a right to his facts. Oh, but she was a bad egg, that one. Jane Clark. Oh yes. She put up a rare oul' fight of it, so she did. But tell me," he squinted into Minogue's eyes. "Alo Crossan. How the hell did he get you into this mess? He'd sooner piss on a Guard than talk to one."

Minogue didn't answer.

"Crossan's a wanker, so he is," Deegan went on. "Matter of fact, he's as bent as a ram's horn."

Minogue's expression prompted Deegan to grin again.

"You didn't know he's a queer? That's what he has the chip on his shoulder about. He's bent, man. He was pally with that bitch. She told me she was going to get Alo and take everyone to court over this. Me, Mrs. Howard here — oops, Sheila — the Howards . . . everyone. It was Dan gave her the clap, she tried to tell me, not the other way around. Funny how things turn out, isn't it?"

Deegan choked off his mirth and threw a glance of knowing candor at the inspector.

"But, sure, who can you depend on these days?" he said.

Ciarán took a step forward, unfolded his arms, and shouted, "Look." With a terrifying, unnatural speed, Deegan turned, brought up the pistol and shot him square in the chest. The shell flew across the room,

Sheila Howard screamed and buckled, Ciarán fell back, and Deegan kept firing. An ejected shell bounced off Minogue's eyebrow as he wrenched himself over, the chair giving way under him. Deegan fired steadily, without pause. Through the deafening reports and the shouts, Minogue heard bodies land heavily on the cement.

Minogue came to rest on his side and opened his eyes. Smoke clouded and shook in the room as Deegan's gun went off. Minogue's cheek was on the cement. He saw legs and a hand, blood on the wall next to the floor. He was shouting himself now and felt his bladder give way. Deegan stopped shooting and stepped toward the arms and legs. Minogue stopped shouting. Kathleen, he thought. His eyes were locked onto Deegan's shoes. As long as the shoes faced away from him, he was still . . . Deegan was whispering hoarsely.

"Christ, Ciarán, you're such a fucking iijit," he gasped, breathing harder. "You poor bastard, you damn near ruined it all with her . . . And as for your mate, God forgive me, I warned you, don't say that I didn't, now . . ."

Deegan's feet shuffled slightly as he fired down. One of the hands fluttered and Minogue went limp. Someone was moaning. Deegan's shoes turned toward Minogue. The piss was warm over his legs, almost a comfort. The clarity of everything in the room, in the world, came to the inspector as something utterly horrifying and familiar. A vision flared in his mind but it did not distract his utter attention from Deegan's gun: the surly, gray-green sea, the stricken ridges of the Burren stretching toward the horizon under clouds that looked like massive slabs themselves. He saw the orange flare as the roof burst into flames impossibly reflected on every wave, the porpoises racing through the black waters of the estuary into the open sea . . . and, always, that face, the young stranger watching.

"As for you, you poor fuck, I don't know . . ." Deegan murmured, and he pointed the gun at Minogue's face.

"Don't," Minogue whispered.

The report seemed louder now since the lull in firing had intervened. Deegan went sideways with a grunt. Minogue tore open his eyes in time to see Deegan's surprised face fall obliquely by him.

"Jesus, Jesus," he heard Deegan wheeze from the floor.

Minogue tugged and drew up his knees to turn the chair but he could not. He turned his head as far as he could and saw Sheila Howard's head resting against the wall. Her chin was jammed down on her breastbone and purple spots were on her face. Though her eyelids looked closed, he thought he saw a liquid glint by her eyelashes. Her arm was lying on her chest and she held the pistol loosely on her thigh. Where she had pulled up her jumper to get the gun out, Minogue saw a band of skin where blood spidered and dripped onto the floor.

Deegan made the wet, choking sound of a smoker summoning phlegm. Minogue heard his clothes rustle slowly along the floor, his huge limbs rubbing as he tried to rise. There was a glottal gasp and the rubbing stopped.

Cold, the floor. Minogue had driven his knee into the cement as he fell and it had that warm watery numbness he knew would turn to pain. An aura of blue smoke, moving slightly, circled the lightbulb. He rested and breathed and watched the layers of smoke forming, sliding across one another, and settling into stillness. The sting of cordite needled the top of his nose as he listened again. An irregular sigh of breathing turned to rasping breath and a short, faint squeal before returning fainter. Jesus, not now, he thought. Was one of them alive and getting up? Schemes flew into his mind, each desperate and quickly discarded. Elbow his way across the room and see if anyone had a penknife or a sharp tool. There must be some tool in the house, in the main rooms — but how to get over these bodies? He felt the cold only as a relief, grudging proof that he was still alive.

Then came a bubbly snore. He stared at Sheila Howard and saw her eyes open, staring across at his. A small new line came from the side of her mouth. She closed her eyes and coughed. A gout of blood oozed down her chin and her body made a spasm. She rolled onto her side and coughed again. Minogue froze and watched her creeping and scraping her way across the floor, heard her gurgling.

"Take it easy now," he whispered and immediately realized how absurd the remark was. She took a deep, rasping breath and whispered in a tone so lucid that Minogue was startled.

"I'm bad. I can't feel where . . ."

"If I can get free," he started to say.

"I warned Ciarán about him." She had squeezed out the words. She gave a wrenching cough and groaned. He closed his eyes. He heard something spill on the floor. He opened his eyes again. She seemed to be resting, her face down on the floor. He began yanking on the chair, scraping and kicking.

Minogue began to jerk the chair, each time sending shooting pains through his shoulder and chest.

Finally, as he rocked the chair, something gave way. The seat of the chair hung loose. Slowly he pulled in his elbows and he heard a spindle hit the cement with a hollow tock. His arms were weak but the cords were now slack. He stood crookedly and spindles from the chair-back fell to the floor. The blood rushed to his head as he stood and he felt the room come at him. Pain surging up from this legs took most of the room's light with it and he lurched to the wall. As the room reappeared, it seemed to swell and the colors take fire. He glanced down at Deegan sprawled over Finbarr. Deegan's head had fallen back and then sideways so that he seemed to be examining the dark stain on Finbarr's jacket. His pistol was on the floor next to his hand. Finbarr lay curled up and half under Deegan. One arm was twisted behind, with the pool of blood spreading from under him.

Still struggling to shake the seat and legs of the chair free, he tottered toward the door. The light flared again and he leaned against a wall to fight the returning surges of dizziness. Suddenly he was gripped by fear. Who was sobbing like that, panting nearby? He turned, a shout already in his throat, expecting to see Deegan in the doorway. No one came. It was his own breath, he realized.

He elbowed away from the wall. *Run.* He was swaying now and the shapes were hanging and falling around the edges of his vision again. With the twine loose, he brought his right hand around. He stumbled toward the front door and pulled it open. He stopped in the doorway and gaped. The roof of the van was like a still lake reflecting the sky. A Ford Escort was parked alongside the van; Deegan's, he guessed. His feet moved under him and he was on his way to the van's door. A buzzer sounded as he pulled it open: keys in the ignition. He left the door hanging and rested his back against the panel. His palms flattened out on the cold metal and he felt his breathing ease. The buzzer filled the sky with its ripping squeak. The colors on the ground had already darkened and the bushes stood out thick against the milky sky. She might still be alive in there, he thought. He listened for sounds but heard only a solitary bird. He stared through the grove of trees and the overgrown bushes at the Burren heights. The stone seemed to be draining light from the sky. Was he going to pass out? He looked at the open door of the cottage. Should he go back for her?

Minogue turned when he heard the distant hum of a car over the tar macadam. He caught glimpses of a dark-colored car coming at a speed up the narrow road. The driver had not turned on his headlights, but Minogue had already spotted the silvered reflections of the sky on the roof-lights of the car. He stumbled back to the van, reached in, and held his hand on the horn. He watched the wheels of the Garda car bounce as it came up the laneway, and he saw a face close up to the window.

The tires bit and skidded as the squad car came to a stop behind the van. Doors opened and he heard voices, a radio. Somebody said his name. He didn't have to go back into that house, he was thinking. He walked haltingly toward the car.

"Yes," he replied to a question. His voice sounded unfamiliar to him now. "Inside . . . There was shooting. I think they're dead."

He wanted to tell them to switch off the noise from the radio. He heard someone say his name on the radio, then repeat it. He knew the voice. The sky jigged and flickered and changed color.

"She's in there and I think maybe —" he began.

His knees pulled him down but it didn't hurt. Hands stopped him falling further. They pulled him up from his knees and grabbed him under his arms.

"Look," he heard someone say as the sky turned and closed over him. "Is he shot?"

CHAPTER 16

I DON'T BELIEVE it," Kilmartin murmured. "It must be a joke." He looked over at Minogue. "Did you ever hear anything so stupid in all your life?"

Minogue shook his head. He dabbed his fingers over his eye. The lump had gone down a little. The X-rays had showed nothing on his knee either. His chest hurt when he breathed in deep. The bruise on his shoulder ran halfway over his shoulder blade. He felt stupid sitting in a hospital bed.

"What?" Hoey asked. He was leaning on the windowsill.

"It says that a man thinks about sex an average of six times every hour."

"Who says?" Hoey said.

"A scientist in the States. Somebody's after codding someone there, by God. Makes you wonder how many millions were wasted on that. God, six times every hour. That's impossible if you're doing a proper day's work."

"Probably only applies in built-up places like Dublin," said Hoey.

Kilmartin folded the newspaper and looked over at the inspector. Minogue decided that no matter what the doctor said he would be walking out the door at three o'clock today.

"How could you hold down a job, though?" Kilmartin went on. "Every ten minutes . . ."

"See what you've missed," said Hoey.

"I'm hitting the road in an hour," Minogue said.

"How?"

"Shea has the getaway car waiting outside."

Kilmartin glanced at Hoey. Minogue had stayed overnight in the County Hospital in Ennis. He had woken up as he was being moved from the squad car to a stretcher at the door of the hospital. Sedated, he had conked out until nine o'clock this morning. His first sight had been Kilmartin's size-eleven brogues resting one over the other on his bed several feet from his own face. Minogue's blinding headache had abated almost completely by lunchtime, but he had no appetite yet. He felt apprehensive, anxious to be on the move again. Several times he had caught Kilmartin and Hoey scrutinizing him from a distance.

"Did you phone Kathleen yet?" Kilmartin asked.

"No. And I hope you didn't either."

The chief inspector raised a hand to mollify. "Course I didn't. And are you sure you're feeling all right?"

Crossan had asked the same question four times that Minogue had counted, a Dr. Leddy three times, Hoey but twice.

"I'm better off out of here, that I know."

"But what about everything here?" Kilmartin was unsure of how to rein in Minogue.

"The X rays are fine. The bruises, well, I'll have to live with them no matter where I am —"

"The other stuff from last night —"

"I'll do it all from Dublin, Jimmy."

Kilmartin frowned. He was not about to give in that easily. "Leave Russell to hear from us in Dublin as to what happened here in his own diocese, is it?"

"Exactly."

"But he's been waiting for the go-ahead to interview you here. If you're well enough to travel, you're well enough to —"

"I told Shea what happened last night. He told you. I told you myself this morning. You told me that you told Russell." Kilmartin was shaking his head before Minogue was through.

"Wait a minute. I don't want to be harrassing you and you laid up here, but there are a million details —"

"Look, Jimmy, they can be had from Dublin later on. I don't want to talk about it anymore right now."

Again Kilmartin looked to Hoey as though expecting a signal. Hoey's eyes went to the window.

"Promise me you'll go straight to the hospital or a doctor up in Dublin then."

"All right."

Kilmartin folded his paper again and tapped the roll on the bed. Minogue had felt the airy calm of the sedative ebbing since midmorning. He had declined more. Leddy, the doctor with Mr. Pickwick glasses, had continued his tests after Minogue's refusal. He had also given Minogue's knee a flex more abrupt than the first tests this morning, the inspector remembered. Minogue was half glad of the returning aches, the stiffness, and the burning bands on his wrists. Kilmartin's final appeal came softly.

"Look, you can't be taking chances now. You know as well as I do about concussion and shock. Stay another night here, can't you? It's for free, man! What's the big hurry back up to Dublin?"

Minogue didn't have an answer. From the silence, Kilmartin suspected some success with his efforts.

"Come on. Jases. Let me phone Kathleen. She can hardly eat the head offa me, now."

"Don't depend on it . . ."

Minogue's thoughts were gone now. He had a floating sensation just before the fear overwhelmed him. The cottage he had stumbled out of, the room full of death. He shuddered and held his breath. Kilmartin looked down at the clenched fists. Hoey stepped away from the window and Kilmartin waved his hand low at him. Hoey slipped out of the room. Minogue's jaw had locked with the strain and his breath was coming fast. He saw Ciarán being thrown to the floor by the bullet, Deegan's face as he fell. And they didn't tell him last night but he knew, the way they said they didn't know, she was dead.

"Where does it hurt?" he heard Kilmartin whisper.

He knew now that he wouldn't make it today. Kilmartin called his name again. Like a lost soul himself, whirling, vagrant, and steadily slipping away as the dawn leaked into the sky. She was dead. He saw the ferry nosing out into the estuary, the Clare shore in the distance and the drizzle turning to rain. He focused on Kilmartin's face. He saw the alarm there and he wanted to reassure him. He opened his mouth. The doctor had appeared. The smug look was gone off his face now. He grabbed Minogue's wrist. A nurse he hadn't seen before elbowed Kilmartin aside and pressed a stethoscope to his chest. Minogue thought of Sheila

Howard pushing the gun into his chest last night. She thought he had been holding out on them.

"If I had known," he began to say. Somebody else came into the room.

· · · · ·

He woke up stunned with a headache the following day to find Kathleen's tired eyes on him. He closed his eyes again. The dream was slipping away too fast. He tried to get back, to see the face. Why was he smiling? He looked more familiar now but Minogue knew that the man intended to go. Who the hell was he? A mustache, black hair, eyes that did the talking. Looked like . . . Iseult? Tell her that sometime, he thought. Then he knew.

He elbowed up and stared at Kathleen. Alarm spread across her face and she came up out of the chair. His eyes left hers and looked beyond her.

"Matt," she called out. Her hands were on his shoulders. "Will I get the doctor?"

He wondered if she still had that snapshot of him when he'd had the mustache. Two years after they were married, he thought: twenty-eight? His eyes returned to study her face.

"Are you awake now, love?" she asked again. "Are you all right?"

That familiar look to the face in the dream. It had to be. His mouth was full of dust, it seemed. He strained to get his tongue around the words.

"If he was here now, I mean, if he was with us, like . . . How old would he be now?"

Kathleen's mouth stayed open and her eyes grew larger still. She leaned in over him and he looked back into her stricken stare. Hoey, he thought, Nolan, Ciarán. The child Superman in Tralee that day, disappearing around the corner of the street. *I'll layve you there.* For a moment he was on the ferry again, searching for the porpoises where the Shannon opened out to the sea.

"What is it, lovey? What's wrong? Who do you mean?"

"Eamonn. Our Eamonn. How old would he be now?"

CHAPTER 17

THE INSPECTOR began to feel claustrophobic. Drinkers continued to pour into the pub. They stood in front of the table where Minogue, Kilmartin, and their wives sat, blocking them in. This idea of Kathleen's seemed to be backfiring. Maybe he should ease off on the drink.

"How and when did this dump ever get to be so popular?" Kilmartin shouted over the din. "A glorified shebeen. They should do it up nice."

Kathleen hadn't slept well for over a week. She had planned this evening out in cahoots with Jim Kilmartin, Minogue guessed. On one of her afternoon visits to her husband in the hospital, she had brought up the topic of putting the house up for sale. Make a fresh start, her logic ran. Though Minogue hadn't yet been able to say what he believed he should, she had read his expression. For over an hour afterward, he recalled, she argued aloud with herself while he listened. Though dopey most of the time, he still marveled that she had read his mind. She had finally declared that it would be good sense to put it off for a year.

A fiddle player tested bow and strings somewhere in the ruck between the foursome and the bar. Minogue was looking up at the men's ponytails, the women's tube skirts. Perfume was thick and sweet in the smoky air. Kilmartin's wife, Maura, answered her husband's question.

"There's a crowd of rock stars and film people living up around here, that's why. Oh, look! Look, Kathleen! That's him! Your man, what's-his-name! Joey Mad-Again. Joey Madigan!"

"They're brilliant!" said Kathleen.

To Minogue, inspired by two Jamesons, it appeared that she and Maura Kilmartin were both levitating. He looked at them crouched, hovering over their seats. Their heads moving from side to side reminded him of hens prospecting for remnants of grain in a farmyard. Invisible in the crowd, a fiddler played two bars of "The Rakes of Mallow." The shouting and laughter dropped to a murmur. A tall, unshaven man turned around to find a spot to place his empty glass. Kathleen waved and caught his eye. Joey Madigan, stage names Joey Mad and Joey Mad Again, lead singer, founder, and guitarist with the hit rock/traditional/folk group Social Welfare, looked around the table and raised his eyebrows.

"Howiya, Joe!" Maura called out.

"Howiya yourself," he called back.

By the way this Joe wiped his mouth with the back of his hand, Minogue pegged him for a man who could drink a lot and had done so tonight. He thought of Hoey. His colleague had taken three weeks' sick leave. Minogue had last seen him the day before yesterday. Hoey had attended four AA meetings, was dry, and looked relaxed. He told Minogue that he was getting his inoculations and booking a flight through to Harare. Hoey assured him several times that it wasn't a joke. Kilmartin believed Hoey, but continued to treat it as a joke.

"Heard you on the radio, Joe!" Kathleen said. "Will you sing? Will you?"

Since when was Kathleen so bold, her husband wondered. And that look on her face. Radiant. An adoring fan? Kilmartin was looking stonily at this recent star on the Irish music scene.

"Go on, can't you?" Maura Kilmartin joined in. Her husband's face set harder as he stared at Joe Mad-Again.

"Give us 'Dublin Town,' Joey. Go on, do," Kathleen pleaded.

"Well, I don't know."

"Ah, go on, can't you?" said Minogue. Kilmartin looked over to his friend in disbelief.

Now he remembered the group. This hit of last summer had launched the group properly. "Dublin Town" was full to the brim of the city's mocking irony. Madigan had a singular talent for belting the lyrics out with angry accusatory snarls. Joey Mad seemed to sense Kilmartin's discomfort. The chief inspector had folded his arms and was studying the empty glass on the table now. Finally, he glared up.

"Ah, go on, do," he growled, and put on a flinty smile. "For your man here with the long face. It's his first day out in a long time. He's a fan of the Dublin crowd."

Joey Mad tapped a shoulder in the crowd. Kathleen Minogue elbowed Kilmartin in the ribs.

"Will you look?" said Kathleen. "It's the other one! The one who used to play with The Goners — Gabby Mac!"

She turned bright, excited eyes on Minogue. For the first time in nearly two weeks, Minogue felt the weight slip a little. Last night was the first night he had slept more than four hours since returning from Clare.

"He looks like a goner, all right," Kilmartin observed. "The narrowback. Get a real job, pal."

Kathleen turned to Maura Kilmartin and Minogue saw his wife's hand splayed down on Maura's forearm.

"God, Maura, it's great! He's going to do it! Fab, isn't it?"

A fiddle launched into a rousing intro. It was soon joined by a guitar and the hollow thuds of a bodhran. Maura and Kathleen were standing up now, trying to see into the crowd.

"Sit down, can't ye?" Kilmartin hissed.

The crowd seemed to heave with the music as Joey Mad began to howl out the words.

> *We sat in Bewley's Restaurant there,*
> *We talked and laughed without a care.*
> *You know, says she, the time just flies*
> *I thought how small talk always lies.*

Joey Mad began to shout out the chorus. Kilmartin rolled his eyes.

> *Oh, Dublin town's a desperate town,*
> *But I'm a desperate man.*

The chief inspector leaned in and shouted into Minogue's ear.

"At least he got that last part right. It *is* fucking desperate!"

Minogue looked at Kathleen and Maura. They were swaying from side to side in their seats, clapping gently, smiling. The whole pub seemed to be lurching somewhere with the music. He felt his heart was beating in an empty space. Other voices joined in louder as Joey Mad bit into another verse. Maybe he'd be better off outside, away from the crush and the racket.

> *What were we then, sixteen or so?*
> *Why did you leave, I'd like to know?*
> *Escape, run, travel — I began.*

But you're back, says she, each chance you can.
Oh, Dublin town's a desperate town,
But I'm a desperate man.

Someone whooped. Kilmartin stood and waded into the crowd. Kathleen, swaying, caught Minogue's eye and winked. Something gave way in his chest then. The music seemed to grow even louder. But as the fiddler let the instrument free and it wandered away from the melody, the guitar fought with the fiddle, soaring and falling with it. The bodhran player was up to the hunt and he smiled and closed his eyes while his hands became a blur. The mob seemed to surge as it moved, egging on the musicians. Kathleen's face had taken on color, Minogue noted. He must write to Daithi tomorrow. She felt his stare and turned. For several seconds her face took on that frown he remembered from that day they'd had a puncture high up over the Burren. There was something beyond anxiety in that look, he believed. He raised an eyebrow at her. He felt the muscles in his cheeks give way. God, he thought, he seemed to be finally climbing out of this. He leaned in toward her and grasped her hand.

"You're the wild woman now to drag me up here. It's like cold water thrown in your face."

"Had to be done," she said. Her eyes had lost the fear and they glistened now. "You were turned in on yourself too long, man."

"We must come here again when it's as mad, so."

Kilmartin was back with a clutch of drinks in his hands. He stooped in over the table and placed the glasses down firmly. For a moment, Minogue thought of tagged exhibits being positioned on the table under the bench.

"I had to walk on a few head-cases to get to the bloody bar," he shouted into Minogue's ear.

Pilgrim, exile, tourist, son,
Leaving here I thought I'd won,
Next time I'm back, I'll bring a sign
Hey, while I'm here, this town is mine!

Voices roared throughout the pub. Still Minogue heard Joey Mad spit out the words.

Oh, Dublin town's a desperate town,
But I'm a desperate man!

{ 302 }

"Jesus," Kilmartin broke in between Kathleen and Minogue. "People buy that, you know!"

More whoops erupted and the fiddle returned to race with the guitar.

"They pay good money to hear this clown tell 'em something like that!" Kilmartin's mockery stopped abruptly.

"Christ," he said, too softly for Minogue to hear, but the inspector turned his head in the direction Kilmartin was looking. John Tynan, Commissioner of Gardai, raised a glass of amber-colored liquid in wry salute. Kathleen had noticed too. She leaned into her husband.

"Are you in trouble? Are we in trouble, I mean?"

Minogue shrugged. He picked up his drink and headed into the crowd, Kilmartin followed. Blocked for several moments by two women executing an impromptu two-step to the repeated chorus, Minogue turned to his colleague.

"How come he's here?"

"Well, he phoned earlier in the day. Asked if you were around or if I'd be in touch with you. I happened to mention that you — well, Kathleen, I mean — had invited us up to this madhouse for a jar. Social, like."

Minogue probed for sincerity in Kilmartin's eyes before making his way toward the Garda Commissioner.

Tynan stepped out the front door of the pub and into the yard. Minogue and Kilmartin ambled with him toward the wall that flanked the Barnacullia road below.

"Lovely," said Tynan.

"Before your man inside started his shouting and screeching," said Kilmartin.

"The view, I was thinking," said Tynan.

The commissioner leaned his elbows on the wall and looked out to the lights mapping the coastline of Dublin. North of the city, a plane's winking lights floated down to meet the waiting airport lights. Behind them came the muffled rumble of the pub. The door opened and blew music out into the night, stealing it back as it slammed shut.

"A lot of our tax-free artists, musicians, and the like, live up around here," Tynan observed.

Minogue guessed that Tynan had attended parties in such houses.

"Social Welfare," Minogue murmured. "Sort of grows on you."

A trill sounded from somewhere on Tynan's upper body.

"Excuse me," he said, and he pulled out a mobile from inside his coat. He fingered a switch and turned away. Kilmartin elbowed Minogue and winked.

"Give me a half an hour, then," Tynan said. The door of the pub opened again.

. . . *a desperate town,*

. . . *and I'm a . . .*

Tynan dropped the phone down the inside of his coat.

"Apparently I'm late for something. So says Rachel."

Why come up here then, Minogue thought. Tynan's clairvoyance startled the inspector.

"I heard you'd be doing some of your recuperating up here tonight," he said. "So I decided to drop by."

Kilmartin took a drink from his glass, shuffled, and looked out over the lights.

"Well. How is it with you?"

"Everything takes time."

"You got off to a false start there in the County Hospital in Ennis," Tynan said.

Minogue had been waiting for Kilmartin's gibe about his mad rush to get out of County Clare but it had yet to be uttered.

"I didn't realize the shape I was really in," Minogue said. "It was almost like a dream, I remember thinking."

"A bad business," said Tynan. "But you did right."

Minogue wanted to contest this. He had already detected in Tynan's gaze that the commissioner knew something about him from talking to others. Minogue had spoken but once to the commissioner, when Tynan had phoned him at home.

"Well, now. Did Jim pass on the word to you?"

Kilmartin was now swaying slightly from the knees. He did not look away from the lights below.

"No."

"The Squad stays as is," said Tynan. "That's what I decided."

He turned to Kilmartin with an eyebrow up.

"After all, I'm top dog. What I say goes."

Minogue noticed that Kilmartin had stopped swaying. Tynan sipped at his whiskey and turned back to Minogue.

"Had a call from Ennis," Tynan resumed. "Superintendent Russell."

He took another sip and his gaze stayed fixed, like Kilmartin's, on the lights.

"Says hello to you, by the way."

"Very nice of him, I'm sure," said Minogue.

"Yes. Tom says you should get in touch with him the next time you're coming down to Clare on business."

"I was on me holidays," Minogue said.

Tynan seemed to ignore Minogue's qualification. "Before you leave Dublin, he was at pains to note."

"I believe I know what you mean."

"What Tom Russell meant," Tynan corrected, "was this. Are you going down on another trip in the near future, maybe?"

Minogue thought of the County Hospital, of Mick and Maura and Eoin in visiting. Mick had smuggled in a half-bottle of whiskey. Maura had slipped as she had kissed her brother-in-law and landed on him. They're talking about the farm at last, she had whispered in his ear. She phoned Kathleen a week later with the news that Eoin had persuaded his father to apply for money to drain the four boggy fields, the Kilshanny quarter as the family knew them. They'd had an agricultural adviser in walking the fields with them. They'd visited the bank.

Minogue thought of Crossan walking from the bed to the window, back to the bed, while he talked about Jamesy Bourke's funeral, the guns found in a field behind the Howards' house, the arrests around Clare. Back in Dublin, Minogue had spent a day mooching around the Art Gallery, hiding in Bewley's. He had admitted to no one how shaky he was. Dan Howard's face, looking empty and older and lined in places Minogue couldn't remember noticing from before, had been on the front page of *The Irish Times* two days in a row.

The inspector had found the box of photos in the wardrobe. He had taken the photos out of the box and kept them in his pocket. He hoped that if he tried harder or sneaked up suddenly on the snapshots, he would spot some semblance of the smiling man from his sleep in the grainy pictures of Eamonn. When he got home that evening, Kathleen told him that Crossan had phoned again. The lawyer wanted to know if Minogue would be coming down for Sheila Howard's funeral. Minogue went first to the cabinet under the sink, then to the front room where he had thought about Crossan's question for almost an hour.

"I think not."

Tynan nodded.

"There's an article in the *Independent*," said Tynan. "Very catchy title too. Credit to a journalist by the name of Hynes, co-written with another one. Do you know Hynes, Jim?"

"He's been a boil on me arse for an undue number of years," said Kilmartin with little malice.

"Must have a good source," said Tynan. "Sharp info. He speaks well of your Squad. Very well indeed."

"Why wouldn't he?" said Kilmartin. "It's only the truth."

"I suppose that they get the *Independent* down in Ennis or thereabouts," Tynan said. Kilmartin gave the commissioner a knowing look.

"'Out with the old Guard, in with the new,'" said Tynan. "Catchy, isn't it?" Kilmartin grunted.

Tynan drew his lapels tighter.

"Oh," he said, and turned to Minogue. "I asked Jim if you'd be long away."

Minogue frowned. Kilmartin began to sway again, but he did not take his eyes from the view to return Minogue's glare. Tynan resumed his prodding.

"Told me he didn't know. You, ah, hadn't told him yet."

Minogue looked beyond Kilmartin to the night city below. The music had stopped. A door opened and the three policemen looked back at two men laughing raucously in the yard. The dark mass of the mountain above the pub seemed closer, larger. Hoey heading for Africa. How things turn out, Hoey had said to him in Bewley's the other day. Hoey hadn't looked at him when he had said that, he recalled. Minogue turned back to the city view.

The lights of the city fell into no overall pattern that he could discern. He let his eyes drift up a little. The few stars he could make out in the city's dull glow did not follow any pattern either. How the hell did people see chariots and horses and plows and goddesses up there? But as he looked, Minogue was startled to find that more stars seemed to be appearing. How did that happen? Kilmartin cleared his throat.

"Two weeks or so, I imagine," Minogue heard himself say. "Then I'm back."

Kilmartin turned. Tynan nodded. Minogue emptied his glass.